The Dragon Knight

The
Dragon
Knight

Gordon R. Dickson

TOR
fantasy

A Tom Doherty Associates Book

New York

THE DRAGON KNIGHT

A Tor Book
Published by Tom Doherty Associates, Inc.
49 West 24th Street
New York, N.Y. 10010

Design by Richard Oriolo

Library of Congress Cataloging-in-Publication Data

Dickson, Gordon R.
      The dragon knight/Gordon R. Dickson.
          p.   cm.
      ISBN 0-312-93129-8
      I. Title.
  PS3554.I328D7   1990   90-38897
  813'.54—dc20   CIP

Printed in the United States of America

First edition: November 1990

10 9 8 7 6 5 4 3 2 1

*This book is dedicated to
Dave Wixon, for a great deal
of effort on a great many books
besides this one.*

Chapter 1

Ⅰt was a frosty March morning just at daybreak in the Malencontri woods, which with a name like that should have been somewhere in France or Italy, but were actually in England.

Not that anyone who had anything to do with those woods—from the three hedgehogs curled up together for warmth in their untidy, leaf-filled hollow under a nearby hedge, to Sir James Eckert, Baron de Bois de Malencontri et Riveroak, asleep with his wife, the Lady Angela, in the castle nearby—ever bothered to use that frenchified name in ordinary conversation, mind you. The title of Malencontri had been pinned on the woods by their previous owner, who was now a landless fugitive, possibly somewhere on the continent; and serve him right.

With Sir Hugh de Malencontri safely out of the way, all the local inhabitants had gone back to referring to the woods by their real name, which was that of Highbramble Forest. All of which was a matter of supreme indifference to the one individual on his feet at the moment and passing through them; not far from the aroused but—happily—safely hidden hedgehogs and close enough to the Castle Malencontri to see it clearly between the trees.

It was a natural indifference, since the early traveler was Aargh, an English wolf, who regarded not only this woods, but a number of others as well, as his own personal territory anyway, and so never bothered to concern himself about what others might call it.

Actually, Aargh very seldom bothered to concern himself about anything. For example, although the early spring morning was bitterly chill, he paid no attention to that fact, except insofar as it increased the possibility of scent trails lying closer than usual to the ground. He showed, in fact, the same sort of unconcern toward the temperature that he did to all other things—wind, rain, brambles, humans, dragons, sandmirks, ogres, and all else. He would have shown it in equal degree to earthquakes, volcanoes, and tidal waves, if he had happened to encounter them, but so far he had not. He was a descendant of dire wolves, as large as a small pony, and his philosophy was that the day anything came along that he could not handle he would be dead, which would take care of any problems that might arise, in either case.

He did pause now, to glance briefly at the castle and at the square box of its solar chamber, with the newfangled glass panes in the arrow slits that were its windows just now beginning to reflect the first light of the dawn sky. But in spite of the strong opinions he had against glassed-in windows, he had a personal fondness for Sir James and Lady Angela, whom he knew to be aslumber right now in the solar, slugabeds though the two were to be wasting a fine crisp dawn like the present one by spending it indoors.

The fondness was one that went back to the time he and Sir James (with some others, admittedly) had been involved in a certain small altercation with an ogre and some other, similarly unwholesome, creatures at the Loathly Tower out on the meres. Sir James had then, through no fault of his own, been inhabiting the body of a friend of Aargh's—a dragon named Gorbash. Aargh allowed himself a few moments of nostalgic recollection of those past, but interesting, times.

Having done so, however, he became unexpectedly aware of a feeling of uneasiness in his bones concerning both James and Angela—but James, in particular. The feeling had not been there a second before, and he turned his full attention upon it, being a wolf who had learned to pay heed to the signals his undersenses sent him.

But the uneasiness neither explained itself, nor disappeared. Sniffing the air and scenting nothing amiss, he accordingly dismissed it, making only a mental note to mention it at the first opportunity to S. Carolinus; the next time he found himself passing close to that magician's cottage, up by the Tinkling Water. Carolinus would be able to tell if the feeling portended anything Aargh might need to bestir himself personally about; though it was hard to imagine what anything like that could be.

Putting the matter sensibly from his mind, therefore, he trotted on; and his lean dark form swiftly disappeared from the view of the hedgehogs, much to their relief, seeming to vanish all at once among the underbrush and tree trunks of the wakening woods.

Chapter 2

James Eckert, now Sir James, Baron de Bois de Malencontri, etc.—though he seldom felt like he really was—awoke in the dawn gloom of the bedchamber he occupied with his wife, Angela, in the Castle de Bois de Malencontri.

Pale slivers of light, showing around the edges of the heavy curtains obscuring the scandalous glazed window of the room, signaled that dawn was at hand. Beside him, under the small mountain of furs and bedcovers that made the unheated stony-walled room bearable, Angie breathed steadily in sleep.

Caught in that odd state that lies between slumber and full awakedness, Jim tried to ignore whatever it was that had woken him. He had a vague sensation of things not quite right, a sort of hangover of the sense of general depression that had been clinging to him the past few dreary weeks. It was a feeling something like the oppressiveness felt by anyone when a storm is just over the horizon and headed his way.

In the last few weeks he had found himself coming close to regretting his decision to stay in this world of dragons, magic, and medieval institutions, instead of returning himself and Angie to the drabber but more familiar world of twentieth-century Earth—wherever in the regions of overlapping probability it might now be.

Contributing, no doubt, to this feeling was the season itself. It was at last the end of a winter that had been stimulating at first; but which had finally seemed to drag on endlessly, with its early twilights, its guttering torches and candles, its icy walls.

Affairs of business to do with the barony he had gained from Sir Hugh de Bois de Malencontri, the previous Baron, had been relentlessly concerning Jim lately. There were buildings and roads to be mended; several hundred serfs, freemen and retainers who looked to him for direction; and all the necessary making of plans for this year's planting. The heavy total of these duties had turned this strange other world about him into a place just about as dull and workaday as the remembered twentieth-century Earth, itself.

Accordingly, Jim's first impulse now was to close his eyes, bury his head under the covers, and push himself back into sleep, leaving whatever had wakened him behind. But when he tried this, sleep refused to return. The sense of something being wrong kept growing until it clamored at last all through him, like a silent alarm bell. Finally, with a snort of exasperation, he lifted his head and opened his eyes again to the light spilling around the edges of the window covering, light which was just bright enough now to dimly show the interior of the bedchamber.

He chilled—and not by reason of the cold bedchamber alone.

He was no longer in his own body. Once more, as it had been when he had originally come to this world by astral projection to rescue Angie, his body had become the body of a very good-sized dragon.

"No!" The word almost escaped from Jim out loud; but he stifled it just in time. Of all things, he did not want to wake Angie now and have her see him as he was.

A frantic feeling possessed him. Had he turned into a dragon for good? If so, why? Anything was possible in this crazy world where magic was part of reality. Perhaps he had only been destined to stay here in his own human body a certain length of time. Perhaps whatever rules governed this kind of thing ordained that he should be a human only half a year and then a dragon half a year. If that was the case, Angie would not like his being a dragon six months of the time at all.

Not at all.

He had to have answers. The one possible source of answers was the Accounting Office, that odd invisible bass voice that seemed to know everything, but chose to tell only what it felt like telling. Apparently, it kept some kind of a record of the magic credit of people who dealt in that commodity—which evidently now included him; first, because he had come to this world by magical means, and second because he had been involved in the frustration of the evil powers at the Loathly Tower less than ten months before.

He opened his mouth to speak to the Accounting Office. As far as he knew they were open twenty-four hours a day—if *they* was the right word for them.

Just in time, he remembered that speaking to the Accounting Office was just about as likely to wake Angie as suddenly shouting *"No,"* the way he had been about to, a moment before.

The only thing to do was to sneak out from under the covers, get out of the room and far enough away so that he could speak to the Accounting Office without waking Angie.

Gradually, he began to ease his enormous body out from under the covers. His tail slid out without trouble. He got one leg out, then the other. He was just starting to move his enormous body when Angie stirred in her sleep beside him, yawned, smiled, and, still without opening her eyes, stretched out a pair of long, lovely arms into the cold air as she arched her body and woke up.

—Just as Jim, by the grace of whoever or whatever was responsible, suddenly reverted to being his own human self again.

Angie had wakened smiling. She continued to smile at Jim for a drowsy moment, then gradually the smile faded and a frown creased a faint line between her eyes.

"I could swear . . ." she said. "You weren't going someplace just now were you? I had a feeling. . . . You sure something unusual wasn't going on with you just a second ago?"

"Me?" said Jim. "Unusual?"

A sense of sudden cunning overcame him.

"Different, me?" he said. "Different, how?"

Angie propped herself up on one elbow just under the blankets, and stared at him with her intense blue eyes. Her dark hair was tumbled by sleep, but still very attractive. He felt a moment's sharp awareness of her trim, naked body only inches away from him. But this emotion was wiped away a second later by apprehension.

"I don't know exactly how," Angie said. "I just have this feeling that there was something different and you were going—why are you practically out of bed?"

"Oh? Am I?" Jim hastily pulled himself completely back under the furs. "Well, I just thought I'd go down and get them started on breakfast and in fact I was thinking of"—he crossed his fingers under the cover of a particularly fine bearskin—"bringing you up a tray."

"Oh, Jim," said Angie. "That's so like you. But it isn't necessary. I feel marvelous, I can't wait to get up."

She had put her hand on his arm under the covers; and he responded to her touch—and then was struck with sudden horror at the thought that his smooth skin suddenly might develop scales under her fingers.

"Fine! Fine!" he yelped, popping out from under the furs and beginning to pull on his clothes. "I'll go down and get them started on breakfast, anyway. You come along as quickly as you can; and maybe we'll have it there waiting for you."

"But Jim, there's not that much hurry—" Jim did not hear the rest of it because he was already out of the door, closing it behind him and moving off down the corridor, still dressing as he went—not for decency's sake, since decency had a rather lower rating in these medieval times he now inhabited—but because the stone-walled corridor following the inner curve of the keep's walls was chillingly cold.

At a safe distance from the solar bedroom door, he stopped, caught his breath, and then spoke to thin air.

"Accounting Office!" he said. "Why did I change into a dragon?"

"Your account has been activated," responded the bass voice about on a level with his thigh; causing him, as usual, to start, even though he knew what to expect.

"Activated? What does that mean?"

"Any account of which the owner is still alive and able to make use, but has not for at least six months, is always activated," said the Accounting Office, rather primly.

"But I still don't understand what 'activated' means!" Jim protested.

"The explanation is self-explanatory," replied the Accounting Office.

It stopped talking. Jim had the uneasy feeling that it had stopped talking permanently, at least on that subject. He called it a couple more times, but it did not answer.

Left not knowing where he stood, he suddenly remembered the business of breakfast and gloomily went down the winding stone stairs from the solar level of the keep.

". . . You might as well tell me the truth," Angie was saying, an hour later over their breakfast platters, at the high table of the castle's main chamber. "Something happened just before I opened my eyes; and I want to know what. I can always tell when you're trying to hide something from me."

"Honestly, Angie," Jim was saying, when his answer became beside the point entirely, as he changed once more into a dragon.

"EEEEE!" exclaimed Angie, at the top of her lungs.

Pandemonium erupted in the hall, which was large enough to contain somewhere between thirty and forty people of both sexes, either concerned with the business of seeing that the Baron and his Lady got their breakfast, or ranging from the armed guard of about eight men-at-arms who were normally there through a selection of other castle personnel and servants down to May Heather, at thirteen years of age the youngest and least-ranked of the kitchen staff.

Danger was something everyone lived with. The unexpected was the expected —in general terms—and weapons of all kinds were never hard to find in an establishment of this kind. Within a couple of minutes, everybody there had some sort of edged or pointed instrument in their hands, had formed into a rough hedgehog-shape with the men-at-arms in point position, and were about to advance on this dragon that had suddenly appeared in the hall.

At this point Angie, having gotten an instinctive, healthy, and rather refreshing scream out of the way, took charge of the matter. The hem of her wine-red morning robe swept the stone floor as she bore down regally upon the hedgehog.

"Stop there!" she ordered it sharply. "There's no danger here. What you see is simply your Lord, who has made use of his magic talents to momentarily put himself into dragon form. May, put that battleaxe back on the wall, at once!"

May had possessed herself of a battleaxe belonging to the former Baron. She was now carrying it on her shoulder like a woodsman's tool; and it was very doubtful if she would have been able to do anything with it, even if she had been able to get it off that shoulder safely. But there was always one thing you could say about May Heather. She was willing.

Abashed now, however, she turned back toward the wall on which the battleaxe had originally been hanging.

The rest of the servants and retainers scattered back to their original duties, looking at each other meaningfully, but bottling up the story they would now be able to tell of Sir James turning himself into a dragon at breakfast time.

Happily, a second later, he was back in human form again, though his robe had split apart and was in rags at his feet.

"Ho, there!" cried Angie to the room at large. "Another robe for His Lordship!"

There was a few minutes of scampering around before another, untorn robe of Jim's was produced. He slipped into it gratefully.

"And now, you, Theoluf!" Angie went on, to the chief of the men-at-arms. "See that Sir James's horse is saddled, provisioned, equipped, his light armor brought down, and everything made ready for him to leave immediately."

Theoluf, having started off with her first words, turned back briefly. He was a man of middling height with a not unfriendly smile when he smiled, but a face badly disfigured by the scars of some form of the pox.

"Right away, m'Lady," he answered. "How many men will m'Lord be taking with him?"

"*None!*" boomed Jim, louder than he had intended. The last thing he wanted was for the people he governed to see him switching back and forth between the human and dragon forms; and possibly come to suspect that he could not control the change.

"You heard your Lord," said Angela to Theoluf.

"Yes, m'Lady," answered the man-at-arms, who would have been very deaf indeed not to have heard. He headed toward the exit door at the end of the great hall. Angie came back to Jim.

"Why are you doing this?" half-whispered Angie angrily, as she came close.

"I wish I knew," answered Jim grouchily, but in an equally low-pitched voice. "You must know I can't control it, or else I wouldn't be doing it."

"What I mean is," insisted Angie, "what do you do just before you turn into a dragon, what makes you do it?"

She paused and stared at him with a suddenly stricken face.

"You're not Gorbash all over again?"

Jim shook his head. Gorbash had been the dragon whose body he had inhabited when he had first come to this strange world.

"No," he answered, "it's just me, in a dragon body. But it just happens to me without warning. I can't control it."

"That's what I was afraid of," said Angie. "That's why I ordered your horse and armor. I want you to talk to Carolinus right away about this."

"Not Carolinus," protested Jim feebly.

"Carolinus!" repeated Angie firmly. "You've got to get to the bottom of this. Do you think you can stay human long enough to put on the armor, get on the horse, and get out of sight, before you do any more changing?"

"I haven't got the slightest idea," said Jim, looking at her unhappily.

Chapter 3

J im was lucky.

He got safely out of sight of the castle and into the woods without changing back into a dragon again. Happily, the Tinkling Water, where S. Carolinus lived, was not far from the castle. Carolinus was the magician who had been involved with Jim in the matter of the Loathly Tower the year before. He had turned out to be a trusty, if equally crusty and short-tempered, friend. He was a magician with a AAA+ rating. There were only three magicians in this world, Jim had been advised by the Accounting Office, who had not only the AAA, which was the highest rating awarded, but the + which lifted it above even the extraordinary level of those three letters.

Jim, by contrast, was a magician—if only an involuntary one—with a mere D rating. Both Carolinus and the Accounting Office had intimated that he would be very lucky indeed if in his lifetime he ever progressed up to the C class. In this world, apparently, as in the twentieth-century one that Jim and Angie had left behind them, you either had it or you did not.

As usual, riding in the woods had a calming effect upon Jim's nerves. There was something marvelously relaxing about being out by yourself alone on a horse, which for the sake for common prudence and economy, you rode at a walk. You were in no hurry, and usually whatever urgency there was in you tended to bleed out gradually.

Furthermore, the fourteenth-century English woodland—even in the early spring of this world—was a pleasant place to be. The trees had all grown high enough to throw enough shade so that only a little grass, by way of ground cover, appeared in the sunnier spots and survived. There were occasional brambles, thickets, and thick stands of willow; but the road sensibly avoided them by simply going around any such obstacles. Like many things here, the road was very pragmatic. It dealt with things as it found them, without trying to adapt them to its own will and circumstances.

Also, it was a very pleasant day. It had been raining for the past three days, but today the sun shone; and the clouds that could occasionally be seen between the treetops were few and far between. It was warm for a late March day, but just enough to make Jim's clothing and armor bearable.

He was not dressed in the suit of plate armor he had acquired by involuntary inheritance from the former Lord of his castle. That armor had required some adjustment. The former Baron de Bois de Malencontri had been heavy-bodied and wide-shouldered enough, but he had not had Jim's height. As a result some changes had been made by an armorer in Stourbridge. But even with these, the suit of plate armor was still uncomfortable to wear for any length of time, and particularly when there was no need to.

Today Jim had felt that there was no need to. Such heavy armor was kept, as Jim's good friend, neighbor, and comrade-in-arms, Sir Brian Neville-Smythe was fond of saying, for hunting mere-dragons, spear-runnings, or otherwise important business. What Jim wore now was essentially a light mail shirt over a leather hauberk, the whole reinforced with rings along the arms and plates over the shoulder, where the impact of an edged weapon might not cut through to him, but could easily break the bone beneath.

He also wore a light helmet covering the upper part of his head, with a nasal projecting down from it in front to protect the bridge of his nose and try to keep it from being broken in case of trouble; also, a pair of equally light greaves on the tops of his thighs.

The end result of all this was that, although the day might have been a little cool for Jim in the kind of clothes he would have been used to wearing in the twentieth century, it was perhaps even a bit on the warm side for him under these conditions. The district was in the English Midlands and already had more than a foot into spring.

Consequently, Jim's spirits rose. What if he was indeed turning into a dragon unexpectedly from time to time? Carolinus would be able to tell him why and set the matter right. The closer he got to the Tinkling Water where Carolinus lived, the more peaceful and cheerful he became. His spirits had lightened to the point where he was almost on the verge of breaking into song, so good was he feeling.

Just at that moment, however, he rounded a curve in the forest track that was the road; and saw, crossing ahead of him, a family of wild boar; the sow first, followed by half a dozen young ones. Meanwhile, facing in Jim's direction almost as if waiting for him, was the father of the family, the boar himself.

The thought of song vanished from Jim's mind, and he reined his horse to a halt.

He was not unarmed. He had learned not to be in the long winter sessions with Sir Brian, as he practiced with that good knight at using the weapons of the period—and picked them up remarkably well and swiftly, which was not surprising, seeing that Jim was a natural athlete, having been a AA-class volleyball player back in his own twentieth-century Earth. But here in a fourteenth-century world it was not wise for a single person or even a group of persons to go unarmed any place. Outside of wild boar, like the one confronting him right now, there were as well unknown wolves, bears, outlaws, unfriendly neighbors; and any of a number of other inimical possibilities.

Consequently, Jim was wearing his regular broadsword, and the smaller of his two shields hung from his saddle. In addition to that, a long poignard in its sheath balanced the sword by hanging down on the other side of his belt—a daggerlike instrument with a blade some eleven inches long. However, none of these were ideal tools for discouraging an attack by a large and well-tusked boar, like the one he saw before him.

Not that a boar like that was likely to be discouraged, even by a knight in full plate armor, with spear. Once a boar made up his mind to charge, as Aargh had once said, that was about all he would be able to think about until everything was over.

There were other weapons more suited to handling a boar than those Jim wore. One was a boar spear, which was a short, but stoutly built spear, made mainly of metal, so that the boar could not bite its shaft in half. It had a crosspiece some three feet behind its wickedly tined head. The purpose of the crosspiece was to keep the boar from charging all the way up the spear, ignoring it completely; and going to work with his tusks on the man who held the spear. Even May Heather's battleaxe would have been welcome at the moment.

Jim sat and waited. He hoped that the family, consisting of the sow and the younger boars, would vanish into the woods on the far side of the road; and that the boar himself would turn to follow them. Nonetheless Jim was conscious of feeling uneasy. His horse was definitely uneasy. Jim wished he could afford a horse like Sir Brian's—which was a highly trained war-horse, with as much instinct to attack on sight as the boar had; and trained to fight anything before it with teeth and hooves.

But horses like that were worth a young fortune; and while Jim had a certain amount of magic credit to his name, plus the castle, his supply of ready coin was small.

The big question was, would the boar's natural desire to attack any potential opponent on sight overcome its other natural desire to move on peaceably with its family? The answer could be given only by the boar itself.

Now, however, the boar had apparently thought the matter over. The sow and the last of the young boars had disappeared into the further woods. It was time, the boar seemed to feel, to put up or shut up. It had been snorting and pawing the turf with its front feet; now it began not merely scratching the earthy surface but throwing up small clods of it. Clearly, it was getting ready to charge. At this moment, Jim's horse literally screamed and, as literally, bolted from under him; so that he fell to the ground with a thump.

As he fell, he felt a second of almost intolerable pressure, which was as suddenly relieved. He found himself looking at the scene from a slightly different angle.

He was a dragon again. In the process of turning into one, he had literally burst out of both his armor and his clothes—with the exception of his hose which, being made of a stretchy, knitted material, instead of tearing or breaking its fastenings, had simply rolled itself down his legs. So that now he gave the rather ridiculous picture of a dragon hobbled by what looked like the lower half of some long underwear equipped with booties.

But at the moment this was unimportant. What was important was that the boar was still there.

Nonetheless, things had clearly changed. The boar had stopped kicking up dirt and snorting. It was frozen, staring at the dragon that now confronted it. For a moment, Jim did not appreciate his good fortune. Then understanding overcame him.

"Get out of here!" he bellowed in full dragon voice at the boar. "Go on. Git!"

The boar, like all its kind, was assuredly no coward. Cornered, even by a dragon, it undoubtedly would have charged. On the other hand, a dragon was not the ideal opponent, even for a boar; and in addition, this dragon had appeared out of nowhere. Combative, the boar might be; but after the manner of all wild animals, it had an instinct for survival. It turned and vanished into the undergrowth in the direction the rest of its family had gone.

Jim looked around for his horse. He found it behind him about twenty yards and a little off into the woods, peering out at him, and to his telescopic dragon vision, clearly shivering.

Thoughtfully, Jim disentangled his hind feet from his hose. He inspected them. They, at least, might be wearable again. He contemplated the rest of his clothing and armor. Even if he had his human body back, it would be difficult to redress and rearmor himself in the pieces that were about him. On the other hand, it would not do to leave them here in the road. He gathered them up and made a small pile, which he tied together with his sword belt. It had broken when he had become a dragon, but its ends could be tied, clumsily.

Gazing at it, he thought that the bundle would probably ride all right on his back, if he fitted the edge of the belt between a couple of the diagonal bony plates that stood up along his spine and out over the top of his tail.

He turned to his horse, gazing at it slantwise out of the corners of his eyes, so as not to alarm it by appearing to put his attention full upon it. It had ceased shivering, though its skin shone damply with sweat. It was definitely not the equivalent of Sir Brian's noble war-horse, Blanchard of Tours, as Jim had been thinking earlier. But it was a valuable beast, the best of his stable; and leaving it loose here in the woods would be the way to lose it, most likely. On the other hand, it was clearly as uneasy about him in his dragon form as the boar had been.

He sat thinking. Any attempt to approach the horse would frighten it away from him. Furthermore, any attempt to speak to it would result in the words coming out in his dragon voice, which would also frighten it. He mulled over the problem.

A sudden inspiration came to him. The horse—in a nostalgic moment Jim had named the stalwart bay gelding "Gorp," after the ancient automobile that had been the only transport Angie and he could afford, back when they had been graduate students in the twentieth-century world—was in no way trained like Blanchard of Tours. But Sir Brian had pointed out that a certain amount of simple, Gorp-level training might still be useful.

One of the most rudimentary bits of training Sir Brian had recommended Jim start off with, had been teaching Gorp to come when Jim whistled. It was highly important to anyone fighting on horseback. If a knight got unhorsed, but his horse was still serviceable, he should be able to call it to him so he could remount. In the noise and shouting of battle, with the clang of swords on armor, one more voice would not be distinctive. On the other hand, a whistle could be heard by the horse over the other sounds, and be immediately identifiable.

Consequently, Jim had worked at training Gorp to come to his whistle; and had, as much to his surprise as to Angie's or anyone else's, succeeded. It was just possible now that the horse would come in this moment also to his whistle. That is, if this other body of his could whistle.

There was no way to find out but by trying it. Jim pursed his lips, which felt very odd in that position to his dragon senses, and blew.

At first he produced no noise at all. Then so suddenly that he himself was startled, his customary come-hither whistle emerged from the dragon lips.

Within the trees Gorp pricked up his ears and stirred uneasily. He stared at the dragon shape in the road; but Jim was still carefully not looking directly at him. Jim whistled again.

In the end it took five whistles. But eventually, almost plodding, Gorp sidled up to the dragon shape; and Jim was able to close one clawed fist on the animal's trailing reins. At last he had what he wanted. He could lead Gorp along with him until he came to Carolinus's. In fact, he could do better than that. He could hook his sword belt to the pommel of the saddle and let Gorp carry the bundle of his clothes, armor, and weapons. He allowed the horse to smell the bundle of clothes first, and Gorp evidently found it reassuring, so that he did not protest when Jim's mighty claws hooked the belt around the pommel of the saddle.

Gently, Jim turned and attempted to lead Gorp slowly forward along the road. Gorp dug in his feet at first, then yielded. He followed.

It was only a little distance to Carolinus's cottage at the Tinkling Water. As he got closer, a feeling of peace began to overcome Jim, at first suddenly and then powerfully. It was always so with anyone approaching the residence of Carolinus; and Jim no longer wondered at it.

He now knew that Carolinus's powers as a magician were such that not only was the spot itself peaceful; but it would remain so in the face of almost any eventuality. Should a forest fire sweep through these woods—an unlikely possibility, because of the relatively small amount of undergrowth in the shadow of these monarchical elms—Jim had no doubt that it would carefully part, well short of the Tinkling Water glade, and pass by at a decent distance on either side before reforming its line once more beyond it.

Jim led Gorp into the glade at last. It was warming, in spite of his situation, to see the tiny clearing among the trees with the stream running through it and tumbling over a small waterfall at its upper end.

Beside the stream and a little off to one side, close to the small house beyond it, was a pool with a fountain. As Jim and Gorp approached the building, a small fish leaped out of the water, made a graceful curve and as gracefully reentered the water headfirst. For a moment Jim could have believed that what he had actually seen was a miniature mermaid. But it was probably just imagination. He put the thought aside.

As usual, the Tinkling Water of the stream and fountain lived up to its name. It did indeed tinkle. Not with the sound of tiny bells, but with the fragile sound of glass chimes stirred by a gentle breeze. Also as usual, on either side of the immaculately-raked gravel walk—though Jim had never seen anyone, let alone Carolinus, actually raking it—were two lines of flower beds filled with a crowded congregation of asters, tulips, zinnias, roses, and lilies-of-the-valley, all blooming in complete disregard for their normal seasons to do so.

In the midst of one of the flower plots rose a post to which was attached a white painted board, on which in black angular letters the name S. CAROLINUS was elegantly imprinted. Jim smiled at it and dropped Gorp's reins, leaving the horse to crop at the thick carpet of green grass which surrounded all else in the glade, and went up to the house by himself. From this spot, he knew Gorp would not stray.

The house was a modest, narrow affair of two stories, with a sharply slanting roof. The walls seemed to be made of pebble-sized stones of a uniform gray color and the roof itself was of light blue tiles, almost the color of the sky. A red-brick chimney rose out of the blue roof. Jim went on up to the front door, which was green and set above a single red-painted stone step.

He had been intending to knock at the door, but as he got close, he saw that it was standing slightly ajar. From within the house came the sound of a voice raised in exasperation, and snarling away in some language Jim could not understand, but which evidently possessed a great number of words that sounded as if they had jagged edges and were anything but complimentary.

The voice was that of Carolinus. The mage was evidently angry about something.

Jim hesitated, suddenly doubtful. Carolinus was seldom numbered among the ranks of patient individuals. It had not occurred to Jim that he might be bringing his problem to the other at a time when Carolinus was having a difficulty of his own.

But the feeling of unease which had come over Jim yielded almost immediately to the general feeling of peace in the environment. He went on up the single red step, knocked diffidently at the door, knocked again when his first knock was apparently ignored, and at last—since Carolinus seemed determined not to pay any attention to the sound of it—pushed open the door and squeezed through it.

The single cluttered room he entered took up the whole ground floor of the building; but right now it had no light coming into it through its windows at all, though no blinds or curtains appeared to have been drawn, and a fairly substantial gloom pervaded it. Only on its curved ceiling were scattered specks of light.

Carolinus, a thin old man in a red robe, wearing a black skullcap and an equally thin, rather dingy-looking, white beard, was standing over what looked like a basketball-sized sphere of ivory color, which glowed with an inner light. From apertures on that sphere, some of the light was escaping to make the flecks on the ceiling. Carolinus was swearing at it in the unknown tongue Jim had heard as he came in.

"Er—" said Jim, hesitantly.

Carolinus stopped cursing—it could be nothing but cursing he was doing— and removed his gaze from the globe to glare at Jim.

"Not my day for drag—" he began fiercely, then broke off, adding in a hardly more friendly note, "So! James!"

"Well, yes," said Jim, diffidently. "If I've come at a bad time—"

"When did anybody ever come to see me at a *good* time?" snapped Carolinus.

"You're here because you're in trouble, aren't you? Don't deny it! That's the only reason anybody ever comes to see me. You're in trouble, aren't you?"

"Well, yes—" said Jim.

"Can you talk without beginning every sentence with 'well'?" demanded Carolinus.

"Of course," said Jim. His own temper was beginning to shorten a little bit. Carolinus sometimes had that effect on people; even normally easygoing characters like Jim.

"Then pray do so," said Carolinus. "Can't you see I've got difficulties of my own?"

"I rather figured you had," said Jim, "from the way you were talking; but I don't really know what it is that's bothering you."

"You don't?" retorted Carolinus. "I should think any fool could see—even a *Master of Arts*." The last word came out with a definitely sarcastic edge. Jim had been incautious enough early in their acquaintance to mention to Carolinus that he had gotten a degree as Master of Arts in Medieval Studies at a midwestern university. It had only been later that Jim had discovered that in this world, and particularly in the exclusive province of magicians, the term *Master of Arts* indicated a great deal more prestige and accomplishment than the academic equivalent he had picked up at Michigan State.

"Can't you see my orrery isn't working right?" went on Carolinus. "It's showing me a view of the heavens that's all turned around. I can tell that by one glance; but I can't put my finger on what's wrong. I'm sure the North Star shouldn't be there," he pointed to a far corner of the room, "but, where should it be?"

"In the north," said Jim innocently.

"Of course, in the—" Carolinus broke off suddenly, stared at Jim, and snorted. Bending over his ivory globe, he rotated it roughly a quarter turn.

The lights on the ceiling flickered to a new position. Carolinus looked up at them and sighed happily.

"Merely a matter of time until I found the right spot myself, of course," he said. For a moment he sounded almost genial.

He looked at Jim again.

"Well now," went on Carolinus in what, for him, was a reasonable tone, "what does bring you to see me, then?"

"Do you mind if we step outside to talk about it?" asked Jim, still diffidently. The fact of the matter was that with his size and the low ceiling of the room, plus its general darkness at the moment, he had a vision of stepping on, or brushing off a table, some priceless object; and sending Carolinus back into his ill-temper once more.

"I suppose I could do that," said Carolinus. "All right then. After you."

Jim turned and squeezed back out the door into the sunlight. Gorp raised his head momentarily from the grass he was cropping to look at the two of them as they emerged; and then went back to the more important business of feeding himself. Jim stepped down from the red step to the pathway and Carolinus joined him there.

"So," said Carolinus, "you're here in dragon body. Why?"

"That's it," answered Jim.

"What do you mean, that's it?" echoed Carolinus.

"I mean," said Jim, "it's the dragon body, that's the reason I'm here. I seem to have started turning into a dragon unexpectedly from time to time. I asked the Accounting Office and all they'd tell me was that my account had been activated."

"Hmmm," said Carolinus, "that's right, been a good bit over six months hasn't it? I'm surprised they didn't do it before now."

"But I don't want my account activated," said Jim. "I don't want to keep changing into a dragon and back again without warning like this. I need your help to stop it."

"Stop it?" Carolinus's white eyebrows climbed up his forehead. "There's no way I can stop an account being activated. Particularly since the time limit's more than run out."

"But I don't even understand what's meant by my account being activated!" said Jim.

"Why, my good James!" said Carolinus, exasperatedly. "You shouldn't need any help to reason that out. You've a certain balance with the Accounting Office. A balance is energy—potential magical energy. And energy is not static. It has to be active, by definition. That means you put it to use, or—as now, very evidently—it puts itself to use. Since you haven't done anything with it; and all it knows as far as your taste and choices of use go, is that you once were in the body of a dragon, it's started turning you into a dragon and from a dragon back again into a human at random. *Quod erat demonstratum.* Or, in language you can understand—"

" '—as has been demonstrated'," translated Jim, a little testily, himself. He might be an ordinary twentieth-century M.A., but he did know Latin.

He forced his voice back into reasonable tones.

"Well, that's all very well," he said, "but how do we get it to stop turning me into a dragon and back again without any warning?"

"*We* don't," said Carolinus. "You've got to do that for yourself."

"But I don't know how!" said Jim. "If I knew how I wouldn't be here asking you for help."

"This isn't the sort of thing I can help," Carolinus said grumpily. "It's your account, not mine. You've got to handle it. If you don't know how, you've got to learn how. Do you want to learn how?"

"I have to learn how!" said Jim.

"Very well then. I'll take you on as my pupil," said Carolinus. "The usual ten percent of your balance for my fee will therefore automatically and immediately be transferred to my balance. Noted?"

"Noted!" said the bass voice of the Accounting Office, from its customary height of a few feet above the ground and with its customary effect on Jim—as if a firecracker had gone off between his toes.

"A pittance," Carolinus was grumbling into his beard. "However, since it's the customary fee . . ."

He raised his voice to a conversational level again.

"You will be counseled by me in all things magical, as was Merlin by the mighty Bleys, his Master?" he said. "Answer *No*, and the bargain is unmade, answer *Yes* and you pledge your total Account to your word to obey!"

"Yes," said Jim, readily enough.

He was thinking he might actually be a great deal better off without that ridiculous Account, so it would hardly break his heart if it came to a matter of disobeying Carolinus on some magical matter.

"Well," said Jim, "now about getting me out of this dragon body and back into my regular one—"

"Not so fast!" snapped Carolinus. "First we've got to feed you with Knowledge."

He turned aside and snapped his fingers at empty air.

"Encyclopedia!" he commanded.

A red-bound volume of the *Encyclopedia Britannica* materialized out of thin air and fell to the gravel below. A second volume was just about to follow it—in fact it had half materialized—when Carolinus's rather brisk attitude changed to one of fury.

"*No!* Not that, you idiot!" he shouted. "*The* Encyclopedia. The *Necroman-tick!*"

"Sorry," said the deep bass voice of the Accounting Office. The already-extant and the half-materialized volume of the *Britannica* disappeared.

Jim stared at Carolinus. He had never spoken at all irritably to the Accounting Office, himself. Something in his bones warned him that it would not be a wise thing to do. Even if he had not remembered the single moment, some nine months ago, in which Earth, sky, and sea had spoken with a single voice, echoing what the Office had just said, he had the feeling that he would know better than to speak up to the Accounting Office voice.

It had been true that the one word the Accounting Office had uttered then had not been addressed to him. But all the same, he would remember it for the rest of his life.

Nor had it been ineffective. The Dark Powers, for all their omnipotence, had been immediate in delivering Angie back to him once that command had been given. Yet here was Carolinus, who regularly treated the Accounting Office voice as if it was some junior employee, and a half-witted one at that.

"Ah!" said Carolinus.

A leather-bound book big enough to make the first volume of the *Britannica* look like a postage stamp appeared out of empty air and fell downwards. Unbelievably, Carolinus caught it as lightly in the palm of one hand as if it had been a feather. Jim was just close enough to read the slanted writing in gold across the cover of the book.

Encyclopedie Necromantick.

"Complete with index. That's right," said Carolinus, balancing the volume in his hand and gazing piercingly at it. "Now you—*small down!*"

The huge volume began to shrink. It got smaller and smaller until it was the size of a sugar cube—until it was no more than the size of a very small medicine tablet. He passed it over to Jim, who automatically braced his arm to receive its weight and was surprised to find that he could hardly feel it in the palm of his dragon's horny paw. He stared at it.

"Well," said Carolinus, "don't just stand there. Swallow it!"

With some misgivings, Jim flicked out a long red dragon tongue, curled it around the tiny pill-sized thing he was holding, drew it back into his mouth, and swallowed.

It vanished down his throat without any feeling; but a moment later he felt rather as if he had eaten an enormous meal.

"There you are," said Carolinus satisfiedly. "Everything a young magician needs to know. In fact, everything any magician needs to know—those who still have to go by spells, of course. You've got the knowledge now, my boy. It's just a matter of your learning how to use it. Practice, practice! That's the answer. Practice!"

He rubbed his thin hands together.

"How—how do I practice?" said Jim, still battling with the feeling of having eaten two Christmas dinners at once.

"How do you do it?" said Carolinus. "I just told you. Practice! Look up the spell you need in the index, find it in the *Encyclopedie*, and apply it. That's what you do. Moreover, you keep on doing it until you have the whole *Encyclopedie* by heart. Then, if you have the talent, you move up a step to the point where needing to use such crutches is no longer necessary. Once you've learned all the spells in that *Encyclopedie*, you can construct your own. Once you know a million spells you can construct a billion, a trillion—however many you want! Not that I think you'll ever reach that point."

Jim agreed. Moreover, he felt as if he didn't particularly care to reach that point.

"How long do I go on feeling like a stuffed goose?" he asked feebly.

"Oh, that," Carolinus waved a hand negligently. "That'll pass off in half an hour or so. You just need to digest what you've swallowed."

He turned back toward the house.

"Well," he said over his shoulder, "that takes care of your matter. I can get back to my orrery. Remember what I told you. Practice! Practice!"

"Wait!" yelped Jim.

Chapter **4**

Carolinus stopped and turned. His white eyebrows were drawn together in a frown and he was looking definitely dangerous.

"Now what?" he asked, enunciating the words slowly and ominously.

"I'm still in my dragon body," said Jim. "I need to get out of this. How do I do it?"

"With Magic!" retorted Carolinus. "Why do you think I took you on as a pupil? Why do you think I had you swallow the *Encyclopedie?* You have the means, use them!"

Jim made a flash examination of his mind. He could feel knowledge there, all right; a lump as indigestible and unavailable as the weight he seem to feel in his stomach.

"You had me swallow it," said Jim desperately, "but I don't know how to use it. How do I turn myself from a dragon back into myself?"

A malicious smile crept across Carolinus's face; but it relaxed from the ominous scowl that had held it a second before.

"Aha!" he said. "As a teaching assistant I naturally assumed you'd know how to make use of resource materials. But clearly you don't."

For a moment the frown came back. He muttered something in his beard about, ". . . disgraceful . . . younger generation . . ."

"However," he said, "I suppose I'll have to walk you through your first use of Magic.

"Look on the inside of your forehead," he added.

Jim stared at him. Then he tried what Carolinus had said. Of course he could not look at the inside of his forehead. But, strangely enough, he now had the feeling that, with a little bit of imagination, he could imagine a curved sheet of darkness, as available as a blackboard to write upon.

"Got it?" demanded Carolinus.

"I think so," answered Jim. "At least I've got a feel for the inside of my forehead."

"Good!" said Carolinus. "Now bring up the index."

Jim concentrated on his imaginary blackboard; and with another imaginative effort he discovered that large golden letters were forming against that dark surface; and that they read:

INDEX

"I think I've got that, too," said Jim, squinting at the scene around him, as if that would help focus his mind on what he was trying to envision.

"Very well," said Carolinus, "now bring up the following, one at a time. Ready?"

"Ready," said Jim.

"*Notshape*," said Carolinus.

Jim made some kind of intellectual effort—there was no way he could describe it, but it was somewhat as if he was trying to remember something that he knew very well. The word INDEX disappeared; and was replaced by a list of words that scrolled past from the bottom of his forehead up out of sight at the top. They seemed to keep on zipping past endlessly. He caught a flash of occasional ones—"fat," "thin," "elsewhere" . . . but none of them made any sense. He assumed that these were somehow attributes of shape he was looking at. But how to slow down the scrolling, or find what he wanted among them—even if he knew what he wanted—was a problem that right now seemed absolutely insoluble.

"*Dragon*," he heard Carolinus's voice barking at him. Jim envisioned it.

It was immediately replaced by more words scrolling, now different. Jim picked out "large," "British," "savage" . . .

"*Arrow*," Carolinus was commanding.

Jim struggled to obey. After a moment he got a straight line with what looked like the literal broad point of a clothyard arrow, on the right end of the line he was looking at. The image on the inside of his forehead now read:

NOTSHAPE DRAGON———>

"Got it," said Jim, beginning to feel a first tendril of pleasure at his own accomplishments. "Got it all so far. 'NOTSHAPE—DRAGON—ARROW—'".

"*Me!*" said Carolinus.

"Me," echoed Jim, summoning up the word just beyond the point of the arrow on the forehead-blackboard of his mind.

It flashed for a moment on the inner forehead of Jim's imagination:

NOTSHAPE DRAGON———>ME

Abruptly, he felt extremely chilly. Forgetting about the blackboard, and returning his attention to his outside surroundings and himself, he discovered he was standing naked on Carolinus's graveled path.

"And there you are," said Carolinus, beginning to turn away once more.

"Hold on!" cried Jim. "What about my clothes? My armor? It's all in pieces!"

Carolinus slowly turned, and the expression on his face was clearly not agreeable. Jim hurried over to Gorp, unhooked his sword belt from the pommel, and brought it back, together with its bundle of weapons and bits and pieces of his clothing and armor, to where the other was standing. The March day was definitely cool. You could almost call it cold after all. The gravel of Carolinus's walk definitely hurt the soles of his feet. Nonetheless, he dumped the package at Carolinus's feet, undid the sword belt and displayed the remnants of his personal wear.

"I see," said Carolinus thoughtfully, stroking his beard.

"I was wearing this when I turned into a dragon," said Jim. "Naturally when I switched to the bigger body it sort of exploded off me."

"Yes. Yes, indeed," said Carolinus, continuing to stroke his beard. "Interesting."

"Well?" asked Jim. "Will you tell me how to put all these things back to the way they were, magically?"

"Heal them, you mean?" Carolinus's bushy eyebrows were making a single line over his eyes once more.

"That's what I had in mind. Yes," said Jim.

"It can be done, of course," said Carolinus slowly, "but there are elements here which you have yet to discover, James. Perhaps, indeed—I think, yes."

"Yes what?" inquired Jim.

"It may just be time for your first lecture as my pupil," said Carolinus, casting a thoughtful glance at the sky overhead before looking back at Jim. "I will now explain to you some of what lies behind the elements of Magic. Pay heed."

Jim shivered. The day was not merely cool or cold, it was positively icy. There were goose bumps all over him. On the other hand, he knew Carolinus well enough to know that the other was now embarked on an action which probably could not be frustrated, diverted, or in fact done anything with, but accepted. He wished he knew whatever spell there was for keeping himself warm. He tried to ignore the goose bumps, and listened.

"Imagine," said Carolinus, "what it must have been like in the beginning. Back when man was a Stone Age savage and before, everything was Magic. If you and the rest of your tribe pounded away on a dangerous bear, let us say, until it fell over and did not move any more, the reason you had conquered it was Magic. Not the clubs. There was no connection between pounding something with clubs and the life going out of the creature that had been a threat to you. That, at least, is the way it was in the beginning."

Carolinus cleared his throat. He was speaking to Jim, but also to the little glade of the Tinkling Water itself and to the sky overhead. Lecturing the world in general, as a matter of fact.

"Conceive this now, James," he said. "This is a time when everything happens by Magic. Rain is Magic, lightning is Magic, thunder is Magic; there is Magic all around you. There is Magic in everything that is done by animals and by other humans. If not directly Magic, it is affected by Magic. You get my point?"

Now he did bend his eyes directly on Jim.

"Er—I think so," said Jim. "You're saying that in the beginning magic was an explanation for everything, everything was done by magic."

"Not *an* explanation!" scowled Carolinus. "Everything was Magical. However, as time went on, those things that were in the common area and used by everybody and about which there was no secret, began to lose their aura of Magic. So the idea came to be that there were things Magic and things that were not-Magic. But they changed over from one area to the other one by one. Consider, that for our purposes—you and I who deal with Magic, James—everything *still* is Magic, at base."

"I—yes," said Jim.

"Very good," went on Carolinus. "Therefore let us imagine the first time someone who was used to just draping himself with furs, happened to get hold of a garment that was made of two furs; one that had been sewed together. And he wore those happily for some time; until some accident or other caused the sewing to tear and the two furs to part. So he took them back to the person from whom he had first gotten the joined furs, or the person he had heard of as being responsible for joining them, who turned out to be the old, wise woman of the tribe."

He stopped and looked severely at Jim. "Every tribe in those days had a wise woman. It was required."

"Yes, yes," said Jim, massaging his upper arms with their opposing hands. "Go on. Go on."

"She took the furs from him," continued Carolinus, "and said, *'Yes I can put these back together again. But it is very secret magic. I will take them into my cave and you must by no means try to follow or watch me. If you do, lightning will tear your skin from your bones, the next storm we have!'*"

Jim had just recalled that his hose, which he now finally remembered had only been stretched, not torn apart, were still essentially wearable. He pulled them on and began to drape himself with bits and pieces of his shirt and doublet. It was not much, but it made the outdoor air a little more bearable.

"Go on," said Jim, looking at his boots, which unfortunately had been rather badly torn apart. He could get them on his feet, all right; but there was no doubt they would not stay on the minute he tried to lift his foot to take a step.

"So," said Carolinus, cheerfully ignoring him and immersed in his own lecture, "the wise woman took the skins into the cave; and after a while brought them out and—Lo, they were joined together again! The man for whom she had done this paid her, and everyone was happy."

Jim was still searching among the fragments of his clothing for more protection from the weather.

"So what do you think had happened?" Carolinus's voice exploded like a bomb in his ear, and he jerked up to find the magician glaring at him from six inches away.

"Well, I—ah—she sewed them together again," said Jim.

"Exactly!" said Carolinus. "But at that time, you now see, sewing was a Magical act. What she did was to pierce holes in the skin and pull sinew through them; and this created a Magic condition in which the two skins had to stay together. *Do you understand?*"

"Yes," said Jim, shocked back into complete attention.

"Now," went on Carolinus almost sweetly, "insofar as this applies to your situation: Yes, within the *Encyclopedie Necromantick*, there is the information that will allow you, or would allow me to show you, how to put your clothes back together with Magic. However, the spell would have to be renewed every sunrise. It would be a problem. It would be vulnerable to any kind of counter-influence from another Magic entity. In short, it is not an ideal solution. Because, my dear James, the moral of what I've been telling you is that those things which have passed from the realm of Magic into the realm of common everyday ways of doing things are always the best forms of Magic!"

He stopped and frowned again at Jim.

"This has ramifications far and beyond the matter of putting clothes back on your body right now," Carolinus went on. "You must always remember what you've just learned from me. Magic that has entered the common domain is the best Magic. It should be used first. The best of Magic that is still unknown to nonprofessionals is liable to mischance and destruction. I will tell you a story."

He glared at Jim again.

"You're listening?"

"Absolutely," said Jim.

"This story concerns a fellow Magician who unfortunately was not the best of us. There are no bad Magicians," said Carolinus, "there are only Magicians gone astray. There are extenuating circumstances, of course; but—I won't tell you his name. You'll find that out after you move up in the ranks—if you ever do—but even though there were extenuating circumstances, what he did was inexcusable."

Carolinus paused importantly. "This Magician chose to use his Magical abilities for mundane ends," he said slowly and impressively. "You must never fall into that trap James. Never."

"Oh, I won't," said Jim quickly.

"Good," said Carolinus. "As I was saying he decided to use his Magic for mundane ends. He thought he saw his way to control a Kingdom by causing the young prince of it, who had just succeeded his father the king as ruler there, to fall in love with a maiden who would be completely under the Magician's control. A contrived maiden who would direct every move the young prince made, and consequently make him a puppet of the Magician."

Carolinus had paused again and Jim felt that he was waiting for Jim to make some kind of comment. Jim could think of nothing to say so he merely clicked his tongue.

"Tch, tch," he said.

"Yes, indeed," said Carolinus. "So the Magician imported the finest and purest snow, from the top of the highest mountain close enough so that the snow would not melt in its journey to him; and fashioned from it the most beautiful maiden that the world has ever seen. He introduced her to the prince, the prince fell deeply in love with her, they were married amidst great rejoicing throughout the kingdom."

Carolinus paused to draw a breath.

"All through the introduction, the courtship, the marriage and so forth," Carolinus went on, "the Magician was very careful to make sure that no moisture touched the maiden—who, of course, being made of snow would melt if it did. He impressed on the prince the fact that the maiden had such delicate skin that she could only be touched by moisture in the form of a Magic potion that he himself imported at great cost from the other side of the world and that even her bathing must remain a secret from the prince."

"But—" began Jim.

"I am talking," said Carolinus frostily.

"Sorry," said Jim. "Go on."

"All other forms of moisture the princess must be shielded from," continued Carolinus. "On the day of the wedding there was a slight shower, but there were plenty of ready coverings to protect the princess. All went well until the newlyweds started to reenter the castle of the prince, who was now king. Without any thought for possible dangers the prince swept up the maiden in his arms to carry her in over the threshold. The Magician was too far away to reach him, even if he had foreseen the danger in this. Unfortunately, the threshold of the castle lay beyond a short bridge that covered the castle moat. The prince started up the slight slope of this bridge. But it was now wet from the rain. He slipped, he fell. He and the maiden were both plunged in the moat—you can guess, I suppose, that he came up alone."

Carolinus paused at last, on a deep and impressive note.

Jim felt vaguely as if he was expected to bare his head at this point and place his hand over his heart. Unfortunately, he had nothing to take off by way of a hat and he decided he would feel decidedly silly putting his hand over his heart.

"She melted in the waters of the moat, of course," Carolinus said. "Tragic."

Jim tried to look properly impressed.

"Particularly for the prince, it was tragic," went on Carolinus. "For the plans of the Magician, of course, it was ruin. For the Accounting Office, there was the necessity of imposing a severe fine upon the Magician—for technical reasons, which are somewhat beyond your reach at the moment, my dear James. The point of the whole story is—Never use Magic when you can better employ some mundane, if no longer recognized as such, form of Magic that exists generally. Now, what I suggest—and I'll coach you through it—is that you use a spell for temporarily sticking together those parts of your apparel and armor that are now—er—dismembered. But when you get home, you have them properly reattached the one to the other, or whatever else needs to be done, by purely mundane means. Do you follow me?"

"Certainly!" cried Jim, relieved to be done with the lecture and overjoyed to know that he was going to be clothed once more. He had been rather sure that Gorp would not be likely to let him mount in his present ragtag appearance; and he did not look forward to a walk all the way back to the castle.

Carolinus accordingly put him through a procedure with the inside of his forehead, the Index, and the *Encyclopedie Necromantick;* and Jim found himself, at last, to all intents and purposes, dressed, armored and on his way home.

A couple of hours later he reached the portal of his own castle, feeling more than a little contented with himself. He had the technique for changing himself back from a dragon to a human firmly in mind now; and he should have no more trouble with that. Under Carolinus's tutelage, he had even experimented with turning himself back into a dragon, simply so he could turn himself back to human again, back and forth several times, to make sure the lesson stuck. It had been, all in all, a good day.

"M'Lord!" said the man-at-arms at watch on the gate. "Sir Brian Neville-Smythe. He's here!"

"Oh?" said Jim. "Good!"

He got rid of his horse and hurried to the great hall, which was where Sir Brian was most likely to be, unless Angie had taken him up into their solar bedroom for privacy. The fact of the matter was, there were not a great many places in the castle that were not essentially public. The result was that both Jim and Angie had fallen into the medieval habit of simply living and talking with all sorts of people around them. Eventually they had simply gotten to the point where they ignored being watched and overheard, except in their most private moments. Sir Brian was seated at the high table in the great hall with Angie, pretty much as Jim had expected. Jim strode up to the table, clasped hands with Sir Brian, and joined them.

"Jim!" said Angie. "What happened to you?"

It was plain, to Jim at least, that the minute the words were out of her mouth, she was wishing that she had not said anything. However, his appearance was bound to be remarked on in any case; and Jim had already come up with a temporary, stopgap answer.

"Oh," he said, "it's a matter of magic gone wrong. Nothing important. We'll just have to get these clothes of mine sewed back together properly and my armor straightened out where it needs to be."

He was conscious of at least twenty other people in the hall drifting close as he spoke.

"Indeed, you do look somewhat the worse for wear, m'Lord," said Sir Brian.

"Nothing important, Brian," Jim said, wincing a little at being "m'Lorded" by Brian. He covered up the reaction by hastily half filling one of the extra flagons on the table with wine from the pitcher that had been placed between Angie and Brian.

When they had first met—nearly a year before, in the matter of the Loathly Tower, and Sir Brian had offered to be the first of Jim's necessary Companions in matching forces with the evil powers within that tower—Jim had informed the other, purely in a spur-of-the-moment attempt to give himself some status, that he was Baron of Riveroak, back in the land he came from.

Sir Brian had accepted this quite naturally; but had always addressed Jim simply as Sir James, until Jim had taken over the castle and lands belonging to the Baron of Malencontri. After that, he had begun using the "m'Lord" term of address to Jim—something that made Jim very uncomfortable indeed. They were old friends now. Close friends. Jim had argued with him on this point of the "m'Lord" several times, asking Brian to simply call him by his first name of James, as he called the other Brian. Still, Brian had a tendency to slip from time to time. Habit was strong.

Sir Brian was now sitting at a forty-five degree angle from Jim, since he, Jim, and Angie were clustered around one corner of the high table, with Jim along the long axis of it, and Brian on the short, with Angie in between. Of the three of them, Sir Brian would have seemed to almost any eye to stand apart from both Angie and Jim.

The good knight was in his twenty-fifth year (as Jim happened to know), actually a good three years younger than Jim. But any observer seeing them together for the first time would have undoubtedly assumed Brian was at least ten years older than Jim.

Partly this was due to his angular, clean-shaven, suntanned face, which showed evidence of exposure to outside weather. But also a great deal was simply due to the fact that Sir Brian radiated an air of confidence, self-possession, and natural authority to command; which Jim simply did not. Brian had grown up taking it for granted he would be a leader. He had always led, he was a leader now; and, a little like Aargh the English wolf, the day that changed for him, he would be dead. In which case any question about his right to his appearance would be beside the point.

Compared to Jim and Angie, he was poor. He was a knight-bachelor, which simply meant he was not a knight-baronet. The "bachelor" part did not refer to his unmarried state. He awaited the return of the father of Geronde Isabel de Chaney, another neighbor, from the Holy Land—which return might never happen—so that Brian could ask for permission to marry Geronde. His castle, Castle Smythe, was old and in poor repair. His lands were small, compared to those of Malencontri. Once married to Isabel, he would eventually, on Lord de Chaney's death, be able to add the de Chaney lands to his possessions. Then he would be more on a par with Jim and Angie. But for the present, as it had been for some years now, he was more or less living on the edge of poverty. It did not, Jim had thought, ever seem to concern him a great deal.

"Well?" said Angie, impatiently. "What about your visit? What did you find out?"

"Oh. Well," said Jim, "it turns out that my magic balance with the Accounting Office—"

He looked at Brian.

"You're familiar with that, aren't you, Brian?" he said.

"Assuredly, James," said Brian.

"Apparently, it can't be allowed just to lie idle. I have to use it, or it'll start using me," he said. "Carolinus fixed me up with the necessary knowledge to use it. If you don't mind, I won't explain any further, because it gets a little complex. But he gave me the knowledge; and what I've got to do now is practice. So, that's what I'll be doing for the next six months, except when necessity keeps me from it. Practicing magic."

"You may not have time, James," said Sir Brian solemnly.

Chapter 5

J im merely blinked at Brian, but Angie was quicker off the mark.

"What do you mean he won't have the time?" she demanded, leaning aggressively toward Sir Brian. "Why shouldn't he have the time? What's going to keep him from it?"

"As a matter of fact," said Brian, "that was what I dropped by to tell you about. I wanted to wait until Jim was also here to tell you both, since it is a matter concerning you both."

There was an absence of any smile on his face and a gravity of manner generally. For a moment Angie said nothing; and so Jim asked the direct question.

"What's this you came to tell us?"

"Why, there's been a great battle fought at a place called Poitiers, in France," answered Sir Brian, "by Edward, eldest son to our King Edward and first Prince of the realm. It was fought against King Jean of France, with all his knights and footmen. And, though it wrings my heart, and that of every loyal Englishman to hear it, Prince Edward has been taken prisoner by that same Jean."

Jim and Angie flashed a glance at each other, in which they agreed they were both at a loss as to how to respond to this. But a response was certainly expected by Brian. They turned back to him.

"Shocking!" said Angie, getting a real note of outrage into her voice.

"Yes, indeed!" added Jim hastily.

"You may well say that, and a good deal more," said Sir Brian grimly. "All England is in an uproar. There is no gentleman worthy of the name who is not now readying horse, armor and troops to recover our Prince and teach that proud Frenchman a lesson!"

"You, too, Brian?" asked Angie.

"Yes, by Saint Dunstan!" said the knight emphatically. He directed a burning blue glance on Jim. "Knights like yourself and myself, James, will not wait for our Liege—whom we all know is somewhat inattentive in matters of state—"

Brian meant, Jim knew of course, that the King was a confirmed alcoholic and usually in a drunken stupor. Confronted with any kind of decision, he could dither and avoid it for months, putting it off until some day he conceived to be decisive. A day which, needless to say, would never come for him.

"—but will start now to ready ourselves for the expedition," went on Sir Brian.

Jim and Angie stared at each other again.

"I've already heard," Brian went on, "that the Earl Marshal, and a few other responsible Lords about the throne, will see to a proper levy being ordered. Meanwhile, there need be as little waiting as possible. We'll gather our forces as quickly as we can, and embark from one or the other of the Cinque Ports— probably Hastings."

The gravity had largely gone from Brian's voice, pushed into the background by what was plainly and unmistakably a note of pure enthusiasm. Jim felt his heart sink. This close friend of his, for all his other sterling qualities, had always shared the glee that those like him in this world and age felt for any prospect of a battle. As Jim had said to Angie once—literally, Sir Brian and those like him would rather fight than eat.

"Jim," Angie appealed to him, "you surely don't need to be caught up in this!"

"Angela," said Brian, "your womanly concern does you credit. But you remember Jim is now bounden in duty to the king, holding these lands of Malencontri in fief directly from His Majesty. As such, James's feudal duty gives him no choice but to submit himself and a certain minimum force to the King's pleasure, for a hundred and twenty days of service during time of war."

"Yes, but—" Angie broke off, still looking appealingly at Jim. Jim hardly knew how to meet her eye. He knew that she knew that there would be many knights who would find some excuse or other for staying home. However, Brian and most of those in this particular district of medieval, rural England, were not of that sort. And if Jim should stay home while his neighbors all answered the call to rescue the Prince, he and she would forever after be isolated and treated as outcasts by those who went and their families.

"I'll have to go," said Jim to Angie, slowly. He turned to Brian.

"Forgive me for seeming less happy to hear this than you, Brian," he said, "but you remember I just learned how to use a sword and shield and a few other weapons this last year. Gorp isn't really a war-horse. My armor doesn't fit me properly. Besides, I don't know the first thing about levying the men I need to fulfill my feudal duty. How many am I supposed to provide, have you any idea?"

"Malencontri can provide no less than yourself and fifty horsemen, fully weaponed and armed," answered Brian. His expression softened to one of sympathy. "What you say is all true, of course, James. I know you fear that your efforts in this endeavor might appear less than you'd like. Just as, no doubt, you fear that m'Lady here will be ill-accustomed to keeping safe this castle in your absence."

"Yes, that too," put in Angie quickly. "Jim may have learned a few things during the winter but I don't know the first thing about defending this castle."

"I hope I may be able to suggest some answers to these problems," said Brian. "First, your problem m'Lady, since—you'll pardon me—it's the lesser one. You've a good friend, as you know, in m'Lady Geronde Isabel de Chaney; who is no novice at maintaining and defending a castle from which the Lord is gone. You've already become a good and capable mistress to all within these walls. In all but the actual matter of defense, you're well qualified. And in that other matter, Geronde will be glad to ride over and spend a week or so; showing you how best to handle any attack, foray, or raid against its walls."

He turned from her to Jim.

"Now, as to you, James," he said. "You're too modest to admit it; but in truth, you're now a fair hand with sword, axe, and dagger. Your shield-work is admittedly ragged. And—I must be truthful—I would not like to see you with lance in hand, in a charge a-horseback against a seasoned knight. Nonetheless, personally you are not ill-equipped to do your duty in this instance, damme if you aren't! You've a fair knowledge of weapons—many men have gone into battle knowing less. And, in addition, you have this magic credit, and are gaining some ability to use it. That, in itself, becomes a weapon which will be of great value to our Liege in this rescue of his royal son."

"But the business of raising men to fight, choosing who's to go, and teaching them what to do, and then leading them in the proper manner . . .," said Jim. "I don't have the first idea—"

"Don't overconcern yourself James," said Sir Brian. "I propose that the two of us join forces and make a unit of ourselves and the men we bring with us. It could be we might even raise the aid of some of those who follow Giles o'the Wold, as well. Outlaws they may be; but in a matter such as this, no one will inquire closely as to their lawfulness."

A wistful look came into his bright blue eyes.

"Would we could also get the use of that master bowman, bowyer, and fletcher,

Dafydd ap Hywel, as well. But these Welshmen all have a chip on their shoulder where good Englishmen are concerned. He's not likely to want to help rescue our Prince, even if Danielle o'the Wold, now that she is his wife, would agree to his going. Besides, he has more of a chip on his shoulder even than most Welsh toward things English—at least as far as our men of the longbow are concerned. But what an archer to have in our ranks!"

"He always said, and Danielle said," put in Angie, harking back to the adventures that had concerned all of them with the Dark Powers and the Loathly Tower, "that he would come to your aid or ours, as we would go to theirs, if needed."

Jim found it hard to believe that Angie had given up on keeping him from going to the war in France. He rather doubted it. Angie did not give up things that easily. But, clearly, if he had to go she wanted him to go with as much skilled protection as possible. And what Brian had just said was the truth. Dafydd ap Hywel was an archer who was too good to be believed, even after you had seen him in action.

"Going to a friend's help is one thing," Jim answered Angie himself. "Going off to a war to help out the king of a country your people have been at war with for some centuries, is something else again. Besides, remember Dafydd was never the kind to get involved in danger just for the adventure of it. You remember he came along with the rest of us to the Loathly Tower only because of Danielle."

Angie sighed, and said nothing.

"You are right, James," said Brian. "However, come to think of it, we lose nothing by asking him. Just as we lose nothing by asking the merry men of Giles o'the Wold if any of them care to come with us to France, for glory and for loot."

"How soon do you actually have to leave?" asked Angie of Sir Brian.

"As soon as possible." The knight rubbed his chin thoughtfully. "Yet, it'll take three weeks, perhaps more, for some good men to reach me. There are those who've said they would follow me in any great endeavor such as this one, but are otherwise in the service of someone else. Those who can get permission to come, will come. They will already have heard of what is happening, and know I have need of them. I would certainly wait about three weeks. Moreover, James—"

He turned to Jim.

"—It will take at least three weeks to instill some small knowledge of weaponry into your levied men, and teach them how to behave on expeditions such as this, into a foreign land. Yet we should be gone as soon as possible. Should be a matter of a few days, only, to reach the nearest port. But then up to possibly several weeks after to find a ship to take us to wherever in France the gathering point's to be. Possibly Bordeaux, though it may be Brittany, which is closer—although the coast along the Brittany shore is perilous."

He turned back to Angie.

"Call it three weeks before we leave our homes, m'Lady," he said, "and you won't be far off. The time's short enough, God knows."

He turned to Jim once more.

"Which is why you should start choosing the men you want to take with you right away, James," he said. "That's one reason I'm here. Not only to bring you the news, but to help you in a few such things. Call in your steward."

Jim turned to the first body he saw lounging close to the platform. It was Theoluf, his chief man-at-arms.

"Get John Steward for me, Theoluf," said Jim.

John Steward appeared with remarkable promptness. It would have been possible to guess that he had been no farther away from the table than Theoluf, except that there was no place in the great hall where he could have been in less than fifty feet, unless he had been hidden by a screen of the bodies of other castle servants.

He was a tall, rectangular-framed, stern-looking man in his forties; but one who had still managed to keep most of his teeth. Only two in front were to be seen missing when he spoke or smiled—although in fact he seldom smiled. His remaining hair was black and long, and combed straight backward. He wore a hat shaped like a loaf of bread and a somewhat food-stained robe that had once been the property of the former Baron de Malencontri. The hat, like the robe, was always on him, so that they seemed like some sort of official uniform.

"Your Lordship desired me?" he said formally.

"Yes, John," said Jim. "How many able-bodied men between the ages of twenty and forty do we have in the castle, and in the outside dwellings beyond the castle walls?"

"How many men . . ." echoed John slowly. He scratched his skull through the fabric of the hat.

"Yes," said Jim, "how many?"

"How many men between twenty and forty . . ." said John again slowly.

"Yes John. That's what I asked," said Jim, puzzled. John Steward was usually not this slow to understand or answer a question. Jim waited.

"Well," said John thoughtfully, counting on his fingers, "there's William by the mill, William of the moat, and William—"

"By your leave, James," interrupted Sir Brian, "this man obviously doesn't know his duties. A steward who can't come up immediately with the number of available men you mentioned is worse than no steward at all. I suggest you hang him and put somebody else in his place."

"No, no," said John swiftly and in something more like his normal rate of speech. "Forgive me m'Lord, m'Lady, noble sir. My mind was elsewhere for a moment. Thirty-eight such men m'Lord, counting the men-at-arms and everybody."

"Strange," snapped Sir Brian, before Jim could say anything, "the last I heard of Malencontri, it had over two hundred able-bodied men. If there are now only thirty-eight, James, even with your men-at-arms, this fief is in parlous state, indeed."

He turned to Jim.

"M'Lord," he said, enunciating the words very clearly, "will you permit that I take over the questioning of this John Steward?"

"Certainly. By all means," said Jim, relieved, "go ahead, Sir Brian."

Brian turned the searchlights of his two piercing blue eyes back on the steward, who now appeared to have shrunk somewhat.

"Now, my man," said Sir Brian, "you'll have heard already of the situation concerning England, and therefore your Lord. Your Lord will need to raise a force of men from the estate, a levy to meet his requirements to his Liege. These will have to be drawn from men fit to march and fit to fight. Men who may well fall within the years he mentioned, although there is none too old nor none too young if they are able, but *fit*. Now, you are required to produce, therefore, a hundred and twenty men within the next two hours."

"Brian—" began Jim, a little uncertainly, "if there's only thirty-eight—"

"I think Master Steward here may be somewhat mistaken about the number of available men on your estate, James. A mistake he now realizes, particularly since his neck will answer for it if he can't raise enough men to fill the necessary levy. Well, Master Steward? Would you care to think again about who might be available? We would want men in good health, sound of wind and body, and in good spirits. Sir James will have no whiners or complainers on this task, by Saint Dunstan! They have a bad effect on the other men. So! You will gather these for us in the courtyard within the next hour, so that your Lord and I may look them over; since we are in haste. You may go."

"But—but—but—" John Steward turned and appealed to Jim, "m'Lord, is this your requirement? I hear the good knight, but what he asks is—well, not possible. Even if we had such a hundred and twenty men, every one of them is needed here and cannot be spared from the castle or the lands. There is the fallow land to be plowed. There are repairs to the castle, which have awaited the spring. There are a thousand and one things that need to be done, for which we are shorthanded already—"

"James," said Brian, turning to him, "may I speak to you privily?"

"Why, of course," said Jim. He raised his voice.

"All of you here—including you John—" He leveled a finger at the steward. "All of you, all the way out of the hall for now. But stay close so I can call you back."

Sir Brian said nothing until all the various staff of the castle had vanished, then turned to Jim. But Angie spoke before the knight could.

"Brian, weren't you a little hard on him?" Angie said. "We've had John Steward since we took over the castle. He's a good, honest man. We've always been able to trust him and he's always given us the best he can. If he says he only has thirty-eight men, that's probably all he's got."

"Never you think it, m'Lady," answered Sir Brian grimly. "I've no doubt he's as you say. A good steward. A good man. That'll be the very reason he does not yield immediately in this matter of giving up whole men to a necessary levy of forces. It is his duty to protect and foster both the castle and the lands; therefore he must try to keep close and protect the best of those beneath him for that use."

He turned to Jim.

"But can you not both see?" he said, "the man only bargains with us. A hundred men is more than we need—granted. It is more than the levy requires. But thirty-eight men is a foolish number. It is far too few. Somewhere between that figure and mine of a hundred and twenty, we will come to agreement on the necessary number. It will be a slow process and he will oppose us all the way, both as to numbers and as to worth of men. You will see that the first group of men he parades in the courtyard will be hardly worthy of leading half a mile down the road, let alone to France and into battle. But at last we will get who we need. Now, do I have your permission to go on?"

Jim and Angie looked at each other. They had lived in this strange world nearly a year now, and that was long enough to know that things were not done by the methods they had been used to all their lives. Also, they knew that Brian did know the proper way of doing things.

"Go ahead, Brian," said Jim. "Once again, as when you were training me to the use of arms, I'm your pupil. You do it; and I'll try to learn how it's done by watching you and listening."

"Good!" said Brian. "Very well, then. I think we'll let Master Steward cool his heels a bit; and wonder if perhaps I wasn't serious about the hundred and twenty men and the chance of his being hanged if he didn't provide them. While he's doing so, call you your chief man-at-arms; and we'll talk to him next."

Jim raised his head.

"Theoluf!" he bellowed.

A figure popped immediately out of the entrance to the solar staircase and came forward to the table. All of the castle people, Jim thought, must be packed like sardines back there, just behind the entrances, out of sight. Theoluf came up to the table and stopped.

"M'Lord?" he said.

Theoluf was in perhaps his mid-thirties. But like Sir Brian, the life he had lived made him look older. Still fit, but older. In many ways, thought Jim, looking at him, he was a great deal similar to John Steward. Both were men of authority, and showed it. Both had courage and knew they had it. Theoluf was, in fact, a smaller man than the steward. Shorter, not as broad across the shoulders, and wiry rather than solid. But he wore his leather hauberk with the steel plates over it, and the sword and dagger balancing at either side of his sword belt, as if they belonged on him. Like the steward, his hair was black, but cut shorter, and he wore a steel cap without a nasal, which he now took off and held in his hands, as a mark of respect.

"Theoluf," said Jim, "I want you to pay attention and give straight and honest answers to the good knight here."

"Aye, m'Lord," said Theoluf.

Theoluf had a touch of accent that Jim could not exactly place. It seemed halfway between Scandinavian and Germanic; which was odd on this world where everybody, including wolves and dragons, seemed to him to speak the same language. But it was only a trace. The dark eyes in his V-shaped face went to Sir Brian.

"Sir Brian?"

"Theoluf," said Sir Brian, "you and I know each other."

"That we do, Sir Brian," answered Theoluf with a slight, harsh grin. "We've even looked at each other from opposite sides of these battlements when Sir Hugh de Malencontri was Baron."

"That is so," said Sir Brian firmly, "but though we have been close to swords' points on occasion, I know you for a good and faithful man to your present Lord, who is Sir James. Am I mistaken in this?"

"You are not, Sir Brian," said Theoluf. "Who Theoluf serves, he serves utterly. I fight now for Sir James, and will die for him if need be—against any."

"You are not required to die this day," said Sir Brian, "but to answer some questions straightly and to the point. You have heard, as all in this castle will have by this time, of what has happened in France and that Sir James and I march thither. We intend to combine our forces. You also know that Sir James must raise a levy of men to meet his duty to his Liege. Now, are any of those, not presently men-at-arms here, fit and good material to be trained for that work?"

"Would I could say there were," answered Theoluf, "but these turf-brains and ladle-skulls have no idea of weapons and less of fighting—let alone any notion of what war can be like."

"I believe you," said Sir Brian, "but I think you take too dark a view, Theoluf. As I was saying to Sir James just a moment past, people have gone to war with less. We will have two to three weeks here, and more time on the road. It will be up to you and the men you take with you to see that those we pick are ready when the time comes. Battles have been fought and won by those who never took weapon in hand in their life before. But, you realize that some of your better men must stay here, for the defense of Malencontri itself and the Lady Angela?"

Theoluf's face darkened. There was a moment's pause.

"If it must be," he said, then. He swung his attention on Jim. "M'Lord, I myself, however, go with you?"

It was not a question as much as a challenge. Jim for once found himself thinking very clearly along fourteenth-century lines.

"You, of all people, go with me," said Jim.

Theoluf's face lit up.

"Why then," he said, looking back at Sir Brian, "we will do our best, Sir Brian. Happen all of the levy are sound of limb and wind and have some small wit—we'll teach them what they ought to do, at any rate."

The light on his face dimmed, and was replaced with a frown, however.

"We lost what few decent crossbowmen we had to that devil of a tall, Welsh archer you had in the matter of the Loathly Tower—Sir Knight, m'Lord and Lady," he said. "We badly need archers of our own. There will be archers in the forces of others who go to rescue Prince Edward, no doubt; but archers who belong to Malencontri—"

"Now, damn my bad memory!" said Sir Brian, turning to Angela. "I had a message to pass on to you: that Dafydd and his wife, Danielle, were on their way to visit you. I was to pass this on; and in the more important matter of the Prince I completely forgot. I crave your pardon."

"Dafydd and Danielle?" echoed Jim. "What would Dafydd have to see me about?"

"As I understood, it was rather Danielle who wished to see Her Ladyship," answered Sir Brian. "However, word came last week that they are on their way. Should be arriving any day now."

"Hmm," said Angie thoughtfully.

"Well," said Jim, "in any case I'll be glad to see them—"

He was interrupted by a noise at the front door of the great hall. A man he recognized as one of Sir Brian's men-at-arms literally stumbled in, with a couple of Jim's own men-at-arms trailing along beside him. The man paid no attention to them, to Jim, or to Angie, but made directly to Brian.

"M'Lord!" he gasped to Sir Brian, catching hold of the far edge of the high table to hold himself upright. "Castle Smythe is attacked, and I have near ridden one of your horses to death to get the news to you as quick as possible."

Chapter 6

"Theoluf!" shouted Jim jumping to his feet, "fetch the men, as many as can be spared! Someone get me some fresh clothes and my plate armor! Brian—"

But Brian had already leaped from the table and was putting on his steel cap.

"Follow me as best you can, James," he threw over his shoulder. "I cannot wait!"

He caught the messenger by the arm and swung him around.

"Can you still ride?"

"Aye, Sir Brian!" answered the man-at-arms who had brought the news. "Give me a fresh horse, only."

"Take what you want from my stables!" shouted Jim, as Brian and the man-at-arms headed out the door, Brian's grip on the other's left upper arm both supporting the man and impelling him forward at what was almost a run.

Jim and Angie followed him to the front door, where someone had already brought Brian's palfrey, plus a fresh horse for the Castle Smythe man-at-arms. Jim and Angie were just in time to see Brian vault from the ground into the saddle of his horse, in spite of the armor he was wearing, and touching only a toe to the near stirrup on the way.

Jim felt a twinge of envy. He could not do that himself. But then, Brian had practiced that vaulting mount since he was a boy.

Jim, on the other hand, had always been proud of his jumping ability. In AA-class volleyball he had been able to outjump anyone else with ease. However, something about that vault onto the horse, particularly wearing heavy armor—which Brian could also do—defeated him. Jim could get up there; but he could not seem to land squarely in the saddle—and it could be very painful not to.

Jim and Angie turned back into the castle.

It was a good fifteen minutes before new ordinary clothes, its separate parts strongly attached to each other with Old Magic, could be brought for Jim to replace those which had been temporarily put back together at Carolinus's home; and Jim had been helped into his inherited, restructured suit of ill-fitting plate armor. He had half-expected objections from Angie; but apparently she was becoming as much a denizen of this world as he himself was. She kissed him good-bye just before he climbed up on Gorp.

"Watch yourself," was all she said.

"Believe me, I will!" answered Jim grimly.

He clambered aboard Gorp and led off his meager, hastily formed troop of some sixteen men-at-arms, Theoluf at their head and riding just behind his own left elbow. They all left the castle for the route that would lead them to Castle Smythe, Jim leading the way at a canter.

"M'Lord," said the voice of Theoluf at his left ear, "we must spare the horses."

"True." Jim reluctantly slowed Gorp to a trot. He had hoped to catch up with Sir Brian and learn more about what was going on at Castle Smythe; but reason now told him that he had no chance of catching them. Brian would be going all out with his single man-at-arms, to get back to whatever people of his own were still free to oppose whoever was doing the attacking.

The two of them could not be caught unless Jim and his men-at-arms also rode their own horses full out; and, as Theoluf had just pointed out, this was not a sensible thing to do. Jim had hoped to learn from Brian's man-at-arms about the attackers and the situation at Brian's castle, but clearly it was not possible. It was best that Jim and his men arrive in the best possible condition to fight.

In fact, Castle Smythe was not that distant; perhaps an hour and a half with a horse at a walk. Jim drew back even further on his reins and slowed Gorp to that pace. Even once they were there, it would be foolish to dive into battle until they had looked over the situation and talked to Sir Brian. The attackers might outnumber them by as much as ten or twenty to one, though it seemed unlikely that a really large force could have penetrated this far without the news of it reaching them from other neighbors.

Jim and all of his men-at-arms were now at a walking pace. He beckoned Theoluf to ride up level with him.

"What do you think?" he asked Theoluf. "Who could be attacking Castle Smythe? It's not as if it was the richest holding in these parts."

"But might be thought by a stranger to be one of the easiest taken," observed Theoluf.

"I see what you mean," answered Jim, suddenly thoughtful. "In that case there're probably not too many making this attack. It wouldn't be one of the neighbors. Sir Brian's on good terms with all of them; and Norman law forbids us to fight each other in any case."

"Law is as law does," answered Theoluf skeptically. "Nonetheless, m'Lord, I think you're right. They'll not be neighbors. Nor are there any bands of outlaws large enough in this area to try such a thing; and we are too far south for raids by Scotsmen. Possibly these attackers were shipborne, and have come from the coast to search inland at a venture, looking for anything that they might take quickly and carry off before this part of England is raised against them."

Jim nodded. The words of the man-at-arms clearly drew the most possible picture. He said no more, and Theoluf let his horse drop back to a more proper position, half a horse length behind Jim and still to his left. They rode on, Jim containing his impatience as best he could.

It had been noon when he had come back from visiting Carolinus. It was now barely afternoon. Jim was suddenly and ridiculously reminded that he had had nothing to eat. Also, almost nothing to drink—except half a flagon of wine, which was now beginning to wear off, leaving him feeling rather dull and dispirited—even though he had of necessity come to adopt the rather heavy drinking standards of those about him.

The thought reminded him of something else. He turned his head and with a jerk of it beckoned Theoluf up beside him, so they could speak without being overheard by the rest of the men-at-arms behind him.

"Theoluf," he said in a voice that was just above the sound of the hoofbeats of their horses, "have the men had anything to eat since daybreak?"

Theoluf gave him a half-grin.

"Never fear, m'Lord," he answered. "A man-at-arms learns to make sure his belly is full at all times against some emergency such as this one." He paused and looked narrowly at Jim. "Has m'Lord eaten?"

"As a matter of fact, I haven't," said Jim, "since breakfast, anyway. I forgot all about it."

"If m'Lord will check the saddlebags on his horse," said Theoluf, "he might perhaps find that they had been provisioned before we left."

Jim checked his left saddlebag; and found that indeed Theoluf was correct. There were some thick slices of bread and cheese; and a large flask of wine. With the wine was a cup.

"Do we pass any streams fairly soon?" asked Jim.

"In another couple of furlongs we cross a small stream," said Theoluf. He looked at Jim questioningly.

The truth of the matter was, right now the last thing Jim wanted was more straight wine—in spite of the well-known idea of the hair of the dog being the cure for even a very small hangover. This notion, which was as current in this world, if not more so than it had been in his original one, was a tribute to the long life of folk remedies.

He was thirsty, and would have happily settled for plain water, if it was clean. Luckily, in this area, the streams were generally safe to drink from. It occurred to him now that something like perhaps a half-and-half combination of the wine in his flask and some stream water would both slake his thirst and help him wash down the bread and cheese. The cheese, particularly, would be pretty dry to swallow unless it was washed down.

When they reached the stream, he sent the troop on ahead, and stopped long enough, with Theoluf beside him, to drink his wine and water and eat some of the cheese and bread. Feeling much more optimistic with something in his stomach, he put away the rest of the food, the flask, and cup; and they rode on to catch up with the troop.

As they got closer to Castle Smythe, they went more slowly; moving off the trail entirely into the woods and spreading out; just in case the attackers were encamped in the vicinity, or had someone on watch.

However, the precaution turned out to have been unnecessary. They made their way right to the edge of the cleared space which, like all castles, Castle Smythe maintained about itself for purposes of defense. Looking out through a screen of leaves, Jim saw a ragtag looking crew, perhaps a few less—but only a few less—than a hundred armed men. These were clustered in an untidy gang before the main entrance to the castle, clearly under the command of a large, black-bearded individual.

Castle Smythe was closed up tight; that is, as tight as it was possible to close it up. Its moat was half dry; there had evidently not been time to draw up the portcullis—or else the machinery that allowed it to be drawn up was not working; and the metal grille that should have defended the pair of heavy main gates was rusted to the point where it clearly would offer little resistance to a determined attack.

The gates themselves, however, were tightly closed; and still looked stout enough to offer some considerable resistance. However, it was just at this point that Jim noticed one reason the gang of attackers was not busy against the castle itself. They had felled a large tree and dragged it up before the gate; and were busy lopping off the last of its branches, to form a makeshift battering ram.

"Where do you suppose Sir Brian and that one man-at-arms of his have gone to?" Jim asked Theoluf.

The other was beside him, peering through the same screen of leaves at the scene before them. Jim had lowered his voice instinctively. They were actually far enough from those assaulting the castle not to be overheard by them; but it was the kind of situation in which lowered voices seemed called for. "I hope those people out there didn't capture the two of them—" Jim said.

"Never fear that, James," said a harsh voice right behind Jim. "They're in the woods just like you, around the other side of the castle, watching."

Jim turned and saw Aargh, the English wolf.

Aargh had appeared, noiselessly as usual for all of his size, behind the two of them. He stood on four legs, his mouth open, his tongue lolling out, and grinned at Jim.

"Aargh!" said Jim, happily and more loudly. "I'm glad to see you!"

"Why?" said Aargh. "Were you expecting me to help you?"

Since this was exactly the first thought that had crossed Jim's mind, he found himself momentarily at a loss for words.

"Well, I'm not," said Aargh. "I'm here to help the knight Brian. He's also a friend, ever since we were Companions together before the Loathly Tower, as well as yourself. Did you think I would abandon a friend?"

"No, of course I didn't think that," said Jim. "I merely meant I was glad to see you, in general."

"In general, or in particular, I'm here," said Aargh. "Fair number of strangers out there, isn't there?"

And he grinned again at Jim, his red tongue lolling out.

"Aargh," said Jim urgently, "you can move faster and more quietly than any of us; and besides you know where Sir Brian and his man-at-arms are right now. Would you go get them and bring them back here to us; so that we can all make plans together?"

"No need," answered Aargh. "They're already on their way here, since I told them sometime since that you were coming. Anyone but humans like yourself would have heard you and those great horses of yours crashing through the undergrowth, ten minutes back. I was speaking no less than the truth, back when you and Gorbash were in his body together, Jim, when I used to tell him he was somewhat slow of wit. But at least his ears would have heard you coming, and his nose smelled you, long before you got here. Not that any dragon was ever a match for any wolf in the matter of nose and ears; but at least his were useful for something. All you humans have are eyes. Or at least, that's all you use. But to answer your question: Sir Brian and that man with him should be here any moment now."

In fact, it was not more than a few moments later that Sir Brian and his man-at-arms showed up, the latter leading his horse and Brian's.

"James!" said Brian, as he came up to Jim. "I'm glad to have you here. How many men did you bring with you?"

"Sixteen, I think, wasn't it Theoluf?" Jim looked around for Theoluf, and the chief man-at-arms nodded. "I left orders for the others to be gathered and follow me as soon as there were at least a dozen of them to come as a group. I'm afraid, more than another twelve we can't count on. A lot of them weren't likely to be back at the castle until the end of the day or even for a day or two. Even if they get here, we'll only have some twenty-eight or thirty men—counting you and I. Of course, there's Aargh here."

"Of course," said Aargh sarcastically. "James, you should know I'm worth half a dozen of your lazy men, all by myself."

"What we really need," said Sir Brian, "are some archers or crossbowmen. With them we could send a message to my people in the castle. As it is they've no knowledge we're out here."

"How many do you have in the castle—who could fight, I mean?" asked Jim.

The minute he said it, he realized that he should have phrased the question a little more delicately. Sir Brian looked definitely embarrassed.

"At *present*," he said, emphasizing the words perhaps a shade more heavily than was necessary, "I have only eleven men-at-arms there, and perhaps half as many of the castle staff, who could use a sword or other weapon if they had to."

"Perhaps another sixteen, all told?" asked Jim.

"Call it seventeen," answered Sir Brian, "though the last is my squire and little more than a boy. Still this is a scurvy lot in front of us. Even the seventeen could be of use, if they could sally at a moment when the rest of us are hitting these reivers from without."

He looked grimly at Jim.

"They and we together make thirty-seven at most, to attack more than double our number," he went on, "for I fear me we've no time to wait for the rest of your men-at-arms to catch up with you. Those out there will be using their tree trunk against my gates within the quarter hour. The gates are good, but they are also all that keep the castle, now. Once these attackers break through, they'll be inside. I fear me we must do what we can with what we have and no further delay. As I say, the gates are stout, but that battering ram will be through them in half an hour."

"Ah," said Aargh beside them, cocking his head on one side. "Two more come—and a pair more used to moving through the woodland at least a little more lightly than the rest of you. Ha!"

There was a note of pleased surprise in his voice—a strange thing for Aargh.

"It is Danielle and that long Welsh arrow-shooter of hers she now calls husband," Aargh went on.

Jim and Sir Brian looked at each other, startled.

"I did pass word to you she was coming to visit—they were coming, I mean," said Brian, "though, come to think of it, Castle Smythe is somewhat on the way they would wend to Malencontri, in any case. But still, how do they know of us being here?"

"If they've anything in the way of ears at all, they've probably heard the lot of you tramping around," said Aargh sourly. "In any case, here they are, now."

A moment later, both she who had been Danielle o'the Wold, daughter of Giles o'the Wold who was leader of the outlaws in the Wold, and Dafydd ap Hywel, a master bowman—indeed, *the* master bowman of all bowmen, if there was any justice in the world, thought Jim—appeared through the greenery. Dafydd's great longbow, that only he could pull and hold steady on target; and which he himself had made, as he had also lovingly and magnificently made his arrows—the stave of that longbow, unslung, was being carried on his back. His left arm was in a green cloth sling.

"Father's on his way with his men," said Danielle without preamble as she came up to them. "He heard about this raiding group, judged it was headed this way and that Castle Smythe might well need aid. But it would take him a little time to get the men together. Dafydd and I came on ahead, both being able to move light and fast. Ah, Aargh!"

She stopped to caress Aargh, who was fawning upon her and doing his best to lick her face at the same time.

"What happened to your arm, man?" commanded Brian.

"A light strain, only—" Dafydd was beginning, when Danielle interrupted sharply.

"A broken collarbone, you mean," she said. "Wrestling two of father's band at once. Showing off, as usual!"

"Well, perhaps it may be," said Dafydd, in that mild, musical voice of his that seemed so at odds with his herculean frame. He tapered from his broad shoulders to his narrow hips like some statue which had aimed to exaggerate the physical attributes of an athlete; and he was even taller than Jim, as well as standing as straight as one of his own arrows. "By myself, I would have thought little of it. Still, sorry I am that I and my bow can be of little use to you in this hap, Sir Brian."

"It can't be helped," said Jim, "though it's sad. Sir Brian here was just hoping we had some means of sending an arrow with a message over the wall to his men within the castle. We need to let them know we're here; and warn them of some signal from us, so that they can sally at the same time as we attack those men from here. If you look, you'll see they're just about to start battering down the main gates of the castle; and Sir Brian says that's all there is to hold them out. Once inside, their sheer numbers will overwhelm anyone there."

"Indeed, I may be of little use," said Dafydd, "but still we do not lack a bow." He looked at his wife.

"Absolutely not!" snapped Danielle, darting an angry glance both at Jim and Brian. "You know perfectly well I can put an arrow inside that castle from here as well as any bowman!"

"To be sure, mistress," said Brian hastily, "I merely had not thought—"

"Well do so, next time!" said Danielle.

Aargh growled an agreement.

"I take it you were thinking of an arrow shaft shot high above the heads of those men out there and also over the walls to drop inside the interior courtyard?" went on Danielle, in a calmer voice, "possibly with a message wrapped around the shaft—can anyone inside your castle read?"

"There is at least one—possibly two," said Brian, "who might be able to understand such scratchings in words as I myself might write. But I can make the message a better way. I—I thank you, mistress Danielle. You make all the difference in the world, if you make it possible for those inside to know when to sally. We are so small in number that we and they must hit these people at the same time to be of any use. Sir James has more men on the way; but in no case can we wait for them."

"Well, make your message then," said Danielle, taking her own bow off her shoulder and stringing it. "I've got thread and needle with me. The thread can be used to tie the writing around the bow shaft. Do you have wherewith and whereon to write?"

Jim had been rummaging in his saddlebags. If those who put in the bread and cheese and wine had not taken out other things at the same time—ah, they had not.

"I have," he announced.

He had taken a charcoal stick and a piece of thin white cloth along with him to Carolinus's; just to be prepared in case Carolinus should give him some kind of directions that he had felt would be better not trusted to memory alone. He pulled these out of the saddlebag now. Sir Brian, he knew—although the good knight would be embarrassed, if only slightly, to admit it—was hardly able to write. Jim, on the other hand, was a product of twentieth-century schools and universities on his own native world.

"What do you want written?" he asked Brian.

"Indeed, I will do it," answered the knight.

He took the cloth and charcoal stick from Jim. Supporting the cloth against the surface of his horse's saddle, on one corner of the cloth's white surface he drew a sort of pictograph.

Jim recognized the figure underneath the horns as a rough representation of Brian's family arms: gules, a saltine sable, differenced by a hart lodged sable which showed his family to be of cadet stock to that of the Nevilles of Raby, Earls of Worcester.

With the point of his dagger, Brian neatly and economically cut off the corner of cloth on which he had drawn, and handed it, together with the unmarked cloth and charcoal, back to Jim.

"This," he said, "they will understand immediately. Three notes from my horn"—he indicated the cowhorn made into an instrument and hanging from a leather loop around the pommel of his saddle—"and they will sally."

"And just how are they going to know it's a true message they can trust?" asked Danielle.

"Hah!" said Sir Brian, suddenly brought up short. He thought for a moment.

"I have put my arms at the end of the message," he said, "as you can see."

"Anyone who knew your arms could do the same," said Jim, "assuming there's someone there in the courtyard to see the fall of the arrow—"

"There will be!" interrupted Sir Brian fiercely. "None of my people would be far behind those gates, with the enemy before them."

"Well, well, even if they see the arrow fall and pick it up, open the message and read it," Jim went on, "they'd still have a right to question whether it actually comes from you. Is there anything we could also attach to the arrow that would make them know that it came from you and nobody else?"

Sir Brian looked unhappy.

"I might once have slid my father's ring upon the shaft," he said. Truthfully, he extended his ten bare, brown fingers before them, "once it was never off my hand. Unfortunately it was—ah—left with the merchant in Coventry three years ago last Shrovetide, less a day."

Jim felt a sudden surge of sympathy for the other man. Pawnbroking was illegal in England, as almost everywhere on the continent, because of the rulings against usury by the Church. But it flourished, nonetheless; and many of its patrons were of the gentle class who found themselves hard up for one reason or another. Jim made a secret mental note to see what he could do about getting Sir Brian's ring back. It would not be hard, provided the pawnbroker had not already resold it. The real problem would be to find a way of giving it back to Sir Brian without offending the other knight by something that looked like an act of charity.

"I have it!" said Jim suddenly. "That kerchief of the Lady Geronde's that she gave you for a favor, Brian! All of your men would recognize that at a glance; and nobody could have such a thing but you!"

Sir Brian looked at him, suddenly pale and fierce.

"Never!" he said. "That favor will never leave me while I live."

"Indeed," said Dafydd, "it would only be for a little while, Sir Brian. Then you will have it back. Surely one of your men will put it in a safe place in the castle, while they await the sound of your horn. It will be as safe there as with you."

"Never!" repeated Brian. "I will see my castle in ashes first!"

"Come, Sir Brian," said Danielle in a gentle voice, "it's as Dafydd says. The favor will be quite safe, both on my arrow and with your men. And it is the only sure sign that the message comes from you alone."

"I cannot!" Brian flung himself half-aside from them. "I have said I will never let it leave me and I shall not!"

"All this fuss over a rag of cloth," growled Aargh.

"Aargh!" said Danielle, rounding upon him, "there are some times that wolves should be seen and not heard!"

Aargh—who would have taken such words from no one but Danielle—put back his ears, dropped his head and lowered his tail between his legs. Danielle turned back to Sir Brian.

"Nonetheless, Sir Brian—" she was beginning; when he burst out, suddenly.

"You comprehend nothing, any of you," he said. "It is all I have of her, do you understand? It is all I have!"

"We know," said Danielle, still in that unusually gentle voice, "but do you think the Lady Isabel would want you to lose your patrimony, for want of letting go of her favor for, at most, an hour? If she were here, would she not rather command you that you attach it to my arrow as a signal to your men?"

She stopped talking. The silence stretched out. Gradually the tension leaked out of Sir Brian. He sighed unhappily, and fished inside his hauberk with one hand, at last pulling up into view a flimsy, saffron-tinted square of cloth with G.d'C. sewn into one corner of it. He kissed it; then, wordlessly, not looking at any of them, he passed the kerchief to Danielle.

"A brave decision, Sir Brian," said Danielle. "Your Lady will be proud of you. We will bind it most carefully with the thread to the shaft of my arrow, so that no harm can come to it in flight, nor from the shock of the moment when the arrow strikes point down into the ground inside the courtyard. And I am sure that all your men will handle it with due respect and gentleness."

"Indeed, that much is so," said Brian in a low voice.

He shook his head, and regained his composure by an obvious effort of will. He stood up straight and looked back at all of them.

"We will do what we have to do," he said, "but I promise you this. No enemies, were they double in number what we see yonder, will be able to keep me from my own courtyard within the hour."

"That also is so," growled Aargh, his tail untucking a bit and his head coming up. "I said a while back that I could reach their leader, even through those around him, and snap his neck. Shall I do that now?"

Brian shook his head.

"Do it, you might well, I doubt not," said Brian, "but come back out alive again—that is not so sure; and we may have need for you in the general fighting. Let justice come to Blackbeard, yonder, when the time shall be. For that matter, it is I who should have first chance at him—"

He checked himself.

"Forgive me," he went on, "in a melee who can choose who his opponent will be? Let anyone who has a chance at Blackbeard then, take him. I will only hope it is myself."

Even as he talked, Danielle had been busy using thread to bind both the message and the kerchief firmly to the shaft of the arrow. Now she bit off the thread.

"Ready," she said. "Shall I shoot the arrow now, or are there arrangements you want to make first?"

"Let us to horse," said Brian. "Other than that, there should be no preparation needed. We will hold ourselves in line just within these woods—" He swept his arm forward to demonstrate what he meant; and Jim's men-at-arms, who were already mounting, began to guide their horses into line just inside the first screen of trees. "—And once the arrow disappears from sight behind the battlements, we will charge!" said Brian. He was again in command of himself and everyone else. "No signal is necessary other than that. When I see the last of the arrow, I will ride—and all the rest of you do likewise. We must come upon those out there as unexpectedly as possible; not only to take them by surprise, but that they may think we are merely the advance guard of more to come!"

Jim had mounted with the rest. Behind him, he heard the twang of Danielle's released bowstring. The arrow came into sight overheard, climbing in a high arc into the sky. It dwindled with height and distance until it was the size of a matchstick, until it seemed it would shrink to a dot and go out of sight entirely.

Then it began to lengthen and grow in size once more, dropping earthward. It fell so rapidly that Jim had the illusion that it was going to fall short and land among the men before the gate. But it did not.

A fraction of a second later it disappeared behind the gray stone walls of Castle Smythe; and at once they were all at a gallop together out of the woods, headed across the cleared space toward the gang of men before the gate, who now were beginning to swing their tree trunk against the gates.

The three notes of Sir Brian's horn rang out loud and clear.

Chapter 7

J im found himself pounding across the open space at the full speed of his horse with everyone else galloping beside him.

In spite of himself, he found it a heady moment. He felt a second's wonder that no one had suggested that he turn himself into a dragon for this part of the attack. Then it came to him that, in any case, he would have to learn this human method of fighting also; and the sooner he got started, the better. The fierce burst of joy he had felt, as Gorbash, flying into the men who had been ravaging the village outside the Castle de Chaney was not there; only his human adrenalin-triggered excitement. So the other had been purely the "dragon fury" identified by the old dragon who was the granduncle of Gorbash's body. But, at least he was not afraid—and that much was good.

Their approach was anything but noiseless. Not only was there the thunder of their horses' hooves, but most of the men-at-arms were also shouting war cries of one kind or another, as was Sir Brian himself. Jim had a glimpse of startled faces as the mob before the gate turned to face them; and those that had been drawing back the battering ram for another swing at the gates dropped it and fumbled at their belts for swords or other weapons.

Then the two groups came together. Certainly, it was an advantage being on horseback. Jim had the impression that he rode down at least three or four opponents before his horse was brought to a standstill so abruptly that he slid forward out of the saddle.

Sheer instinct, backed by his athletic training, caused him to land on his feet rather than his nose; and the lessons with Sir Brian automatically put him in a position with his shield up and his sword ready. For the moment he had his horse at his back, which protected him from that direction, and, taking advantage of that protected position, he waded into the two men with swords in front of him.

Both clearly knew how to handle their weapons, but neither had been a student of Brian's. Nor did either of them have shields. They were simply hewing away at him. Jim simply fended off the one on his shield side and thrust at the one on his right, and was almost surprised to see him disappear, going down before him. He turned toward the one on his left, but that man had already moved off and he found himself facing another opponent, who was whirling an axe around his head.

Jim dodged aside and the axe missed him. He thrust but did not see the result. The fight was becoming a blur in which he merely reacted automatically.

He caught a momentary glimpse of Aargh, who was not wasting his time on any one opponent, but gliding between them snapping right and left at whatever was within reach of his jaws. The power of those jaws was clearly awesome, for Jim saw them close, apparently fully shut, on the arms and legs they seized, which must have meant that Aargh's long teeth were penetrating right to, and even into, the bones of those he bit. Certainly, he left behind him men with an arm or leg suddenly become useless.

Then all at once, strangely, Jim found himself in a small open area of the general fighting. The invaders and his men-at-arms, plus some men dressed and armored like men-at-arms whom he did not recognize, and who he assumed must be part of those who had sallied from Castle Smythe, were fighting with the raiders all around him. But for some reason, at this moment, there seemed no one left over to attack him. It was almost ridiculous.

. . . a bass bellow of rage jarred him abruptly out of his moment of inaction. He turned just in time to get his shield up as a huge axe in the hands of the black-bearded leader of the group, himself, crashed its edge down the shield's outer face.

The metal held, but Jim was driven almost to his knees by the force of the blow. Somehow he disengaged. This was that same "raggedness" of his shield-work that Brian had been speaking about. Jim had not yet picked up the ability to instinctively angle his shield to a coming blow, so as to cause the enemy's weapon to glance off to right or left, up or down. He merely shoved the shield out between him and his opponent, as if to push the other's weapon back.

Now, his shield had caved in, but protected him. However, his arm had paid a price for that protection. It was numb from fingertips to shoulder, and the next blow of his opponent's axe swept it out of his now-feeble grasp. Jim suddenly found himself facing a man as large as himself and weighing at least fifty pounds more, with a much heavier weapon to oppose the broadsword that was now Jim's only defense as well as means of offense.

The axe swept down again, appearing to aim for his head; then, at the last moment, changing to a cut at his legs. Jim reacted instinctively. He jumped.

For once he could be as proud of the ability of his leg muscles as he had used to be. He went up in the air well over the axe, which whistled below him. The black-bearded man kept after him. He was evidently skilled with his heavy weapon; but equally plainly, he had never encountered someone dressed in a knight's armor who acted like a jumping jack.

Jim dodged, ducked and leaped; and the other continued to miss him. Meanwhile Jim searched for an opening through which he could put the point of his own broadsword. But the other was too skillful to give him one. Jim was too busy to pay attention to what was going on in the battle around him; but his real worry was not whether he would be able to stop his present evasive tactics, and continue to search for an opening, but that eventually someone from the other side would come up and bury a blade in his back.

Blackbeard, having apparently tried all the blows in his repertoire, once more tried the cut for the head that was merely a feint preliminary to a slice at Jim's legs.

Whether he had forgotten what had happened the first time, or thought that Jim was beginning to get tired and more likely to be caught by the axe's sharp edge, Jim never knew. What Jim did know was that he could keep this jumping up all day. He had often used jumping-jack exercises, in which he leaped into the air and while up touched the toes of his extended feet with his fingertips, to psyche out the members of an opposing team. And now he had gone up until his legs were level with the head of his opponent. For once, inspiration struck. He kicked out hard with both legs.

His opponent was momentarily lucky, in that the suit of armor Jim had inherited did not include steel over and around Jim's feet. Nonetheless, both the heels of Jim's boots caught him, one on each side of the jaw, with all the kicking power of Jim's legs behind them.

A second after, Jim landed lightly on the ground again.

Blackbeard would not have been human if that blow had not dazed him. When Jim faced him again, the man was still standing with the axe down; on his feet, but staring at Jim with unfocused eyes.

Jim, however, was too geared up to notice details. He only knew that he had been fighting for his life; and that his enemy was still standing before him with a weapon that could destroy him with a single blow. Without even stopping to think, almost by reflex action, he drove the point of his broadsword through the leather jerkin that was the only protection the other wore, into the thick body.

The blade went in with what seemed surprising ease; and the leader of the attackers tottered and fell.

Jim stood, staring down at him. He had slain men when he was in the body of Gorbash the dragon; but this was the first time when *as a man* he had killed another man; and Blackbeard was undeniably dead.

He came out of his daze in the nick of time to dodge a sword blade coming at him from his left. Once more, by reflex rather than by conscious thought, he spun away from the line of its blow and struck back. He missed the body of the tall, thin, almost white-haired swordsman who was now engaging him; but his blade came down on the other's arm and half cut it off. The man, not killed, but badly wounded, fell to his knees trying to stop the flow of blood from his wounded arm.

For a brief few seconds Jim had a chance to look about him.

The fight was still on; but it was not going well for his side. Neither Sir Brian nor Aargh were to be seen, but those whom he assumed to be Castle Smythe's people were hotly engaged; some of them with two or more defenders at once.

Jim suddenly woke up to his obligations. His dented but still serviceable shield was only a couple of paces away. Surprisingly, the place where he had first encountered the leader of the attackers was still fairly clear. Jim could only guess that the leader had originally called to those with him to leave Jim to him; and the others had obeyed. After that, they had all been caught up in the general fighting, so that only the man whose arm he had just wounded had bothered to attack him.

He picked up the shield and took on one of the two men nearby who were attacking one of his own men-at-arms. The opponent began to back off almost immediately, sliding away through the press. Jim had encountered someone almost as agile as himself—not necessarily in the sense that he could jump as Jim could, but that he could twist and dodge as well, if not better. Jim, heady now from the fight, pressed after him with only one thought, to destroy him. Jim was in full armor and the other man had nothing but a leather jerkin and a sword. No wonder the other was running, thought Jim.

Jim was still thinking this when his opponent, having dodged one of his sword blows, suddenly reversed directions, stopped, came forward, and kneed Jim cruelly in the crotch. Jim fell to the ground in agony. His opponent fell on top of him, his sword now shortened, so that its point glimmered a few inches above Jim's face.

"Surrender!" the man yelled. "Yield, or I'll cut your throat!"

Even through the haze of pain that enveloped him at the moment, Jim belatedly recognized that, wearing armor as he was, he would of course be taken for somebody worth holding to ransom. Come to think of it, with Malencontri in his holding, he probably was. However, before he could answer, the matter was settled for him.

There was an audible thud, and the broadhead of a clothyard shaft suddenly emerged from the man's chest, sticking out several inches. The man choked, fell off Jim, and lay still.

Jim's first thought was that somehow, miraculously, Dafydd had overcome his broken collarbone and was pumping arrows into the fight with almost the rapidity of bullets from a fully automatic weapon of Jim's time—something only Dafydd would be able to do.

Then Jim became aware of two other things. The attackers had broken off the fight and were now running for the security of the forest edge behind Castle Smythe. Through the open spaces their leaving made, Jim could see not only that Aargh and Sir Brian were still on their feet, but that beyond them a number of brown-jerkined archers were coming toward the castle; running forward, pausing to draw bow and shoot, running forward once more and pausing to shoot again, and so continuing directly toward the spot where all the fighting had been going on.

Brian loomed suddenly over him, took one of Jim's hands in the firm grip of his own and helped him to his feet.

"Are you wounded, James?" queried the knight.

"Not . . . wounded, exactly," grunted Jim, still bent over like an old man. He was making a mental note now—as he had once made a mental note after discovering that even a dragon could not fly with impunity into an armored knight on horseback charging with a lance at rest—never to make the same mistake again. As long as he lived, he would never assume, simply because an opponent was unarmored and lightly weaponed, that it would be safe to get close to him simply because Jim himself was in armor. "Who's helping us?"

"I believe," said Sir Brian, "it is Giles o'the Wold and his men, come to meet his daughter and Dafydd, and also offering me his help in this time of need."

Now Dafydd and Danielle had also emerged from the woods and were coming toward them; Dafydd still with his sling and Danielle carrying her bow down but with an arrow still notched to the string. Jim was walking around in circles, trying to straighten up.

"You're sure you're not wounded, James?" asked Brian concernedly, following him along. Jim shook his head. "In that case, what has happened to you?"

Jim told him, in simple, plain, Anglo-Saxon words.

Sir Brian broke into a roar of hearty laughter. Jim glared at the knight in very unfriendly fashion. He would have thought the occasion called for a little sympathy, rather than this robust humor at his expense.

"Come, James," said Brian, slapping him on the shoulder. "You'll not die from it!"

He caught the eye of one of Jim's own men-at-arms who was standing not too far off.

"You!" Sir Brian said. "Sir James's palfrey is just over there. Run see if there is not some wine in the saddlebags."

The man-at-arms turned and set off, in fact, at a run. It had taken Jim some months to get used to the fact that, in this world, whenever any superior sent an inferior on an errand, the inferior did it at a run—even though he might be a fully grown man, or she a fully grown woman. Stranger still, was the realization that Jim came to accept eventually, that if someone of superior rank should send him on an errand, he also would be expected to run. In fact it was a highly structured world. Inferiors invariably stood in the presence of a superior, even if the inferior was simply the second son of the Lord of the estate and the superior was his older brother.

He had begun to feel a little better, when the man-at-arms came running back with the wine flask that Jim had drunk from earlier. Sir Brian had him swallow a fair amount of the straight wine; and Jim, after a few moments, found that either it did make him feel better, or else it helped him to imagine he was feeling better. Gradually he was recovering, and in the process straightening up, so that he did not advertise his mishap to everyone within sight.

This was just as well because Danielle and Dafydd were upon them, now flanked by Giles o'the Wold himself—and Jim knew Danielle. She would have no inhibitions about inquiring as to what had happened to him; and would probably laugh just as uproariously as Brian had on hearing what the cause was.

As it happened, Danielle did not get a chance to ask any questions after all; because Sir Brian spoke first.

"Welcome friends! Welcome, and my thanks!" he said. "Without the help of all of you I don't know how Castle Smythe could have been saved!"

"It couldn't have," said Aargh, who had just now joined the rest of them.

"Indeed, Sir Wolf," said Brian, "I think you may be right. Nonetheless, it is saved; and this is a festive occasion. Let us all repair within my castle, where I can feast you and entertain you in proper style—"

He was interrupted by a large, rather fat man, in clothing that was a walking structure of grease stains, and who carried a strange knife in his hand, one that was either a very odd axe or a rather ornate cleaver.

"What—?" began Sir Brian irritably, as the other man plucked at the elbow of his sleeve and whispered in his ear. "There must be—"

He stopped speaking, and allowed himself to be drawn off to one side by the man with the cleaver. From a little distance the rest of them could see a sort of violent, whispered argument going on between Brian and this man, who was plainly one of his people from the castle.

"Winning a battle may be one thing," said Aargh grimly, "feasting your guests, something else."

"Hush," said Danielle.

The truth suddenly burst upon Jim's mind. He should have realized it before this. It was the most ordinary sort of hospitality for the owner of a castle to invite inside those who had just helped him save it from raiders. But the truth would be that there was not the wherewithal in Brian's castle to put forth the kind of feast he had in mind. Jim was fairly sure that the knight drank small beer and ate coarse bread as an ordinary dinner repast by himself, right along with the rest of his people in the castle.

Jim knew how indifferent Brian was to his hard life, ordinarily. He would think nothing of such a diet for himself. But when it came to entertaining guests, it would be a totally different matter. His family pride, let alone his own, would be shamed utterly if he had to bring guests into a ruined hall and feed them the sort of rough fare that kept him alive from day to day. Jim had an inspiration.

"Sir Brian!" he called, "if I could interrupt your talk with your man there for just a moment—"

Brian turned an unhappy face to him, muttered an order to his retainer to stay put, and came back to the rest of them, trying to smile as he approached.

"I just had an idea, Brian," Jim said. "I didn't get a chance to tell you sooner; but after you left so suddenly and I had to follow after you, the Lady Angela made me promise that I would bring Danielle to her immediately. 'Without any delay,' she said, as soon as Danielle and Dafydd should be met with. I wouldn't miss this feast of yours, myself, on any account, but I can hardly disobey my Lady. Though it seems equally impossible to take away, not only myself, but one of the other guests, perhaps two of the other guests. I was at my wits' end just now; and then this idea came to me."

"James, I'm sure—" Brian began, unhappily, but Jim hurried to cut him short.

"But listen to this notion of mine first, Brian," he said. "Why shouldn't you just change the location of your feast to my castle? You can use any of my castle stores for the moment; and simply replace them whenever it's convenient for you. That way all of us will be together, there. Not only that, but Angie herself will be able to be one of us; and she'd never forgive me if she wasn't."

The look of unhappiness on Brian's face slowly drained away, to be replaced by one of growing joy.

"James," he said, "this is too good of you. No. I really can't allow—"

"I know it's an imposition," said Jim hastily, "in fact, I fully realize how rude it is of me to keep your guests from your castle on this occasion. But perhaps, just this once, you could make an exception?"

"Jim," said Brian, shaking his head, "I don't know what to say. But—thank you, thank you. Yes, I will accept your kind offer; and we will move to your castle for the feast. And I pledge my honor as a knight that you will be repaid every—"

"Never mind that," said Jim, turning away and starting to lead the way toward where the horses were. "We don't need pledges from each other, Brian. Surely we know each other well enough by this time to simply take such things for granted. Now, let's get back to Malencontri."

C h a p t e r **8**

J im and Angie had started a number
of new customs unheard of before in castles like Malencontri. One of them had to
do with seating small parties around one end of the high table, so that everybody
could talk to everybody else comfortably; something not easily possible when
they all sat side by side along one long edge. Their new way worked very well
unless the number dining at the high table was so large that the whole table-length
was required.

In this case, happily, it was not. Jim, Angie and Sir Brian—in that order—were
seated along the upper edge of the table, with Jim next to the table-end. Across
from them sat, again in order from the table-end, Dafydd, Danielle and Giles
o'the Wold. Occupying the table-end itself, on a bench which allowed him to lie
at length, but at the same time have his head and shoulders above table level, was
Aargh.

Down below them was the low table that stretched the length of the hall, at
right angles to the high table. Its upper end was just below the center of the high
table, so that together they had the shape of a very large *T*. Along both sides of
the low table sat the men-at-arms of both Malencontri and Castle Smythe, as well
as the members of Giles's band who were participating in the victory feast.

In either case, at low table or high, Jim's kitchen—with Angie in company with

Danielle making frequent excursions to keep an eagle eye on its work—had done both Malencontri and Sir Brian's honor proud. Now, those at the high table, after a good two hours of eating and drinking, had finally reached the stuffed stage—a point where any physical activity was out of the question; and serious talking could begin. Aargh, who had gulped down about twelve pounds of boneless meat in what Jim estimated to be the first thirty seconds of his presence at the table, had been merely lying, lazily watching the rest of them during most of this time, only interjecting an occasional, acid comment.

Now, as the men loosened their belts and the ladies their waistbands, and all leaned back against the newfangled seatbacks that Jim had caused to be attached to the benches that served not only the high table but the low, Brian worked the conversation around to the matter of the coming expedition to France.

". . . Lord James and I have determined to make a single unit of our forces and both travel and fight together," he was saying to the three across the table. "We wait only a few weeks for some good men who have promised earlier to serve me in such a case as this. In those weeks, of course, we will be training some of the untutored lads from James's holding, here. James will have his full levy; and I, of course, will bring all but a few of my men-at-arms, along with perhaps some of my other people who will wish to come. But it cannot be denied that we could also use some good archers."

He looked across the table at Dafydd.

"It would be a wondrous thing, of course, if you could join us, Dafydd," he said. His eyes shifted to Giles, "and you and as many of your lads as might wish to come."

Giles's face darkened.

"No," he said briefly, "I and any of my men would be fools to leave a life which is sure, only to go out and scrabble with half of England for whatever loot is left in the fought-over regions of France."

"And as for me," said Dafydd mildly, "I and my people have little enough cause to love the kings and princes of England that I should go to rescue of one of them. As for the making of war for its own use, you know my feelings on that. So there is all this against my going, even if I would consider leaving my wife for any cause whatsoever other than our own good."

He looked fondly, if a trifle ruefully, at Danielle.

"Even if she would allow me, I think," he added.

"You're right!" said Danielle, "I'd not have you going off on any such business."

"It certainly wouldn't be wise," murmured Angie, but with a note in her voice that caused Jim to look at her curiously. Angie was gazing down at her plate and toying with a few morsels that were left of the very rich dessert they had been served, and which it was quite beyond the capability of either Jim or Angie to finish.

At the end of the table Aargh yawned hugely, showing his wicked, yellow, canine teeth.

"You know better than to ask me," he said.

"I didn't intend to, Sir Wolf!" said Brian, a little sharply. "In any case it's archers we need, not wolves."

"If this was a world of wolves, there would be no wars," said Aargh.

"Because you'd kill each other off first," said Brian.

"No," said Aargh, almost lazily, "because there'd be nothing to be gained by such fighting. If your Prince cannot win a battle, of what use is he? Let the French have him."

"We do not do things so." Brian's voice was sharp.

He controlled the slight edge that had crept into his voice.

"Well, well," he said, after a second, his voice calm again. "I blame no one for not going who has no duty to go. For James and myself, it *is* a duty, of course."

"Also a pleasure," put in Aargh. His golden eyes and the furry mask of his face gave a hint of wicked humor. Brian ignored him.

"As for our need of archers," said Brian, "we should be able to supply that once our forces are gathered together on French soil. The gathering will attract many worthy people. The best of knights will not want to miss such an opportunity; and there will be free lances, as well as men of foot—crossbowmen, men-at-arms and archers who have been given leave by their feudal Lords to fight where and as they will. The best of them will be drawn to such a gathering; simply because they are the best, and will let pass no opportunity to be among others of their own skill and rank."

"There are always those who choose to live by war and pillage, I know," remarked Dafydd, "but I knew of none except knights who choose to engage in such bloody work for the sheer pleasure of it."

"It is not so much a pleasure as a pride, in knight and man alike," said Brian. "Would the greatest crossbowman of Genoa sit at home there at ease; while men who are not perhaps as skilled as he are doing deeds of great worth, and being acclaimed where he is not? As I say, many will be there. We will have some of the worst, no doubt. But certainly, also, we will have the best."

"Do you say so, now?" said Dafydd, toying with the meat knife beside his plate.

"I have seen it myself," answered Brian, "on other such occasions; though it's true I've never seen any as great as this. But as you yourself will have seen, every fair of any size draws out the best archers from the country around to compete."

"I've been in some small contests in archery, myself," said Dafydd, still playing with the knife. "You say both crossbowmen and men of the bow who are also men of great worth and skill will be there?"

"You are letting him cozen you!" said Danielle to Dafydd angrily. "He is merely tempting you with this idea of great bowmen. You are so easily tempted to any trial between yourself and someone who thinks himself a better man than you."

Dafydd pushed the knife away, raised his head, and smiled at her.

"Indeed," he said, "you know me too well, my golden bird. I am, indeed, easily tempted by such things."

His free hand reached out and played for a second with the soft ends of the blond hair on the back of her head.

"Fear not," he said, "for you I will resist all temptation. And that will always be true, mark you."

"Your pardon, mistress," said Brian. "I own I was indeed trying to tempt your husband. But I now own that to have been an unworthy attempt; and I crave your forgiveness, and his."

"Indeed, there is no need, Sir Brian," said Dafydd quickly. "Is there, Danielle?"

"Of course not," said Danielle. But the tone of her voice did not quite match her words.

That was, in fact, just about the last of the words spoken at the table about the war. The combination of the heavy meal, plus the fact that the day had almost worn itself out, put an end to the grouping at the high table shortly after. Jim and Angie, like the others of this time and world, had come to see sundown as a signal to fold up for the night; just as they took sunrise for an alarm clock. Not until they were in their own solar chamber, however, did Angie drop a bombshell into their desultory and sleepy conversation.

"She's pregnant, you know," Angie said.

Jim paused in the act of pulling his undershirt off over his head.

"What?" he said.

"I said," repeated Angie, enunciating clearly, "Danielle is pregnant."

Jim absorbed this in the process of finishing the pulling-off of the undershirt.

"I didn't think Brian had any real chance of recruiting him, any way," Jim said, "but of course, with a baby on the way he's not going to leave his wife."

Angie dropped her second bombshell.

"He doesn't know."

Jim stared at her, for a moment not understanding. Then he did.

"Dafydd doesn't know his wife is pregnant?" he asked.

"That's what I said," answered Angie.

"I'd think the first thing she'd do would be to tell him," said Jim. "Isn't that the natural thing to do?"

"Usually," said Angie.

Jim finished undressing and crawled in under the pile of furs, watching Angie cautiously. He knew Angie. At the moment she was either very angry, or at least emotionally worked up over someone or something. Jim's instincts were betting on anger.

In such instances, Jim had learned, the trick was to avoid saying something that might sound as if he were at least unconsciously on the side of whoever or whatever Angie was angry with. Further, the best way for him to do that was to establish as quickly as possible just who the target of her anger was, and the situation involved. This was best done by judicious questioning; but even that was like walking through a mine field. Very often a question could turn out to be the wrong question.

"Why hasn't it happened in this case, then?" asked Jim.

"Because she hasn't told him, of course," snapped Angie. She seemed in no hurry to come to bed; and to have suddenly decided that her hair needed brushing. One of the few luxuries that the former Baron of Malencontri had possessed was a mirror. It was set up now in their solar, with a chair before it. Angie sat looking into it, brushing out her hair with short, angry strokes.

"But I mean," said Jim, "why hasn't she told him?"

"I'd think that would be obvious," answered Angie to the mirror.

"Well, you know how unobservant I am," said Jim with a little laugh. "I didn't see any change in her, and of course it never occurred to me that she was. But you say she told you."

"Who else could she tell?" said Angie. "She's got no close women friends; and besides, I'm an old, wise married woman."

"Old?" said Jim in honest astonishment. He had never thought of himself as anything else but a very young man; and Angie was three years younger than he was. "You? Old?"

"On this world, and to someone Danielle's age—yes, I'm old!" said Angie. "A middle-aged, wedded woman!"

"I see," said Jim; although he did not really see at all. There was nothing for it but to ask a direct question.

"Then," he asked, "why hasn't she told him?"

"Because she thinks he won't love her anymore!" snapped Angie.

"Why not?"

"Because she'll swell up with the baby and turn ugly; and he'll fall out of love with her. Just like that!"

"Dafydd?" Jim was honestly bewildered. "Even the little time I've had with him, I can tell Dafydd's not the kind to change like that. How can she know that he'd suddenly fall out of love with her, just because she's carrying a baby?"

"Oh, for pity's sake!" said Angie to the mirror. "Because she believes it was her looks, and her looks only, he fell in love with. If she loses those, she'll lose him."

"But that's ridiculous!" said Jim.

"Why?" retorted Angie. "You were there when it happened. We all came through the door of the inn, he took one look at her and said 'I'm going to marry you.'"

"It wasn't quite that fast," protested Jim.

"No," said Angie with sarcastic edge to her voice. "First he had the landlord bring a lantern so he could look her over closely."

"That's not the way it was," said Jim. "If I remember rightly it wasn't until the next day that he gave any signs of being in love with her."

"What's the difference?" said Angie. "She knows she's beautiful. She *is* beautiful and attractive to men, isn't she?"

Angie swung around in the chair and looked at him directly.

A prickly question.

"Well, yes, I guess so," said Jim.

"Well then," Angie swung back to the mirror, "knowing how she attracts men, and having him fall in love with her at first sight, what else was she to think except that it was her looks he'd fallen in love with?"

"But why should she still think it now?" asked Jim. "After all, they've been married nearly a year. In that length of time she must have gotten to know him better than that."

"Of course she has," said Angie, "but she can't help how she feels, can she?"

Another prickly question. It was Jim's opinion that in many cases people could help how they felt, if they realized that what they were feeling was incorrect. But maybe he was wrong about that. In any case, something told him it would not be a wise point of argument to raise with Angie, right now.

"You saw her face a little while ago downstairs, when he called her his golden bird," said Angie. "Didn't you see how that made her feel? It was written all over her!"

Jim actually had not seen anything written all over Danielle, simply because he hadn't been paying any attention to her at the time. He had been concentrating his attention on Dafydd.

"As a matter of fact, I didn't," he said. "At any rate, what could she expect you to do about it?"

"Give her advice," said Angie. "She knows Dafydd wants to go off to this war, just to see if there's anyone there who thinks he's better than Dafydd with a bow. So she's torn between not wanting to let him go and not wanting to keep him around, where he'll see her get big with her pregnancy and fall out of love with her. She expected me to have an answer."

"Have you?" asked Jim.

"Well, have *you?*" said Angie.

"No," said Jim. He was tempted to add that he was not a woman and these were waters where he was out of his depth; but thought better of it.

"*Nobody* can answer that question but her!" said Angie.

She put down the brush and blew out the candle by which she had been brushing her hair. The room was plunged into a dimness barely relieved by the last light of sunset beyond its windows. Jim felt, rather than saw, her climb into bed beside him. But she lay down and covered herself up far enough away so that she did not touch any part of him.

She said no more on the subject. And Jim asked no more questions; although he would very much have liked to have known if Angie also believed that Dafydd was in love with Danielle only for her looks. Because he, Jim, did not believe that for a second.

Chapter 9

The next three weeks passed swiftly. Dafydd, Danielle, and Giles o' the Wold with his men, departed. Brian became a regular resident of the castle, together with a number of his men-at-arms, busily engaged with Jim in training the sixty men that had been chosen from the men of the lands, and staff of the castle, to help fill out Jim's levy requirement of fifty lances.

Of the sixty, only the twenty-two most promising would actually end up being classed as men-at-arms. For this, they had to show that they could ride and handle weapons with some promise of skill in the future, if not a great deal of skill now. The rest of the sixty would be horse handlers and personal servants for Jim, Brian, Brian's squire—a pleasant, open-faced, blond sixteen-year-old lad named John Chester—and the present and soon-to-be men-at-arms generally.

The fifty "lances" that Jim was required to supply technically meant fifty fighting men, each one of them horsed and able to handle a full complement of weapons, consisting of heavy dagger, broadsword, shield, and—in the case of the men-at-arms—a light lance or "spear."

Brian ended up adding twenty-six men to the total strength; these being made up by his own force of all but five of his castle men-at-arms, plus five others who were recruits from his household staff; and the rest consisting of experienced men-at-arms who had come from elsewhere to fight under his command.

Properly speaking, Jim as well as Brian should have had a squire. But there was no hope on this short notice of getting one of the sons of a neighboring noble family to train as one, even if there had been time to train him. Brian's counsel was that Jim take one of his men-at-arms whom he got along particularly well with, and name him squire; since it was unlikely anyone they were likely to encounter would know the difference.

England—as Jim remembered from his medieval studies back in his original world—unlike France and some other continental countries, did allow a common man to rise to knighthood; and the preparatory stage for knighthood was that of squire. So it was not unheard of for a man-at-arms to become a squire, although he would have to do something exceptionally remarkable to go on to become a knight.

At most, as Brian pointed out, if it became common knowledge that Jim's squire was a former man-at-arms, nothing about the situation would be altered; except that Jim would be a little less respected than he might be, if some son from a house of gentle blood was holding that office for him.

The first two weeks proceeded pretty much as expected. But the last week was enlivened by two visitors, each with a separate word of particular importance to Jim.

The first of these was Secoh, the mere-dragon. He belonged to that unfortunate branch of the local dragons which had suffered from the Dark Powers which had chosen to locate themselves in the Loathly Tower. This was the same Tower by the seashore to which the renegade dragon Bryagh had stolen away Angie, when she and Jim had first ended up in this world.

Secoh's tribe as a result had become small, weak, and timid, as dragons went; and Secoh had been no exception. He changed, however, when old Smrgol, a dragon who was the granduncle of Gorbash, the dragon whose body Jim had inadvertently taken over, shamed him into standing up for himself as a dragon should—mere, or not.

Secoh had ended by helping old Smrgol, after Smrgol had been crippled by a stroke, to battle and kill the powerful rogue dragon, Bryagh, in the final battle at the Loathly Tower. Meanwhile Jim, in the dragon body of Gorbash, fought and slew an Ogre, Sir Brian killed a Worm, and Dafydd's arrows shot any of the Tower's harpies who flew down to attack them, Aargh kept off the sandmirks, and Carolinus held back the emanations of the Dark Powers.

So Secoh had ended up being one of Jim's Companions and had helped him deliver Angie from the Dark Powers.

Since then, Secoh had been a different dragon. He did not hesitate to challenge any other dragon, regardless of size. They, on their part, usually backed away from him. Physically, they were almost certain to win a fight with him; but winning would not be worth the certainty of being badly torn up in the process, by a mere-dragon who did not acknowledge the words "surrender" or "retreat."

Secoh landed outside in the courtyard one afternoon; and without asking around, stumped into the main hall on his hind legs, looking for Jim. Undersized by usual dragon standards as he was, he had to duck his head to get through the great main door; and the people in the hall, quite naturally, ran for all the other exits.

Disappointed at not finding Jim and having everybody else run from him, Secoh merely raised his voice. This, again for a dragon, was a rather light voice; but by human standards would have put the foghorn of a good-sized ship to shame.

"Sir James!" roared Secoh. *"Or, Lord James, I mean! Where are you? It's Secoh. I need to talk to you!"*

Confident of having more or less spread the word, Secoh stumped forward to the high table, where his nose told him that a pitcher left there was about half full of wine. He picked this up and poured it down his throat, smacking his lips. Wine, for a mere-dragon, was more than an unusual luxury. Jim had not so far appeared, so he sniffed at the empty pitcher regretfully, put it down on the table, and curled up behind it, with only his chin resting upon the board so he could keep an eye out for his host, and went into the pleasant half-doze that dragons are capable of doing at any time when there is nothing else in particular to do.

It was about five minutes before Jim and Sir Brian, hastily summoned from the exercise ground outside where the new recruits were being trained, came at a run into the hall, backed up by about a dozen of their veteran men-at-arms.

Secoh sat up suddenly behind the high table.

"Lord," he boomed—then remembered that Jim in his human body did not have a dragon's capacity for listening to another dragon's voice. He made an effort to lower his tones to only a bass rumble. "A matter of high importance brings me to you, m'Lord."

"It's Secoh," said Jim. He turned to the men-at-arms behind him. "The rest of you can get back to the exercise yard."

He watched them go; then he and Sir Brian came up to the high table.

"It *is* you, Secoh, isn't it?" said Jim, as the two of them came around the end of the high table and halted before the dragon. He was aware out of the corner of his eye of Sir Brian looking at him a little admiringly. The knight's hand was firmly on his sword hilt.

Jim felt a little guilty. Sir Brian either had not realized, or did not recollect, that Jim should be able to change himself into a dragon a good deal larger than Secoh, on a moment's notice. Actually, thought Jim to himself a little ashamedly, even a couple of weeks ago, he would not have been that sure of his ability to make the change so quickly. But in between he had, as Carolinus had suggested, been practicing all sorts of small magics; and in particular, since it was something he was already familiar with, he had turned himself into a dragon and back to human again several dozen times over—when nobody else was looking, of course.

"The same, m'Lord," whispered Secoh. "There's something you need to know right away, James."

"*Lord* James, Dragon!" corrected Brian automatically.

"That's all right, Brian," said Jim. "Anyone who was with us at the Loathly Tower can speak to me as an equal. You know how I feel about this."

"Well, well, have it your own way," said the knight. "Seems a damn lack of manners when a dragon does it, though."

"I apologize, Lord James," whispered Secoh.

"No apology needed, Secoh," said Jim. "You want to talk? Brian, pull up a chair."

Jim grabbed a chair from the table, turned it to face Secoh, and sat down himself. Brian followed suit and Secoh sat back on his haunches.

"Is there anything I can offer you, Secoh?" said Jim. "Half a cow? A small keg of wine, perhaps?"

"If you don't mind"—Secoh's eyes almost visibly lit up like lamps—"a drop of the wine."

Jim shouted for his castle servants. They came, after a little delay, but slowly, and approached gingerly, stopping a good dozen feet from Secoh.

"Know you," said Jim sternly to the closest servant, "this good dragon is Secoh, who was one of my Companions at the Loathly Tower. He is classed among the most favored of my guests. Give him anything he wishes. Right now a small keg of burgundy will do."

"A keg, m'Lord?" stammered the servant.

"That's what I said," said Jim. "Just take the top off and bring it in."

The servant went off and a little after the wine was delivered. Secoh sipped daintily at the open keg, no more than a quart or so, a sip. Clearly, he meant to make the wine last, under the impression that there would be no more forthcoming. He put the keg down.

"M'Lord," he began.

"James," Jim corrected him.

Secoh bobbed his head.

"Sir James," he began again, "you're going to France, I understand, to fight in a war there. There's something that you should understand and do something about right away."

"What's that?" asked Jim, "as far as I know—"

He broke off.

"Angela!" he said. "Look who's come to see us. Secoh!"

Angie had just swept in wearing her third best, royal blue dress. Clearly the word had reached her as well. She came right up to Secoh, who got up off his haunches, with his tail carefully tucked close to his back so that it would not knock anything over, and turned to face her.

"My Lady." He attempted a bow, which with his dragon's body was not all that successful. It looked more like a dart of his fearsome head toward her as if he was going to bite her in half. Angie, however, was not flustered, having encountered this bit of manners from Secoh before. She curtsied in return, knowing that that would please Secoh enormously.

"You are welcome to our hall, Secoh," she said demurely.

"Secoh has come to tell me something important," said Jim, getting a chair for her and bringing it around so that she sat with Brian and himself, facing the dragon. They sat. Secoh, himself, sat down again.

"I never thought, at first, that James might not know about this," said Secoh in a cautiously low voice, "then it struck me that maybe he didn't. So I came right away."

He turned directly to Jim.

"James," he began again, "I hear you're headed toward this humans' war in France?"

"That's right, Secoh," answered Jim. "In fact we're getting ready for it right now, Sir Brian and I, as you might've noticed when you were flying in."

"So that's what all the running around was about outside the walls," said Secoh. "I should have realized. But, my real question is, James, while you're in France, do you intend to be a dragon for any length of time? We dragons understand that with the magic at your disposal you can become one of us at any time."

"I hadn't planned on it," answered Jim slowly, "but I suppose the need might arise. Why do you ask?"

"Well, there's some rules and regulations to all this," said Secoh. "I know most people think we dragons don't have much order and discipline; but there are a few things that we're pretty strict about. Now to begin with, if you plan to be a dragon in France, even for a short while—at least long enough for the local dragons to discover you're there as a dragon—certain matters come up."

"What sort of matters?" challenged Sir Brian.

"Well—matters—Sir Brian," said Secoh. He looked almost apologetically at Jim. "For one thing, James, you can't just be a lone dragon, a dragon with no affiliations. There's no such thing; unless you're a rogue dragon, like Bryagh turned out to be. So, you've got to belong to one of our communities."

"I hadn't realized I had to do that," answered Jim.

"Oh, but you do," said Secoh earnestly, "and there's no choice about it. Since you were in the body of one of our local dragons, and since you live in the territory of the Cliffside Dragons, here, you're a member of that community whenever you turn into a dragon—like it or not."

"I see," said Jim.

"Exactly," said Secoh. "Naturally, I—we'd love to have you be one of us mere-dragons. But aside from the fact that you're really—er, too large—the rules won't allow it. A Cliffside Dragon you were to begin with. A Cliffside Dragon you will always be, no matter how much of a magician or sorcerer you become, or where you go. That's the way we dragon people have been for forty thousand years. You can check with your Accounting Office, if you like."

"No need," said Jim. "I'll be glad to take your word for it. I wouldn't doubt you in any case, Secoh."

"Well, thank you," said Secoh. "Now your belonging to the Cliffside Dragons is going to be something of great importance when you're in France, because it gives you an identity, a homeland. You aren't just, as I say, any lone dragon—an outlaw dragon—but a respectable member of a dragon community. So the only way you can be in France safely as a dragon, is to be there with the consent of your community. In short, you need a passport."

"What the bloody hell's a passport?" demanded Sir Brian.

"Permission to travel, Sir Brian," Secoh answered. "What it means is, Sir James here—Lord James here—has the permission of his community to travel to France, and his community as a whole vouches for his good conduct, dragonwise, while he's there."

"What wouldn't be good behavior?" asked Jim.

"Oh, for example," said Secoh, "getting yourself into some trouble that left the dragons of that particular neighborhood in trouble too, and then flying away and leaving them to deal with it."

"I see," said Jim. "What does a passport consist of, then?"

"Well, that's the thing," said Secoh. "Your passport would have to consist of the best jewel from the hoard of every dragon in the community."

There was a moment of silence in the Great Hall. Having been a dragon long enough to understand what the least jewel in a hoard would mean to the dragon owning it, Jim had some idea of what would be involved in the Cliffside ones lending him the best one each owned.

"Are the rest of the dragons likely to all part with their best jewel? To let me carry it," said Jim, "to France?"

"It is asking a bit of them, I know," said Secoh. "Usually a dragon going someplace else like that has some official business to transact for the community; or else he's got a great deal of respect and power in the community. But I'll help you talk to them; and I think we can talk them into it. But we ought to go right now."

"You mean this minute?" asked Angie sharply.

"I'm afraid, m'Lady," said Secoh, "I do. I really believe we can talk them into it in one session. But they just might want to talk it over among themselves, and think about it and delay things for some time. Maybe even a month or so. So, the sooner we get started the better; and this minute is a better time than any because it's the soonest we've got."

Jim looked at Angie. Angie looked at Jim.

"I think I ought to go," said Jim.

"You could just not be a dragon, while you're in France," put in Brian.

"And what if my turning into a dragon turned out to be a useful way—perhaps the only way—to rescue the Prince?" asked Jim.

"Damme!" said Brian uneasily. "Yes, I suppose you must go, then."

So it was that a very short while later Jim found himself in company with Secoh; winging his way toward the cliff, from one of the high dragon entrances of which he had first emerged in his present shape into this medieval world. It had been so long since he had flown in a dragon body, that he had forgotten the sheer pleasure of soaring.

Flying—that is, using his wings to gain altitude until he could catch a thermal so as to ride higher up until he was ready to start gliding toward his destination, with stiffly outstretched wings—was work. Soaring—gliding silently over the surface of the earth with unmoving wings—was sheer joy. He made a mental note that he would make time in the future to get off by himself and do a little flying, just for the sheer pleasure of it. Perhaps, he thought, he could even become a good enough magician so that he could change Angie into a dragon also, and the two of them could go soaring together.

"There it is, right ahead of us." Secoh's voice woke him out of his thoughts.

The cliff face and one of the high entrances to the caves was straight ahead of them. Secoh, who was a trifle in advance of Jim, made a neat landing on the lip of the opening and disappeared inside.

Jim had a moment of panic over whether he remembered how to land under such conditions; but his dragon body seemed to have reflexes that took care of that for him. His hind feet grasped the lip of the entrance and his wings folded almost simultaneously, as he touched down and moved inside.

They had entered a completely empty, small cave. The sort of a place, Jim remembered, in which he had awakened in the body of Gorbash. The sort which dragons liked for curling up and sleeping.

"No one close around here," commented Secoh, cocking an ear toward the further entrance of the cave. "They must be down in the main cavern. Do you remember the way?"

"I don't know," said Jim hesitantly. "I don't think so."

"Never mind, I'll find it," said Secoh. He led the way out of the cave in which they had landed, into a tunnel in the rock which wound down into the bowels of the cliff.

They went down and around for quite some distance; farther than Jim remembered having gone to reach that central chamber of the dragons when he had woken up in the body of Gorbash. But Secoh seemed perfectly confident about the route he took, and the branching tunnel openings he chose among. This suggested that he either had been here before or was following his nose in some way that Jim did not quite understand. Jim also had a dragon sense of smell now, but to him all the tunnels smelled of dragon. However, he had to admit that as they went on the smell grew stronger; and after a while he began to be conscious of the distant rumble of voices, which steadily mounted in volume as they got closer and closer to what was obviously their goal; until it was perfectly clear to Jim that a very loud argument was going on, with a great many voices, dragon-style, talking at once.

Jim and Secoh came out on the scene at last, emerging from a tunnel high on the rim of the bowl-like amphitheater that was the base of the great cavern. It was indeed an enormous place. Its walls were of some dark granite, but they were patterned with a perfect lacework of streams of what appeared to be molten silver, each no thicker than a pencil, but covering the walls densely. All of them radiated light. The result was that the full cavern, including its dark, overarching natural roof, was lit by it. It was not as bright as day, but very close to it. Right now, it was filled with dragons, all of whom seemed to be in hot argument with each other, but as Jim knew, were actually just chatting.

The noise was deafening—or, it should have been deafening. Dragon hearing was much better than human, Jim had discovered, but also, rather strangely, it could endure more in the way of a sound. A human would have been dazed in the great cavern at that moment. Jim found that in his dragon body he simply found the roar of sound somewhat exciting.

He and Secoh stood where they were and waited. Gradually, one by one, the dragons below became aware of them; those who had caught sight of them jogging the dragon body next to them and pointing out the newcomers. Eventually an unaccustomed silence fell on the whole huge chamber. All the dragons were staring particularly at Jim. They ignored Secoh. But their eyes on Jim seemed to express both nonrecognition, and astonishment.

Jim was just thinking about introducing himself; when one of those before him did speak up at the top of his dragon voice.

"*Jim!*" cried a dragon halfway up the opposite wall of the amphitheater, and as large as Jim himself.

Chapter 10

It was the dragon called Gorbash.

Jim remembered then that the largest dragons in this community had always been Gorbash, whose body he had once been in; Smrgol, Gorbash's granduncle; and Bryagh, the dragon who had turned rogue and stolen away Angie.

Hearing his name called, Jim remembered with almost painful clarity those days shared with the other. Gorbash was the only one in this medieval world who called him always by the name his friends and acquaintances had used, once upon a time, back on the world he and Angie had come from. Why Gorbash preferred *Jim* to *James*, Jim had never really found out. Certainly there was adequate excuse. He and Gorbash had shared the same body and brain—the body being Gorbash's—and it was hardly possible to get closer than that. So it would be natural that Gorbash would have come to think of him as Jim, and as Jim only.

Now, all the other dragons switched their stares of astonishment and incredulity from Jim to Gorbash.

"What's the matter with you all?" roared Gorbash. "It's the mage-george, who shared my body when we defeated Bryagh and the Dark Powers at the Tower! He was right in there with me all the time, while I—*we*—won the victory! I've told you all about it many times!"

As one, the dragons of the amphitheater craned their necks around to look at Jim once more.

"It's good to see you, Jim!" boomed Gorbash. "The dragons of Cliffside welcome you back among us! Don't just stand there! Come on down!"

Jim felt Secoh nudging him forward and downward. He realized he was being invited to take center stage; to go down and stand in the very center of the amphitheater where all the rest could examine him in comfort.

He picked his way down between the bodies of the dragons before him. Secoh followed demurely—if a dragon could ever be said to do anything in a demure manner—and they both descended until they were at the lowest point in the center of the cavern. Jim stopped and looked around him. He suspected that a few words from him were called for.

"It's good to see you again, too, Gorbash," he roared back, "and good to be back among the rest of you!"

"Yes," thundered Gorbash, "and a credit to all the Cliffside Dragons to have as one of their members not only a dragon of courage like myself, but one who is also a Mage among the georges, and one of their respected leaders. It gives us all stature and standing in the eyes of the georges and the world in general!"

There was quite a difference here, Jim thought. Secoh had predicted after the fight at the Tower, and after Jim had finally separated from the body of Gorbash, that the large dragon would make good use of his share of the glory resulting from his body being present in the fight there. Up until then, Jim had come to understand from Gorbash's granduncle, Gorbash had not been much looked up to by his fellow Cliffside Dragons.

In fact, just the opposite. Gorbash was generally regarded—correctly—as somewhat slow of wit; and also something of an unnatural dragon, in that he spent a great deal of time out of the caves—"above ground," as the dragons referred to it—with non-dragons. Characters such as Aargh the wolf.

Jim had consequently expected some improvement in Gorbash's position among his fellow dragons, particularly since his granduncle, who had been the acknowledged leader, was now dead. But he had never expected anything like this. Gorbash was clearly respected; and apparently listened to.

Jim was beginning to conclude that dragons had a tendency to believe in what they wanted to believe in, whether it was obviously true or not. Gorbash had evidently convinced most of those there that he was at least one of, if not the greatest of the heroes to be involved in the battle of the Tower.

Most, but not all, evidently.

"That's right!" Secoh interrupted him now. "Only not just because you say it, Gorbash! It may have been your body; but it was James who made it fight and win! I know, remember? I was there. And I *did* fight!"

He suddenly whirled about in a circle, scorching all the other dragons there with his gaze.

"You all know me," he said. "I'm Secoh! And I'm a mere-dragon! And proud of it. Any of you got anything to say about that or about me? If so, you know what you can do about it!"

There was a rumble of muttering and an uneasy stirring among the Cliffside Dragons; but nobody moved forward to take up Secoh's challenge; and none of them spoke up. Not, Jim noticed, even Gorbash.

"Now," went on Secoh after a moment, "I'll tell you why James is here. He's going to France; and that means he'll need a passport from Cliffside. From all of you!"

This announcement was certainly enough to stir the Cliffside Dragons out of their silence. A babble of cries exploded all around Jim and Secoh. Shouts of *"Wait!" "Just a minute, here!" "Who does he think he is?" "Why's he got to go to France?"* arose. These, and a few score other questions and comments reverberated from the rocky, rough-cut walls of the Great Cave.

For a good four or five minutes there was pandemonium. Then Gorbash's voice managed to rise above the rest of them, by sheer lung power dominating the uproar. One by one, the other dragons sank into silence; and Gorbash was left, the only one talking.

"Hold on, now! Hold on!" he boomed into the new silence. "Are we the Cliffside Dragons or a bunch of mere—I mean an unruly bunch of other dragons?"

"That's better," muttered Secoh audibly.

Gorbash chose not to hear the comment.

"Secoh, here, has some right to speak," announced Gorbash. "After all, as he says, he was indeed there at the Loathly Tower. I saw him myself, helping my granduncle, the great Smrgol of revered memory, destroy the traitor Bryagh. Don't forget that we, all of us, every dragon here, every george in this area, everyone, gained by that fight. If we hadn't won, then the Dark Powers would have reached out and touched many more things, possibly including us right here in the cliff. We might have ended up like the—Like Secoh's people."

There was an uneasy movement among the other dragons, but none of them spoke.

"So what it amounts to," said Gorbash, "is that Jim, and—of course—Secoh, deserve to be heard. What we decide, of course, is something else again. But first we all ought to listen. Perhaps the Dark Powers are trying to make a move toward us from the direction of France. Ever think of that?"

Not only an uneasy movement but an uneasy murmuring agitated the Cliffside Dragons now.

"That's right!" said Secoh, "and we all know we've got no defenses, personally, against the Dark Powers. Only the georges and the magicians among them have ever had any luck meeting them head-on. But here we are, lucky enough to have one among us who is not only a dragon, but a george, and not only a george but a mage."

He coughed, a little self-consciously.

"A mage-in-training, that is," he stuck in rather hurriedly, "but nonetheless, someone who can handle magic." He turned to Jim. "Show them James. Turn yourself into a george and then back into a dragon again."

Jim thanked his lucky stars that Secoh had happened to choose the one thing he had practiced the most. He had had no warning about this. What if Secoh had asked him to suddenly produce a ton of gold or something impossible like that?

"Very well," Jim said, in his most slow and solemn dragon voice. He paused a few moments for effect; and then turned himself back into his normal shape.

He was able—but barely able—to repress a start. Because one of the immediate effects of the change was that all the dragons around him suddenly seemed to jump into being four times the size they had been before. He was abruptly aware of being a very lone, and eminently eatable, human surrounded by somewhere between fifty and a hundred dragons, any one of which could snap him in half with one snap of his or her jaws.

He had been trying to think of something trenchant he could say to impress the dragons while he was in his human form. But now he suddenly recognized how unimpressive his relatively high-pitched voice would be in this particular place and time. So he only waited a few more—hopefully still impressive—moments before turning back into his comfortably large dragon shape, where he was physically at least a match for the largest dragon there.

There was a babble of excited comment in sub–basso profundo voices. There was no doubt, thought Jim, he had impressed them. The babble finally died down.

"Mage," inquired a respectful dragon voice halfway up the slope to Jim's left, "how did you first discover that the Dark Powers were attempting to attack us from France?"

"Yes," put in another voice before he could answer. "Is there some reason they were headed directly for us Cliffside Dragons?"

"Don't be foolish," snapped a voice from Jim's far right. "What do you suppose they're after? Our hoards!"

"Dark Powers haven't any use for hoards!" put in yet one more voice; and the babble broke out all over again into full-voiced argument, this time about whether or not the Dark Powers had a use for gold or jewels.

"Let's ask the mage," put in the first, respectful voice, finally making itself heard. Silence fell.

"Well?" demanded a dragon voice after a second, "Are they after our hoards or not, Mage?"

Jim realized two things almost simultaneously. One, it would probably make things infinitely easier for them if he should tell them "yes." The truth of the matter was he did not know; but he strongly suspected—in fact he was just about sure—that they didn't.

"I don't think they do," he said.

There was another babble, of triumph this time from those who had never believed that the Dark Powers would be interested in dragon's hoards. It was quelled by Gorbash's strong voice.

"James!" he roared. "Maybe you'd better tell us then exactly why you do want to go to France!"

"Actually . . ." Jim would have cleared his throat at this point, but apparently dragons never needed to. He went on rather lamely, "To rescue a Prince. An English Prince—of the georges."

"Nothing to do with us!" roared someone immediately; and Gorbash got a new outburst of voices quelled just in time to get his own next question in.

"James," he said, "do you actually mean to tell us that you want us to give you the best jewel each one of us has, just so you can go rescue a george prince?"

"That's right!" cried Secoh. "Why don't you learn? Why don't any of you ever learn? What affects the georges affects us dragons too! Smrgol knew that! Just before that last fight, he was talking to one of the georges who lives right around here, a george called Sir Brian, that's hunted a lot of us mere-dragons in his day. Smrgol thought georges and dragons should work together."

"But to give Jim my best jewel—" mumbled Gorbash, finally aghast.

"You wouldn't be *giving* it to him!" said Secoh. "You'd just be lending him these jewels, all of you. Just so that he can deposit them with the French dragons as proof that he won't do anything that will cause them harm."

With a flourish he produced from among his scales a pearl the size of a robin's egg and handed it to the astonished Jim.

"Here, James!" he announced grandly, "just to show these others the way. Here's my best jewel!"

Jim stared in astonishment at the pearl. He had been under the impression that Secoh was so poor that he did not know where his next meal was coming from.

There was a sighing, grumbling mutter from the crowd. Secoh's gesture had impressed them all right, but, Jim noted, more with horror than with admiration.

"Crazy mere-dragon!" Jim heard one grumble.

The comment was a signal for another full-fledged, full-voiced argument among the dragons in the Great Cave. Listening to them, Jim felt his heart sink. Clearly almost all, if not every one of them, were against giving up their best jewels, even temporarily. To a certain extent, particularly now that he was in his dragon form, Jim could feel how the idea might effect them. A dragon's hoard was passed down through the generations, growing as it went. The best jewel that any dragon owned might well be one first gained hundreds of years before. It would be as much an heirloom as something of quality and value.

To put that heirloom at any risk at all would be almost unthinkable to the individual dragon. They might quite honestly believe that Jim was trustworthy; and that, furthermore, he was capable of guarding their jewels as well as they could themselves. Nevertheless, the world they shared with the georges, the Dark Powers, and all the other elements in it—this medieval, fourteenth-century type of world—was one in which the unexpected could happen all too easily.

It was that unexpected that would frighten them now. With all Jim's trustworthiness, with all his capabilities, they still had to take into account the fact that somehow, somewhere, something could go wrong and none of them would ever see his or her prize jewel again. In a sense, and he knew it, he was asking too much of them.

On the other hand, in that same chancy world, they knew as well as he that sometimes it was necessary to take a desperate risk. The mere fact of existence forced such risks upon you. If only there was some way he could point out to all of them that his having the passport when he went to France involved one of these necessary and unavoidable risks—

It was at this point that his thoughts were interrupted, as he noticed that the argument around him had taken a rather ugly turn. Certain dragons of definitely anti-passport persuasion were developing their arguments; not so much against the purpose of the trip for which Jim needed the passport, as against Jim himself, his first defiance of the Dark Powers and his involving dragons in that. Also, not to put too fine a point on it, his personal character.

This argument Gorbash was not so much supporting or opposing, as cautiously hanging back from. His voice was not being heard.

"It never had anything to do with us, anyway!" one dragon halfway up the amphitheater on Jim's left was bellowing.

This individual was fat rather than large, but his or her voice had almost as much resonance and carrying power as that of Gorbash.

"All right, so Bryagh was a Cliffside Dragon before he went rogue and stole the female george away!" this dragon went on, to an increasing crowd of listeners. "All right, so Gorbash just happened to be invaded by the mage, here. He couldn't help it. That's magic and nobody, not even a dragon, can stop magic. But were we asked about getting involved anywhere along the line? Was the Cliffside Community asked if it wanted to attack the creatures of the Dark Powers at the Loathly Tower? No! We were simply dragged into it whether we liked it or not. As if we had no rights at all!

"In fact, the whole business was george business right from the beginning!" the shouter went on. "This mage invaded Gorbash without asking his leave. None of us asked to be visited by that skinny, bony, no-good female george that began the whole problem in the first place! If it hadn't been for that useless, smelly, female george—"

"All right! Just hold it right there!" roared Jim with the full power of his lungs.

He was a dragon as big as Gorbash; and in this moment he discovered that his voice could be equally, if not more, powerful. The truth of the matter was that, being in dragon form, he had fallen victim to that same instinctive dragon fury that Smrgol had warned him about when he had been in the body of Gorbash. In human terms, he was seeing red; and not stopping to think of the consequences. His sudden outburst silenced everybody, even the dragon who had been doing the shouting.

"You're talking about my mate!" thundered Jim.

He felt a definite warmness in the region of his stomach, as if the fires of a boiler down there were stoking up. He had never himself experienced the breathing of flames; and he had never seen any other dragon of this world do it. Possibly it was only a form of speech. But it was a feeling that suited his present mood and he enjoyed it. If he had been able to breathe flames at that moment, he would have been doing so.

"No one—dragon or anybody else—" he roared, "is going to talk that way about Angie! Try it and you'll see what happens to you! And something else. I've been patient. I've sat here and listened to you all argue and make excuses and do everything else to get out of giving me the passport I need; a passport that in the long run is going to be as much for your good as for anybody else's. This is England and what happens to one happens to everyone here, george and dragon and everybody else alike!

"Well, I've had enough!" he bellowed at them all. "I've waited for you to listen to reason; and you're not doing it. Now I'm through waiting! Secoh told you, and I showed you, I'm a magician; a mage-in-training. I hadn't wanted to use that; but you're not leaving me any choice!"

He had a sudden inspiration, remembering something Carolinus had once said to a watchbeetle less than a year before, when trying to get answers for Jim as to where Bryagh had taken Angie. The watchbeetle had given an incomplete answer, then ducked back out of sight under the ground. Carolinus's words, only slightly altered, came conveniently to Jim at this moment.

"So you won't be dragons of integrity and valor, won't you?" he roared. "Well, there's other things than being dragons. There's watchbeetles!"

He snapped his jaws shut in the midst of an awful silence.

The dragons before him were as silent and still as statues carved from the rock of the Great Cave around them. They stared, frozen, at him.

As the silence stretched out, Jim began to come slightly out of the red rage that had possessed him. He began to appreciate the effect of what he had said. The threat had come out of him without any real idea of what he was saying. He had absolutely no knowledge of how to turn dragons into beetles. No doubt, the proper magic was locked up in the miniaturized volume of the *Encyclopedie Necromantick*, somewhere within him. But he had never gone looking for it; and he did not know it now. If these dragons challenged him to be as good as his word, he could only show himself completely incapable of making good on it.

For a moment a spasm of anger at himself flashed through him. How could he have been so stupid as to lay himself wide open this way? Effectively, his whole purpose in coming here was lost.

Then, looking at the still unmoving dragons and the nearly a hundred pair of eyes fixed fascinated on him, his understanding of the situation suddenly changed. Perhaps he had not lost, after all.

Just because he knew that it was impossible for him to carry through his threat and turn them all into beetles didn't mean that they knew that he could not. They had no evidence that would indicate that he couldn't; and they had a great deal of evidence that he might be able to. He had been identified as a magician, a mage-in-training. Before their eyes he had turned himself from a dragon into a human and back into a dragon again. If he could do that much, what was there that he could not do?

In fact, considering the available evidence they had, the indications might well be that his ability to turn them all into beetles was child's play, compared to turning himself from dragon to human and back to dragon again.

The more he looked at them, the more convinced he became that this was the fact. Conviction spilled over into a deeper understanding of dragon nature than he had ever had before. He suddenly understood how much more powerful the nature of his threat had been than he had ever intended.

Now, in his dragon body, he could appreciate dragon feelings. Dragons were a race apart; neither bird, animal, nor flying mammal, like a bat. They were a people powerful, apart, and with pride.

It was not just their size. They were bigger than almost any other creatures, but they were not the biggest by any means. Sea serpents, for example were larger.

He could hear in the back of his head, almost as if it was yesterday, Smrgol speaking to him in that split-second before the fight started with the Worm, the harpies, and the Ogre, nearly a year ago now.

"Remember," Smrgol had said almost softly, "*that you are the descendant of Ortosh and Aqtval, and of Gleingul who slew the sea serpent on the tide banks of the gray sands, and be therefore valiant. . . .*"

Under their avariciousness, their laziness, their self-centeredness and a great many of the other unprepossessing things about them, the dragons had pride in themselves. Sea serpents were larger, but Gleingul had slain one. Ogres were both larger and more dangerous, but Smrgol had killed one in his youth; and Jim in Gorbash's body had killed one at the Loathly Tower. To be a dragon meant a great deal to a dragon.

To become a beetle was to loose all that being a dragon meant to each of these winged monsters before him. Even more than their hoards, that was precious to them. For a moment he felt a twinge of guilt at how he had threatened them. Then he realized that it had been necessary. He did need the passport. He might have to be a dragon and this was the only way to get it.

"Well?" he said. The sound of his voice broke the spell that held them all.

They turned without a word, all of them; and slowly began to shuffle up the amphitheater and out the many exits near the top of the Great Cave. There was not a word from them. In fact Jim's one-syllable question was about the last thing said until they were all back; and the favorite jewel of each had been gathered and put into a sack before Jim. The jewels were not small ones; and to Jim's surprise the sack gave the appearance of being somewhat larger than a sack bulging with a hundred pounds of potatoes. After the last jewel had been added, by the last Cliffside Dragon, Secoh reached out and took his own large pearl back from Jim's hand and put it delicately on top of the rest, then closed and tied the top of the sack.

"Well," said Jim, feeling something ought to be said, "thank you Cliffside Dragons, one and all. I'll take good care of these jewels and get them all back safely to you."

The only answer from the assemblage before him was a general heavy sigh. The dragons there, including Gorbash, watched him somberly; and with Secoh at his side he mounted the side of the amphitheater down which he had come; and went out, directed by Secoh, through the doorway by which he had entered. A few moments later he was on wing, with the sack clutched to his scaly chest with one clawed hand, headed back toward Malencontri.

The voice of Secoh roused him out of his thoughts.

"Jim!"

Jim turned his head to see Secoh soaring beside him.

"I'll peel off here," said Secoh. "You've got your passport now. I knew you would. You were magnificent there, threatening to turn them all into beetles. Serve them right too, if you had! Anyway, good luck, James—while in France!"

At that, Secoh went into a wingover and swooped down and away from Jim, leaving him traveling on by himself toward his castle.

Jim found the mere-dragon's comments did not exactly soothe his somewhat guilty conscience. Something inside him seemed to insist that he had obtained his passport jewels not only under false pretenses, but by definitely bullying the Cliffside Dragons.

He pushed the voice from him and told himself that somewhere along the line he would make it up to the Cliffsiders. He remembered, then, that Smrgol had tried to get them to come and back up himself, Secoh, Carolinus, Brian, Dafydd, and the others at the Loathly Tower; and they had not come. In a sense, his borrowing their jewels this way might be regarded as just retribution for that refusal to help.

But while this was true, the fact was it did not make him feel a great deal better.

It was only a matter of minutes before he swooped down to land on the top of the tower above the Great Hall, just over the solar that was his bedroom and Angie's. The one man-at-arms on the tower, after bringing his spear around to ready position at Jim's approach, now saluted with it. He, like everyone else in the castle, was aware that Jim was wearing his dragon shape, and was determined not to show alarm at a large fanged monster landing within feet of him.

"Good," said Jim. "You can leave me alone up here, now."

The man-at-arms immediately disappeared down the stairs, on his way through the solar and farther down into the Great Hall.

The reason for his being ordered to leave would probably not make much sense to the castle people; but then, it did not have to. The fact of the matter was, thought Jim, as he turned back from a dragon into his own body, and carefully picked up the sack of jewels, that he was simply not used to appearing naked before even the people of his own castle.

The medieval attitude toward something like this was very indifferent. Clothes, people seemed to feel, were for warmth and convenience; and all very well for that. But modesty was a notion that had yet to take root among them. It would have meant nothing to them if Jim had made a habit of not wearing clothes most of the time. It would be merely one of their Lord's eccentricities. But Jim himself felt differently.

He carried the jewels down into the solar, put them in a corner and covered them up with some of the furs—though he was quite sure that they would be absolutely safe in this room, in any case. In the first place, none of the people of his castle would dare to touch any of his things, being as much in awe of him as a magician as the dragons had been. Secondly, a sack that size, with jewels in it of a size that could scarce be believed, would be enough to give any would-be thief pause.

Jim pulled on hose, shirt, doublet, and boots; and hurried down the rest of the winding stone stairs jutting out from the walls of the tower, and into the Great Hall.

Arriving there, he was surprised to see, with Angie at the high table, the second of their unexpected visitors.

Carolinus.

"Mage!" he cried happily, hurrying forward to the end of the high table, where Carolinus and Angie were seated on two sides of that end. Jim pulled a chair up to the third side. "You're just the person I want to see!"

"That's what they all say to me," muttered Carolinus. "Matter of fact, I came by because I had something to tell you. Can't think of it right at the moment though."

"Carolinus just got here, Jim," said Angie. She turned graciously back to the magician, who was clad as usual in a long, rather dingy red gown and black skull cap, contrasting with his wispy pointed, white beard, above which his blue eyes glared fiercely at both of them, "or will you take milk, instead?"

"No, the ulcer-demon seems to be exorcised finally, thanks to that milk-spell of yours, James," said Carolinus. He helped himself to wine from the pitcher on the table, half filling the wine cup before him. "Must say I'm glad to get away from it, too. Milk's the worst-tasting food ever invented. And they force it on helpless babes! Barbarous!"

"I think the babes have a different attitude toward it than someone like yourself, Mage," said Angie soothingly.

"Not old enough to think yet, that's why," said Carolinus. He set down his wine cup, after taking a small drink from it. "What *was* it that I was going to mention to you? It's about this business of your going to France."

"Oh," said Jim, "you heard about that?"

"Who hasn't heard about it anywhere within fifty miles?" retorted Carolinus. "Not that I'd have to wait for common gossip to inform me. It came to me immediately you'd made your decision to go. It was then that it struck me that if you're going to do something foolish like that, then you ought to be warned about—"

He broke off, drumming his fingertips irritatedly on the tabletop.

"About what, now?" he asked himself; and fell silent, evidently busy exploring his memory.

Jim and Angie sat politely silent for a few moments; and then, as it seemed that Carolinus had gone off completely into his own thoughts, Angie spoke again.

"I take it you don't exactly approve of Jim going to France, Mage?" she asked.

"Oh! That!" said Carolinus coming to with a start. "Oh, I don't know. Good experience and all that. Particularly for a young magician with a lot to learn in every direction anyway."

He looked sharply at Jim.

"Don't go getting yourself killed, though, now!" he said. "Absolute waste, people getting killed right and left, for no good reason. Now what we did at the Loathly Tower had some purpose to it. But this business of galloping off to France to bring back some youngster who shouldn't have been there in the first place—ridiculous!"

"I'm going to do my best not to," said Jim sincerely. "But, speaking of that business of going to France, I'm awfully glad you're here. You couldn't have come at a better time. I've got a very important question to ask you—"

"I'm sure I could remember it, if I could just stop trying to remember it," muttered Carolinus to himself. "Right on the tip of my tongue, but I can't seem to think of the words."

"You see," Jim cleared his throat, "I have a slight problem. I've got a large sack of superb jewels upstairs—"

"Like jewels, do you?" said Carolinus, still absentmindedly. "Never cared much for them myself, I must say. Still, lots of people do like them—*there*, I almost had it! Beelzebub and Black Thunder-Bells!"

"Jewels!" echoed Angie, staring at Jim. "Did you say jewels, Jim?"

"Yes, yes," said Jim, "tell you all about it later, Angie. The point is, Carolinus, it's the best jewel from the hoard of every one of the Cliffside Dragons."

"Ah, yes," said Carolinus, drinking again from his flagon, "passport. Of course. Should have thought of that myself. But then I can't think of everything; and it's not as if it's important like this other thing I'm trying to bring back to mind here."

"Jim! You got the jewels for the passport?" Angie said. "Where are they? I'd like to look at them."

"Upstairs in the solar," said Jim, still concentrating on Carolinus. "The point is, Mage, they make a pretty bulky package. Now I was thinking, if you could just point me in the direction of finding that spell that allowed you to shrink down the *Encyclopedie Necromantick*—"

"Impossible!" snapped Carolinus. "Remember you're only a D-class magician James! And a pretty ignorant D-class, to be truthful about it. That shrinking spell is C-class at the very least—Unless, of course, you're talented enough to find it in the *Necromantick* yourself, and teach yourself how to use it. No, no, it's out of the question. Step by step, James. That's the only way to progress. Learn how to walk before you try to run."

"But this sack of jewels is practically half as tall as I am!" protested Jim.

"It is!" said Angie.

"Yes, yes, Angie," said Jim, a little irritably, "as I say, it's up in the solar. I'll show it to you as soon as we're through here."

"In the solar?" said Angie, rising. "I need to run up there for something, anyway. I'll just be gone a moment—"

"Mage, you have to help me," said Jim seriously. "I'm responsible for jewels that must be worth more than the whole treasury of the kingdom of England added up together. How am I going to carry that around and keep it safe from thieves? Almost anyone who would even entertain the thought of robbery would risk his neck for just one of those jewels. Can you imagine the position I'm going to be in, if I lose even one of them?"

"Well, well," said Carolinus. "Perhaps I'll have to help, after all. I'll shrink the jewels down for you."

"I'll go get them," Jim said.

"No, no, never mind that!" Carolinus waved his hand and the sack Jim had so carefully covered with furs up in the solar appeared upon the high table, between him and Carolinus. Angie abruptly sat down again.

"Would you open—" she was beginning, when the sack abruptly shrank down to what appeared to be a speck on the table. Carolinus reached down and picked it up. If anything, it was smaller than the *Encyclopedie Necromantick* had been after he had shrunk it so that Jim could swallow it.

"Here you are." Carolinus handed it over to Jim. His tone became testy. "Well, don't just sit there. Swallow it."

"Swallow this, too?" echoed Jim, thinking uncomfortably of the bulk of this, plus the bulk of the *Encyclopedie Necromantick*, even though shrunk, inside him. What if something happened and they suddenly decided to explode to their natural size? He would explode right with them.

"Of course!" said Carolinus. "You want to carry it safely, don't you? What safer way is there than inside you? Don't worry, it won't pass on through you any more than the *Necromantick* did."

Jim put the tiny object on his tongue and swallowed. It stuck a little in his throat. He washed it down with some wine. Angie sighed, a little bitterly.

"But," continued Carolinus to Jim, "that's the last time I small anything down for you. You've got to learn to stand on your own feet. Study. Study. Practice! Practice!"

He stood up abruptly.

"Well, I must be going," he said. "By the way, James. If you want to produce those jewels simply cough twice, sneeze once, and then cough once again. To small them down, cough once. If you should ever need to produce the *Necromantick*, it's three coughs to start off with, two sneezes, and then a single sneeze—"

Jim fumbled in his doublet pouch for a charcoal stick and hastily noted this information on the tabletop.

"But actually that *Necromantick* should stay with you for life—however long you choose that to be," Carolinus concluded. "Farewell then."

He turned about and started stalking toward the distant entrance to the Great Hall. Both Jim and Angie got up and hurried after him.

They caught up with him halfway to the front door. For someone of his age and apparent fragility, Carolinus could move with surprising briskness. He took long strides and he covered ground.

"Ah, spring," he said to them as they appeared one on each side of him, "always been my favorite season. For a little while my flowers and the season match better than at any other time—by Sagittarius!"

He slapped his forehead without breaking stride.

"Edelweiss!" he ejaculated. "Why didn't I ever think of edelweiss? The one thing that's missing from among the rest of my flowers. Edelweiss. Yes, I must have it by all means . . . Edelweiss, edelweiss . . ."

Carolinus sang the last two words in a hoarse and incredibly tuneless voice.

"Beautiful flower! Beautiful!" he went on. They had reached the front door. Jim pushed the right-hand half of it open to let the three of them out onto the courtyard. Together they walked to the drawbridge entrance; and their footsteps sounded hollowly on the drawbridge's wooden surface as they passed over the waters of the moat which, in spite of all of Jim's and Angie's efforts and orders to the castle people, still contrived to smell pretty badly, particularly close up. Jim and Angie both had hopes that continued dredging, a redirection of sewage disposal, and a few other things could eventually get it to the point where it would be—if nowhere near swimmable—at least bearable to be close to. Not for the first time Jim blessed his magician's credentials. Any ordinary castle staff would have been up in arms long before this at the type of changes he and Angie were trying to make.

The sound of their feet ceased almost immediately as they stepped off the end of the drawbridge onto the soft spring earth, unfortunately a little muddy and entirely free of grass in this particular area.

"Well, thank you for your hospitality. Good to see you both again. I think I'll just dematerialize back to my cottage—quickest way—" He extended both his arms full out at shoulder level and began slowly to rotate, beginning to turn a little dim around the edges even as they watched.

"Farewell!" Even his voice had dimmed, seeming to sound thin and a little bit farther away than it should have.

"Ha!" he cried, distant and far away.

He stopped revolving suddenly. His outline firmed up, his arms fell to his sides, and his voice, when he spoke again, was at its usual strength. His blue eyes snapped at Jim.

"I've just remembered, James," he said, "the reason I came over to see you. King Jean of France has a very powerful minister named Malvinne."

"Oh?" said Jim. "Will that be important to me?"

"It could be," said Carolinus. "He's a mage. Triple A, doesn't have the plus after his three A's the way I do, of course. Has a large estate on the Loire there below Orléans. You'd be well advised to steer clear of it. An excellent master-of-arts. Great grasp of thaumaturgy. Brilliant. Stinky, we used to call him in college—"

Jim started. It was the first he had heard of any school, let alone a college, existing upon this other world.

"Obnoxious little beast." Carolinus was winding up. "Never could stand him myself. Look out for him."

With that he spread his arms again, spun rapidly into a blur, and disappeared.

Chapter 11

Five days later, Jim and Brian marshaled their forces and left for Hastings, the closest of the Cinque Ports, that confederation of seaports which acted as shore headquarters for the English navy of the time. Hastings was the chief of these ports, which included New Romney, Hythe, Dover, and Sandwich; to which Jim knew would afterwards be added Winchelsea and Rye.

Their leaving was almost a festive occasion. For several weeks now Angie had shown almost a lighthearted attitude toward Jim's going. But the night before he was to leave she suddenly burst into tears in the solar under their heap of furs, and clutched him tightly to her.

"Don't go!" she said.

He did his best to comfort her; but he also had to point out how impractical it would be for him to change his mind at this late date. It was only at the very beginning that he might have refused to go—and even then at the expense of being scorned by everyone else in the region, very probably including Brian himself.

"I have to go, now," he said to her.

But it was a long time before her storm of emotion passed.

"There's that Malvinne, Carolinus warned you against," she said.

"Don't be silly," answered Jim, stroking her hair. "I won't be going within of miles of him. Why should I?"

"I don't know!" wept Angie. "I just know if you go I won't like what's happened to you after you get back—if you get back!"

There was no good answer for this. Jim merely continued to hold her; and eventually, they both fell asleep.

The next day Angie was as cheerful as ever. Whether it was a real cheerfulness, or simply a front she was putting up for his benefit, was impossible to tell. Jim suspected it was only a front. But what he had said to her the night before was incontestable. He could not change now.

So they left, he and Brian leading the way on their palfreys, with their war-horses being led behind them by their squires. They went almost directly south, avoiding London, since Brian had feared that the men might be tempted by the attractions of that metropolis. Most of them had never been to anyplace larger than Worcester or Northampton. Below Reading they swung eastward, passed through Gilford and out onto the north downs, and then headed directly southeast to Hastings.

It was a port town that had built up in two converging valleys running seaward, that split through the shoreline of chalk cliffs. Most of the important buildings, were clustered near the shore; including the inn to which Brian had sent a couple of his men-at-arms ahead, two and a half weeks earlier, to reserve space for them. It was an inn called the Broken Anchor and both Brian and his father had used it before on trips to Hastings.

The space in the inn would be only for Jim, Brian, and their squires. The rest of their men would be making do with whatever space the stables afforded, or neighboring stables, if the inn's were too small. They could expect, Brian had said, that Hastings would be swarming with gentlemen and their troops headed for France.

The landlord was a powerful, genial, but shrewd-looking man in his midforties. His hair was already growing thin but the muscles on his half-bare arms swelled like cords as he stood with those same arms folded to welcome them to his inn.

"Well pleased am I," Brian greeted him, "that you had room for us, Master Sel. As we foresaw, the town is overloaded with visitors."

"Indeed so, Sir Brian," answered the landlord, "but if room there was, it would be yours for your father's sake, if not your own. He was a worthy gentleman, and much respected by my own father who had this inn before me."

He turned to Jim.

"And this will be Lord James of Malencontri," he said, ducking his head in the shadow of a bow. "Welcome, my Lord. If you will just follow me, Sir Brian and m'Lord, I'll take you to your quarters upstairs."

Their quarters turned out, Jim thought, to be nothing special. They consisted of one fairly large, almost empty room, with a rather small bed in one corner. But they did have two casement windows that opened on the street below.

"You'll not be disturbed here, Sir Brian, m'Lord," said the landlord. "The bed, of course, is for your noble selves; and there is plenty of floor space for your squires and any belongings you might wish to bring up. As for stable space, I can take care of a good half of your men. I have made arrangements for several of my neighbors to make stable room for the rest."

"You do us well, Master Landlord," said Brian. "We are not only housed, but well housed."

"This inn has always taken good care of its guests," answered the landlord modestly, and bowed his way out of the room. The door, Jim noted, had neither lock nor latch. But then, he had already learned enough about this world and its people to realize that the landlord would assume that if they had valuables there, somebody would be with them at all times.

"You stay here for the present," Brian said to Jim. "I'll take my squire and seek out the king's representatives in this town, to find out what I can about our chances of sailing soon. For the moment, if you wish it, the bed is all yours."

Jim politely declined the bed, on the grounds that he had made a vow that until he had achieved something toward the rescue of the Prince, he would sleep on the floor. His real reason was that he knew without checking that the bed would be full of lice and fleas. Sir Brian might be able to lie there all night, and even sleep soundly, ignoring the bites and the itching. Jim had never learned how to do this; and profoundly hoped he would never have to.

Brian went out, taking his squire John Chester along with him in case it should be expedient to send a message back by the young man to Jim. Jim rather liked John Chester. He was obviously not the brightest of youngsters; and the fact showed in his wide, innocent gray eyes, white-blond hair, and a face that would have looked well on someone four years younger than his sixteen years. Nonetheless, he was loyal and honest to a fault; and clearly worshiped Sir Brian.

Jim was left alone with Theoluf, whom he had elevated to the post of his own squire. A man-at-arms named Yves Mortain had replaced Theoluf as chief man-at-arms.

"Theoluf," said Jim now, "go out to my sumpter horse. It's probably in the stables by now. Bring in my valuables and necessary goods, and in particular that pallet stuffed with soft cloths that Lady Angela had made for me. Bring them up here."

"Yes m'Lord," said Theoluf, and was gone.

Left alone, Jim looked around the room and congratulated himself on not making the mistake of trying to share the bed with Brian. Aside from the fleas, lice, bedbugs, and what all else there might be in its furnishings, the structure was barely big enough for a single person, let alone two. The idea of sleeping as entangled with Sir Brian as he might with Angie, was a rather uncomfortable prospect.

He was just turning his attention away from the bed when an uproar arose downstairs, the noise of which filtered up through the thin floor of his room. He could hear the voice of their landlord and someone else clearly enough so that, while he could not understand everything that was being said, he got the gist of the argument.

Whoever the unknown voice was, it was demanding that the landlord give it the very room that Jim and Brian had been assigned.

In spite of the wisdom acquired in the last year that had taught him to prudently keep his distance from any disagreements, he found himself feeling a certain responsibility in this situation. He reached for his sword belt, which he had taken off a moment before, and strapped it back around his waist so that he was now armed. It was not that he had any intention of using it—in fact he fervently hoped that no occasion like that would come up—but a gentleman just did not appear in public without one. He went downstairs.

In the large common room that took up most of the ground floor of the inn, just inside the front door, their landlord was being confronted by a somewhat stout-bodied young man a few years younger than Jim, with a beaklike nose above a flourishing mustache, and taffy-colored hair on a round skull.

"Did or did not your great-grandfather run this inn?" this individual was demanding fiercely as Jim came down the stairs. His thick mustache went out to points that bristled as fiercely as the tones of his voice. It was of even a paler blond than his hair. Below this was a generous mouth and a strong, determined chin. In spite of the fact that he was possibly half a head shorter than Jim, he struck Jim as possibly a rather tough customer.

"Of course, Sir Giles," the landlord answered him, "but that was eighty years ago; and never a word have I heard from one of your family from that day to this."

"Nonetheless," snapped the other, "did or did not your great-grandsire promise my grandsire that there would always be room for him under this roof?"

"Well, yes he did, Sir Giles," said the landlord, "but it never occurred to him that your respected great-grandfather or any of his family would show up without sending a message in advance to prepare for them. Also, it happens that I have just given out the last private room I had to a worthy knight and Lord from western parts."

"Which was the first promise?" roared the short gentleman, "the one to my great-grandfather, or this recent one of yours to these two gentlemen—whoever they may be?"

"To your grandsire, of course," said the landlord, "but as I have explained already, Sir Giles, I received no message that you were coming; and I did receive a message from them. Also, you see how full the town is with gentlemen of rank from every part of England, all eager to find quarters for themselves and their men until they can take ship to France. What else could I do, not knowing one of your family was coming, but give out a room which otherwise would have stood vacant when many would like it?"

"Confront me with them!" roared Sir Giles. "Let them show themselves to me. If so be it they are willing to abandon peaceably what is rightfully mine, then they may go their way. If not—I, Sir Giles, will prove my right to have that room upon their bodies!"

He twisted the right end of his mustache savagely.

"Sad I would be, to be the occasion of a dispute between gentlemen over room in my house," said the landlord. "Further, with all respects, Sir Giles, I must say that I do feel they have a better right to the room than yourself—under the circumstances, that is—"

He broke off suddenly, catching sight of Jim approaching.

"M'Lord!" he said, "I am dismayed—"

"I do not know this gentleman!" snapped Sir Giles, glaring at Jim.

Jim felt a slight prickle of temper beginning to germinate inside himself, in spite of his better intentions. There was something so firey and combative about this Sir Giles, that he seemed to automatically heat up anyone who came within range of his voice or eyes.

"M'Lord," stammered the landlord, "may I introduce Sir Giles de Mer. Sir Giles, this is the noble Lord James, Baron of Malencontri et Riveroak."

"Hah!" said Sir Giles, twisting his mustache and shooting glances of fire at Jim. "M'Lord, you are occupying my room!"

"As I keep pointing out, Sir Giles," interrupted the landlord, "it is not your room. It has already been given to Sir James and his companion-at-arms, Sir Brian Neville-Smythe."

"And where is this Sir Brian?" demanded Sir Giles.

"He is momentarily gone," said the landlord. "Nonetheless, he will be back shortly to the room that most assuredly is his and Sir James's."

Sir Giles advanced his left foot, put his left hand on his hip and jutted out his jaw pugnaciously, his eyes boring into Jim.

"Sir James," boomed Sir Giles, "I dispute your right to my room! I challenge you to defend with your body your right to it. Let us step into the courtyard. You may arm yourself as you like. I will do likewise; or failing the convenience of the proper arms and armor to me, I will meet you even as I am!"

Things had turned very nasty indeed. Even as he finished speaking, Sir Giles had turned around and stamped out the door into the courtyard. There he turned again and stood waiting for Jim to follow him. Seeing no other choice, Jim did so.

As he stepped onto the cobbles of the courtyard, he was acutely conscious of how they had been worn smooth and round, and were rather greasy for reasons he felt he would rather not speculate upon. It was a bright, cheerful day with a sky as blue as the sea and with little white tufts of clouds scattered here and there about it.

"Well, damme, sir!" snapped Sir Giles, "have you no voice? Answer me! Do you wish to cry recreant and abandon the quarters, or will you meet me, man to man, with weapons of your choice?"

Sir Giles, like Jim, had only the single broadsword hanging from his belt, and was wearing no armor. Jim was uncomfortably aware of what Sir Brian's response would have been—an enthusiastic agreement to fight. At the same time, his memory was uncomfortably reminding him of Sir Brian's voice tactfully referring to Jim's shield-work as ragged; and in no way really praising what skills Jim had learned during this last year in the use of the weapons of this world and time. Could he stand a chance against someone as explosive as this Sir Giles; who had probably been trained from the time he could toddle in the use of those same weapons? Jim rather thought not. But answer he must—or fight. His mind galloped.

"I have been somewhat laggard in answering you, Sir Giles," said Jim at last, slowly, "because I was thinking of a way to explain the matter to you without giving offense to such a knight as yourself—"

"Hah!" interrupted Sir Giles, his hand, which had dropped from his hip, going back to it and perching there as a fist.

"The fact is," said Jim, "I'm under a vow. I've vowed never to draw my blade until it first crosses the blade of a French knight."

The minute the words were out of his mouth, Jim felt how weak and silly they must sound; particularly to such a martial figure as this Sir Giles. It was the poorest sort of excuse, but the first he could think of at the moment. He braced himself for having to draw the sword and fight after all; but was abruptly astonished by the sudden change in the attitude of the man facing him.

It was as if all the fire and fury in Sir Giles had suddenly run out of him, to be replaced by overwhelming understanding and sympathy. Tears literally shone in Sir Giles's eyes.

"A noble vow, by all the Saints!" exclaimed Sir Giles staring at him. He took a step forward toward Jim. "Would I had but the faith in myself to merely attempt such a vow! Give me your hand, sir. A gentleman who can endure all provocations, any and all slights and shames, in order to keep his eyes fixed firmly on that goal toward which all good Englishmen are now set is a brave man, indeed!"

He grasped Jim's automatically extended hand and wrung it gratefully. "You could never have given me offense, Sir James, by telling me of such a vow. I would give my right hand to have thought of such a vow for myself; and to have faith in myself to keep it—eternal damnation as penalty for failure, notwithstanding!"

Jim was stunned. He had completely forgotten how men of the class of Brian and Sir Giles in this world literally idolized courage in any form. In fact, with most of them, it was almost a reflex. His sudden relief was almost enough to make him shaky. But not enough to rob him entirely of the opportunity he saw now flickering before him.

"Perhaps then, Sir Giles," he said, "you'd be agreeable to resolving this difficulty by sharing the room with Sir Brian and myself. Indeed, you can share the room's bed with Sir Brian, if you wish; for I've taken another vow that restricts me to sleeping only on the floor."

"Why damme! Damme!" replied Sir Giles, grinding Jim's fingers almost to powder in the excess of his emotion. "Noble and generous! So should a knight be, always. I'd be honored, m'Lord. I'd be happy and honored to share with both of you, as you suggest!"

"Then perhaps you'd have someone bring your things up to it now," said Jim. "I'll tell our landlord—" He was turning around as he talked; and he broke off to discover, not merely the landlord, but what must be nearly everyone else in the inn, either right behind him or peering out through doorways or windows at Sir Giles and himself.

"I trust you have no objection to Sir Giles joining us in the room, Master Landlord?" he said.

"None in the least, m'Lord. None at all. I, myself, will send someone for Sir Giles's things if he will only tell me where they may be found."

"A man of mine has them with our horses outside the courtyard," said Sir Giles with a negligent wave of his hand. He coughed, a little embarrassedly. "Others, of course, will be along in due time."

"Then let me take you upstairs, Sir Giles," said Jim, "and perhaps the landlord can send us up some wine."

He led the way upstairs, and the wine was quick to follow them. Deftly avoiding the bed, he sat down on one of the piles of clothes and saddlecloths that were on the floor. Sir Giles, quick to take cue that Jim was restricted in all things to floor level, chose another pile close to him.

"Your pardon, m'Lord," said Sir Giles, as they embarked on their first brimming cups of the rough red wine with which the landlord had supplied them. Jim winced inside as he saw most of the contents of the other's cup disappear within his companion at the first gulp. Sir Giles, clearly, like most of the knights of this time, appeared to drink like someone lost in the desert who has at last stumbled across a water hole. "But I fear I do not know where your family home may be. Also, it shames me to say, I do not recognize either—what was that—Malencontri? Nor does my memory recall the name of Riveroak."

"Malencontri lies in the Malvern hills," answered Jim, "not far in fact from Worcester. Actually, it lies within the lands of the Malvern chase, most of which is in the holding of the Earl of Gloucester. But I myself hold Malencontri direct from the King."

"I am indebted to you for your gentle courtesy in telling me," answered Sir Giles. "Myself, I am a knight of Northumberland. Our family for many generations has lived on the coast of the German Sea, what some call the North Sea, but a little ways south of Berwick. And your companion is the good knight Sir Brian Neville-Smythe? I do not know of his holding, either."

"Actually, Castle Smythe, his home," said Jim, watching Sir Giles refill his cup absently for the third time, "is quite close to mine of Malencontri and also in the Malvern area. We first became companions in a small matter having to do with a place of the Dark Powers, called the Loathly Tower."

"By Saint Dunstan!" Sir Giles leaned toward him eagerly, spilling a little wine in his excitement, "are you then that Dragon Knight of whom the story before the Loathly Tower is told? It is said you killed an Ogre in single combat."

"As a matter of fact, that did happen," said Jim. "Of course, I was in dragon body at the time, if you happened to have heard the story."

"Heard it, m'Lord?" said Sir Giles. "All England and Scotland have heard of it! A most honorable endeavor."

"It's good of you to say so," said Jim. "Actually it was a matter of necessity. My wife, the Lady Angela—"

He broke off at the sound of a familiar voice filtering up through the thin floor beneath them, "but unless I mistake myself," he said, "Sir Brian is just about to join us now."

He got hastily to his feet. "Will you excuse me for a few moments while I speak to him privately—"

"Privately?" echoed Sir Giles, with a puzzled look.

"Privily, I should have said," answered Jim. "It'll just take a minute or two. Then we'll both be back. I'm sure he'll be glad to find you here."

"Hah!" said Sir Giles, kindling for a moment. However, he evidently thought better of gearing up to any objection by Brian to his presence, and merely settled back with his wine cup. "By all means, m'Lord. I will await you here."

Jim was already halfway out of the room. He met Brian coming up the stairs and stopped him. In as few words as possible, he explained what had happened, and why somebody else was now sharing their chamber at the inn.

"Ah," said Brian, nodding understandingly, when Jim explained how the other had challenged him. Then he looked at Jim a little dubiously. "Did you indeed make such a vow about your sword, James? You said nothing of it to me."

"Forgive me Brian," said Jim. "There're some things . . . you understand . . ."

he dropped his voice conspiratorially, ". . . the vow mentioned my broadsword, only . . ."

Brian's face broke into a happy smile.

"Say no more, James," he said. "A matter of Magic, or somewhat between your Lady and yourself, I have no doubt. Forgive me if I seemed to pry."

"Not at all, Brian," Jim said, with a twinge of conscience, "but come on upstairs and meet this Sir Giles de Mer. He's a little quick-tempered, but he cools down just as fast. I think you'll like him."

The last few words were as much an inner prayer as a comment on Jim's part. In the back of his mind was an uncomfortable image of Brian and Sir Giles striking immediate sparks off each other. To his surprise, however, Brian seemed already to be acquainted with the name of the other knight.

"Sir Giles de Mer," he echoed thoughtfully. "But this is convenient. I have somewhat to tell you Jim; and curiously, it affects this Sir Giles as well. By all means, bring me to the gentleman."

C h a p t e r 12

J im's fear that Giles and Brian might
immediately strike sparks off each other had some reason behind it, both knights
being very definite-minded individuals, if in slightly different ways. But it turned
out he had no need to concern himself.

"Sir Giles," he said, introducing them up in the room, "this is my old friend Sir
Brian Neville-Smythe. Brian, this is the worthy knight Sir Giles, whom I've just
invited to share our quarters, since he'd expected lodging here; and the inn is
unfortunately filled up."

"Hah!" said Sir Giles, genially twisting the right end of his mustache. "An honor
and pleasure to make your acquaintance, Sir Brian."

"An equal honor to meet and make yours, Sir Giles," responded Brian. "I was
just about to tell Sir James that I am charged with an important message for him.
Curiously enough, I am charged also with one for you, Sir Giles."

"Say you so? One for me?" Giles's face showed a mixture of puzzlement and
mild belligerence. "That's passing strange. No one in Hastings at this moment
would know I was here, I should think, let alone send a message to me."

"It may seem less strange when you hear who the message is from," said Sir
Brian. "The messages to both of you are from the noble knight, Sir John
Chandos."

The name produced a reaction not only in Sir Giles, but in Jim as well. Sir John Chandos, he remembered from his historical studies of the fourteenth century in his own world, had been a brilliant military captain and a close friend of the Black Prince, as the Crown Prince of England had been known. He had been among the founding members of the Order of the Garter; which knightly Order the Black Prince had established in Jim's world somewhat in imitation of King Arthur's Round Table. Chandos was also spoken of as the "Flower of Chivalry." What such a man could have to do with someone like himself, Jim thought, was beyond guessing.

Meanwhile, after uttering a feeble "hah!" Sir Giles was almost twisting the hairs on the right side of his mustache out by the roots. Either, thought Jim, he must have some reason for knowing why Sir John Chandos would send a message to him; or else he was as completely overwhelmed by the source as well as the unexplainable nature of the summons as I am.

"The message in either case is the same," Sir Brian went on. "Sir John wishes each of you to come to him as quickly as possible."

"That means right now?" asked Jim uncertainly.

"It could hardly mean anything else, James," said Sir Brian, frowning at him; and with a mild note of reproof in his voice.

"Naturally! At once. Of course," echoed Sir Giles, his voice still slightly muted by the tone of shock in it. "Where is the gracious Sir John, that Sir James and I may find him?"

"I'll take you to him," responded Brian.

He led them out into the street. Their destination turned out to be another, larger inn, some little distance back from the waterfront, which seemed to have been completely taken over by someone of importance.

Half a dozen flags, with coats-of-arms none of which Jim could identify, hung over its front entrance. Jim made a mental note to start studying up on his heraldry. He had been paying some attention to it, but mainly to the arms of those in his own neighborhood. Here, where a good share of the knighthood of England was gathered, and where nearly all of them recognized at least the arms of the important personages among them on sight, he could find himself in trouble if he showed too blatant an ignorance.

Brian slipped them through the front door and Jim discovered that the large common room of this establishment was almost filled shoulder-to-shoulder— standing room only—with men, most of them in quite resplendent clothing. Jim, not someone who ordinarily paid much attention to how he was dressed, was suddenly very aware that neither he, Brian, nor Sir Giles were anywhere near respectably adorned, in terms of their present company.

Brian was leading them around the walls toward the staircase to the upper floors at the far end of the room, when his sleeve was suddenly caught by one of the brilliantly dressed men there.

"Hold, fellow!" said this individual. "Keep your place. Speak to the steward when he comes by, and if so be it you have some business here, speak it to him!"

"Did you call me "fellow'?" flared Brian. "Take your damned hand off me. And just who the bloody hell do I have the dishonor of addressing?"

The other's hand let go.

"I am Viscount Sir Mortimer Verweather, f . . ."—the other trembled on a reiteration of the word "fellow," but avoided it—"and not to be spoken so by any hedge-knight! I can trace my lineage back to King Arthur."

Sir Brian told him in fulsome scatological terms what he could do with his lineage.

"As for me, m'Lord," he concluded, "I am of the Nevilles of Raby; and need look down in the presence of no man. You will answer to me for this!"

Both men were now grasping the hilts of their swords.

"Willingly—" Sir Mortimer was beginning, when a stout, very well dressed man with a heavy silver chain around his neck and some sort of medallion hanging from it pushed his way between them.

"Stop this at once, gentlemen!" he ordered fiercely. "What? Brawling in this of all chambers—" He checked himself suddenly. "Sir Brian!"

His eyes had rested on Brian's face.

The change in his tone of voice was surprising, although the sternness remained. "You left us but half an hour since. I did not look to see you back so soon—"

"As it happens, Sir William," answered Brian, letting go of his sword and speaking in a calmer voice, "I've already found and have with me both the gentlemen that were spoken of."

"Excellent!" said Sir William, smiling. "Sir John will want to see you immediately. Come with me."

About to leave, he turned back to look at Sir Mortimer.

"As for you, m'Lord," he said sternly, "it would not bear you amiss to remember to mind your manners in this place. Sir John will see you when he sees you."

He turned back to Brian. "Come, you and the two you bring." He led the three of them to and up the staircase, with the gaze of all eyes in the room following.

Jim found himself feeling ill at ease as he mounted the staircase behind the substantial and dignified figure of their guide. In fact, "uneasy" would not be too strong a word to put on the present state of his emotions.

He had been aware of, and also found useful, the instinctive dragon fury of his dragon body. He had also found himself thoroughly caught up in the battle with the raiders outside Sir Brian's castle, to the point where he had not noticed until some time afterward, some cuts and bruises, and the places where his ill-fitting plate armor had scraped his skin raw.

But a twentieth-century upbringing on his own world had badly prepared him for this kind of society; where it seemed you had to be ready to explode into fury at a second's notice. His training as he was growing up had been the other way around.

In fact, when James and Sir Mortimer had been standing toe-to-toe downstairs, Jim's first thought had been how he could smooth over the confrontation, though he found himself beginning to get his back up in response to Sir Mortimer Verweather, as the exchange continued.

He decided now that, somewhere along the line, he was going to have to develop quicker responses—whether it went against the grain of his upbringing or not. He had a role to play in this society; and evidently that was a part of it.

On the upper floor of the building, they were ushered into a room not much larger than the bedroom back at their own inn, and furnished very much the same. A typical undersized bed fitted in one corner of the room, the bedding on it tumbled about. A thin, middle-aged man, with a few lank strands of black hair remaining on his nearly bald skull, stood at a sort of tall lectern, writing with a quill pen on what to Jim looked like parchment. Another man, in a dark blue doublet, managed to lounge, somehow, in a perfectly straight-backed, unpadded chair at a small square table on which were some papers, plus the omnipresent pitcher and wine cups. The man in the blue doublet was drinking from one of these cups and set it down as they came in.

A stool of a height to make convenient sitting at the table was pulled up to an adjacent side of that table, and four more stools like it stood around the room against the walls.

"Sir John," said Sir William, as the three with him halted just in front of the desk, "here, at your pleasure, is Sir Brian Neville-Smythe, back again with the two you mentioned."

The man behind the table—who could only be Sir John Chandos, himself, thought Jim—straightened up a trifle and leaned forward, with his forearms on the table.

"Good, William," he said, "leave me with them."

He looked across at the man busily writing.

"Cedric," he said.

The man put down his quill pen with care and followed Sir William out of the room.

Sir John's eyes left the door as it closed, and came back to the three men before him.

He had the lean body of a teenager in good shape; though Jim would have guessed him to be at least in his middle thirties, if not into his early forties. There was a sort of languid grace about him, but nothing of the fop, or the sort of pretentiousness that Sir Mortimer Verweather had shown downstairs. Rather, it was like the intimidating relaxation of one of the large and dangerous members of the cat family.

Jim found himself studying the man, fascinated. When he had been a graduate student, there had been no known picture or description of Sir John Chandos which agreed with the man he was facing, now. That this man was not only intelligent and capable, but accustomed to command, radiated from him like heat from a fireplace.

He did not invite them to sit down. Nor did he offer them the wine cups that stood available on the table.

"Gentlemen," he said, still in that soft voice, "wars are not won by fighting, alone. In particular, this war; where the main object is to recover safely our sovereign Prince, whom may God protect. It is in one of the other necessary ways that I require the services of all three of you. Although you, Sir Brian, may find that your part may require somewhat more in the way of combat than that of these other two knights."

Sir John looked at them each in turn, his eyes moving from one to the other as if he would judge and weigh them with his glance. His eyes were brown flecked with gold, as was the thinning dark brown hair upon his head.

"To bring our Prince home safely," he went on, "we must undoubtedly meet the forces of King Jean of France in battle. We will win or lose that battle as God wills. Nonetheless, the actual immediate recovery of the Prince will be in great measure up to you three gentlemen and some others."

He paused, as if to give them a moment to digest this information.

"None of you, I'm afraid," he went on, "will have had experience with work of this sort. But you must understand that the stability of this kingdom does not rest merely on charging with sword and lance at full gallop against the first enemy in sight; but on many things done quietly, and often, by necessity, secretly. Which means that they are not spoken about by those engaged in them, either at the time of their doing, or afterward. I will require that type of silence from all three of you, most particularly with regard to any connection between your actions and myself and the crown of England. Do you understand me, gentlemen?"

They all said they did. Jim was a little surprised to find his voice as respectful as those of the other two. He had not expected to meet this kind of authority in any knight or noble of this world.

"Very well, then," said Sir John. He glanced down at one of the papers in an untidy pile on the table by the wine pitcher. "What I tell you now must remain forever untold. We have certain advisers in France who can supply us with information which you will need to carry out the work I'll give you; and whose lives may depend on the closeness of your mouths."

He glanced up at them for a moment with a slight frown, then looked back at the paper.

"These advisers are friends of ours, who in France are thought to be wholeheartedly in the service of the French Crown," he went on. "Some may say that the work they do is not work for gentlemen, and that this must also be true of the work on which I send you."

He looked up at them again, but this time without any frown.

"I tell you that such a judgment lies," he said. "Rather it is work that only true gentlemen can do; since it calls on everyone concerned to fight, not easily and in the open, but with difficulty and in darkness. Your job, Sir Giles and Sir James, will be to actually recover the person of our Prince from wherever the French king may have him held prisoner. Yours, Sir Brian—"

His eyes moved to Brian.

"—will be to come to the aid of these gentlemen if and when they need you, with what small force with which you may be provided. You will therefore follow them, by markings and indications they shall leave as to their routes, at perhaps a day's distance behind; and rendezvous with them at Amboise, which is deep in France. Then you will make such plans to rescue the Prince as you may think necessary. Is this understood?"

"It is, Sir John," said Sir Brian.

"You, Sir Giles, and Sir James," Chandos continued, "have been chosen for the actual work of rescue because of certain special . . . talents that you each possess. You each know what these are, without my mentioning them; and if either of you does not know of the other's talent in this respect, then it may remain that way, unless at some time you wish to exchange confidences on the matter. Enough to say that the Earl of Northumberland has spoken at length to me about you, Sir Giles; and you, Sir James, are already well known from your bicker at the Loathly Tower, in song and story, to all England. The three of you will leave on tomorrow's early tide for the port of Brest in France. Can you both read and write?"

"I have been taught my letters," said Sir Giles, twisting the right side of his mustache with a touch of pride, "and can both read and write some little Latin. Also I can use those same letters to write somewhat in English."

Sir John nodded, pleased. He turned to Jim.

"Yes," answered Jim.

Sir John's eyebrows went up.

"You speak as one oddly sure of yourself, Sir James," he said. "Am I to take it you write and read very well?"

"I can write both Latin and English; and also French, come to think of it," said Jim.

Sir John turned over one of the sheets on the table in front of him, so that its blank side was upward.

"Fetch the quill from where Cedric left it, if you will, Sir James," said Sir John, "and write on this paper as I speak the words to you."

Jim went and got the quill and, seeing that there was a small pot of ink also on the lecternlike piece of furniture Cedric had been using, he brought that back with him also to Sir John's table.

He dipped the quill in the ink, wiped off the excess fluid from the nib, and poised the quill over the paper. A thought suddenly occurred to him.

"Forgive me, Sir John," he said. "I had forgotten that perhaps my style of writing and manner of spelling might not be familiar to you. If you wish, I can print the letters, although it will be slower than if I wrote in script."

Sir John smiled. Jim got the uneasy feeling that the knight thought he was trying to back away from too exaggerated a claim. However, Chandos made no comment, but leaned back in his chair.

"Write this," he said. "'There are five French ships on the sea—'"

Jim printed the words in block letters on the parchment, leaving a good space between the words, so that there could be no doubt of what letters belonged to which word. He paused and looked up to hear the rest of what Sir John had planned to dictate, and saw the knight looking at him with his eyebrows raised once more.

"You are certainly fast with a quill, Sir James," he said. "Rarely have I seen a clerk move one so speedily. I think perhaps I will look at this before giving you the rest of the sentence—it may not be necessary."

He turned the paper around so that the letters faced properly toward him, and frowned at them.

"You do indeed write oddly, Sir James," he murmured, "but if one makes allowances it is easily readable. But you spoke of two ways of writing?"

"Yes, Sir John," Jim said. "I printed these words. Commonly, however, I and the people where I come from write rather than print when they wish to put information on paper—or parchment, as in this case."

"I would see this other way of writing. You called it—?"

"*Script*, Sir John," said Jim. "By your leave, I'll write the same words again in script below the ones I printed, so you can see the difference."

"By all means. Do so," said Sir John, watching him narrowly.

Jim turned the piece of parchment around and wrote the same words in as clear a flowing hand as he could manage. Then he turned the paper about so that it faced properly for Chandos, who looked at it.

"This is indeed difficult, if not impossible, for me to read," said Chandos. "Though I make little doubt we have scribes who would be able to puzzle it out. But I must be truthful with you, Sir James, and say that you amaze me with the speed of this latter form of writing. It will not do in this instance, however. You had best write the first way—what was that called again?"

"Printing," said Jim. "I printed the words the first time I wrote them for you."

"The more I look at them, the more they seem marvelously clear, if a little oddly made," said Sir John. "Certainly it will be excellent for our purpose, which may require the passing back and forth of short, written messages. But for my own pleasure, would you also demonstrate your writing in Latin and in French?"

"Gladly, Sir John," said Jim. He did so, using the same words.

"Wonderful!" said Sir John, shaking his head in admiration over the other two lines, which Jim had also both printed and laid out in ordinary handwriting. "I cannot say that I can read either one of them in script; but I have no doubt that you yourself can. And possibly a cleric, and particularly a French cleric, could read them both; at least those lines done in the manner you call printing. This will be excellent."

He looked almost narrowly at Jim.

"I take it the ability you show me here has something to do with that special talent I spoke of earlier?"

Jim was tempted to answer that in his own place and time there were multitudes of people who could write as he had just demonstrated. Caution reined in his tongue.

"If you will forgive me, Sir John," he said, "that is a question I am enjoined not to answer."

"Ah," said Sir John, looking very serious. He nodded. "Of course. It will have to do with that *talent* of yours. I understand. We will say no more. There remains only a couple of other matters."

He took from one finger one of the several rings that he wore on his hands and handed it over to Jim.

"Sir James," he said, "you, as the gentleman of rank here, will wear this ring. When you get to Brest, you and Sir Giles will both take quarters at an inn with a green door. In fact it is referred to as the Inn of the Green Door, in the French tongue. You will find there is space available. Wait there until you are contacted by someone who can show you the like of this ring. I would suggest you wear it on entering the inn, then keep it visible until you see someone wearing its fellow. That man will have word for you on what your next move should be. Now, the only other matter is that of your device."

"Device?" echoed Jim, bewildered.

But Sir John had already turned toward the door and lifted his voice. He had spoken so softly until now, that it had not fully registered on Jim that he was a tenor. Now that he chose to shout, he was revealed to have vocal equipment capable of a remarkable carrying quality. Jim was suddenly reminded of the fact that up through something like the nineteenth century, infantry officers benefited from being tenors, since their higher-pitched voices could be heard by their men more clearly over the noise of battle and gunfire. Sir John had a tenor with the penetration of an operatic singer.

"Cedric!" he called.

The door opened almost immediately and the thin, balding man whose pen Jim had borrowed appeared in the opening.

"Sir John?" he said.

"Fetch Sir James's shield and the painter," said Sir John.

Cedric went out, closing the door behind him.

"The Earl of Northumberland," said Sir John, turning back to Jim, "on consultation with His Majesty, was pleased to learn that His Majesty had granted you a coat-of-arms. No doubt, you have arms of your own in the land from which you came. Nonetheless, it was felt that while you are one of us and in our England, you should by right have English arms. These are to some extent prescribed by law. In any case, a man of experience in the painting of arms has been sent down with the necessary information from London and has just finished displaying those arms on your shield."

"My shield?" echoed Jim. The last he had known of his shield, it had been back at the inn under the surveillance of Theoluf, along with all the rest of the baggage belonging to the three men.

"I sent John Chester back for it after I first spoke to Sir John," explained Sir Brian. "He told me that you were in conversation in the courtyard with Sir Giles at that moment, so not wishing to interrupt, he merely went upstairs, spoke to Theoluf, and took away the shield to bring it back here."

"Oh," said Jim.

The fact of the matter was, he had been carrying his shield cased ever since they had left Malencontri—that is, with a linen cover over it. He had never gotten around to putting any kind of arms on its blank metal surface before, though Sir Brian had assured him that probably he could put any arms he wanted on them without objection from others, unless he happened to duplicate somebody else's arms. The fact was, Sir Brian seemed a little bit puzzled that Jim had not immediately put onto his shield the arms he had undoubtedly possessed in that far-off land of Riveroak from which he had come. Jim's hesitation in this matter had been due to a sense of guilt over claiming both a nonexistent rank and a false coat-of-arms that he had made up on the spur of the moment when he had first met Sir Brian.

While he had been thinking, the door had opened again and Cedric had returned, followed by a little man, arthritically bent-backed, who may have only been in his forties, because his hair was just beginning to turn gray and he still had most of his teeth; but who, in his general actions and the leatheriness of his skin, looked seventy.

The little man was carrying Jim's shield, no longer cased but with its face turned away from Jim. Cedric went to the table, silently recaptured his quill pen and returned to his desk. The little man came forward, bobbed his head at Sir John, and then at the other three, and rested the shield on its point, with its face still turned away.

"Well, Master Arms-painter," asked Sir John, "are you finished?"

"Finished indeed, Sir John," answered the little man in a creaky voice, "though the paint is still wet so that I would caution any of you gentles not to touch it for another hour or so. Shall I show the device?"

"That's what you're here for, man," said Sir John, a little testily.

The small man did not seem either intimidated or offended by Sir John's reaction. He merely turned the shield around to display its front side to them all.

Jim stared. What he saw on the metal surface was a dragon rampant surrounded by a border, a very thin border, of gold, which looked like the actual metal rather than paint, for it did not glisten with the wetness that the other colors showed. The rest of the shield was a uniform dark red.

"You understand that it's the law of England, and of all Christian countries," said Sir John, "that one of your—er—talent, should always show some red upon his arms, so that any other worthy knight having cause of dispute with you, will be duly warned of whatever advantage you might have by cause of that talent."

Jim understood immediately. He hardly knew enough magic now to make him dangerous under ordinary battle conditions—if you excepted the fact that he could change from a human being into a dragon—but it was not surprising that someone who could work any form of a magician's art would be considered to have what amounted to an unfair advantage over a knight who could not. It was rather a nice piece of caution, he thought, considering the fact that large knights might be considered quite fair in attacking a knight much smaller and weaker than themselves, as long as the one attacked actually was a knight and carried weapons. But he had learned a good many months back not to question the ways of this world, but to merely accept and fit himself to them.

Some gesture of appreciation was required, however.

He turned to Sir John.

"I'm indebted to His Majesty and the Earl of Northumberland for this coat-of-arms," he said, "and also to yourself, Sir John"—he turned toward the little man—"and to yourself, Master Painter. I shall be honored to bear these arms granted to me by the King of England. Would you convey my deep appreciation and thanks both to His Majesty and the noble Earl, if you should ever find yourself in a position to do so, Sir John? I would appreciate it most highly."

"Indeed, I shall be glad to, Sir James," said Sir John. "You speak your gratitude in a manner most gentle, it seems to me; and I am sure the Earl of Northumberland and His Majesty will feel likewise."

Over at the writing stand, Cedric cleared his throat. Sir John glanced at him for a second and then back to the three.

"But I see time presses," he said. "I have much to do, getting all things ready and embarking as many of our forces as is possible. So, you may go gentlemen. With God's help we will all be reunited in France."

Jim, Brian, and Sir Giles bowed themselves out of the room.

Chapter 13

Dawn was just breaking.

Jim stood by the port gunwale of the very small, definitely tub-shaped vessel on which they had labored through the night down the English Channel and along the coast of France. The shipmaster, in contrast to what Sir John had said about traveling on tomorrow's tide, had insisted that they take off instead on the late night tide that same day on which they had had their interview with Sir John Chandos.

His reasons were very definite. On both sides of the Channel between England and France, shipowners and shipmasters were aware that England and France were about to be actively at war again. That meant that there would be a good deal of shipping passing southward. Apparently, on the high seas, every ship was a pirate ship if it saw another vessel which was smaller or looked to be easily taken; and this shipmaster, like most, was the sole owner of his ship. If he lost it, he lost his livelihood.

Night, the shipowner and master had insisted, swearing by a number of saints to witness that his words were true, would be the only safe and sensible time to take three such men as themselves to Brest. In bad weather this would not be so; but both wind and a near-full moon favored them.

The construction of the ship and the waters they were traversing, however, in spite of these good conditions, combined to make for a very choppy voyage. Sir Brian was sick almost from the moment they left Hastings harbor, though Sir Giles was fine. Jim had discovered at an early age that for some strange reason he was immune to seasickness; so he was merely concerned over how such a cockleshell as this could survive if any kind of a storm blew up. Luckily the weather during the night continued to be, as the shipmaster had claimed it would, almost too good to be true.

They had passed the Channel Islands during the latter part of the night. After that, the shipmaster had kept his vessel well out from land, although he was obviously one of those navigators—for all Jim knew all navigators at this time were that way—who preferred to see a coastline on the horizon at all times. But with the lightening of the sky, he was moving in closer toward a dark line that Jim finally identified beyond any doubt as land, rather than a bank of low-lying, dark clouds.

Now, as the day broke cloudless and clear, Jim saw that they were quite close to a coast that seemed to stretch to the horizon on either side.

He walked down the side of the boat until he came to the square, powerful shape of the shipmaster, who was standing with legs apart in the bow, staring ahead of him.

"Where are we?" he asked.

"Entering the Rade of Brest," answered the shipmaster, without taking his eyes off the water and land ahead. "God be with us now"—he crossed himself—"for this water is full of rock and I must—"

He did not finish his sentence. There was a sudden, grating shock that ran all through the vessel and it stopped abruptly.

"What is it?" demanded Jim.

"Saints preserve us!" cried the shipmaster, literally wringing his hands, "we are caught, as I feared! We are held fast!"

Jim stared at the man, for he made no move to do anything, simply stood where he was, twisting his hands together, with tears starting in his eyes. Behind Jim there was a quick thunder of feet and the half-dozen men who made up the ship's crew came running, crowding up to the bow to stand with the shipmaster, staring down into the water ahead. It was true that now the ship stood, solidly unmoving in spite of the taut single sail overhead.

"Can you see anything?" Jim heard one saying.

"Nothing," replied the man beside him, still staring into the water.

"What's the matter?" Jim demanded of the shipmaster. "Why aren't you doing anything?"

"There's nothing to be done, Sir Knight!" answered the shipmaster, still not looking at him. "These rocks are like iron. We are stuck fast here until we perish from lack of food and drink, or a wind finally blows us off and we sink through the hole surely torn in our bottom."

"There must be something you can do," said Jim. "You've got that small boat on deck. Why don't you put it overside, tie a rope between it and this ship and see if you can't row us loose?"

But the shipmaster merely shook his head wordlessly, the tears now streaming down his face.

"What's amiss?" said the voice of Sir Brian in Jim's ear.

Jim turned to find the other knight at his elbow.

"We seem to have run onto a rock, Brian, an underwater rock," Jim said. "I've been trying to get the shipmaster to do something, but he seems to think it's no use."

"Land no more than two or three miles away, and he thinks it's no use?" snorted Sir Brian. "What sort of poltroon is he, to give up so easily?" He raised his voice. "Here you—"

He punched the shipmaster on the shoulder hard enough to rock the man on his feet, but the other still did not respond. He seemed lost in a frenzy of sorrow and despair.

Brian continued to shout at him, but the seaman paid him no attention. Jim looked back over his shoulder. He put a hand on Brian's arm to attract his attention.

"Where's Sir Giles?" he asked.

"Damned if I know!" growled Brian, punching the shipmaster again. "Pay me some mind, you! Are you a man or some puking child to stand there and weep and do nothing?"

He might as well have talked to a man in a trance. Jim, driven by a sudden curiosity, left him to deal with the shipmaster and walked back the length of the ship, looking for Giles. It was most odd that the other knight had not joined all the rest of them up in the front of the vessel where the excitement was.

The neck of the small vessel, as well as its hold, was loaded with boxes and bales, all strongly tied down so that they would not shift as the vessel moved about. As a result, Jim had to thread his way among these goods, some of which were piled higher than his head, and look out that his feet did not get caught and tripped up on the anchoring ropes that held this deck cargo in place. The result was that he did not find Sir Giles until he was nearly to the back of the ship; and came on the other knight suddenly, around the corner of a large stack of kegs.

To his surprise Sir Giles was just taking off the last of his clothing. He was very round and pink without it, so that he looked rather like a white-mustached cherub. Jim stared at him in surprise.

"What are you up to, Giles?" he asked.

"All right then, damme, watch if you want!" Sir Giles glared at him. "It's good blood, been in my family for generations. Not the least ashamed of it—just don't go around announcing it to any Tom, Will, or Hal. If you want to know, I'm going to have a look at the underside of this boat and see what it's hung up on!"

Completely naked, he ran to the near side of the ship, clambered up on it, poised outwardly there for a minute, and then flopped off it to land with a resounding splash in the water below. Jim, who had followed him automatically in his dash, reached the side just in time to see Giles turn, on contact with the sea, into the sleek gray shape of a harbor seal. The seal righted itself, stuck its head out of the water momentarily to look up at Jim with the eyes of Sir Giles, barked once, then turned, dived, and was gone.

Jim stood staring at the dark sea surface for a long moment. So—that was Sir Giles's particular virtue or talent. He was what was known as a *silkie;* someone who was, to quote the old definition, *"a man upon the land, a seal upon the sea."*

Jim turned and hurried back up front, to find Brian literally cuffing the poor shipmaster about. The rest of the crew stood back and showed no inclination to interfere. There were six of them; and a long knife hung in a scabbard from the belt of each. But because of either the sword at Sir Brian's side, or merely the fact that he was a knight—or possibly even the fact that they blamed the shipmaster for their running aground, so that they were not amiss to seeing him take a certain amount of punishment—they were being nothing more than spectators.

Jim winced. In some ways Sir Brian was the gentlest and kindest of men; but he also lived by a hard set of rules that both Jim and Angie had had their greatest difficulty in adjusting to. Coming up to Brian, Jim caught the other's arm to stop him.

"Brian!" he said urgently. "What are you doing?"

Brian's head jerked around sternly, but his face relaxed when he saw it was Jim.

"Why, James," he said, "this fellow has lost his wits. I'm merely trying to knock some sense back into him."

"That won't do it," said Jim. "He's in deep emotional shock."

"Deep . . ." Brian stared at him. "Er . . . James, is this something magical, you mean?"

Jim had used the words that had come naturally to his tongue, without thinking how they would translate into whatever language he spoke on this world; or if, even if they did translate properly, they would convey any real meaning to Brian. For a moment he was tempted to explain; and then a number of occasions before this in which he had tried, and failed, to bridge the gap between a medieval society and a twentieth-century technological one, laid the finger of caution on his tongue.

The chances were that nothing he could say would make Brian understand. From Brian's point of view it made perfectly good sense to knock a disturbed head around until its parts were jarred back into proper working order, the same way someone in Jim's original world might hit or kick a piece of machinery in the hope of jarring it out of a nonworking state back into a working one.

Also, there were more important matters to discuss. Unreasonable as it seemed, this was one more case where it was simpler, simply, to lie.

"You could call it that, Brian," said Jim, "but there's something more important at the moment. We must talk about it privily."

"Quite right," said Brian, turning from the still unresponding shipmaster. "Let us step aside to a back part of the ship—*hold!*"

The last word was a shout that came from him with all the authority of someone in command over troops.

"The first man who touches that small boat, without orders from Sir James or myself, will have his arm cut off!" snapped Brian.

Some four of the crew members, who had begun to move in the direction of the little boat, which was designed to carry no more than three bodies ordinarily but could possibly have accommodated one more, checked immediately.

"All of you, into the point of the deck there, with your shipmaster!" ordered Brian. "If I look back and see one of you not as close there as herring in a dish, the one I see shall be dealt with!"

"Now, James," said Brian, turning back to Jim, "let us step aside."

They headed back among the bundles and bales, Brian glancing, once or twice, over his shoulder to make sure none of the crew had moved away from the position to which he had sent them. He let himself be led by Jim around the pile of kegs to the spot where Sir Giles's clothes lay on the deck.

"What's this?" said Brian, seeing them and bending over to pick up a doublet. "Where's Giles? And what are his garments doing here without him?"

"That's what I want to tell you," said Jim. "He dived overboard to swim under the ship and see how stuck it is on the rock, or whatever is holding it."

"Has he?" said Sir Brian, dropping the doublet and gazing over the near side of the ship. "Indeed, I had no idea the gentleman could swim so, almost like a fish to go down beneath the water to the depth to which this ship's bottom must lie."

"That's what I wanted to tell you, Brian," said Jim. "Normally I'd respect Giles's confidence. However, you'll see for yourself; since I think—"

He was interrupted by Brian turning and sticking his head around the edge of the kegs and shouting toward the bow of the boat.

"Hah!" He stood staring where he was for a second, then turned back to Jim.

"One of them looked as if he were trying to slip away toward the small boat after all. It will be *sauve qui peut* with them. And once several are in that boat and headed for the coast, it is not likely they will come back, as gentlemen might, to ferry the rest of us to safety. Now, what were you saying, James?"

"I was about to tell you something about Giles," said Jim, "a sort of family secret of his. As I say, normally I wouldn't breach his confidence; but it'll take the two of us to throw him a rope and help him on board when he comes back. So you'll see for yourself, anyway. Brian, Sir Giles can turn into a seal when he dives into the sea."

"Ah," replied Brian thoughtfully, "a silkie. When he mentioned his Northumberland seashore home, I half-suspected it. James—"

He had turned and stuck his head around the corner of the kegs again. Jim could not see the expression on his face but he kept looking forward for a long moment before turning back again.

"James, those rascally fellows up there will be in that little boat and away unless we keep our eyes almost always on them," he said. "If we are both to be needed here at the rail, they may well have time to get it into the water and some of them get away; and we may need that boat. I can hold them where they are as long as I keep looking at them from moment to moment; but the minute they think I've forgotten them for longer than that, they'll bestir themselves and away."

"Yes," said Jim. "What do you suppose we can do?"

"I could simply stand over them," said Brian, "but as you say I'm needed here. It's you can put them in such fear that they will not dare stir. Show them your shield. Tell them you are a sorcerer and will put some spell upon them that will turn them into toads or somewhat if they move. Then we can turn our backs on them with safety. None will dare shift from where he is, to save his soul."

Jim felt a touch of inner chagrin. Brian's innocent faith in Jim's ability to work magic of any degree desired, had made small troubles for him on previous occasions. Apparently, from Brian's point of view, you were either not a magician or you were a magician. If you were a magician, you ought to be able to do all the things a magician could do. This, in spite of the fact that Sir Brian had been fully informed that Jim had only a D rating with the Accounting Office, whereas someone like Carolinus was one of the three AAA+ magicians in the world.

Jim had not the first idea of how to turn people into toads, whether they moved or not to trigger off the change. On second thought, it occurred to him, if Brian so thoroughly believed in what he could do, the seamen would probably believe no less.

"Excellent idea, Brian," he said. "I'll do just that. Meanwhile, do you want to watch for Giles over the side of the boat there?"

He pointed.

"Gladly," said Brian, hurrying to the ship's side and leaning over it to look at the water.

Jim went back around the barrels, seeing a sudden uneasy shift of the fairly loose group in the bow back into a tighter one; located his own belongings on the deck, and dug out his shield. He uncased it and carried it forward to the seamen. The master was still weeping, still in shock.

"Do you see this shield?" said Jim, giving the seamen his best scowl.

They stared.

"Do you know what the red on it means?" demanded Jim. "Answer me, one of you!"

"You—you are a magician, m'Lord?" stammered one of them after a long pause.

"Good!" said Jim. "I see you have some common understanding. Very well." He let go of the shield with his right hand and made several elaborate passes in the air between himself and them. They shrank away from him. *"Urntay intotay oadstay!"* he intoned solemnly. "Now, the first one of you who stirs so much as one step from the bow in which you now stand will be turned forever into a toad. It shall remain thus until I come back and lift the enchantment from you!"

Terror was obvious among the seamen. They seemed already about as close together as they could get; but now they huddled even closer. Jim turned and carried his shield back, recasing it as he went; and put it with the rest of his belongings. He could now hear Brian's voice shouting something from farther back. He hurried to reach his friend.

Sir Brian was leaning over the rail as Jim rounded the corner of the kegs.

"Wait but a moment until James gets back!" Brian was calling down to the water alongside the vessel. Jim came up with him just in time to see the seal down there swimming in place and looking up at them.

"You might have thought about how to get back aboard, before you went into the sea," said Brian to the seal. "If that's an example of Northumbrian sense—"

Down below him the seal barked twice, and the barks did not sound complimentary.

"Oh, there you are, James," said Brian. "Here is Giles. I've just been telling him you'd be back in a moment. Did you bring a rope with you?"

"No," said Jim. "I didn't stop to think about it in the midst of putting a spell on those sailors up there to keep them in place. Would you like to look for one? I'll keep an eye on Sir Giles, meanwhile."

"I'll be back in a moment," answered Brian, disappearing from beside Jim. "It shouldn't take longer than that. There are hundreds of the pesky things around the deck."

"Are you all right, Giles?" Jim asked, leaning over the rail. "Did you find out anything useful?"

The seal barked up at him. The barks were still testy, but did not carry quite as sharp-edged a tone as those which had replied to Brian. But they were still, at the very least, impatient.

"Here we are," said Brian, reappearing at Jim's elbow. He was holding the end of what looked like a half-inch line.

Together, they dangled it over the side to the seal, who lunged out of the water at it. As the seal emerged, it sprouted a couple of arms, with which it grasped the rope. As it pulled itself farther out of the water, it resolved itself back into the complete, naked Sir Giles; who with some struggle and swearing, half-climbed, was half-pulled, up the side of the boat and helped over the gunwale onto the deck.

"Damn cold up here!" said Giles, shivering. "All of a sudden I'm chilled to the bone! Help me to somewhat wherewith I can dry myself."

"I thought of that, too," said Brian. "Slashed open one of the bales. Here you have a length of cloth in lincoln green that I cut off with my sword."

Giles snatched it from Brian's grasp, his teeth chattering, and proceeded to rub himself dry.

"Cold up here?" asked Jim. "It must have been freezing in the water, then."

"Not at all. Quite pleasant, really," said Sir Giles, as he rubbed himself down. "But, of course, I was in my other body."

Since the sea in this particular area was far from what an unclothed man might consider warm, Jim could well believe that wearing a seal body instead of a human one would be the only possible reason for finding immersion in it comfortable.

"What did you find?" demanded Brian eagerly.

"One moment, Brian," interrupted Jim. "Giles, Brian here, of course, now shares the knowledge of the—uh—talent in your family to which Sir John Chandos referred. You both know mine. I am a magician."

"Indeed," said Giles humbly, "I learned as much back at the inn. If I have offended through my ignorance of your true rank, m'Lord Mage, I do most heartily beg pardon—"

"Nonsense!" Jim cut him short. He had expected the other, being a silkie, not to take the fact of magic in Jim as seriously as Brian and others did. "I only have a D rating, which makes me a very junior sort of magician."

"Nonetheless," put in Brian swiftly, "he was able to put a spell upon the sailors up front so that they should not escape with the small boat we have on deck, thus leaving us free to lift you from the water."

"Hah?" said Sir Giles, "That's good. That's very good. If you would hand me my underclothing and hose, m'Lord—"

"Giles," said Jim, handing the clothing to him, "to get back to what I was just saying, we were at the point of first names between us, if you remember. Please, let's stay on that level. You're a silkie. I'm a beginning magician. Sir Brian is simply a worthy and valiant knight. Nonetheless, we are all three equal here, and all good friends. Call me James, then."

"If you wish. Very kind of you, m'—James," said Sir Giles, rapidly dressing. "Very good indeed, considering that I was merely *born* a silkie, whereas to understand magic, so I understand, takes great and terrible study. But if you wish, James"—he hastened to stop Jim, who was about to speak again—"so it shall be.

And Brian, if my language was a little overrough just now when I was in the sea and you were above me—"

"Barked a couple of times," said Brian. "I heard nothing to be offended at."

"Good of you too, Brian," said Giles, completing his process of dressing. "Now, about the ship. It is really not badly aground at all, and it is not holed in the least."

"The shipmaster will be overjoyed to hear that," said Jim, "but—go on. What's the situation down there, then?"

"Why, we have simply run our bow up on one small spire of rock, as we might on a sandy shore," answered Giles. "It is an outward piece of a larger rock that goes down to the sea bottom; but we are not strongly fixed, for all that the ship seems solidly set. Still, a rising tide will not lift us off it, because of the way we are held. The only way we can get free is to back the ship up. But that can be done if we are men enough. If the shipmaster and his lads will give me a longer rope, I can swim out with it from the stern and tie it around another spur of rock not too far off and by using this apparatus they have on board for lifting weights and such—"

"Block-and-tackle," supplied Jim.

"No matter. Whatever the name. The sail will have to be lowered, for with the wind in this quarter it would work against our effort, pressing us farther on the rock. But if they will take it down and use the block-and-tackle to multiply their strength, and pull against the rope which is tied to the other rock, I am sure we can pull the ship loose."

"Then that we shall do," said Sir Brian decisively. "Let us be about it immediately."

The crew was moved from the bow of the boat to its stern. The sail was dropped; and a long, stout, hawserlike length of rope firmly attached to the stern, it having been explained to the shipmaster, who had returned to life on hearing that there was hope for his ship, what they intended to do. The three knights carried the other end of the rope far enough forward so that Giles could enter the sea once more and be turned into a seal again in privacy. The stout young knight once more disrobed.

"But how are you going to tie something like this to the other rock with no hands?" Jim asked him.

"I see no difficulty," answered Giles. "I will carry the end of the rope out in my teeth, beyond the farther rock; then around it, over it, and around that part of the rope which stretches from the ship, until I have made a knot, then simply pull the knot tight. It should slide up the other length of the rope; and fasten itself firmly to the anchoring rock. You will see," said Sir Giles, "there will be no trouble to it. It remains only for the seamen to put their backs in it and do their part of the work."

"Over you go, then," said Brian, for Giles was now once more unclothed. "We will wait for your return and see you dried and dressed after it. Then we will all return to the stern of the ship and give the shipmaster his orders."

It all went as Giles had explained. Jim had suggested, as they were returning, that they could help the crew pull on the loose end of the shorter, anchoring rope that was attached to the block-and-tackle, which was in turn attached to the cable Giles had tied around the other underwater rock. But this suggestion was brushed aside airily by Sir Brian.

"We are knights, and men of rank," said Sir Brian. "Were it necessary, we could help. But let them first bend their backs to it with a will. Surely they can do some such small thing as pulling a ship like this off a place as Giles has described."

Jim reserved his opinion, but let it go at that.

The seamen were already attaching a block-and-tackle and a shorter rope to the line. The block-and-tackle line they would be hauling on went around a sort of narrow drum, with a brake that could be operated by a foot-pedal by the most forward man on the line, to lock in position any gain on the hawser they might make. The shipmaster was busy questioning Sir Giles.

"And how exactly did you say the stem of the ship lies on the rock?" he was asking.

Giles described it in an almost kindly voice. It occurred to Jim that, living close to the sea as Giles had all his life, he had probably had something to do with ships and the men who sailed them before this.

"It is merely a speck of rock," he answered, "with a little trough in it, slanting upward; and it is in this trough that the stem of your vessel has pushed itself—but only by a matter of inches. The sides of the trough hold the keel in an upright position, but pinch it only on the end. Therefore the ship seems fixed. But it is barely so. A short pull backward will bring her off."

"Praise God and all saints!" said the shipmaster. "Do you hear that lads? A strong haul, but a short one. One good effort and we're afloat again! So, put your backs into it, if all is ready, and heave!"

Apparently all was ready, for the men spat on their hands, took up the rope, and all together moved back half a step, straining against the rope they held. The drum gave a half turn as the hawser straightened, lifting higher out of the water, so that it was closer to a straight line than the sagging curve it had held originally. Twice more they gained some distance on it this way. Still the ship itself had not moved.

"On! On!" the shipmaster encouraged them. "Heave and haul, my lads!"

The men heaved and grunted. A few more inches were gained, but still the ship had not moved, and the line, stretching out until its farther end disappeared in the water, seemed as immovable as if it were a rigid rather than flexible thing.

"Perhaps we should beat them, and so get more effort from them," suggested Sir Brian thoughtfully.

"Perhaps we might," agreed Giles.

"No!" cried Jim; and the shipmaster turned to face the two knights, as if he would interpose his own broad body between the two of them and any attempt by them to reach the men.

"Nay, nay, messires," he said. "My lads do not lack for willingness. No offense, but you who are always on land have no idea of what it takes to move a ship this size even inches, were it caught only on the point of a needle. But we will do it!"

"We *can* do it, lads," he cried, turning to his sailors and snatching up the loose end of the rope on which they strained. "Come on, all together. With me, now—"

Hoarsely, he began to chant.

"No sea sarpent hath a Master . . ."

Six other voices roughly joined in with him, so that they chanted all together.

> *But ye sea-lads hath,*
> *So ye sea-lads hold him fast there,*
> *—Haul him in at last!*
> *Heave and haul! Ye sea-lads all!*
> *Heave, and haul him in!*
> *Heave and haul! Ye brave lads all!*
> *Bring ye sarpent in!*

Nothing had happened during the earlier part of the chanting and heaving; but with the last line the boat gave a sharp jerk and shudder. It did not seem to have moved backward at all, however, but merely to have shaken itself in place. But the chant was infectious. Jim found himself snatching up a length of the line behind the shipmaster's thick body, and heaving with the rest, chanting with the rest. Then, behind him, Brian was heaving on the line, and then behind him, Giles.

The effort, the joined, musically-roaring male voices, bound them together and seemed to give them a strength they had not realized they had.

> *No sea sarpent hath a Master,*
> *But ye sea-lads hath,*
> *So ye sea-lads hold him fast there,*
> *—Haul him in at last,*
> *Heave and haul! Ye sea-lads all!*
> *Heave and haul him in!*
> *Heave and haul! Ye brave lads all!*
> *Bring ye sarpent in!*

Somewhere among all that sweat, and effort beyond effort, the ship suddenly shuddered and moved a little backward. A second later, it floated to the motion of the waves; and they all dropped the line exhaustedly, lapsing into silence.

"We are afloat!" cried the shipmaster. He sank on both his knees, joining his hands and raising his eyes toward heaven. His lips began to move as he prayed silently.

One by one, the sailors followed his example; and, looking around, Jim saw that both Brian and Giles were now also on their knees behind him.

Awkward, bemused, not really sure why he was doing it, Jim went down on his own knees, joined his hands, and stayed kneeling, although there was no prayer in him. Yet, somehow, he could not bring himself to simply go on standing.

After a while, the shipmaster rose; and they all rose. The master's voice was lifted and the men scurried about their duties.

A little over two hours later, the vessel was docked in Brest, and Jim, with Brian and Giles and certain of the seamen, went down the gangplank into the city.

Chapter 14

The shipmaster had told them where to find the Inn of the Green Door and sent three sailors along to carry their belongings. It was pushing past midmorning here in Brest and it was warm. The sun beamed down out of a bright sky, and the heat did not improve the stench either of the harbor or of the streets through which they slogged.

The streets of medieval cities, Jim thought, had taken some getting used to, on his part and Angie's. On second thought, he was not used to them yet. His thoughts went off on a tangent.

The sailors carrying their possessions behind them were all very well; but they would be leaving once those possessions had been delivered to a room at the Inn of the Green Door. Jim found himself wishing that his new squire Theoluf was with him; but that had been impossible.

Both his men and Sir Brian's, in a single group, had had to wait for a later and bigger ship. Meanwhile, someone had to take command of them; and in this world, the command was always given to the person with the highest social rank. Or, if there were two of equal rank, the one with the greatest seniority.

Unfortunately, the only one they could leave behind with any rank at all was Brian's squire, John Chester. When Jim had first understood this, he had felt definitely uneasy at the thought of that innocent-eyed sixteen-year-old being in sole command of eighty-three men-at-arms, all older than he, some in their late thirties, with years of experience in warfare and savage living behind them.

His protesting would have done no good; and in any case there was no one else to take over if he, Brian, and Giles were to travel by themselves, as Sir John Chandos wanted. It was the only way for them to be as inconspicuous as possible. He had been tempted to protest John Chester's appointment. But nearly a year of living here had taught him that there were many things he simply had to accept.

John Chester was a gentleman. A very young and inexperienced gentleman, but a gentleman nonetheless. It was not right that he should be put under the command of a common man-at-arms, no matter how experienced the commoner was. Ergo, John Chester would have to learn to command, whether he was capable of it or not. Jim had mentally chewed his nails over the situation, until he had seen Brian talking urgently with his own chief man-at-arms in a low voice, at some distance from everybody else in the common room of the inn back at Hastings.

Suddenly understanding how these things might be worked, he looked around for Theoluf; and, not seeing him, went up to the room he shared with Giles and Sir Brian. The former man-at-arms was there. Theoluf got to his feet as Jim entered.

"Theoluf," said Jim, "I take it you're going to be second-in-command to young John Chester?"

"Indeed, m'Lord," said Theoluf, "I am a squire now and outrank any ordinary man-at-arms such as Tom Seiver, who commands the men of Castle Smythe."

"And, as I know," Jim went on, "you know how to keep a group of men like this in line and how to get them where you want them to go. You're not likely to let them get out of hand and start drinking too much, or fighting, or stray."

"No, m'Lord," said Theoluf with a grim smile. "Was m'Lord afeared that the men might not get wherever they're supposed to be going, with all their weapons and ready to fight?"

"Well, not exactly afeared, Theoluf," Jim had said. "I like John Chester, as you probably know, but he hasn't seen as much of the world as you and most of the men you and Tom will be taking with him overseas. He will face some decisions which may be a bit difficult. . . ."

Jim's voice had trailed off. He had not known really how to approach this subject with Theoluf, in the terms it should be made according to the social rules. But the other man was already well ahead of him.

"I take m'Lord's meaning," said Theoluf. He gave another of his grim smiles. "Is a good young gentleman, Master John Chester. Let m'Lord rest assured that he will see John Chester and all the men at whatever appointed place is set, when the time comes. I and Tom Seiver will give you our heads on it, if it not be so."

"Thanks, Theoluf," Jim had said. "I trust you."

"No Lord or Master of mine," said Theoluf, "has ever found that trust misplaced, m'Lord. It will not be now."

Jim had returned to the common room below with a much lighter heart.

The thought returned to him now, as they tramped along toward the Inn of the Green Door. His own position here was not unlike John Chester's with the men-at-arms. Here he was, wearing the ring that would identify them all to whatever English spy was due to contact them in this place; and he was doing so only because he had the word "Baron" before his name.

Both Sir Brian, who knew him so well by this time, and Sir Giles, must surely have seen through Jim's ineptness at being a fourteenth-century man of rank, to say nothing of a fighting knight. Yet they had both seemed to accept his being so with no trouble. Possibly, it was that sort of double-valued thinking that allowed Brian to see his king as a drunkard and a thoroughly indecisive man; and at the same time give him credit for all the virtues a monarch could traditionally command.

It struck Jim suddenly that possibly Brian was able to do this simply because the king was *his* King, and therefore special allowances—not to say arrangements—could be made mentally. Certainly it was a fact in the case of the Lady Geronde Isabel de Chaney, who was Brian's love. He could speak of her in one breath as if she was as unreal and super-perfect as the best product of a troubador's imagination; and a moment later talk of her as a very real and earthy woman indeed. He apparently saw no argument between these two points of view, held side by side. Isabel was *his* Lady. Possibly—just possibly—it was the fact that Sir James Eckert, knight and Baron de Malencontri; and the half-magical, thoroughly-untrained-in-all-things James, was *Brian's* friend, that made a special view of Jim possible.

Jim also wondered whether by this time Brian and Giles, who looked to be on their way to becoming friends themselves, had possibly done what Theoluf and Tom Seiver had done about John Chester. They might have made a sort of silent agreement to take care of Jim and steer him in the right direction, while carefully not allowing him to lose any prestige in the process.

His thoughts had finally lasted him until they were at the entrance to the Inn of the Green Door. They stepped into its large common room filled with long, picnic-rough tables supplied with benches on either side. The shade within was welcome after the mounting warmth of the day outside; but the smell of the common room was hardly better, if different from the reek of streets and harbor; and the landlord who came to greet them was a far cry from the one they had known at the Broken Anchor in Hastings.

His name was René Peran. He was a young man, but fattish rather than stout, with a stubble of dark beard that apparently had not been shaved too recently. There was an equally dark suspiciousness about his eyes. He gave the impression of mistrusting them on sight. Perhaps he did not like the English.

Nonetheless he went through the regular innkeeper motions of greeting them, but with patently false warmth. His manner seemed to say that they were unwanted interruptions in his work; and he would be glad to get rid of them and back to it.

He ushered them to an upstairs chamber that was, if not quite as big as the one at the Broken Anchor, almost as clean. The bed was not so much a bed as simply a platform of about the same shape and size as the actual medieval beds Jim had seen; and as usual it was in the corner of the room.

There were also a table and a couple of stools. Grudgingly, it seemed to Jim, the innkeeper sent one of his servitors for another couple of stools, since Brian pointed out that there were three of them, and they might well have a visitor, at least one. The sailors settled their gear where they asked to have it put, and left, each with a small tip from Jim. He was quick to offer these tips, since he knew Sir Brian did not have much, if any, money; and he rather suspected that Sir Giles was in very much the same condition, from the fact that his talk of a servant who was supposed to be with him had never produced an actual person. While he was at it, Jim ordered up some wine.

The wine came promptly enough. Both the pitcher and the wine cups were far from what Jim would consider clean. He openly rinsed one out with some of the wine and wiped it with a clean cloth from his gear. He had come to do this frequently in this world; and Sir Brian, and evidently Sir Giles, accepted it as also having something to do with Magic.

But the wine itself was a surprise. When they sat down to it at the table, Jim was startled to discover that it was as good as anything he had tasted anywhere in England. It appeared to be a young wine, with a light red color and a fresh taste. He was tempted to remark on how good it was; but since neither Brian nor Giles made a point of mentioning it, he thought perhaps it was wiser to simply take it for granted.

"Well," said Sir Giles, drinking generously from his cup before continuing, "now we're here, what's first to do?"

"Wait, I should think," Brian said.

They both looked at Jim. He had been asking himself the same question; and now for the first time it occurred to him that perhaps after all he had advantages that the other two lacked in dealing with this situation. Sir John seemed to be, in this world, at least, in the position of being a sort of spymaster for the English. As such, he struck Jim as a cross between a man of his own historical period, who simply gave an inferior an order to accomplish something without going into detail about how it was to be accomplished; and a truly intelligent, thinking man of Jim's original century. Half-medieval, half-modern, in a sense.

"We can hardly do anything else," said Jim. He looked down at the ring which fitted a little loosely on the middle finger of his right hand. "I'll stay around the inn here and let myself be seen wearing this ring; and we'll see what happens."

"Plague take it!" said Sir Brian. "I much dislike this sort of waiting."

"Still," said Jim, looking at him and Sir Giles, "I think it's necessary. Remember, we were to be as quiet and attract as little attention as possible—except for the attention of the one who should contact us."

"True," growled Brian, "and I do not quarrel with Sir John on the wisdom of that. Nonetheless, it's not easy for one of my nature!"

"Nor mine!" said Sir Giles.

He and Brian touched cups on the statement ceremoniously.

Indeed in the next few days, Brian had adequate cause to complain; and Jim could hardly blame him. He and Giles were not built for undercover work. Their proper field of endeavor was the open field of battle, and an enemy plainly in sight before them. Nonetheless, they conducted themselves well. Although, with nothing to do but drinking, they did what Jim considered perhaps a little too much of this; including cruising the various inns and drinking places of Brest.

By the third day both knights were bored with drinking.

This followed a pattern that Jim had remarked in this world. Its population seemed to do a tremendous amount of imbibing, by twentieth-century standards; but the beer was weak and the wine not exceptionally strong. Also they had a different attitude toward alcoholic liquors than Jim had been used to in the twentieth century. Beer or wine were drunk to help get food down, in preference to water (which could make you sick), and because each acted as an all-purpose stimulant, relaxant, analgesic, and a means of generally making you feel better.

Enough wine, for example—Jim had discovered this in spite of all his precautions—could put you in a condition to ignore the biting and itching of the lice and fleas which you carried around in your clothes and hair. It also made it easier for you to forget the hardness of the benches or stools you sat on, the cold or heat you happen to be enduring at the moment, and various other uncomfortable things.

The result seemed to be, from what Jim could tell, that although almost every knight he knew was a heavy drinker, he did not know of one alcoholic among them except King Edward. No doubt when they got too old to do anything but sit at home by the fire, they would drink themselves into alcoholism. But both social custom and their own bounding energy, which seemed to come from living a very physical sort of life, militated against sitting still too long, even for the pleasure that wine could give.

He also mentally apologized to his two companions, after finding that their three-day drinking bout had enabled them to gather a remarkable fund of information about the other English in Brest; as well as about the general condition of the town, and even something of France in general, according to the latest talk and rumors.

Almost to a man, the English forces in Brest reflected Brian and Giles's boredom. There had been much talk over the wine jugs of forays and raids, including the idea of marching on the French without waiting for the rest of the Expeditionary Force to arrive from England. My Lord the Earl of Cumberland, who was in command here, had been having great trouble restraining them from such a move—particularly since, basically, he secretly felt the same way himself.

Meanwhile, Brian and Giles were eager to get busy at anything useful Jim might suggest.

"I take it you've had no contact from this man, whoever he is, who is to meet us here?" asked Brian, the morning of the fourth day, as they were seated in their room, working away at some smoked fish, tough boiled mutton, and some very excellent fresh bread that had been sent up to them by way of breakfast.

"No sign of him at all," said Jim.

"It may well take a week or several," Sir Giles put in, his mouth full of bread and mutton. "We may have outrun the word to whoever it is who is to meet us here; or perhaps he is being delayed in coming to meet us."

"Nonetheless," said Sir Brian, drinking from his wine cup and setting it down with a bang on the table, "it is none too soon that we start looking for horses. Also, for what other gear will be necessary for us to travel to wherever we may need to go."

"You don't think it likely Sir John arranged for transportation for us?" Jim asked his friend. "After all he arranged for our lodging at this particular inn."

"Lodging . . . simple," replied Sir Brian, now with his mouth as full as Sir Giles's had been earlier. He chewed a couple of times and swallowed; then spoke clearly. "For such things as the means of getting wherever we may need to go, someone such as Sir John would trust us to find them for ourselves, even as he would trust himself to find such things, were he in our position."

He looked meaningfully at Jim.

"It means, then, that we must buy at least three horses," he said. "Six would be better, so that we may use the others as sumpter animals to carry our belongings. But the price will be high for anything on four legs worth taking."

Jim got the message very clearly. He was the only one with money. Indeed, he had some gold coins sewn into the clothing he wore, with lesser-value coins hidden in the lining of other clothes or within the scabbard of his sword; more than ample means for them to make this trip into France and back out again. He, himself, was no great shakes as a landowner, in the sense of making his holdings pay him well. On the other hand, Sir Hugh de Bois de Malencontri, the knight who had fled to France, leaving Malencontri for Jim to take, had had taking ways, to say the least. The castle was well supplied with a number of valuable items, some of which looked suspiciously like the sort of silver vessels that would have been used by some church in its celebration of divine services.

In preparation for his trip, Jim had had some of these objects sold for coin in Worcester. The coins came in various denominations, copper, silver, and gold; and were French as well as English, with even some German and Italian ones. But in this age coins were assessed and accepted for their weight of precious metal, whatever their source.

What Brian was hinting, none too delicately, was that it was time for Jim to produce funds for the shopping that Brian had just suggested.

This was not, Jim had come to understand, necessarily mercenary on Sir Brian's part. If the other knight had had money with which to buy, he probably would have simply gone ahead and bought; and never thought about how much wealth remained to him, until his purse was empty. At which point he would have turned to his companion or companions, if they were of gentlemanly rank, and simply accepted the fact that they would supply his needs.

It was the way things seemed to be done by many people of his class; just as one knight might pay a visit to another and spend six months as a guest, helping himself while there to whatever he needed without giving a moment's thought to what he might be costing his host; his host would pay no attention to the expense of keeping his guest, in return.

Accordingly, the three of them discussed the horse-buying situation. The news, Jim discovered, was not good. There were two possible markets in which horses might be had. One—a source of potentially good horses—was to buy from their fellow Englishmen already in Brest, who had brought in their own horses from England. The other was the local horse market.

The imported English horses were owned by knights or others who would be very reluctant to part with them, since they could not be replaced. Therefore their prices would be high. An awareness on the part of the other English in residence that such horses were hard to come by, would have a tendency to put the prices even higher. The local market, on the other hand, in the opinion of both Sir Brian and Sir Giles, could supply horses, but these would be generally in poor condition, barely fit to act even as baggage animals.

The natural conclusion was to buy three good horses, if they could be got, from other English; and buy three baggage animals from the local market.

It appeared that Brian and Giles had been thinking ahead, and exploring the possibilities of these particular purchases. They had concluded on a possible price for both of them. Jim was somewhat jarred when he heard it, since even at his worst he had not imagined that horses could cost so much. It was true, he had money and to spare to pay for this, but he had no way of gauging how many other expenses lay ahead of them.

Nonetheless, he produced the necessary coins and handed them to Brian, who as his older friend had a sort of seniority in this kind of situation over Sir Giles.

The two went out. Jim was left with his fleas, his lice, and the temptation to drink enough more wine so that he would not notice them. What held him back was a lifetime of training, and the fact that it was still barely midmorning. Though the other two could not suspect it, his waiting was a good deal more wearying than theirs, partly because he could not take solace in alcohol the way they could; and also because he was tied to the inn, with a landlord that he found more sour and repulsive every day.

Nonetheless, he went downstairs to the common room, where he would be more visible to anyone who might be looking for someone like himself wearing a certain ring. He found a seat at one of the empty tables, and ordered another pitcher of wine and a cup—meanwhile passing the word that the remnants of the breakfast should be cleared out of their room.

In doing this he was necessarily taking a chance. Their baggage was up there, unprotected and open to pilfering, not only by the inn staff, but by some outside source.

However, he had taken a position where he could watch the stairway and know if anyone other than one of the inn's people went up. Also, he had made sure the people of the inn knew him to be a magician; and finally, he had left his shield uncased up in the room, so that its device and colors could be seen.

The average man in the street might not be able to read—"might" was a kindly word, considering that most knights and most of the nobility could not read—but at every level they had learned to read devices and arms. He had no doubt that the color red, with its indication that its owner was a magician, would be enough to deter anybody tempted to take anything from the room.

From the evidence on the shield that one of the three knights had magical powers, it would be natural for any thief to deduce that the goods were protected by some kind of spell; or, if there was no spell, that the magician himself had some way of knowing if anyone attempted to take what was there.

So, all in all, Jim felt fairly safe about their goods. Which was a bonus, since there were only the three of them; and one could not always be on watch in the room. Nor was there anyone in this French port that they could safely hire to guard the goods. The chances were that they would be simply hiring someone who would help himself to whatever he was supposed to guard.

The threat of magic was much more potent, much more real, and much more reliable. Not only that; but people had a tendency to fear more what they did not know and could not see, than something they could see and know.

He settled down with his pitcher of wine, prepared to put in another day pretending to drink, while simply being available for whatever English spy should come seeking him.

Jim had developed the habit of practicing his magic during these long days of waiting. He confined his practice to small magics: moving an inconspicuous bench slightly from across the room, or slightly changing the color of a piece of woodwork.

He had also practiced, and finally become fairly successful at, causing the wine in his pitcher to vanish, by small amounts. Since he could not sit drinking all day without getting incapably drunk, something like this was a necessity.

He found that it was not simply a matter of making the wine vanish. He had to send it someplace. Accordingly he would send the equivalent of a cupful of wine out into the waters of the harbor, some three hundred yards away. This neatly disposed of it; and gave him an excuse to order a refill of his pitcher from time to time, so that the servants and the innkeeper would not think it remarkable that he simply sat there all day killing time—obviously waiting.

His twentieth-century academic training automatically impelled him to look for principles behind what he was learning to do, Principles on which the Magic operated. Carolinus, in directing him how to turn himself from a human into a dragon shape and back from the dragon shape into his human one, had actually given him very little information as to how to make use of the powers contained in the huge *Encyclopedie Necromantick* he had swallowed.

He was beginning now to suspect that this lack of information had been deliberate. For some reason, Carolinus had wanted him to find his own way to use the *Encyclopedie*. This pointed to Magic being an art rather than a science, in which no two practitioners did things exactly the same way. What Carolinus had given Jim had been the end product of a magical operation, not the operation itself.

That left it up to Jim to find the means of doing these things himself. He had discovered further evidence of the fact that that was what he was intended to do. For one thing, the business of simply "writing" the command, as Carolinus had suggested, on the blackboard that was the imagined inside of his forehead, worked perfectly well with certain pieces of magic, and not at all with others.

For example, he had found he could change into dragon shape and back again. He could also move a bench, here in the central room of the inn, as long as he was looking at it. The minute he looked away, he did not seem to be able to move it.

His attempts to dispose of wine from his pitcher did not work at all until he visualized the harbor in the moment when he had looked overside at it, just as the ship docked. It was as if there had to be a receptor at the far end in his mind, or else a clear image of one; as well as a clear image of what he wished to send or change or move.

He began to test this theory now by seeing if he could memorize a particular bench across the room and the particular position it was in, in relation to the table it was at and the rest of the room around it. After working at this for some twenty or thirty minutes, he finally succeeded in moving it while not watching it.

He had become thoroughly wrapped up in his magical practice. It was more by chance than otherwise, that at the moment following that in which he had finally moved the bench unseen, he noticed a man entering the common room of the inn; which at this hour was almost deserted, only two other people besides Jim being seated there, at good distances from each other.

The newcomer caught and held Jim's attention at once.

There was something unlikely about him—unlikely, at least in the sense that he did not seem like the kind of person who might choose such an inn as this for a destination. Also, he paused just inside the entrance to let his eyes adjust to the gloom of the interior, which was relieved only by the few small windows that fronted on the street.

This was a common enough thing for anyone who entered the inn to do, a customary thing. However in the case of this individual, the pause lasted a little longer than Jim would have expected; and, because he was watching closely, he saw that the man was also examining the people who were in the room.

Jim had been sitting these last few days with his right hand laid out on the table, the ring visible upon his third finger. Its top was a seal cut into a blood-red stone, and the stone picked up what little light there was from the nearest window, so that it was clearly visible across the room, even in the reduced light within.

The newcomer's eyes touched on it, moved on. Then, almost casually, he turned and moved in Jim's direction.

He was a tall, slim man in his middle thirties, but with the skin of his face somewhat tanned and aged. A scar several inches long puckered his left cheek.

He would have been remarkably handsome, except for the fact that his nose was hooked like Sir Giles's; but it was nowhere near as fleshy as Giles's. In fact all the bones of his face seemed thin and sharp. There was an air of authority about him that the ordinary clothes could not disguise; and he moved with a looseness and sureness that gave evidence of someone in excellent physical condition. He was wide shouldered and very erect.

He reached Jim's table and, without invitation, dropped onto the bench on the other side of it, across from Jim.

Without a word, he turned his left hand palm upward to reveal that what had appeared merely a circlet of gold from the top, carried a stone on the palm side with the same crest engraved in it that Jim had in his. After exposing it to Jim's gaze for a moment, he closed his hand into a fist again, hiding it.

"You will be the Dragon Knight," he said in a low, clear, baritone, "from Sir John Chandos?"

"That's right," said Jim. He had not moved. "But I'm afraid I don't know your name, mesire."

"My name has no importance in this," said the other. "Do you have a privy place where we can talk?"

"Certainly," said Jim. "Upstairs."

Jim had started to rise, but the other shook his head sharply; and Jim sat down again.

"Not now," the other said. "This evening. I'll be back. A private room, I take it?"

His eyes flicked toward the stairway.

Jim nodded.

"This evening, then," said the man, rising. "When there are more people around, so that not so much attention will be paid to my coming and going. Wait for me upstairs, then."

He turned, made his way to the door, and went out. For a moment he stood outlined in the bright rectangle of the doorway, a dark outline without further features. Then he was gone.

C h a p t e r 15

I t was late afternoon before Brian and
Giles returned. They had found and bought the necessary horses; and were
obviously overjoyed with their purchases. They insisted on Jim coming out into
the courtyard to look at them before they were put away in the stables.

When Jim saw the beasts, he understood why they had wanted him to look. It
was not so much that they felt a responsibility toward the money he had given
them to spend, as a desire to prove to him they had returned with usable animals.

There were six horses in the courtyard. Jim had not been in this world long
enough to become a real judge of horseflesh; but he had picked up enough to
know and recognize large differences between animals. There was no mistaking
which were the riding horses and which were to be the baggage animals. The
baggage animals were smaller, more roughly coated, and looked underfed. Of the
riding horses, two were good and one was an excellent beast, already equipped—
as were the other two—with saddles and bridles that Brian and Giles had also
evidently bought this day.

Unfortunately, the other two riding horses, while they did not look as if they
had been underfed or mistreated in any way, were very ordinary horses. Not up,
according to Jim's limited judgment, to the level of a gentleman's or lady's palfrey.
Rather the sort of beasts that might be given to men-at-arms to ride.

"This," said Brian, patting the saddle of the best riding horse, "is yours, m'Lord."

The title at the end of the sentence tipped Jim off just in time. It was not because of his money that the best horse was to be his to ride. Nor was it because he was the leader of the expedition. It was simply, once again, a matter of rank. He outranked the others, therefore he had to have the better horse. It was the John Chester situation cropping up again.

But there were all sorts of things wrong with his being given the best horse to ride. This past winter, under Brian's teaching, he had learned to use a knight's weapons while fighting on his feet. But he still knew next to nothing about using them while fighting on horseback.

If the three of them ran into trouble, which was more than likely under the conditions of the time and place of their journey, that one good horse should be between the knees of someone like Sir Brian or Sir Giles, who could be useful with it. James's best use in a case like that would be either to simply get out of the way, or to try to keep one attacker busy so that Giles and Brian could deal with the rest. But he foresaw trouble in putting this point across to the other two knights.

Since there were more important things to be talked about, such as the spy having finally made his connection with Jim, he decided to let the matter go for the present. Possibly a way would occur to him to politely urge one of the others—Jim secretly favored Sir Brian, whose abilities with weapons he knew—to take the best horse. In any case, he had been brought out here to have the animals shown off to him; and it was up to him to respond appropriately.

"Excellent!" he said. "Excellent! You did much better than I'd expected. Especially that first horse!"

The others beamed; and Brian shouted for stableboys to come and take the horses to the stable.

"It was all Brian's doing," said Giles. "Never have I seen sweeter throws. But, let us upstairs where we can talk about it. I think some wine is called for, do you not Brian?"

"I do, Giles. I do," said Brian.

The stableboys having arrived at a run, Brian turned over the lead reins of the horses to them, with a few fierce admonitions to be sure they were well taken care of. The three went inside, crossed the common room, and mounted the stairs.

The other two were evidently in high good spirits, Jim noted. And both his congratulations outside and their cheerful spirits were certainly justified. In this strange town, and with his limited knowledge of all things medieval, including the bargaining that must go into the buying of horseflesh, Jim had to admit to himself that, left alone, he would have been lucky to buy the equivalent of one of the baggage horses; and probably he would have ended up spending all of his money to purchase that one animal.

But, once in the room, a further surprise was in store for him. Reaching both hands into the purse that hung from his sword belt, Brian brought out two bulging fists; and dumped on the table a pile of money.

As the coins danced and chinked against each other, Jim stared at them in astonishment.

"But there's more here than I gave you when you left!" he said.

The other two burst into uproarious laughter, slapping each other on the back, delighted with his surprise. At this moment the woman bringing the wine knocked at the door and immediately walked in, as was apparently the custom on both sides of the English Channel. Quickly turning his back on her to hide the money, Brian hastily swept it off the table and back into his purse again.

She looked at them strangely as she put the wine on the table, then lit up as Brian gave her what was clearly more money than she had been expecting. She curtsied and went out.

The two knights seated themselves at the table and poured wine cups full. Jim joined them and imitated their example.

"Tell me what happened," said Jim.

They laughed again, slapping each other on the back in further exultation.

"As I said below," said Giles to Jim, "was all Brian's doing. Tell him, Brian!"

"Why, none of the English here with horses worthy of sale—and Saint Stephen knows that the local people have none," said Brian, "would sell four legs of anything to us."

He paused to drink deeply from his wine cup.

"As is not surprising," he went on, "seeing such horses are not replaceable, except by ship from home. We tried hither, we tried thither; but not a seller could we find."

He paused, obviously for dramatic effect.

"Go on," Giles urged him impatiently.

"Then a stroke of luck came upon us," went on Brian to Jim. "We found Percy, the younger son of Lord Belmont, who had a full string of horses just by ship from England, which he was about to take with him to his father and his father's retinue. My Lord Belmont has already taken a small but comfortable holding for his entourage, some five miles beyond the town. Sir Percy and the beasts were fresh off the boat; and we met him before his father had had a chance to see him, or them."

Once more he paused, obviously again for dramatic effect. Once more Giles urged him on.

They were acting, thought Jim, with inward amusement, like a pair of well-rehearsed amateur comedians.

"Well . . ." began Brian, drawing the word out with malicious humor. The delay was too much for Giles.

"You see, James," Giles put in hastily, "Sir Percy had certain debts of which his father would disapprove—"

"I will tell it, Giles," broke in Brian hurriedly. "Sir Percy had private debts that Lord Belmont would have been exceeding wroth about. In short, he needed money."

"So you bought the horses from him?" asked Jim.

"That was my first thought," said Giles, "but Brian, here, had a better idea. Sir Percy's debts were from the dice."

"He was a gambler?" Jim asked.

"A greater one I vow there never was," said Sir Brian. "The mere touch of the dice in his hand made his eyes light up. Though I did not see that until after I had suggested to him that we dice for the horses, their price against the beasts themselves; and the winner to take both."

Jim blinked and hoped that that was all the expression he had shown. The sudden realization that Brian had been cheerfully ready to lose the relatively large amount of cash Jim had given him, in an attempt to win the horses they needed by gambling, hit him like one of Brian's blows on his helm during their practice bouts of the winter before.

"At first," said Brian, "I lost, it seemed, on every throw of the dice I made. Percy was overjoyed."

Jim's heart sank. In spite of his having guessed the outcome of this matter, the thought of his money being cheerfully gambled away when there was no possible means of replenishing it until they were back in England, left him with a cold feeling. But Brian went on.

"In fact, finally the moneys I still held had gotten so low that I told Percy that I would cease gambling unless he was willing to wager double the amount against what I put forward, so as to give me a chance to recoup my losses."

"Brian!" said Jim. "That was taking a chance! All he had to do was sit tight and you would not only not have horses, you'd be left without enough money to buy some anyplace else."

"Not at all, James," answered Brian. "As I told you, the mere feel of the dice in his hand made his eyes light up. I had the measure of the man. He could no more stop gambling than most men could pass up a lusty tourney, to sit idle in the stands, watching whilst others traded good blows before the eyes of all. Oh, he complained that this was not the way things were done; but when I pointed out that he had no choice in the matter, he gave in."

"And then, you began winning?" Jim asked.

"Well, no. At first, on every pass I continued to lose," said Brian.

"Indeed," put in Giles, "I was thinking it had become a most serious matter. But—hah! I had faith in Brian. And that faith—"

"—was justified," said Brian quickly. "In short, James, at the last I began to win. Percy sweated; and finally, when our funds on the table were equal again, in decency I had to go back to even stakes with him. But I had his measure now. A man who needs to win, never does. He was desperate to win. Therefore he lost. And lost. And lost. And lost . . . until I had won back not only all my money but all that he had with him as well."

"Whereupon, with our regrets that his fortune had been so ill," said Giles, "we told him we must take our leave together with our winnings."

"And he let you take his horses too?" Jim said.

"What else could he do," said Brian, "being a gentleman? I did him some small favor, by buying the saddles and bridles from him and paying him back in money for these. Still, it is not to be denied that it was an unhappy man we left."

In fact, Jim was feeling a good deal of sympathy, and a certain amount of guilt, toward the hapless Sir Percy, who now had to face his irate father without either horses or money. Obviously, however, his two companions did not share these feelings of his at all.

"Is it not a day of great luck for us, James?" beamed Sir Brian. "I cannot, at the moment, remember, and Giles likewise, which Saint's Day this is. But I shall find out and mark it down for future notice when I have things of risk to consider; since obviously the good Saint aids me—whoever he may be—at this particular time. We should order up some more wine, I think. But first—"

He dived into his purse again, once more spilled the money from it on the table, and pushed it in Jim's direction.

"My Lord," he said grandly, "the money you entrusted to me, and a trifle more, as witness that your true and loyal servant Sir Brian has fulfilled his duty!"

Jim looked at the pile of money almost with dismay. There should be some way he could take advantage of this moment, he thought—and then he had it.

"Since this has been handled so well," he replied in roughly the same formal tone Brian had used, "I can see no better use for it than to leave it in such able hands."

He reached out and roughly with the side of his hand divided the coins into two groups.

"Do each of you take half," he said, "and keep or use it as necessary to our common need."

Inside he felt a private glee. For once he had been able to take a social custom of the upper classes in this world and use it to gain his own end. One of the strongly ingrained elements of this society was generosity on the part of superiors toward inferiors. Not only were the recipients inclined to be grateful; but it would be almost an insult for them to refuse such gifts.

He had judged rightly.

With happiness and properly expressed thanks, Brian and Giles took their individual piles of the money, making no attempt to count the coins to see if one pile's worth equaled that of the other, and stuffed the coins into their purses. Jim was thoroughly pleased. He had succeeded in doing what he had wanted to do for some time; which was to find an acceptable way of supplying the other two with pocket cash to get around in this strange country.

"And now for the wine!" said Giles.

Jim's two companions were clearly in the mood for a celebration. It was not exactly what Jim wanted—to meet the spy with two half-drunken companions. The spy would be giving them information they would need to remember. Also, Jim wanted them to hear what he heard, so that he could check his own memory against them.

"By all means," he seconded Giles's suggestion. "However, I'd suggest that we all drink rather lightly. We have an important evening ahead of us. The spy who was supposed to get in touch with me did so, today, this afternoon. He'll be back at evening, here in this room, to talk to us all."

This news, as he had guessed, caught their imagination immediately. All thoughts of a celebration were put aside. The time until evening passed in impatient waiting, particularly on the part of Brian and Giles, and discussion of what might be involved in the rescue of the Prince.

The conclusion reached by all this conjecture was no more than a general agreement that the Prince must be being held secretly someplace, undoubtedly well guarded against any rescue attempt. Particularly since the French King Jean would realize that, by keeping the young man secure, he held a high card that could be played at whatever time was most useful. If the English army should end up by defeating all opposition and overrunning France, then the English might be bought off by a return of the Prince. Or, if the English were defeated a second time, decisively, then the Prince could be held to very high ransom indeed—including the English Crown giving up its claim to a great deal of France. Specifically, the old Kingdom of Aquitaine and the cities of Calais and Guines.

But where the Prince might be held, and how strongly guarded, was something that could only be guessed at. They would have to await the coming of the spy who might be able to tell them more about these things.

He came at last. It was still early evening—what Jim would have guessed as no more than seven or eight o'clock at night—but it seemed quite late to the fretting Brian and Giles. Jim introduced the visitor to his two companions; and ordered up enough wine to last them for some time, with cups for everyone. He then sent down the news that they did not want to be disturbed; and put his shield outside the door of the room as warning against any such intrusion.

The spy watched him with an only half-concealed sneer as he put the shield outside.

"Why the shield, mesire?" he asked. "It will only draw attention to us and our meeting."

"Because I consider it necessary, mesire," retorted Jim.

They adjourned to the table and sat down. The wine cups were filled in a somewhat strained silence. The spy was obviously looking both Brian and Giles over with a critical eye; and they were examining him with undisguised hostility.

"It sits ill with me," said Brian, breaking the silence before Jim could start some sort of more reasonable conversation, "to sit at table with a man who will not tell me his name and rank. How do I know indeed that you are a gentleman?"

"I have satisfied mesire, here," said the spy, nodding at Jim, "of my credentials, this afternoon."

He looked directly at Jim.

"Are you satisfied, mesire, that I am what I claim to be and at least a gentleman, since Sir John would employ none other in such an instance?"

"Yes," said Jim. "Certainly. Brian, I'm sure our visitor here is a gentleman and I know him to be the one who was sent to meet us. It only remains for us to hear what he has to tell us."

The spy looked back at Brian.

"Satisfied, mesire?" he asked.

"I see I must be," said Brian grimly, "but considering your activities you can understand how one like myself might doubt it."

The half-sneer was now in Brian's tone. It was a tone of voice rare on Brian's part. But when roused, he could be as rough and deliberately offensive as any other medieval knight. Nonetheless the implication was underplayed enough so their visitor could have ignored it. He did no such thing.

He was suddenly on his feet on his side of the table; and his fists crashed down on it as he glared at them all.

"Before God!" he swore. "I will be treated as a man of honor, which I am! Were it not for special circumstances I would not be here this moment. I am a loyal servant to King Jean and would see all Englishmen like yourselves dead or in the sea, before you ever set foot in France. If it were not for special circumstances, I vow I would rather have you English at the point of my sword than across the table from me. You have been a plague and a disaster upon our France. I would see you dead in the sea before any one of you set foot in this fair country. It is that snake—that magician Malvinne—that puts me into this moment's unhappy alliance with you. He, and he alone, is the only thing worse than the English; and has been the destruction of my family and the death of my father. It is my father's blood that calls for his confounding—and his death, could I but encompass it. Therefore I will do this much for you English. But that is all! I have no love for you. Nor for that worthless stripling you call a Prince, which you are here to take back safely to the cradle where he belongs."

Now both Sir Giles and Sir Brian were on their feet.

"No one speaks so of our Crown Prince to my face!" snarled Brian with his hand on his sword hilt, leaning across the table toward the other man. "Before Heaven, you will apologize now and here to him, for having uttered such words!"

The visitor was still as a dancer about to leap, his hand also on his sword. His face was completely expressionless and his eyes never moved from Brian's face.

Chapter 16

"**S**it down all three of you," said Jim, who was now the only one not standing. The sound of his own voice startled him. It had a ring of authority that he would never have believed was in him. It did more than command, it took for granted the command would be obeyed.

Slowly, after a moment, all three men sat down, wordless and still staring at each other, but seated again.

"We are here," said Jim, "to see what can be done about a certain matter. Brian, Giles, we need this gentleman here. And you, mesire—"

He changed his gaze to match eyes with the visitor.

"You need us, or you would not have had to do with we English in the first place. What we are up against does not require that we have any great affection for each other, or for what any of us are or may be. It requires only an exchange of information!" His palm slapped the table. "For that reason we are met and for that reason we will set about doing what we are met for. Now—"

His eyes were still on the visitor.

"Your likes and dislikes, and your reasons for being here are yours, mesire," he said. "The same, likewise, is true for the three of us. Such things are not for discussion. We are here to rescue our Prince and take him safely home if possible.

You are here to give us whatever information you have that will help us do that. So, begin by telling us what you have come to tell us."

For a long moment the spy sat tensely on his stool, and the dark brown eyes in his narrow face glittered back into Jim's. Then the tension went out of him. He relaxed, picked up his untouched wine cup, and drank deeply from it, then set it back down on the table.

"As you will," he said in a flat voice. "I will say no more of how I feel if others say none of such to me."

He took another drink of wine and this time Giles and Brian and—a little behind them—Jim, picked up their cups and also drank at the same moment. Their movement became a kind of silent pledge around the table.

"You may call me Sir Raoul, if that will make our conversation easier," said their visitor. He shifted a little on his stool to extend his long legs to one side of the table leg; and leaned his elbows on the table's surface, holding his cup thoughtfully between his two hands. He spoke over the rim of it. "Well, I have found your Prince. Though that was little enough to do since he was exactly where I expected him to be. The difficult part has been since, in trying to discover some way to get you to him; and give you all a chance of getting away again with your lives."

He put down the cup and reached inside his doublet to pull out a small folded piece of white cloth.

"I have here a map."

He unfolded the cloth on the tabletop as they all craned forward to get a look at it.

From Jim's point of view it was hardly more than the sort of map a third-grader might have drawn in the classroom, back in the world he came from. It showed a rough scribble that obviously was the coast, with the upper half of some sort of fish sticking its head out of the sea portion. Inland from that, up a V-shaped indentation that Jim took to be the estuary up which they had sailed, was the name of the town itself, BREST, printed in ink in curiously drawn block letters, but readable. The lines drawn on it all ran directly from point to point.

From the ink dot below the name of Brest, a line led around the southern coastal plain of Brittany and inland to another ink dot named Angers, on the Loire river. Then, following the Loire all the way, it led eastward to another dot called Tours.

From there it ran still eastward but a little northward, once more following the Loire, past a dot marked Amboise to one close to it named Blois. From Blois a line ran to a further dot, some distance up, marked Orléans. Some three-quarters of the distance from Blois to Orléans, was a dot with a capital *M*, and a very rough sketch of some kind of tree beside it. Beyond this, on the river, was a square building with towers and turrets sketched in.

Sir Raoul tapped a slim forefinger on the large letter *M*, the tree, and the towered representation of the building.

"The château—what you English would call castle—of Malvinne the sorcerer," he said. "You'll find it in outward appearance a very pretty place, surrounded by arbors, walks and plesaunces. Beyond these, you'll come upon the château itself, which is as stoutly built as any strong point in Christendom; strong enough to repel an army. Within are great, rich rooms; but also dungeons, terrible beyond the describing, and other things no man knows."

He paused to look at them for a moment, a little sardonically.

"But you are all paladins, are you not?" he said; then caught himself up short. "Nay, forgive me. I have a bitter tongue and it runs away before I can rein it in, sometimes. But in truth, the château of Malvinne is no place such as any good soul would wish to visit willingly."

He paused, looking at them.

"No offense taken," muttered Sir Brian.

"I am in debt to you for your courtesy, mesire," said Sir Raoul. "I will try to speak more gently from now on. The fact of the matter is, though, that you will be lucky to reach the pretty grounds of the château. First, you must penetrate a wood that Malvinne has caused to be grown all about that place. A wood of tangled trees, wherein you may be caught and held by branches until you starve to death unless you are wary. Also, through that wood roam at all times some of the hundreds of armed servants that he has created about himself—beings half-animal, half-human that once were men and women—"

"Good God!" said Jim, jolted entirely out of his ordinary caution, so that he spoke without thinking to the empty air beside him. "Accounting Office! Is that sort of use of magic allowed?"

"It is not forbidden, though not approved, to magicians of AA class and higher," replied the invisible bass voice some three feet above the floor to Jim's left.

"Saints defend us!" said Sir Raoul. His eyes stared at Jim with the pupils enlarged; and he quickly crossed himself. "I have delivered myself into Malvinne's hands, after all!"

Jim looked guiltily at the other two. Of them, Sir Brian was not affected, having heard that voice several times before in the company of either Jim or Carolinus. But Sir Giles was almost as badly shaken as Sir Raoul. It was the latter, however, whom Jim hurried to reassure first.

"That's just the voice of an accounting office that all magicians have to report to; and can ask questions of," he said to Sir Raoul. "Malvinne undoubtedly uses it, too; but he couldn't use it to find us any more than we could use it to find him. It simply keeps track of how much magic each one of us has. Besides, I told you I was just an apprentice magician."

"All the angels defend me from such an apprentice!" said Sir Raoul.

But the color was coming back into his face, and the pupils of his eyes had dwindled back to normal size. He filled his wine cup again, with a hand that shook slightly, and drank off the contents at a gulp.

"I would not hear that voice again," he said, "nor does your explanation really satisfy me. It proves once again that all magicians, like Malvinne, are the same at the core. As he is evil, they are evil."

"No, no. Listen to me please, Sir Raoul," said Jim earnestly, "it's all a matter of the character of the individual magician. I know another magician, a very high-ranking one, who told me just the other day how much he detested Malvinne and his ways."

Jim was embroidering a little on what Carolinus had said. Nonetheless, after the difficulty in getting Sir Raoul to be even as companionable as he had been for the few previous moments, before the Accounting Office had spoken, Jim did not want to lose whatever little goodwill had been achieved with the French knight. Under such conditions, he thought, a little embroidery of the facts would do no harm. Besides, Carolinus probably felt the way Jim had reported him feeling, judging by his last words to Jim on the subject.

"You'll not convince me," said Sir Raoul grimly. "All magicians are creatures of evil. How could they not be and deal with what goes beyond all ordinary belief and understanding?"

"Oh, come now," said Jim. "There've been good magicians."

"Indeed!" put in Sir Brian, "How about the mighty Merlin? And Carolinus? Men who did great good and were always on the side of those who served the right."

"Hah, yes," answered Sir Raoul, glancing aside at him. "Always I am quoted the names of magicians who are but memories and fables."

"Carolinus is no fable," said Jim. "In fact he's my tutor in the subject of magic. He lives less than seven leagues from my own Castle de Bois de Malencontri."

Sir Raoul looked him squarely in the eye. "He is a fable, as all in this country know!"

"I tell you," said Jim, "he isn't! He's a wise magician who's alive this moment!"

"And what reason might I have to believe that, except that you say it to me and are a magician yourself—and I have learned not to trust magicians?" retorted Sir Raoul.

"Sir James speaks the truth," growled Brian. "From my own Castle Smythe to the place of Carolinus is less than nine leagues. I have seen it, and him, often."

Sir Raoul looked from one to the other, from Brian to Jim.

"You would tell me that this Carolinus, then, who is known everywhere in our France as a fable only, not only lives but is alive today in England?" he said. "How can I believe that?"

"Whether you believe it or not is up to you," answered Jim, "but come to England sometime and be my guest at Malencontri. I'll introduce you to Carolinus myself. You'll find that his home is a lot different from Malvinne's. So is he different. Do your fables say he's evil?"

"No," admitted Sir Raoul slowly. "Like Merlin, they credit him with all sorts of good things. You swear he lives?"

"I do," said Jim and Brian, in chorus.

"Then I will say you this," said Sir Raoul, sitting upright on his stool and speaking deliberately, looking at each one of them in turn. "If you indeed win alive into the castle of Malvinne, rescue your Prince, and bring him safely out and back to England; then as soon as may be I will make the visit that you suggested; and see this Carolinus for myself."

He held up a finger.

"Not merely to see someone who calls himself Carolinus," he went on, "but to see a magician of that name, who will prove to be as good as Malvinne is bad, as good as the legends about Carolinus say. So much I pledge myself to do."

"You'll be welcome anytime," said Jim. "Now can we get back to what you were going to tell us about how we might be able to penetrate this forest, pass all these armed creatures he's made, and enter the castle to find our Prince?"

"Yes. Very well," said Sir Raoul after a moment. He leaned forward once more on the table. "Mark me, now."

He again tapped his finger where the *M* was on the map.

"As I have said," he went on, "I was sure your Prince would be kept in Malvinne's castle. Malvinne leads the King in all things, as a sighted man leads a blind one. Malvinne would want your Prince under his thumb, rather than under the royal one, where he might be too lightly kept and loosely held. But even if it were not for Malvinne's influence on our King Jean, he would see the advantage of your Prince—Edward, I think his name is? He would see the advantage of your Prince Edward being held in Malvinne's grasp; where it would take something more than ordinary rescue to steal him back."

He paused and drank from his wine cup.

"As I say, I was sure this Prince Edward was there," he went on, "but could not be absolutely certain. Neither could I penetrate to the castle myself and make sure. I told you Malvinne has destroyed my family. I meant that. All—all are dead. But the most foully slain of all was my father; though that is not a story that need concern you now. Enough to know that if one of my blood moved within the grounds of that castle, Malvinne would be warned of it immediately through his magic; and would, without doubt, secure me at any cost to make sure my race was exterminated forever.

"I'd only one hope," he said, looking up at them. "It lay in one of Malvinne's poor enchanted creatures, with the upper parts of a toad and the lower parts of a man, who once was one of my father's most able servants, leader of his men-at-arms. When Malvinne destroyed my family home, it pleased him to take those of our servants who survived to be made into his creatures. There were a dozen, no more. Of those, all but one died within the first year, for having been magicked like that, they do not have a strong hold on life. At a passing breeze they sicken and die; or some small accident that would merely keep an ordinary man or woman from their work for a week, will kill them in hours."

"'Fore God!" swore Sir Brian. "It is an evil doing!"

Sir Raoul glanced at Brian for a moment with some surprise and possibly even a tinge of gratitude. His face had been so trained to conceal his emotions that it was hard to read. He went on.

"Malvinne's castle is deadly to me," said Sir Raoul. "The woods, however, threaten me with no more danger than they would any other man who lacked Malvinne's permission to come there. Accordingly, for a number of weeks I have haunted that wood, hiding whenever one of his armed creatures came by, so that I should not be found except by the one I looked for. I would know him when I saw him by the sword cut on his toad-face; for either by some whim of Malvinne's or some limitation of the magic that had made him so, a scar that he had taken as a man was still with him in his new shape."

"And he came at last?" Jim asked.

"He did—Bernard, his name is—and knew me. He was willing to help though it cost him his life, for any chance to strike against Malvinne."

Sir Raoul sat back on his stool and took a deep breath.

"To make it short," he said, "if you go to a certain spot in the wood, of which I shall advise you, and wait there, night after night, at certain hours; in the end Bernard will be able to reach you there. Having once found you, he will then conduct you by safe ways through the wood, into the castle. But then he will leave you. He dare go no farther with you; for part of his enchantment makes it that he shall be someone who guards the wood outside and the exterior of the castle; and he would be able to give no good reason for being in the tower itself. From there on you must depend upon yourselves."

The others considered this. Sir Raoul thoughtfully filled and drank another half-cup of wine.

"This Bernard will tell us how to reach the room where the Prince is held, you said?" said Brian finally. "And, I suppose, give us some ideas for getting him free from that place? After that, how do we find our way out?"

"I'm afraid much of that will be up to you," answered Sir Raoul. "If you can make it back down out of the tower, there will be a place at which Bernard will be waiting for you, if so be it he is not ordered to other duties. He can then lead you and your Prince back out through the woods again."

"And no more aid is available to us than this?" Sir Giles tugged at his mustache.

"If I could give you more, willingly I would do so," said Sir Raoul. "As it is, were it not for Bernard, I would have nothing to offer you but the location of the castle itself, and my prayers that you should be successful in getting inside and getting out again with your Prince."

"If that's all there is, then that's all there is," said Jim.

He put his hand on the map.

"But there are a number of other things," he said, "that you can help us with. For one thing you can give us a clearer idea of the kind of country we're going to travel through. Also, how much time it'll take. Also, what we're likely to run into along the way in the shape of other enemies or problems."

"That I can do," answered Sir Raoul, once more moving forward to put his elbows on the table.

He began to talk. His knowledge of the terrain and the country to be traversed was as encyclopedic as his map had been sketchy. Jim desperately wished that he had the materials for taking notes. Then he remembered, from past experience with Sir Brian, that both Brian and Giles, being men of their unlettered time, were used to absorbing and remembering such heard information. This was still a period in which long messages would be spoken by one Lord to a messenger; who would then, some days or even weeks or months later, deliver it word for word to someone else in a different place. In short, their ears were trained to listen and their minds were trained to remember.

Accordingly, he did the best he could to keep up with what he was being told; but realized that he would have to depend on the other two for much of the specific information. He made a mental note that after Sir Raoul had gone he would find writing materials and make his own map and set of notes, both from what he remembered and from what Brian and Giles could tell him.

The telling occupied several hours. Both Giles and Brian had some very important questions about the country and any opponents they might encounter. They thought in terms of such things as men, horses, and weapons that might come against them; the prevalence of large and dangerous wild beasts; the availability of food and drink along the way; and a number of other things that might eventually have occurred to Jim—but probably would not have while he had Sir Raoul before him.

In the same process, Sir Raoul also mellowed, until they were all quite friendly by the time the talk wound up.

"We will need to buy provisions and possibly even hire some servants to deal with the horses," said Brian, all business once Sir Raoul had left. "If the men we left behind with John Chester were here, we could use some of them. As it is, there is a slim chance I might be able to borrow one or two men for a short while from one of the other English in the city—but it is a very slim chance indeed."

"In any case," said Sir Giles cheerfully, "we will begin to be as busy as knights should, starting early tomorrow morning. As soon as we've decided on the provisions and other necessaries, I can see about purchasing those. You, Brian, can meanwhile see if men of trust can be borrowed. To hire any of the local people is taking a chance; but perhaps, with a sharp eye on them, we should be all right; since they will be as dependent on us for protection as we will be upon them to be good servants."

On that note the evening broke up. The next morning, Brian and Giles were up and out at dawn, after a hasty if—at least by Jim's standard—gargantuan breakfast. He wondered how men could eat like this and not put on weight. Then he remembered that there were times in between the periods of such eating, when food was scarce indeed—even for knights. The people of this time had the instinct of wild animals: to fill their stomachs while the chance was good, against the possibility there would not be another chance for some time.

After the other two had left, he went on his own search for materials with which to write down what he remembered from the night before. Searching about Brest—he had hardly been out of the inn since he had arrived—he finally found a shop that boasted not only someone with a clerkly ability to write letters on dictation, but who could be brought to part with pen, ink, and charcoal sticks, as well as thin sheets of parchment; for what Jim considered to be a rather extravagant sum. Jim bargained him down to a certain extent, but he was painfully conscious that he was nowhere near the class of Giles or Brian at this.

He returned to the inn, and spent the rest of the morning with the table pushed against the one window of their room to get adequate light; putting down everything he could remember Raoul saying, in as good an order as was possible. He left spaces between his lines, so that he would be able to write in whatever extra information Brian and Giles would be able to give him later on.

He also made a stab at drawing a map, putting down what geographical features he could remember Raoul mentioning. It was an improvement over Raoul's map, but not to any great extent, since Jim had never been much of a draftsman. But it would help; and on this particular sheet of parchment there was plenty of room to write in extra information gleaned from his two companions. He made three copies of the information and the map.

Over dinner that night the three made their final plans. Only Giles and Jim were to leave immediately. Brian, as Sir John had ordered, would stay in Brest to take charge of their men when they arrived on a later ship, before following in their path. It was arranged that Sir Giles and Jim would leave signs by which Brian would be able to check that he was indeed on their trail, since he would have to travel relatively fast to catch up with them—at least at first.

So it was that their last dinner turned into a celebration after all; even though no servants had been found to help Giles and Jim along their way. Men to be hired in town, there certainly were. But they were all locals, and none that Jim's two companions trusted. Nonetheless, both Giles and Brian were in high spirits. Jim could not have changed this if he had wanted to. The other two were built for action; and finally, after sitting on their hands for several days, they were about to engage in some—or at least Jim and Giles were and Brian hoped to be, within the next few days.

"I can't think," said Brian, as they sat over the remnants of their meal, the other two knights still cheerfully drinking wine, "but that Sir John will see them sent to us just as quickly as possible. Clearly this matter of the rescue of the Prince was of first importance to him. I think the two of you can leave without fearing that I will be far behind you in starting out."

For the first time the whole storybook unreality of the adventure of rescuing a Prince began to assume the hard structure of reality in Jim's mind. For some reason he could not name, he felt suddenly chilled.

Chapter 17

The route that Jim and Sir Giles took, following Jim's improved version of Sir Raoul's map, led them across the Aulne River southeast to Quimper and along the southern coast, through Lorient, Hennebont, Vannes, and at last inland to Redon. The coastal areas were fairly cheerful grounds to traverse; but Jim was a little shocked when they began to move into the interior of France. Here, the devastation of warring armies was too visible for comfort.

They passed more ruins than were pleasant to see. The populace, generally, hid from them in the open country; and were inclined to be distant if not cool with them when they stopped in the towns. This situation continued as they went on toward Angers, where they at last came up to the Loire River.

For two weeks they had been completely alone. This did not seem to bother Giles at all. Like Brian, he seemed to regard the world simply as a stage for one huge, continuous adventure. Even more than Brian, he seemed to get enormous pleasure simply out of being alive. Jim, however, worried about whether Brian had managed to join up with their men and follow behind, as Sir John had ordered. But he had an even larger, secret, worry on his mind.

In all this distance, he had neither seen, smelt, nor felt the presence of any French dragons.

To say that this was peculiar was the least of it. Jim had been conscious, every time he had been in his dragon body at home, of the fact that other dragons were in the vicinity. How, exactly, he could not say, but the feeling was a real one. Secoh had assured him that when he got to France he would feel the presence of local dragons; and he was to contact the first ones he ran across.

Each night when they had been in open country, Jim had left Sir Giles by the campfire and gone off into the woods far enough to safely change into his dragon form. In this he had made every possible effort to feel the nearby presence of other dragons. But he had felt nothing.

It puzzled him. He could think of only two possible explanations. Either the dragons were clustered elsewhere—continual warfare in this area might well have led them to move out—or they were somehow managing to hide so well from him that he could not even feel their presence.

The latter explanation he doubted. There would be no point in dragons being able to sense that others of their own kind were nearby, if that sense could in any way be blocked out. Certainly earth and stone could not do it. Every time he had been in his dragon body at Malencontri, he had been as conscious of Cliffside, with its community of dragons within it, as he might have been of thunderclouds on the horizon on an otherwise bright summer day. This, in spite of the fact that Malencontri was a good five leagues—or fifteen English miles—from Cliffside's upthrust of heavy rock.

However, on the first day's ride he and Giles made beyond Tours toward Amboise on the direct road to Orléans and Malvinne's castle, Jim, on turning into his dragon shape in the darkness away from the fire, got a strong feeling of dragon presence. It was almost directly north of where they had set up camp for the night. He changed back into his human form, put his clothes back on and, thinking deeply, rejoined Sir Giles by the fire.

"Giles," he said, "there's something that I had to keep to myself up until this point, and still need to keep mostly a secret. But I'm going to have to separate from you for a little while. Why don't you go on to Amboise and take a room big enough for two of us at the best inn there. It may take a few days, but I'll join you there. If I haven't joined you in three days, go on to Blois and wait for me there. Sorry about having to keep this secret from you, but it's part of my part of this matter."

"Hah!" said Sir Giles, sipping genially at the wine cup he had filled from one of the bottles of wine they had supplied themselves with in Tours—their supply having grown low by the time they got there. "Indeed!"

He did not, Jim thought with relief, sound in the least offended at not being taken into the secret.

"Yes," Jim said. "In Blois, do the same thing. Take a room and wait. If for some reason I never catch up with you at all, then stay put until Brian shows up. If I haven't shown up by that time, it'll be up to you and Brian to do what you can to rescue the Prince. You remember the directions Sir Raoul gave us for finding the spot in the forest where we're to meet this Bernard—that former man-at-arms of Sir Raoul's father, who was changed by Malvinne's magic?"

"Hah! Yes," said Giles, twisting his mustache, "but you mean Brian and I should make no effort to find you?"

"I think that the rescue of Prince Edward is of more importance," said Jim.

"True. It must be so," said Giles. "But I am not happy to think that we might lose you, James. I had thought that someday you might come visit me in my home in Northumberland."

Jim was deeply touched. He had run into this same sort of thing with Brian. These knights were as quick to make deep friendships as they were to make lifelong enemies; and there was a suspicious shine to Giles's rather liquid brown eyes. Jim had never gotten quite used to the freedom with which these fourteenth-century men broke into tears.

"I—." He had to stop to clear his throat. "I think there's no danger of that. It's just that unforeseen things may slow me up to the point where it's better that the two of you go ahead. I was just making sure that we agreed on all possibilities ahead of time. I'm really expecting to see you at Amboise; and, if not there, I ought to be at Blois within a day or so of when you stop there."

"I am much relieved to hear you think so," said Giles, "much relieved, indeed. You're a gentleman I have come to like and admire, James."

"And I, you," said Jim. He took refuge in the universal escape route of this world. "Come, let's have a glass of wine upon it!"

"Willingly!" said Giles, almost fiercely.

They filled their cups and drank; and by the time the wine cups were empty, the moment of emotion had passed.

"I'll be leaving all my horses and gear with you," said Jim. "The only things I'll be taking will be my clothes, my sword belt, sword, and poignard. And a short length of rope for which I'll have a special need."

"Hah! Rope?" said Giles, then checked himself. "Forgive me, James. This going off of yours is secret, as you say; and I should not inquire. Will you not also need some provisions?"

"Thanks," said Jim. "To tell the truth I hadn't stopped to think about that, myself. But yes, some easily carried meat, bread, and wine might not be a bad idea—but only a small amount. The sort of emergency rations a knight might take to help him through a day's hunting."

"So little," murmured Sir Giles. "Hah! Excuse me James, I am intruding again on something that's your matter, entirely."

He looked at his empty wine cup. From what Jim could see he had drunk about a bottle and a half of the wine they had been carrying with them.

"Best probably we should get to bed early, then," Giles said. "You'll leave at dawn, James? Or somewhat later?"

"At dawn I think. Yes," said Jim. He thought he detected in Giles's voice a sort of wistful note on the suggestion that Jim might not leave until later on in the day. But the dragon feel Jim had sensed had not been close. He might have to cover some distance to find its source.

He was very grateful that Carolinus had shrunk the sack of jewels that was his passport to a size he could swallow. He could make a bundle with his clothes, his sword, his poignard, and whatever food and drink he was carrying, and tie it all about his neck so that it would be fairly secure while he was flying. But to carry the jewels as well was more than he liked to contemplate.

He settled down on the opposite side of the fire from Sir Giles, bundled up in several spare cloaks. To such an extent had he accustomed himself to the rough living of this world and century, that he was asleep shortly after the other man was. They both woke at dawn and had breakfast, and Jim agreed to have Giles accompany him to the parting point.

The suggestion provided a happy solution to a problem he had not thought of until he was ready to leave. Before, it had been only necessary to get away from the firelight to take off his clothes and change into a dragon in darkness. But it was now daylight, and there were no woods nearby in which he could make the change.

He could, of course, leave Giles here; and, carrying his food, drink, and rope, tramp off the road into the open wasteland that followed it on both sides until he came to some dip in the landscape, or some other place where Giles would not see him in his changed form.

On the other hand, tramping across an open landscape with nothing but his sword and dagger for protection—he would even be leaving his shield with Giles—posed a problem of personal safety.

After all these years of war, the local peasants were as quick to prey on unprotected travelers as anyone else might be. Two knights on horseback, with arms and shield, might be enough to keep them from trying. But a man alone, on foot, would be in danger. There was no reason why Giles should not accompany him to a place where he was hidden from the road, leave him there, and go back. Jim could wait until the other was out of sight before making the change.

He had reached this point in his thinking when his conscience suddenly struck him amidships. He had seen Giles change into a silkie. They were brothers-in-arms. Moreover, Giles was aware not only that Jim was a magician but that he was known as the Dragon Knight; and the other had heard the stories about the fight at the Loathly Tower.

There was no reason not to turn into a dragon right here with Giles watching. The only problem was that of scaring the horses. He remembered how Gorp had acted when he had unexpectedly turned into a dragon on the way to Carolinus's. And Gorp had been used to him—although, admittedly, not used to him turning into a dragon.

"Giles," said Jim, as he tied up the bundle that would hold his food and drink, "for what I have to do now, I need to change myself into a dragon. I don't want to alarm the horses; so maybe we should leave them here and walk off some little distance before I make the change."

"Hah?" said Sir Giles. "Certainly they would not take kindly to your turning into a dragon a few feet from them. I think we should tie them securely to that dead tree yonder, so that they cannot pull loose, before you go off to change shape, as long as you plan to do so anywhere within their sight."

"You're quite right, Giles," Jim answered.

There were no living trees nearby, but the tree Giles had mentioned was a dead fragment which looked as if it had been struck by lightning. It stood not ten yards off down the road behind them. They fastened their horses securely, then walked off together through the knee-high, unkept grass of the fields; until they were a good hundred yards from the animals.

"This far away I ought not panic them," said Jim, halting at last.

"Can't pull loose, anyway," replied Giles. He watched as Jim stripped off his clothes; and took them from Jim. Giles made them up as a bundle with the rope that already held the food and drink.

"Tie all these things tight about my dragon neck once I make the change," said Jim. Giles nodded.

Standing clothesless, Jim wrote the equation on the inside of his skull, and was instantly a dragon.

"I vow!" said Giles, staring at him. "I'd thought myself prepared for your change, James; but I did not expect you to be quite so big a dragon."

"I don't know why I am," answered Jim from his dragon body, "unless it's got something to do with my size as a human. Will you tie that bundle tightly around my neck? Thanks. Then I'll be off."

Giles finished fastening the bundle to Jim's scaly neck.

"Is that tight enough, James?" he asked, stepping back out of the way.

"It couldn't be better," answered Jim. "Farewell temporarily, Giles. I'll look forward to seeing you soon."

"And I, you, James," answered Giles. "Godspeed!"

Jim sprang into the air, beating down with his wings; and almost instantly began to mount with that speed that had astonished him the first time he had tried to fly in a dragon body. Reaching a height where there was a thermal, an updraft of air, he soared in a circle for a moment, with wings outstretched extending his dragon's telescopic vision to locate the tiny figure of Giles far below. The figure waved. Jim waggled his wings.

Then he pumped his wings again, reaching for greater altitude. He had to climb some distance before he found a higher thermal and began his glide, following the feeling that was attracting him to whatever dragons there were in the vicinity.

As had happened on his flight with Secoh to Cliffside, he found himself responding with exhilaration to the pleasures of soaring. Certainly it seemed to him the most enjoyable way to travel that had ever been created. Again, he found himself making a mental note to get off by himself and do more such traveling.

The day was cloudless and was going to be unseasonably warm. Already, the temperature was rising rapidly. It was noticeable even at his present altitude. in fact, if it had not been for the breeze created by his own passage, he might have felt a little warmer than was comfortable. As it was, he gave himself over to the sheer joy of flight.

His mind wandered off on various unconnected issues. He thought of Angie back in England; and regretted that there was no way to send a letter to her with any certainty that it would reach her before his own return—if it reached her at all. Letters here were simply handed from one person to another until they reached their destination. Consequently, their reaching such a destination was often more luck than anything else. He thought about Giles; and how, in spite of the short knight's explosive temper and the single-mindedness he shared with Brian and just about every other such person Jim had met in this world, Giles was a very likable sort of character.

Partially, he told himself now, it was because the other had, along with the excessive temper, an equally excessive dose of the common trait here of being very open, direct, and immediate with his emotions. He, Brian, and others like them, were almost like children in this. They could be suddenly very happy, or suddenly very sad, or suddenly very outraged—and just as suddenly return to good temper again.

To Giles, the world was a never-ending series of interesting things. There were surprises at every turn. Not only that, but Giles expected it to be so. Anything could happen, from Giles's point of view.

It often happened that when Jim's mind was puttering along on something entirely different, the solution to an earlier puzzle would suddenly occur to him. It was as if the back of his mind chewed on the problem all the time; and finally delivered a solution.

Jim found himself thinking once more about Carolinus, and magic; and Carolinus's evident attempt to make him learn the magician's trade for himself.

The possible reason that occurred to him now was an extension of a thought that had crossed his mind, briefly, once before. Magic was not science but art. It turned into science only when it was adopted into the domain of common use and became universally understood. Like the sewing of furs into a garment, that Carolinus had used as an example in his lecture.

The fact that magic was an art and nothing but an art, went far to explain a great many things. For one thing, there was essentially no one particular magic, no one particular spell for any situation. Each magician reached into that available pool of energy that the Accounting Office kept track of, and fashioned out of nothing more than pure energy, a *Magical* solution to whatever problem he had in hand.

After all, what was art? Jim asked himself. He tried to think of a definition that would include writers, painters, actors, musicians, composers, sculptors . . . everyone who could possibly come under the umbrella of that word.

The answer had to be that art was a process. A development. Rather like the equationlike process Carolinus had suggested he envision on the inside of his forehead in order to change from dragon to human and back again.

Art, Jim told himself—a little surprised to find himself in such an intense philosophical vein—was a process, and whatever the process the artist had chosen to work with, it had to follow a certain pattern.

First the artist had to imagine something that had not been imagined before. Like a Stone Age man standing on a hill, watching birds in the sky, and dreaming of himself flying. That was simple, direct imagination at work. Then from this chunk of raw imagination must come something that was unique to art: a conceptualization; which was something more specific than just a general imaginative wish.

It must throw up some fanciful means by which the imagination could become reality; as Leonardo de Vinci's drawing of an ornithopter was an attempt to conceptualize a human flying machine. Then that conceptualization had to be refined by a number of generations and experiments, until finally it became a clear visualization of whatever was the ultimate conclusion.

It suddenly occurred to Jim that those three steps—imagination, conceptualization, and the envisioning of a working solution—celebrated the very faculties that medieval life taught people like Brian and Giles to avoid. Medieval people were not supposed to think of altering the environment around them, but rather accept and put up with it. The better they were at simply accepting and reacting to things as they saw them, the more they tended to be a success within the structure and terms of their own society.

No wonder the road of learning down which Carolinus had pointed Jim was called Magic.

And no wonder, being a product of a civilization in which much of this magic had become scientific and technological reality, he was in a better position to travel down it than someone like his two friends, with all their courage and other good points.

He woke out of his thoughts to realize that he was getting very close to the source of the feeling that had drawn him in this direction. In fact that feeling now pointed him only a little ways ahead and back down to the surface of the earth.

He looked in that direction now; and saw, perhaps a mile or two ahead, a scattering of trees that could hardly be called a wood, but which enclosed an open space at its center in which sat what looked like a castle.

Jim adjusted his vision to the best of a dragon's telescopic eyesight; and was barely able to make out that the castle, while real enough, was to a large extent in ruins. The moat around it was empty; and while most of its roof seemed intact from this distance, in some cases the outer wall had fallen down. He put himself into a glide toward it.

The day had fulfilled its promise by becoming hot. As he neared the ground, what air was moving tended to die away, so that he planed downward merely on the spread of his wings and the speed of his descent. He pulled up with a jerk just above the earth; and landed with a thump just outside the dry moat of the ruined castle. A drawbridge, in surprisingly good repair, spanned the moat and pointed the way to a large pair of double doors, one of which stood a little ajar, revealing a narrow, vertical gap of darkness beyond.

Here at ground level the air was absolutely still, so that the day seemed breathless. In spite of the bright sun beaming down on everything, and the small blades of grass trying here and there to sprout through the bare earth, the stillness and the ruined aspect of the castle had an ominous feel to it. But it was from inside the building that the dragon feeling was reaching out to Jim.

He stumped ahead—a dragon walking on his hind legs could hardly do anything else but stump when he walked—and the sound of his feet, with all his weight upon them, boomed heavily in the utter silence about him. He reached the two tall doors and knocked. They were large enough to reach half again his own height above his head. Either one of them, opened, could let him pass through.

He thumped with his knuckles on the door. And waited.

After a bit he knocked again. But there was still no response.

He pushed the door all the way open and stepped into a space that turned out not to be entirely lightless, after all. It was a dimly-lit, large hall illuminated only by a couple of slitlike windows, one beyond the hinge side of each of the doors through which he had entered.

"Anybody home?" he shouted—although he knew very well that somebody was home. He could feel him, her, or them there. After a moment, still with no response, he grew tired of waiting.

"I know you're here," he called. "You didn't expect to fool another dragon did you? Come out, come out, wherever you are!"

In spite of himself the last words ended up in the singsong in which he had spoken them in his childhood.

There was a second more of silence and then a long length of white cloth—it must be forty or more feet, Jim thought, to reach up to wherever it was attached, out of sight in the darkness at the top of the hall—fell down before him and began to ripple as it was waved back and forth.

"Go away!" boomed an enormous, hollow dragon voice. "If you value your life, go awaaay!"

The crude attempt of exaggerated voice and the rippling white cloth, which plainly was being made to move from above, reminded Jim of his Halloween-party days as a child. He almost laughed.

"Don't be ridiculous!" Jim shouted back. "I'm not going away!" He had upped his own voice a notch. It did not match what he was hearing; but it came fairly close.

"You're an English dragon!" boomed the voice. "You've got no business here! Go awaaay!"

"I'm an English dragon all right," Jim roared back, "but I've got a passport to turn over to a responsible French dragon!"

There was a second's pause. Then the voice he was listening to spoke again, on another note.

"Passport?" the voice said. "Stay there."

The white cloth was whisked upward, and there was a scrabbling sound, at first overhead, then moving toward the back of the hall, and at last descending toward Jim. He waited. After a moment, there was the sound of heavy dragon footsteps approaching; and there appeared not one, but two dragons, one noticeably smaller than the other. They both looked underfed. The larger dragon must once have been as big as Jim, but he was now showing signs of age and his body had shrunken on his great bones.

"What's your name?" he demanded of Jim in a rusty, deep, bass voice.

No wonder, thought Jim, that the other had sounded hollow shouting down from the ceiling of the hall. He was himself hollow; a bag of bones was not an unfair way to describe him. He must be older than Smrgol had been. This, however, was no such kindly old dragon as Smrgol. He looked old and wicked.

"James," said Jim shortly.

The bigger dragon looked at the lesser.

"Crazy English name," he said, to his companion. The smaller dragon nodded her wickedly narrow head—for Jim could now see that she was a female—in agreement. It struck Jim suddenly that he had run across something that was an oddity among the English dragons. A mated pair who lived apart from any dragon community.

But the larger dragon's eyes were gleaming avariciously. "Where's the passport?" he demanded.

Jim felt a sense of caution.

"Outside," he answered. "I'll get it. But you two stay here while I do."

The larger dragon grunted unwillingly. But neither stirred when Jim turned about, went out the door again, crossed the moat, and ended up on the bare earth and sparse grass before the castle. He turned his back on the doorway.

He was trying desperately to remember just what Carolinus's directions had been for his getting the passport up out of him and back to proper size again. If only Carolinus hadn't complicated the matter by telling him in the same breath the routine for getting up the *Encyclopedie Necromantick.*

His mind scrambled and found it.

To produce the bag of passport jewels, Jim was to cough twice, sneeze once, and then cough once again. He had not stopped to think that he might be in his dragon body at the time he did this. Of course, he could always change back to his human form; but after seeing the two inside he held a strong inclination not to give up, even temporarily, the protection of his strong, young, dragon body.

Well, there was nothing to be lost by trying.

He attempted to cough. To his joy, dragons could cough. He coughed very well, in fact. Having done it once, he did it again. What was next? Oh yes, the sneeze.

However, it seemed a legitimate sneeze was not easy to produce on demand. Jim began to feel uncomfortable. In spite of the fact that the other two dragons had not moved as he went out the door, he was now almost certain he could feel their eyes on him through the door that still stood ajar—in fact, Jim had found that it would not close any further.

"*Atchoo!*" he said hopefully.

Nothing happened. No sack of jewels began to bulk inside him. Jim began to feel a bit frantic. What if Carolinus, absentminded as he seemed to be from time to time, had simply not taken into account the fact that dragons were incapable of sneezing? In fact, who had ever heard of a dragon sneezing?

In desperation, Jim reached down, plucked one of the sparse blades of grass and attempted to tickle the inside of one of his nostrils with it. But he could scarcely feel the grass within the capacious nostril. That was no answer.

Perhaps if he had something a little longer and firmer. . . . His eyes searched the ground and finally spotted, about fifteen feet away, a dry and ancient twig, which had the virtue of being at least twelve inches long.

He walked over to it, trying to do so as casually as he could while still keeping his back to the open slit in the doorway. Having reached it, he looked around at the landscape and up at the sky before—as casually as possible—reaching down to scoop up the stick. Keeping it hidden by the bulk of his body he tried tickling the inside of his nostril with it.

This, his nostril could feel. But it produced no sneeze. The dry stick, that had several corners of once-budded joints, scratched at the inside of his nostril and brought momentary tears to his eyes.

But still, it did not make him sneeze.

Well, a dragon's muzzle was long, and therefore his nostrils were long. There was still plenty of nostril to go. He pushed the stick as far up as he could. There was a moment of sharp pain, then a horrendous tickle. Then an enormous sneeze that blew the twig somewhere out of sight. Hastily, Jim coughed.

When he at last blinked his watering eyes clear, he saw the sack of jewels that was the passport standing on the ground in front of him. He snatched it up, turned, and went back into the castle.

By the time he came through the front door again, carrying the sack, the other two were back where he had left them. But their eyes fastened almost as if hypnotized on the sack.

"Look!" cried the smaller dragon.

Her voice was as rusty as that of her companion. They also looked to be about the same age. It was a much higher voice, however, and it did not have the tremendous booming quality of the other.

"Those Phoenicians," rumbled the larger dragon, "coming up to the Isle of Scilly and other places about nineteen hundred years ago. And those English dragons getting all the best of it."

He looked directly at Jim.

"So," he said, "hand over the passport!"

"Hold on a minute," retorted Jim, still holding the sack to him. "What are your names?"

"Sorpil," grumbled the big dragon after a moment's pause. "I'm Sorpil. This is my wife, Maigra. Now give me that passport."

"Give *us* the passport!" snapped Maigra.

"Not just yet," said Jim. He was suddenly grateful that on their flight back from the Cliffside dragon community to Malencontri, Secoh had briefed him on both the obligations he would have toward his French hosts, and the corresponding obligations they were supposed to have toward him. "Do you assure me that the two of you are in good standing with your fellow dragons and that you are qualified to accept this passport on their behalf?"

"Of course, of course," grumbled Sorpil. "Now hand it over."

"Don't be in such a sulfurous hurry!" said Jim, borrowing one of Gorbash's granduncle's favorite dragonish swearwords. "We'll go through the whole ritual of transfer, if you don't mind. You're agreeable to that, aren't you?"

The two looked sour. But Jim knew they had no choice. If they wanted to get their claws on his passport, it was incumbent upon them not only to give Jim the right answers, but even to feed and house him, in a supposedly friendly gesture, overnight. It was a way of sealing the bargain.

"Now, you've assured me you're in good standing with your fellow dragons," Jim said. "You understand that I'll be checking this statement of yours with the next French dragon I meet?"

"Yes, yes!" shrilled Maigra—or at least her voice was shrill by dragon standards. She was almost jumping up and down in excitement, with her eyes on the passport.

"I do," growled Sorpil. "We both do."

"Yes, yes!" said Maigra again.

"On my part," said Jim, now well into the ritual, "I give my word not to do anything that will cause difficulties or trouble for the dragons of France, and if accidentally I should do so, I will undertake to correct or dispose of this difficulty or problem, before I leave France and without imposing upon the dragons of France for help. You have heard and noted this declaration from me?"

"We have," said Sorpil disgustedly.

"On the other hand," said Jim, "in case I should run into mistreatment in France, as a result of attitudes or actions by French georges, or others native to this land, I can if need be call for help upon all French dragons; and will be given the courtesy of that help."

This time there was no immediate answer. Sorpil and Maigra looked at each other, then looked at the passport, then looked at each other again. The moments stretched out without a response from them.

"Well?" demanded Jim, at last. "Is the answer yes, or not? Perhaps I should just go back to England."

"No, no," said Maigra quickly.

"Now *you* don't be in such a sulfurous hurry," muttered Sorpil. He turned to Maigra. "Do you think the others—"

"We'd have to pay, of course—" said Maigra.

They looked at each other for a long moment, then back at the passport, then at each other again. Finally their eyes came once more to Jim's.

"We accept," said Sorpil, heavily, "we agree."

"Fine," said Jim.

"Just what are you planning to do here?" asked Sorpil.

Jim, who had been about to hand over the passport, held on to it instead.

"I don't have to tell you that," he said.

Sorpil swore, in a manner rather more georgelike than dragonlike.

"Just thought we might be able to be of some use to you, that's all," he said disgruntledly.

"Well, thanks anyway," said Jim, "but what I do here is my own affair; and I expect not to be followed or spied upon by any local French dragons. Is that understood?"

"Yes!" shrilled Maigra.

"Then I hereby give you this passport to hold until I leave," said Jim. "At which time, providing I have not violated the terms of our accord, you will return it to me exactly as it is. You understand that it is merely security for my good conduct while I am here."

"Of course!" said Sorpil. "Now, hand it over and we'll take you in and feed you. Isn't that what you want?"

"As I understood, it was customary," said Jim, passing over the passport.

"Oh, it is," said Maigra, in no particularly inviting voice. "Come along, then."

Jim followed them; and they went back through the dim hall, into the even dimmer recesses of the rest of the castle.

Chapter 18

Over dinner Sorpil and Maigra made a belated attempt to play the genial hosts. It was not largely successful because, as Jim discovered while the meal, the wine-drinking, and the talk went on, the two were about as sour-mouthed toward each other as they were toward anybody and anything else—except their guest of the moment.

Small, cutting remarks aimed at each other had a tendency to creep into their conversations, even while they were trying to pour conversational syrup over the social situation. In addition, they were obviously both very interested in enticing or tricking Jim into revealing why he was in France and what he intended to do here.

However, they were exceedingly clumsy at it, probably as a result of not having had much practice. In fact, Jim suspected them of having gone without any kind of contact, even with other dragons, for a very long time.

Maigra, the faster talker, had a tendency to slip into the middle of sentences being slowly enunciated by her husband. Sorpil would occasionally take time off to rebuke her for this. The result was that their efforts to worm Jim's secrets from him were sadly hampered because they could not act as a team; in fact, they had rather a tendency to act at cross purposes.

Meanwhile, Jim learned something about them.

"This château?" Sorpil responded in answer to one of Jim's questions. "It belonged to georges, originally, of course. I took it from them, about a hundred and twenty years ago. I'd had about enough of them sitting and milking the peasants dry, and leaving nothing for a couple of dragons to live on, but a few scrawny goats. So—"

"Actually, by the time Sorpil made his attack on the georges in the château," Maigra cut in, "they'd already taken a rather bad beating from a group of your English georges. That's why the château's so damaged—"

"I was speaking, Maigra, if you don't mind," came in Sorpil, heavily. "As I was saying, the minute these georges Maigra mentioned had left, I waited for a time when everybody in the château should be asleep; and entering through the part of the château that had been broken into, I, alone—"

"I was with him," said Maigra, "but he doesn't count that, naturally. The fact of the matter is—"

"It was at night," said Sorpil, "and most of their little lights—what do they call those things, now—"

"Candles!" snapped Maigra.

"Their candles were all out," said Sorpil, "and of course they're practically blind unless they've got some light to see by."

Jim and the other two were dining in a hall almost as large as the one he had entered through the front door, lit only by the moonlight coming through some tall windows along one side of the room. This, of course, did not bother Jim in his dragon body—dragons being quite comfortable in near-darkness, or even in complete darkness; although it was a little more convenient to get around with a small amount of light. The amount of moonlight coming in the windows was ideal.

"So I caught them, most of them, one by one, in their rooms and corridors, and had no trouble killing them off. There were one or two who gave me some trouble; but of course they were on foot, and not wearing their shells, so—"

"So actually he almost had no trouble at all," sneered Maigra. Sorpil turned his head briefly to scowl at her before turning back to Jim.

"So we took over this château over a hundred years ago," he went on, "and since then the peasants bring their taxes to us, instead of to the georges. The result is the fine food and drink we're able to offer you tonight."

The statement about food and drink was something of an exaggeration, Jim thought. It was true the three sheep that Maigra had brought freshly slaughtered to the table, hide, bones, and innards intact, had been relatively fat and quite tasty from a dragon's point of view. The wine was not bad; and Jim would actually have never thought to look at it otherwise than with approval, if he had not already had some weeks of experience with what was actually available in the way of wines, here in France itself.

The large keg, the top of which Sorpil had stove in with something of a ceremonial flourish, so that they could each dip into it with the human-made pitchers they used as drinking cups, contained a wine that was a bit better than some of the worst Jim had tasted since he had stepped ashore in Brest. It was also a long way from being the best that Jim had tasted since that moment.

Jim suspected that he was being given the type of wine they kept for their ordinary dining, figuring that an English dragon wouldn't know the difference. This was cutting very close to the line of insulting their guest. The assumption behind the passport was that, for temporary purposes, Jim owned the gems in it, and therefore was a dragon to be treated with the utmost respect.

"Where're you going from here?" Maigra asked suddenly in her sharp voice, breaking into and putting an end to Sorpil's no doubt largely-embroidered account of how he had conquered the château.

"East," said Jim with deliberate vagueness, coiling himself up more comfortably on the floor around the end of the george-sized table. The eating was over now; and Jim had taken enough of the wine, even as a dragon, to begin to feel rather relaxed and comfortable. He judged that the keg Sorpil had broached was at least half empty by this time.

"But I mean by what way, what route?" demanded Maigra.

"Oh," said Jim, "I thought I'd just pick my way generally eastward, you know. I'm not particular about exactly which route I travel."

"Well, you ought to be!" said Maigra. "After over a hundred years with no one but us to rule them, the peasants for miles around have gotten very bold. Sorpil and I never touch land outside unless we're together. Twenty or thirty peasants attacking you all at once with pitchforks and reaping hooks and things like that if you're alone—particularly if you're a little dragon like I am—is something you need to take seriously."

"Well, if you'll tell me the limits of your territory," said Jim, "I'll simply fly beyond them before I go down to earth. Not but what I don't think I could probably handle even twenty or thirty armed peasants if I had to."

In spite of himself, the wine was bringing out some of Jim's instinctive dragon's pride in his own size and power. In fact, right now in a sleepy, wine-induced, sort of way, he found rather attractive the idea of having to deal with twenty or thirty armed peasants. He had little doubt that he could kill a good number of them and drive the rest off.

He remembered the first time he had flown into a mounted group of men-at-arms belonging to Hugh de Bois de Malencontri, the former owner of his castle and then his enemy, and scattered them like tenpins. Of course, that had been before Sir Hugh, in armor, on a war-horse and with a lance, had taught him that there were situations in which even a dragon might want to back off from a single george—human, that was.

The memory of the spear he had gotten through him on that occasion, that had nearly taken his life and the life of Gorbash, who owned the body he had been in, had a sobering effect on him.

"What do you suggest?" he asked Maigra.

"Well, to start off with," she answered, "you should let me tell you the best way to go, the safest way to go. Then you should travel on foot, so you can't be seen by a lot of peasants from underneath, so that they can gather and lay in wait for you. Now the best route for you after you leave here, would be through the woods to our northwest and then back again to a westerly line until you come to a large lake."

She paused to see if he was following her.

"Go on," he said.

"Follow the edge of that lake around it on your way west," she said. "For some reason the local peasants aren't as likely to attack you if you're close to the lake. None of them can swim; and of course none of them ever learned that we dragons are heavier than water and don't swim, either. So even if you are attacked you can jump into the lake itself—it's quite shallow near shore for someone like us; but it would be up to the neck on a george—and be safe from anything except what they might try to throw at you."

Jim grinned a little wickedly inside himself. Maigra did not know that he was that anomaly, a dragon who could and would swim. He found this out when crossing the Fens on foot on his way to the Loathly Tower, where he had had to swim to get from one piece of land to another. He had not learned yet, then, that his dragon body would be heavier than water, so he had tried to swim across a stretch of water without thinking. Once in the water, after the first moment of panic, he had discovered that if he simply moved his legs and tail hard enough—swishing his tail back and forth the way a sea serpent would—he could not only keep afloat but make progress. It was tiring; but it was possible. No other dragon that Jim knew had ever attempted it; and all of them believed firmly that they would go to the bottom like a stone if they stepped into water too deep for them to stand up and keep their head out in the air.

Nonetheless, Maigra's advice, he decided, was good. He mentally apologized to her for thinking that neither she nor Sorpil had any real interest in being useful to him. It had been a natural assumption, dragon nature being what it was; since if anything happened to him, they got to keep the passport. On the other hand, she had also had a number of pitchersful of the wine from the keg; and maybe the alcohol had softened her up, also.

She must have had an attractive and gentler side, at least when she was younger, he thought. It did not stand to reason that someone like Sorpil, who would have been a mighty dragon when they both were young, would have married her otherwise.

"Thank you, Maigra," he said; and heard the words come out very sleepily indeed. It had been before noon when he had entered the château; but their eating and drinking, as was usual with dragons when they got down to it, had been an extensive affair. The moonlight should have warned him that they had been at it for eight or nine hours. Still, the time had rather seemed to have flown.

In any case, he was undeniably sleepy.

"Have you got a spot for me," he asked, "or shall I just curl up here?"

He had no great objection to curling up where he was. On the other hand, it was dragon instinct to find a small enclosed place in which to sleep. It would be only hostly of Sorpil and Maigra to find him such a place—possibly one of the smaller original rooms of the castle, no matter in what condition it was now.

"I'll show you a spot!" said Maigra, getting to her feet rather spryly.

Sorpil stayed where he was, merely rumbling something that sounded like "good night" intermixed with a dragon-sized belch. Jim followed Maigra off. She led him through a number of corridors and up and down several staircases, all in almost complete darkness. But with his nose and ears telling him where she was, Jim followed her without any worry of making a misstep or going astray.

She brought him at last to what Jim had expected, a bedroom of one of the original inhabitants of the castle. She left him there, and he curled up among the ruins of its original, rather sparse furniture. His last thought before falling asleep was that castles in France seemed to have more individual rooms than castles in England.

He slept, as all dragons normally did, dreamlessly and soundly. When he awoke the room was bright with daylight. It had only one slit of a window, but the sun seemed to be beaming directly through it, so that the room was probably as bright as it ever got. The difference from the darkness of the night before was a little startling to Jim, to whom the hours between the moment when he fell asleep and this moment of waking seemed hardly more than an instant.

He yawned, his long red tongue flickering out in the dusty air of the room as his great jaws gaped. Then he uncoiled himself, stretched—all but his wings, there wasn't room enough to stretch them—and by using his nose and memory together, followed back down the path he had been brought up the night before.

He found his way back to the room where they had eaten, drunk, and talked. Neither Maigra nor Sorpil was around. There was nothing left of the sheep, except a few bones cracked open, the marrow licked out of them. The keg Sorpil had opened the night before was four-fifths empty.

Jim treated himself to a pitcher of the wine, poured down at a gulp, and found it wonderfully revivifying. He had another, just on general principles.

It was probably time he got started. There would be nothing more to gain from his two hosts. Maigra, under the mellowing influence of the wine, had evidently given him the best advice he was likely to get from either one of them.

About to go out the double front doors, he turned for a last time and shouted a farewell to his hosts, since neither had bothered to show up to see him off.

"This is James!" Jim shouted. *"I'm leaving now. Thank you for your hospitality; and I'll be back to pick up the passport before too long. Farewell!"*

His voice went off, echoing and reechoing from distant, and more distant yet, corners of the castle. No sound came back in return.

He turned and went out.

It was another hot, cloudless day. He started off on foot according to the directions that Maigra had given him. He was getting started at a later hour today due to the food and wine of the previous evening. He had slept well into midmorning.

Two hours later he sighted a patch of blue that was evidently one end of the lake Maigra had mentioned. He paused to concentrate on his panting.

He had been panting so heavily that anyone within fifty feet would have been able to hear him sounding like a steam locomotive on its way uphill. His jaws were wide open and his red tongue lolled limply from between his front teeth like a dispirited flag.

He had forgotten the plain and simple fact that dragons were not really built for foot travel. By nature they were creatures of the air if traveling had to be done. And the day was hot.

Something Jim had never had to consider before was the fact that dragons, with their nearly-impenetrable hide, had no sweat glands over the outer surface of their body, like a human or some animals. They got rid of excess heat by panting, the way a dog does. Unfortunately, they had a great deal more size and body weight than a dog, and therefore more mass. Movement like this on foot accumulated heat in the body rather quickly; and this particular day was not one in which heat dissipated easily.

Jim had simply not encountered this problem before. The two previous foot-trips he had made as a dragon had been in a cooler climate; and both times it had been under conditions in which he was emotionally wrought-up and not paying much attention to the effort of his travel.

The first time he had been frantic with worry over what might be happening to Angie as a prisoner in the Loathly Tower. The other had been on the abortive march to retake the castle of Malencontri from Sir Hugh. On that occasion he had been full of bitterness and self-hate. But the big difference between those trips and this one had been the temperature of the day. The march to Malencontri, in fact, had ended in a fairly heavy rain which had kept him cool.

In this case, however, there was nothing to take his attention off how extraordinarily hot, bothered, and uncomfortable he was feeling. In fact, he thought, standing there and panting, he was damned if he would put up with it anymore.

Maigra had naturally assumed that he had only two choices: to fly or to travel on foot; on his hind legs, specifically. She had not, of course, recognized that she was talking to a magician who was just temporarily wearing a dragon body and therefore had a third option: to turn back into his human form.

Jim wrote the necessary magical equation on the inside of his forehead; and a second later stood there, blessedly naked and radiating heat from all over his body, with the rope that had secured his belongings now hanging loosely from his much smaller neck and shoulders.

He took the burden off and dressed; retying one end of the rope around the cloth that held the wine flask and the food and then making the rest of the rope into a loose sling, that he slung over his head and off one shoulder, so that it hung off his opposite hip like a baldric above the handle of his poignard.

He might not now be in as good a shape to face the attack of half a dozen or more armed French peasants; but on the other hand he was nowhere near as conspicuous now as he had been walking along as a dragon.

Also, in case he really got attacked, there was always the option of turning back into his dragon form again for self-protection. If the local people were as ready to believe in magic as everybody else he had met in this world so far, the very fact of his turning into a dragon before their eyes would be enough to send them scattering.

He felt much better—except for a tremendous thirst, engendered not only by last night's wine but the pitchersful he had drunk this morning. Accordingly, he headed hastily on toward the lake, where he hoped to be able to fill himself to the brim with cool water.

The closer he got to the lake the more achingly clear and beautiful the taste of that cool water grew in his imagination. Finally, he could hardly stop himself from breaking into a run. He did not, not because he was afraid of building up too much body heat once more—he was cooling off rather nicely, as a matter of fact, in his human shape—but because a certain sense of pride stopped him.

Would Brian have burst into a run simply to cover the last few yards to water he would reach in a second or two anyway? No, thought Jim, his friend would disdain any such human weakness. In learning to be the fourteenth-century equivalent of a wartime officer, Jim should be capable of showing no less restraint. After all, it was not as if he were dying of thirst. He was simply parched from having drunk too much wine.

So he managed to walk sedately to a point on the lake edge where he could lie on the bank and reach over and drink from the surface. The water was just as attractively blue and beautiful as he had imagined. And the first few swallows were so delicious that he lost control after all and began to gulp the water up as quickly as he could.

Pausing at last for breath, he had time finally to notice how the water, once it had ceased being disturbed by his drinking, showed his own image staring back up at him, it seemed, from just below the surface. He gazed at it, bemused—then suddenly stared at it in something much more than bemusement.

The face staring up at him was not his. It was the face of a beautiful girl with long blond hair. She was smiling up at him—or rather her face was smiling up at him—from what seemed only inches below the surface of the water. The image was far too sharp to be any kind of a hallucination.

"Wait a minute!" said Jim out loud, scrabbling up onto his hands and knees, but still staring into the water.

The face came out of the water, proving to be attached to a head and, as it emerged further, the complete rest of the beautiful girl. She smiled at him and his head swam.

"There you are, my love," she breathed. "Finally, you are here at last. Come with me."

Her voice tinkled softly in his ears. She reached out and wrapped one of her little hands around Jim's; and the next thing Jim knew—he had no clear idea of how it happened—he was being towed down into the lake itself.

He had time to notice that the underwater banks of the lake were nowhere near as shallow as Maigra had said. They fell precipitously to an unknown depth; in fact, so far that he could not at this moment see the bottom below them. A dragon who believed he couldn't swim, falling or being pulled into this water, would sink immediately and drown without a hope.

But he had no time to dwell upon the perfidiousness of Maigra's directions; and the possibly unhappy end that he had avoided only because the warmth of the day had spurred him to change into a human being. He was too concerned with the fact that he was being steadily pulled deeper into the lake.

He could swim passably well in his human body. He had even been snorkeling in water fifteen or twenty feet deep. But at the present moment he had no face-mask, no snorkel, and for some strange reason, the girl's ability to draw him deep into the lake was completely irresistible. Even if he had struggled, he had the feeling that it would have done no good; and he had no will to struggle.

He would drown. It was inevitable.

No sooner had he thought this, however, than he realized that if he was going to drown he should have started to feel some symptoms of it by this time. He had assumed he was holding his breath; but he was not. He was breathing quite normally, here, underwater.

This made no sense at all. Either the water had been replaced by some sort of bubble of air around him, which was impossible. Or else he was breathing water as if it was air, which was even more impossible.

"It's wonderful your turning up like this at last," the golden-haired girl was saying in front of him, without bothering to turn her head. "You're the last thing I was expecting. I had my eye on a nasty dragon that was getting closer and closer. Then suddenly he disappeared."

Her tone became thoughtful.

"I don't understand that at all," she said, more to herself than to Jim. "I've never known a dragon to do that before. And he was headed right for the lake, too. I could have drowned him so easily!"

"Why—why would you want to drown a dragon?" asked Jim bewilderedly.

"Why, because they're such nasty things!" said the girl. "Those great, ugly, batlike wings and scaly hides. Ugh! Wish I knew a way to get rid of all of them. As it is I simply do what I can by drowning any who come close. I draw them to the water's edge with my magic; and then, of course, once I've laid hold of them they can't get away. I can pull them right into the water and—"

Her tone became girlishly happy.

"They drown just all by themselves!"

Jim shuddered inside.

"The fishes are so grateful," the girl went on. "They find a lot to eat in one of those dragons. You'd be surprised. It's one reason they all love me so much. And of course they do. I mean—they'd love me anyway, because they have to. But they love me all the more because I give them nice dead dragons to eat all the time."

She paused.

"Well, perhaps not all the time. But every so often I give them a dragon."

They had reached the bottom of the lake and were descending into a sort of underwater castle, which, however, was wide rather than high. Its walls seemed made of shells and shiny gemlike stones, and many panels of what seemed to be pure mother-of-pearl, that gleamed irridescently underwater. A school of small blue fish shot toward them through the water, or air, or whatever it was that surrounded them, and went into a sort of elaborate dance around the golden-haired girl.

"Oh, you!" said the girl to them playfully, "you knew I'd be right back. I've brought the most beautiful man in the world. And he's going to stay with us forever and ever. Won't that be wonderful?"

It occurred to Jim that it might have been nice if she had stopped to consult him about staying down where he was now, forever and ever. He could see drawbacks that could make this far from the most wonderful thing to happen to him.

Aside from everything else he had things to do up on land. Not that the girl wasn't breathtakingly lovely. Jim had thought once upon a time that Danielle was possibly the most beautiful woman he had ever seen in his life. But this little creature radiated something beyond ordinary beauty. He could no more keep himself from being attracted to her than he could release her grip on his wrist that had brought him down here.

The girl was still talking to her small fish.

"I would never leave you for any real length of time, you know that," she was telling them. "Leave my dear little ones? Never! You know I love you and everything in this lake and the lake itself. It's just that I couldn't resist this magnificent man I found up on the bank. You can't blame me for that, can you?"

By this time they were well within the palace-like structure, entering a room walled with mother-of-pearl and draped, padded, and furnished with gossamerlike fabrics in all shades of blue and green, that seemed to shimmer in the underwater light. The chairs were not chairs so much as large, soft, multicolored lounging platforms. But the central piece of furniture in the room—if it could be called furniture—was a great, opulent structure, like a round bed with no head- or footboard, but with mounds of fluffy pillows piled high at one point on the edge of it.

It was to these pillows that the girl towed Jim. He could not be sure whether they were actually walking now, or floating, swimming, or simply skimming through this strange, water-colored, breathable atmosphere. At any rate they came eventually to rest against the pillow piles. Here she released Jim, so that he sank into the pillows. They were softer than anything he had ever touched before, so that he went half out of sight into them, in a semi-propped up, stretched-out position.

"Now," said the golden-haired girl, sitting down cross-legged on the surface of the bed—or perhaps just a few inches above it—it was hard for Jim to tell. Although the water-air atmosphere that surrounded them seemed transparent, there was a sort of shimmer to everything that made exact details uncertain. "What would my dearest love like first?"

"Well, er, if you don't mind," said Jim, "some explanations."

She looked at him, her mouth in a perfect O of astonishment.

"Explanations?"

"Yes," said Jim, "I mean, it's nice of you to call me the handsomest man in the world. But anybody knows I'm not. In fact if anything I'm one of the . . ."

He searched for a word.

"One of the most unhandsomest you're likely to meet."

"Why, you are not!" said the girl. "But, even if you were, I'd still love you just the same, with the same great passion. I am a person of great passions, you know."

"I see," said Jim.

"Indeed, yes," said the girl earnestly. "All we elementals—actually there's only just a few of us but all of us, in any case—are beings of great, great passion!"

"Oh, I believe you," said Jim.

"Yes." She sighed softly. "Foolish people call us water fairies. But that's just because they don't understand the difference between a mere water fairy and an elemental. An elemental is something far, far finer than a mere water fairy. Water fairies are merely fairies that live in the water. They have a little magic, it's true. They are immortal, that's true. But they have no great capacities. They have no ability to have the great passions elementals have; and of all elementals, if I do say it myself, I'm capable of the greatest passion. I always have been and I always will be."

She looked at Jim curiously.

"What's your name, my beloved?"

"Well—it's James," said Jim.

"James . . ." She tried the name out on her tongue. "An odd name but it has its charm. *James.* It does not sing the way some names do; but nonetheless it's a good name. *James* . . ."

"If you don't mind, I'd like to know your name too," said Jim.

"My name?" She looked astonished. "I thought everyone knew my name. I'm Melusine. How could you not know it? After all, I'm the only one there is. There are no other Melusines."

"Well, you see," said Jim, "I'm English."

"Ah, English!" said Melusine. "I've heard of England and the English. So you're one of those. You don't seem too different—except for that strange name. But enough about names."

She gazed into Jim's eyes with her own deep blue ones, turning the wattage of her attractiveness up from what seemed to Jim some five hundred watts to about a thousand watts.

"Let's talk of more immediate things," she purred. "Oh my dear one, what is it you desire most in the world right now?"

And she turned the wattage up another five hundred watts.

Jim closed his eyes desperately.

No, he thought! I mustn't. I don't want to stay here forever and ever and make love to an elemental. I want to go home to my own castle, to Angie, and every so often kill an ogre or rescue a Prince or something . . . what am I thinking? Anyway I mustn't. If I give in just once, I'll give in again; then I might get to like it. Then I might want to stay here forever at the bottom of the lake. And what then? What happens if she gets tired of me, as she must get tired of the men she falls in love with from time to time? She probably does something unspeakable to them. I've got to get out of this. Angie, help me!

"I've got a headache," Jim said feebly.

Chapter 19

He had not expected it to work;
but it had. Melusine had turned overwhelmingly solicitous at his mention of a
headache; and insisted that he rest and sleep. There would be all the time in the
world for other things later on.

It might be, thought Jim, that her attraction-magic worked even on her; so that
when she thought she was in love, she was really and actually in love, and ready to
sacrifice herself for the good of the loved object. In this world where he had
discovered that an individual could be tremendously gentle and caring one
moment and literally vicious the next, and those around him or her would not see
anything the slightest bit contradictory about it, he would believe anything. She
had left him alone and he had slept.

When he woke up, she was still not there. However, within a few minutes of his
waking, some of the little fish that had done acrobatics around Melusine, showed
up. They swam in to surround him in midair and bring him things. Some brought
badly cut but good-sized jewels in their mouths. One brought a large bunch of
grapes depending from one stem, heavy enough so that it had to labor with its fins
to swim (or fly) its way to him.

"I don't like grapes," Jim told it.

It was quite true. He had never really cared for grapes; and, as a matter of fact, as a human he did not even care too much for wine. It was only as a dragon that he had discovered an enjoyability in the latter.

The fish dropped the grapes on the bed, as if in exhaustion, and swam off. But it returned a moment later with a second bunch.

The same determination seemed to operate with all the rest of the fish. They might listen to Melusine, but they certainly did not listen to him. They only kept piling unwanted gifts on him. Eventually, a whole school of them labored toward him with flailing fins, carrying some iridescent green clothing.

That was followed by a ridiculous hat that looked halfway between a chef's cap and a rather angular top hat.

As this piled up around him, he was grateful that Melusine was not around, so that he had freedom to think without that magical attractiveness of hers beaming at him with the power of an oversized sunlamp.

His reaction when she had tried to entice him into sexual congress with her had been purely instinctive; but with a cool head, he realized how sensible he had been. Even if she was willing to keep him forever as she had said—and he really did not believe that for a second—someone like her must fall in love afresh, the minute a new male face showed up on the horizon. But even if she did intend to keep him around forever, the fact of the matter was he did not want to stay around forever. For many, many reasons.

The chief of these was Angie. There was a great deal of difference between being sexually attracted to someone like Melusine and the deep emotional response—the love—he had for Angie.

He actually could not imagine life without Angie. It would be like having half of himself amputated down the middle, from the crown of his head to the soles of his feet. Angie had something that Melusine would never have. He did not know exactly what it was; but it made life entirely different for him, knowing she was there. Even when he was off like this in France, the fact that he knew she was at Malencontri and that he would be getting back to her eventually—for he had no intention of letting anything happen to him along the way—made his response to living entirely different.

He had to get out of here. Out of this lake and away from Melusine. His mind chased frantically after reasons he could give her for taking him back up onto the shore of the lake.

It was true, she had exerted that magical pull on him, even when he was on the bank and she was in the water. But it had been nowhere near as strong as what he had felt down here on the bottom of the lake.

He had a feeling that once he got up on dry land, he might be able to grit his teeth, turn around, and walk away from her until the magic no longer affected him. He assumed someone like her would not follow him. But if she did, something seemed to tell him that she would not have the kind of power she had while in the lake.

He had reached this point in his thinking when it suddenly came back to him, like the eruption of a grenade in the back of his mind, that he was at least an apprentice practitioner of magic, himself. If her advantage over him lay in the area of her magic; then he ought to be able to counter it with magic of his own, if he only knew what magic, and how to apply it.

That last, was the tricky part. The information he wanted was no doubt buried in the *Encyclopedie Necromantick,* but he had already learned that he could not simply reach in and get it simply because he wanted to.

First, he had to have a clear definition of what he wanted. Then he had to go after it by the route he had already figured out for himself. For all he knew every other magician used every other possible method, each to his own, but for him the method seemed to be the one he had worked out of imagination, conceptualization, and visualization.

All right then, he told himself. He sat up cross-legged on the bed; and tried to apply his method to his problem.

First question: What was the magic he needed to get out of here?

No, on second thought that was the second question. The first question was: What was the magic that was keeping him here?

For the first time it occurred to him that it might be a different kind of magic than the kind he would use. Melusine had called herself an elemental. She might be an elemental in the same sense that Giles was a silkie. So that what was magic about her was something inborn, not something that she had learned.

If that was the case, the question became: What exactly was this innate magic of hers?

Well, it seemed to be divided into two areas. One was that which gave her power over any other beings in or near water. The other was her ability to make water and breathable air interchangeable.

Apparently, it was immaterial whether Jim was breathing water right now and getting away with it; or whether the water right around him had turned into air and he was breathing that.

He had it!

Melusine's primary control over people like himself was the fact that she could choose to make it possible for them to breathe underwater or not. Apparently, she had it in for dragons. She clearly preferred that they be stuck with breathing water once they were under the surface. On the other hand, in his case, she had preferred that he breathe water as if it were air, or water that had been turned into air. That meant that all he had to do—

"Ouch!" cried Jim.

He rubbed the right side of his skull. A dozen laboring little fish had just dropped a small ingot of gold on his head. He glared at them.

"I don't want this!" he shouted at them. "I don't want any gold, or jewels, or grapes, or all this other stuff you're bringing me. I don't want it, do you understand me? *I do not want it!*"

The fish went off again in a body—judging from past performance, to find something else to bring him. He rubbed his head again and tried to recapture the thought that had been interrupted by the gold brick.

He had the first step of his system. He had something to imagine. He must imagine that there was a way he could walk, underwater, out of here and up the side of the lake into the air—with the water around him staying as breathable as air until he got out in the open and could breathe the real atmosphere.

He concentrated on the image of his doing just that. Here am I, he thought, strolling along the lake bed, breathing water perfectly well, even though I am escaping from Melusine. My own magic turns the water around me into the most breathable possible air. I have as much air as I want. I can breathe deep into my lungs. I could even run as fast as I wanted to, and there would still be plenty of air with plenty of oxygen in it for my lungs to pump into my body and keep it going. Here I am, running along the floor of the lake, beginning to climb up the side, breathing nicely—

Now, what do I write on the inside of my forehead to make myself be able to breathe water this way? I know I have the answer right inside me, in the *Encyclopedie Necromantick;* but I just can't seem to bring the exact thing to mind that I need—

"Oh! You're awake," said the voice of Melusine behind him. She bounced onto the bed beside him, landing on her knees. "Shoo!"

The last word was addressed to a small school of fish which was now laboring up with what looked like a crown made entirely out of mother-of-pearl.

They turned about and swam away with it again.

"I'm so glad to have you awake, my dearest," purred Melusine. "Are you feeling all better now?"

"Yes," said Jim; and then decided that he ought to put some enthusiasm into it, "Yes, yes indeed. Very much better indeed."

"Well, that's just fine," said Melusine. "Now, perhaps—"

"And how was your day?" asked Jim.

She looked at him, startled.

"My day?" she said.

"Well, day or night, whatever time you've been away from me while I was sleeping," said Jim.

"You want to know how things have been with me since you fell asleep?" said Melusine, staring at him. "Nobody ever—I mean, usually nobody ever asks me that kind of question."

"Well, you see," said Jim, "when two people, like you and I—"

"Oh, yes," sighed Melusine.

"When two people like you and I," said Jim, "are attracted to each other as we are, it makes their love a bigger, finer thing if they're interested in each other's doings, even when they aren't together."

Melusine looked at him in extreme puzzlement and shook her head.

"This is most strange of you, James," she said. "Does it come of being English?"

"Oh yes," said Jim, "we all feel this way in England. That's why people are so much in love with each other there."

"Ugly, brutal savages, with dragons all over the place, are very much in love with each other, in England?" said Melusine unbelievingly.

"Oh yes. Very, very much in love. Take my word for it," said Jim.

"Of course, I'll take your word for anything, my dearest heart," said Melusine. "It's just a little hard to accept, that's all. Ugly, brutal . . . why do they think that knowing about what they've done when they're apart makes their love stronger?"

"Oh it does much more than make their love stronger," said Jim. "It adds an entirely new dimension to their love. Anyone who hasn't experienced it can't imagine what a difference it makes. But to answer your question, the reason it improves their love is because it means that they're thinking about each other, even when they're apart and longing to be together again. Because of that they want to know everything there is to know about each other, even what the other does when they're not around."

"It is a most strange notion, James," said Melusine earnestly. "I begin to see, however, that there might be something to it. I'm just terribly surprised that if there's something like that, it didn't occur to me before this."

"It's because your ability to love is so large," Jim assured her. "It's so large that it never occurred to you to look beyond it for anything that would make it larger."

"That's true," said Melusine, "at least the part about my love being so large is true, so I suppose the other could be true too."

She put her hands together in her lap.

"Well," she said, "I assume I know how your time went since I last saw you. You've been asleep until just recently, haven't you?"

"Yes," answered Jim, "but how did you know that?"

She waved one hand negligently over the gold bricks, garments, jewels, and other items scattered over the bed.

"Oh, there'd be a great deal more of these things here, if you'd been awake earlier," she said. "I told my fish to watch you very carefully and start giving you things as soon as you woke up."

"I see," said Jim. "Well, that takes care of me. Your day is much more interesting, anyway, I'm sure. Tell me about it."

"Well, I can't just lie around all the time the way you can, darling," said

Melusine. She placed a comforting hand on Jim's forearm, "not that I begrudge you being able to lie around. I want you to have the best of everything. But for me—well, this is really a very big lake you know, much deeper than it looks from on top and I have my hands full taking care of it. My dear little people—my fish and the other underwater creatures who live here—are all very good; but they'd never really keep a tidy lake unless I had charge of things."

She turned her compelling eyes on him for a moment. Jim nodded to show he thoroughly understood.

"So I'm always busy moving around the lake and making sure that everything is the way it should be," she went on. "Now, today—or rather the part of the day, the night and the part of a morning you've been sleeping—I've been busy all around the lake. The deep-growing waterweeds are doing just fine; but the weeds up near the surface are not quite as happy as they should be. There are three rather small streams that feed into this lake, as well as some natural springs of water in the lake bottom itself; but this last winter was rather dry. Not much snow piled up; and the result was that the lake level has dropped just a bit. Not much, you understand; not enough to hurt my high-growing weeds—those like the bulrushes that stretch up out of the water—but enough to make them feel a little uncomfortable, particularly those already at their full height."

She paused and sighed.

"There's always something," she said. "Well, naturally, there isn't much I could do about the streams unless I wanted to travel up each one of them to their source. But I did cause the lake-bottom springs to work a little harder and put out some more water. I think that in about four or five days, the bulrushes will be completely happy again. Then there was the matter of the bones of the last dragon I drowned in the lake."

She stopped and made a face.

"I hate even to look at their ugly bones; and all my fish know that. They're supposed to go down and fan mud and silt, as much as they can, over the bones until they're hidden; but they haven't been working at it as they should. I hate to be hard on them; but I did talk to the ones in the immediate area of those bones pretty sternly. However, after I'd lectured them, I used some of my own abilities to bring silt up over the bones, this one time. I'm sure they'll do better next time."

"I'm sure," echoed Jim. "How could anything not put out extra effort after you had spoken to it like that?"

"Nothing, of course," Melusine agreed. "They all promised to do better; and I know they will. The thing is, we had several dragons all at once about a month ago and there was quite a bit for them to eat so they didn't get it all cleaned up earlier. So it wasn't completely their fault. At any rate that's taken care of. Then I checked on the pearl nursery; and that's coming along fine. I do prefer freshwater pearls to that hideous saltwater kind that georges seem to like—oh, I don't mean georges like you, James. Much less sensitive georges, the way most of them are. Almost as bad as dragons, some of them."

"I know," said Jim. "Some of us georges—but then, it's not for me to say. I really wish I could see this marvelous lake of yours. You make it sound so real that I can almost imagine it."

"You would?" Melusine stared at him. "You're a most strange man, James. But I'd love to show it to you. I really adore my little lake and I've never actually had the chance to show it off to anyone. We can go right now, if you want. That is, if you're rested and if your headache is over?"

"I'm just fine," said Jim, "and I can't wait to see the rest of the lake."

"Come along then," trilled Melusine, floating off the bed. Jim found himself floating off with her. She had him by the wrist again.

"You don't have to hold on to me," said Jim, as she towed him through the palace and out into the lake bed. "I'll come along with you."

"Oh, that's right," Melusine let his wrist go. "Just concentrate on staying with me, and you won't have to bother walking."

Jim did so; and found she was right. Together they moved out through a patch of tall, feathery, underwater weeds, and emerged finally into an open space beyond. Black, flat, and level, it seemed to stretch off until its farther parts were lost in the shimmer of the water.

"These are my mud-flats," said Melusine. "It's the lowest part of the lake. Aren't they beautiful?"

"Er—yes," said Jim. "They're so . . . so . . . ."

"Thick and clean," Melusine supplemented for him. "I know what you mean. It's a continual job making sure that everything that lands on them gets covered up or pushed down under the surface. But I don't think there's a better stretch of mud-flats anywhere, certainly not in France."

"I can believe you," said Jim.

They floated over the mud-flats.

"The far end of the lake is shallower," Melusine said as they went along. "That's where the oyster beds are, and a lot more of the vegetation. It's also where those dragon bones were that I had to speak sharply to those fishes about. Usually I try to get the dragon bones down to the mud-flats. They disappear so nicely into the mud. They're gone in a day or two. That's the trouble in a way. Just about anything on the mud-flats gets sucked down so quickly. I want to make sure that my fish have all they want to eat off the dragon before what's left gets taken out here. If there's any weight at all left to the carcass it pops down out of sight almost while you watch."

She laughed suddenly, a high, happy gust of girlish laughter.

"Can you imagine what it's like when a full-sized dragon happens to fall directly into the mud-flats? It almost never happens, but can you imagine it?" Melusine said. "They just go right down. You should see the expression on their faces—that is if you can call what they have, faces!"

"Oh, yes," said Jim, "that reminds me. I never did ask you why you dislike dragons so much."

"Well," said Melusine, "for one thing they're about as far from underwater as you can get. They're not even on land most of the time but up above it in that terrible stuff called air. Not that air is completely bad, I mean. I can breathe it myself, of course, but it can really be very nasty stuff, dry and sour and smelly."

They had reached the far end of the mud-flats now and were entering a territory carved into small gullies and mounts, all leading generally upward. Melusine showed him her pearl oysters—all of which obediently yawned open at her command, and contorted their soft inner parts to display their pearls. Jim duly admired them; and then carefully investigated the various waterweeds to which she introduced him.

They had started out followed by the horde of the little fishes that usually hung around her in the palace; but these had fallen behind shortly after they had ventured out over the mud-flats; and now the only fish they saw were of varying sizes, right up to some monster pike. One of these must have been four-and-one-half feet long, estimated Jim. It swam up to her, made a sort of bow of obeisance in the water-air, then swam away again after being spoken to and petted by Melusine.

At last, Melusine turned back.

"Isn't it all wonderful?" Melusine sighed, as she and Jim skimmed along together over the lake bottom.

"It certainly is," agreed Jim with feeling. In fact there was reason for the feeling; because in the process of examining this end of the lake, he had seen that it would be much easier to climb out here than to mount the almost vertical underwater shore walls where he had first entered it.

If he could get away from Melusine and get this far, he told himself, he should have no trouble climbing up to the top of the lake and getting out on the land again. Then once on land he would take his chances of getting away from her. Possibly, after a short distance, beyond the point where she could sense that a dragon was nearby, he could turn himself back into one and fly well beyond her reach in a hurry.

As they sped back over the mud-flats toward the palace his mind was fumbling at what felt like the outline of a solution to the magical command—*spell* seemed like entirely the wrong word, to him now—that would keep air around him, if he got away from Melusine. He had made subtle little tests while she was enthusiastically showing him around, deliberately going some distance from her, to see how far away he had to get before he lost the envelope of water turned to air that she evidently produced for him. The critical distance did not seem much more than about ten feet.

On the other hand, back at the palace, even when she had been gone, he had continued to be surrounded by a breathable atmosphere. And there was still the curious matter of the fish seeming to swim through this atmosphere as if it were actual water.

But that was a minor question. The solution to his breathing underwater by use of his own magic had just taken form in his mind.

What he needed was something he could imagine out of his own experience—and he suddenly had it, out of an experiment in his chemistry class back when he had been in high school. It was the simple experiment in which a metal armature had been lowered into ordinary water and an electric current run through it. Bubbles of gas had been produced at either end as the water broke down into the two gases—hydrogen and oxygen—which were its component parts.

The formula had been simple.

$$2H_2O \longrightarrow 2H_2 + O_2$$

In fact, the process suggested a ridiculous little rhyme to him.

I'm an O_2 armature, thin or stout,
Come, you little O_2 bubbles, pop right out!

It was terrible poetry, but it let him visualize what he needed. Secretly, as they went along, he extended an arm on the side away from Melusine, who was chattering away in any case, and not noticing. He wrote on the inside of his forehead.

$$ME \longrightarrow O_2 \text{ ARMATURE}$$

Immediately, bubbles began to stream up from the ends of his fingertips. Hastily, he rewrote the command inside his forehead, reversing it. The bubbles ceased immediately.

He sighed silently with relief. One problem solved.

Now he needed the answer to that other question, which was how to leave the lake without Melusine knowing.

He woke suddenly to the fact that at the moment, however, neither problem was the immediate one. He should be concentrating on what he could do to elude what was clearly on Melusine's mind as they got closer and closer to the room with the large bed. He could not pull the headache trick again. Even if she might give in to it a second time, she would certainly begin to get suspicious. It was too bad he did not know some way to put her into a deep sleep—or at least make her so sleepy that the thought of lovemaking would be put off for a while. His mind galloped desperately down that particular trail.

The only thing that came to mind was the fact that he had mastered Carolinus's trick of turning wine into milk as a treatment for his stomach ulcer. One of the first little pieces of magic that Jim had tried after he got back from seeing Carolinus and learning how to turn himself from a dragon back into a human being again and vice versa, had been the business of trying to turn wine into milk, himself.

Jim liked milk as much as he did not care for grapes. But milk was not something ordinarily on the menu at Malencontri. In fact nobody, including the servants as far as he knew, drank it. Although out in the cottages, the people who belonged to his estate probably chewed or swallowed anything that was food at all, since the idea was to keep themselves alive with whatever was available.

At any rate, he had never quite gotten up the courage to order milk for himself at Malencontri. Instead, he had striven to master Carolinus's turning wine into milk.

And succeeded.

It had turned out to be rather simple. He understood more now how it could be. He already knew what milk tasted like, and he could imagine the taste on his tongue. He also knew what wine tasted like. It was fairly simple therefore to write on the inside of his forehead:

$$\text{WINE} \longrightarrow \text{MILK}$$

And have whatever vessel he was holding turn white and prove to contain milk instead.

The reason he had been able to do it so easily, he was beginning to understand now, was because both wine and milk could be clearly envisioned by him. Now, if only Melusine drank milk, he could change it to wine in her stomach, and possibly she might get drunk. Drunk enough so that she would lose interest in affectionate embraces with Jim. Although, come to think of it, if she was at all like these other medieval characters, he would probably have to fill her full of wine to make her pass out.

Unfortunately, he was sure that she did not drink milk. Down here under the lake would be the last place that a cow would be available—or anything else that gave milk for that matter. Some of the sea mammals produced milk; but this was a freshwater lake.

By this time they were back in the palace and approaching the bed. They settled down on it.

"My love," said Melusine, looking at him amorously, "you're quite right. I love you all the more for being interested in my lake."

"That's good," said Jim. "I mean I'm very happy; because I feel exactly the same way."

"You do?" she said; and her magical attraction shot up a good thousand watts.

Jim's mind searched desperately for a way out. Today's trip around the lake had only reinforced his original instinctive conviction that once he had given in to Melusine's emotion, he would be hooked by it and never have the courage and will to get away from her. His mind scrambled desperately once more and, under the pressure of great emergency, as minds will do, came up with an idea.

"Why don't we have a little wine together, first," he said. "We can toast our being together today, looking at the lake, the lake itself. I think it's a fine idea. Don't you?"

"Why . . . yes," said Melusine. She was kneeling as before, at his side on the bed. "You are most unusual James; and you do have the finest ideas."

She turned to the little school of fish that was always hovering around her here.

"Wine," she ordered, "and two crystal goblets. The very nicest crystal goblets I have."

She beamed at Jim.

The wine came, the small fish struggling with the full bottle, which they put down on the bed beside her, along with two very ornate, convoluted goblets of a type of sculptured glass Jim had not seen anywhere so far in this world.

"I think we ought to have two bottles, don't you?" asked Jim.

"Why not," said Melusine with a trace of a giggle. She clapped her hands and looked at her fish. "Another bottle."

"And something to open them with," suggested Jim.

"Pooh!" said Melusine with a soft wave of her hand. "If I tell a bottle to open up, it'll open up."

She picked up one of the ornate glasses and handed it to Jim, picked up the other in her left hand and picked up the bottle in her right.

"Cork!" she said, frowning at the top of the bottle, "come out!"

The cork obediently popped up in the air, leaving the top of the bottle open. Melusine filled her own glass, then filled Jim's. She evidently, Jim saw, liked white wines that fizzed. She set the bottle back down on the bed.

"Now stand upright," she warned it.

She turned away from the bottle and raised her glass to clink it with Jim's.

"To us, beloved," she said.

She drank. Jim drank. As he had suspected, the wine was a champagne—a rather sweet champagne, but an unusually tasty one. Even he, in his human body, found himself appreciating it.

They looked at each other, their glasses half-empty.

"Oh, I'm so happy," said Melusine, with a slight glisten in her eyes. "I've got my lovely lake and I've got lovely you and everything is going to be perfect forever and ever."

For a moment, inexplicably, Jim's conscience struck him. He had seen this individual before him talking cheerfully about pulling down dragons to their death and making sure their bones were well sunk into the mud-flat. At the same time, she seemed so wholeheartedly happy and deeply in love with her lake and him at this moment, that he suddenly felt like a dirty dog for thinking about escaping from her.

He put that feeling away from him as the last emotion he should feel, if he was going to escape.

He reached for the wine bottle, refilled their glasses, and set the bottle down. It stayed upright on its own this time.

"To your magnificent lake and all the magnificent plants and creatures in it," he said.

Again they drank, about half as much as they had drunk the first time, but still a noticeable amount.

The fish arrived with the second bottle and set it down beside the one already opened. It emulated the open one by standing upright. The fish then rose and circled just above their heads.

"This is just wonderful," said Melusine, as they finished the first bottle. Jim had been right. She did drink like the rest of the medieval people he had met. "The most wonderful day I ever had. Have some more wine."

She filled Jim's still three-quarters-full glass to the brim and completely refilled her own empty one.

"And, that's the difference," she said, leaning toward Jim. The wine in her glass started to slosh out, stopped in midair, turned around, and went back into the glass again. "Nobody before has ever understood what it's like to be Melusine. Nobody has the slightest understanding of Melusine. Poor Melusine!"

"Yes," said Jim, a little absently, "it must be hard. It must be very hard for you."

Most of his mind was off busily trying to put together an idea that had come to him on the wings of the memory of Carolinus's changing wine into milk. The recall did not come easily. Just to look good, he had drunk about a glass and a half of wine, himself; and these glasses were deceptive. They must hold at least a good pint of liquid each.

Jim concentrated. What was necessary was that he transmute something that was nonintoxicating into something that was intoxicating.

Or—the idea burst on him suddenly like a bright light in the back of his skull—from a less-intoxicating substance to a more-intoxicating substance!

"Hundreds and hundreds and hundreds of years," Melusine was saying, staring down at the cover of the bed, "and not really my fault at all. After all, somebody like me, with royal blood in them— I have royal blood in me, you know?"

She tugged at Jim's sleeve to attract his attention.

"Royal blood?" echoed Jim. "Oh, I was almost sure of it, from the way you look."

"That's right," said Melusine, "royal blood. I am the true daughter of Elinas, King of Albania. My mother was the fairy Pressine. But he was so cruel, my father. You just can't imagine how cruel he was. So I just had to shut him up in a mountain. I mean, what would you do? I'm sure you'd shut him up in a mountain too!"

She tugged at Jim's sleeve again.

"Don't you agree?"

Brandy! The thought exploded in Jim's mind. Yes, from wine to brandy would be the most natural step in the world, seeing brandy was made from wine. But Melusine already had abandoned the subject.

"Don't you think we've had enough wine?" she asked.

She put down her glass and waved her hand. The little fish congregated and took away not only her glass and the two bottles but the glass out of Jim's hand that was still better than two-thirds full.

Jim looked at her and saw that her attractiveness had suddenly glowed clear up to at least two thousand watts. He faced the fact that it was now or never.

Hastily he wrote on the inside of his forehead:

MELUSINE-WINE——→MELUSINE-BRANDY

Melusine threw herself into his arms.

"Oh, I'm so lonely!" she wailed.

Jim closed his eyes, desperate and helpless. Too late. He had been just a little too late. His mind felt empty. He could not think of anything left to do that might still save him. He sat there for a long minute or so, waiting for her to make another demand on him, or move in his arms; but she did not.

Cautiously, he opened his eyes and looked down at her.

Her own eyes were closed, her long lashes down on her cheeks. She looked like a sleeping child; and when Jim spoke to her, she neither opened her eyes nor answered.

The sudden change of well over two and a half pints of wine into brandy in her stomach—fairy or not—had had its effect. She was out cold.

Chapter 20

Melusine's fish gathered about her worriedly as he laid her down. They paid no attention to Jim, which was just as well. He was already on his feet and on his way out of the palace. He had barely escaped beyond the limits of the palace when he went, in a single breath, from breathing what seemed like normal air to what seemed like something that was half-water. Hastily, he wrote the magic formula on the inside of his forehead that would change him into an oxygen-producing electrode, and the atmosphere around him cleared. Bubbles streamed up from the end of his arm. Experimentally, he tried extending the other arm and that also produced bubbles. In fact, now that he stopped to notice it, he had a prickly sensation all over his body including his scalp. He was apparently exuding oxygen from every point on the surface of his body.

He headed toward the far end of the lake. Since he was not with Melusine, he no longer skimmed along above the surface of the lake bottom, but had to tramp it as if it were ordinary dry ground. He thought with a shudder of the mud-flats, and remembered that they did not stretch quite to the walls of the lake. He therefore angled toward the nearest lakeside, which was the one from which Melusine had originally pulled him down, and found there enough rocky surface—even if sharply angled upward, into the nearly vertical cliffs that walled in the lake at this point—so that he could continue toward the far end of the lake, where it would be possible to get out of it entirely.

It was not until he got into the far end of the lake with its gullies and its mounts, and away from the mud, that he began to be conscious of potential opposition to his leaving. The edge on which he walked had lasted all the way around the sea of mud and he was traveling nicely up the underwater slopes among the weeds and other growth, before he was aware that those accompanying him had been getting definitely more threatening—and able to threaten.

Somewhere along the line the little fish, like those that served Melusine in her palace, had begun to cluster about him, apparently held at a distance by the bubble of oxygen around him. Happily, the magic that produced it was making it stay with him on the lake bottom, instead of streaming up to the surface and leaving him exposed not only to the lake water, but its inhabitants.

These fish were none of them friendly, for all of their tiny size. He paid them very little mind until he reached the far end of the lake, when their numbers began to be swelled by much larger fish. By the time the water was getting quite light around him and he felt the surface could be only about fifteen or twenty feet away, he was completely surrounded, not by little fish, but by pike the size of that four-and-a-half-foot specimen that had greeted Melusine when she had brought Jim here earlier.

There was no doubt about the fact that the pike were not friendly. They clashed their jaws at the extremity of the bubble, but either could not or did not want to enter it. Jim wondered fleetingly whether it was the magic that kept them from coming through, or the fact that the bubble was effectively pure oxygen. In fact, if it had not been for a certain amount of moistening of the gas by the water around it, he suspected he would have been uncomfortable breathing it before this. As it was, his mouth and throat and nose felt increasingly dry.

But now, the surface was not far away. Very soon his head broke water and he saw that he was only about twenty yards from shore. He waded toward it, his bubble clinging to those parts of him that were still below the surface, until he came at last upon a rocky shoal that led him abruptly up and out of the lake entirely. He stood at last on shore, unnaturally and ridiculously dry from the top of his head to the soles of his feet, while a large school of disappointed pike prowled angrily along the shoreline behind him.

His first feeling was one of immense relief. Then came one of apprehension. After all, Melusine was not just any other human. She was an elemental—or, if her father actually had been the King of Albania, perhaps she was only half an elemental.

In any case, there was no telling how quickly she would recover from a large dose of brandy. Nor what her reaction would be. She would hardly be happy with

Jim for having tricked and escaped her. The question was, what would she do about it?

Would she simply sit there in the lake and hold a grudge, hoping for some future time to pay him back? Or would she actually make an attempt to follow and recapture him? With all these unknowns, the smartest thing he could think of to do was to get out of this area as quickly as possible.

He had intended to stay on foot until he was beyond the range of her dragon perception. But if she was still sleeping the sleep of the well-brandied just, then there was no reason for him to delay getting back on wing and gaining some distance from her. He stripped off his clothes, remade his bundle, and hung it around his neck loosely enough so that it would not choke him once he became a dragon—and changed bodies.

It was a great relief being back in his dragon body again, he found. Along with that body went a whole set of dragon emotions and dragon attitudes. And where he, in his human body, had perhaps too much imagination for his own good; in his dragon body he had a lot less imagination, so that his worry over how Melusine might react dwindled considerably; and he had a great deal more confidence in his own size, strength, and readiness to take care of himself.

It struck Jim that in his dragon body he was a lot closer to the human medieval point of view, than he was in his human one.

In any case, it was time to fly. He leaped into the air, spread his wings, and climbed for altitude.

He found convenient thermals only about two thousand feet above the ground, and commenced soaring in the general direction of Amboise and the road toward Orléans, somewhere below which Malvinne's castle stood.

It was late afternoon; and in spite of the fact that this was only reasonable, since he could count back over his time in Melusine's bed and the time he had spent examining the interior of her lake with her, the lateness of the day was disorienting. Instinctively he found himself feeling that he ought to have come out of the lake at roughly the same time of day at which he had gone in—to wit, noon.

In essence, although he knew better it felt as if no time should have gone by at all while he was under the water. Actually he knew very well that he had lost at least two nights, one with Melusine and one with Sorpil and Maigra. The distance from where he had left Giles to Amboise was not really that far. Giles had undoubtedly reached it by this time and set himself up at an inn. But the lateness of the day had aspects that might pose problems.

Sir Raoul had given them some information on Amboise, but in any case Jim would have been sure that it would be a walled city. Almost all the medieval towns were. Usually, the wall was nothing more than a tall palisade running completely

around the important part of the city, with a scattering of dwelling places taking
their chances outside those walls.

The walls would not be for defense alone. They were also useful for keeping
people in, and regulating who came in. The gates would be shut at sundown; and
that meant that anyone in the town who wanted to sneak out and not be
recognized by the gate guards, would be penned up where he or she was until
morning.

Similarly, anyone attempting to enter who seemed at all suspicious, or
threatening, could be arrested by the gate guards and disarmed, and/or taken into
the city to have judgment pronounced upon him or her. Further, the gates allowed
the city to collect taxes on goods coming and going for sale within the city. This
was both a neat and necessary matter from the viewpoint of the city treasury.

On wing, as he was, Jim was covering ground much faster than Giles would
have, even on horseback, down on the surface. Nonetheless, it was very close to
sunset, and once the gates were barred, it would be unwise of him to try to get
in—either flying in as a dragon, for fear someone would see him; or as a human
being attempting to bribe the guards to open the gate momentarily, or otherwise
allow him an entrance—simply because they would remember particularly anyone
who came in under those circumstances.

If he could not get in before the gates were closed, the only sensible thing to do
would be to spend the night outside in dragon form. Then, turning back into his
human shape, he could mingle with those coming and going through the gate in
the daylight. He had his story ready for this. He was a little too well dressed to be
a simple man-at-arms; but he could claim to be a knight whose horse had had an
accident or otherwise died under him; and say his retainers had gone on ahead into
the city the day before. He could even give them Sir Giles's name, although that
probably would not be necessary. This, plus a small bribe—there was no hope of
getting away with no bribe at all—should get him in without fuss.

At a city gate you either paid taxes or a bribe, if you came in through it at all.
This way he could slip through and be forgotten in a short while. Then it would
be simply a matter of looking up Giles.

He had reached this point in his thoughts when a new sense of caution took
hold of him. He had been following the road to Amboise from the air for some
time now, trusting to his distance above the surface, and his similarity to other
flying creatures such as birds, to make him unremarkable to anyone who might be
below.

But now it occurred to him that anyone who looked closely at him from the
ground was bound to make out fairly quickly that he was no bird, but a dragon.
Birds might be unremarkable. Dragons were not. Since his chances of making it
through the Amboise gates before sunset were small anyway, perhaps it would be

wiser of him to go back down to the ground now, change into his human form and clothes, and proceed on foot as far as he could, until night fell.

Then, under cover of darkness, he could change back into a dragon—since dragons could sleep quite comfortably in the outdoors, ignoring small things like changes in temperature and occasional rainfalls—get a good night's sleep, and be up at dawn and back into his human shape and clothes to go in with the early crowd to the gate.

It fact, it would not be a bad idea to be among the first crowd that came in through the gate. At that time the guards would have a lot of people to check; and they would probably want to deal with these people as quickly as possible, get their tax or bribe or whatever was coming from them, and let them in.

He must have, Jim estimated, at least a couple of days' beard by now, which would back up his story of being a knight who had lost his horse at some point back on the road. Perhaps he could tell a story about being attracted by some wild animal that he thought he could ride down and dispatch with sword or lance; and it had been while chasing this animal away from the road that his horse had broken a leg and needed to be killed and left.

Accordingly, he looked around for a patch of trees, and did a quick descent. There he changed back into being Sir James Eckert, Dragon Knight; and set forth on foot once more toward the road and the rest of the way into Amboise, which he had estimated from the air as being about five miles distant.

The road was nothing to write home about. It was dry and dusty this time of year, but it was also deeply rutted and pocked with potholes that he could avoid, possibly a horse could avoid, but a cart would have a very rough time with. Yet carts must travel regularly up this route which led eventually to Paris.

Still, it was slower going than he had estimated. He resigned himself to the fact that there was no real hope of reaching the village gate before it closed. He began, indeed, to look around for someplace to spend the night as a dragon, and saw that just ahead the road curved into a fairly thick woods and, somewhat to his surprise, suddenly improved as far as its surface went. Somone had been at work on this stretch of it.

He was well into the woods, and just thinking that this might indeed be the very place that he would want to curl up for the night, when he began to hear the sound of the bell, like a church bell, coming from ahead of him.

He was still too far from Amboise for it to be one of the churches inside the city walls. Intrigued, he picked up his pace a little, aided by the now much smoother surface of the road which compensated for the fact that here, shaded by the fully summer-leafed trees, it was not so easy to judge the depths of ruts and potholes as it had been out in the full late sunlight of the day.

The bell continued to toll. It was really very close indeed, and the trees were thinning. A moment later Jim had stepped out from underneath them into a full moment of sunset, with the rays striking red across an open field to gild a whole complex of large buildings, most of them built of a brown stone. Into a sharp-roofed wing of one of these large buildings a group of figures in brown robes, their hands tucked in their sleeves, was proceeding single file.

At their head walked a heavier man dressed as they were, with the cowl piled up behind his head and the hooked top of an abbatical staff carried in his right hand. Before him walked a smaller, single figure carrying a pole which supported a crucifix which seemed to be of gold, for it caught the final red light of the sun and burned brilliantly against the dark stone of the building.

Jim halted. He was seeing a monastery, with its monks filing in for some special service at the normal evening prayer-time of vespers.

He stood watching. The sunset, the solid buildings, the black and open doorway, the file of slowly moving figures, and the steady, slow tolling of the bell overhead struck some unexpected, deep chord of feeling in him. The road that he had been following led toward the buildings and then away from them again. It was as if the moment and the whole image of it was a picture of that retreat from the bloody outside world that the medieval Church alone offered at this time.

For a moment, strangely, he felt drawn toward the figures and toward the buildings. He was not built to be one of them; but for the first time he felt deeply within him how a man of this time could want to turn his back on the rest of the world and enter this special and secluded sanctuary where the battles of knights and princes and Dark powers did not enter.

He could not help himself. He stood watching until the last of them had disappeared inside, the door had closed, and the bell at last ceased to sound. The sun was now setting squarely upon the open horizon to his left. He cut across from the part of the road he was on, that still pointed toward the monastery; to the part beyond, that carried back into the outside world.

Shortly, he was on it, and heading toward the town beyond, which was still not in sight. For a little while the road continued to be cared for and well surfaced, but in a bit it went back to its ruts and potholes again, and the general state of disrepair in which it had been since he had first begun to follow it.

Chapter 21

Within minutes after leaving the monastery, the road took Jim through another band of trees and into a wide, open space; A cleared space, in effect, as there were cleared spaces around all castles and dwellings of any size anywhere for defensive purposes, beyond which Amboise was fully visible.

The gates were shut.

It was no more than he expected, but he felt an instinctive irritation at the idea of a night's delay. Nonetheless, since there was nothing to be done for it, he turned back on the road to find himself a place for the night.

The last patch of trees was too thin to provide any real cover or security. Jim went all the way back past the monastery into the growth of trees beyond, that was much deeper and wider. Penetrating into these, and after having been lashed in the face by a number of branches and tripped up by a number of roots, he decided he might as well change into dragon form now as later, and did so.

Now he was much better off. Not only was he more at home in the dark, but he had a nose, a pair of ears, and a sort of animal sense of ground underfoot that he had not had before, all of which made his penetration through the woods easier. He simply shoved through patches of brush and small growths of sapling with his heavier dragon body, not only able to push the lighter stems aside, but able to ignore those that rebounded to hit his thick, scaled hide as he passed.

The wood was wider than it was deep; and he found this to his advantage. He went several hundred yards off the road, to be on the safe side, and was just looking for a convenient hollow in which he could curl up, when he all but ran into an upthrust of rock.

It was not a large upthrust. It was rather like a large, rectangular chunk of rock that had been tipped up on one end, so that a little less than a hundred feet of it stuck up through the earth. The rock itself was naked of vegetation except around its base, where some weeds and small bushes gathered like a fringe of circular beard. Its sides were not the sort that his dragon body would find easy to climb. He backed off a small distance to find a spot that would give him wing space; then spread his wings and leaped into the air, flying upward toward the top of the rock.

He came to it almost immediately. It was no more than a hundred feet high. But it did reach up above the treetops, and it did have a relatively flat top itself—in fact, not only was there a flat space there; but one that had been somewhat dished out by time and weather, so that it would make a natural curling-up place. He proceeded to settle himself down into it.

Comfortable in spite of the rough stone underneath him, because of his tough dragon hide, Jim gazed drowsily across the trees, adjusting his telescopic dragon vision for a view of the city of Amboise, in which lights were now beginning to glimmer. A freak of the darkness and the lights made it seem closer than it was, almost as if it lay only a short distance from the foot of the spire of rock on which he nested. He was drowsily amusing himself with the thought of lying in a place from which he essentially overlooked the city walls at close quarters, when a voice spoke from just below him.

"What are you here for?" asked the voice.

It was the voice of a dragon.

Jim woke up completely and looked down. Even through the darkness he was able to make out the winged shape clinging to the outswell of the rock spire some fifteen feet below him, almost in the manner of a bat clinging to the rough wall of a cave.

"For that matter," he answered, "what are you doing here?"

"I've got a right to be here," the shadowy dragon form retorted. "I'm a French dragon. And you're in my territory."

Jim's dragon temper, as ready to respond to a challenge as the human tempers of Brian or Giles, went up a few degrees.

"I'm a guest in your country," he said. "I've left a passport, which was accepted by two French dragons named Sorpil and Maigra—"

"We know all about that," the other dragon began. Jim reinterrupted this interrupter.

"And that gives me the freedom of your country. I don't have to tell you what I'm doing here. That's my affair. Who are you to question me anyway?"

"Never mind who I am," said the other. His or her voice was definitely more highly pitched than Jim's; and from what Jim could make out of the other's shape, he or she was also a considerably smaller dragon. "It's only natural for a French dragon to want to know what you're doing in his area."

"It may be natural," said Jim, "but I'm afraid any French dragon that wants to know anything like that is going to have to go on not knowing. As I said, my affair is my affair—and nobody else's. 'Nobody else' includes you."

There was a long silence. Jim waited for the other to say or do something more, telling himself that all it needed was one more prying question, and he would launch himself off the top of this rock down upon his questioner.

But, evidently, that was not to be.

"You'll regret not being friendly and telling us. Wait and see!" said the other finally. With a sudden flapping of wings it disappeared from the rock spire into the night.

It took Jim a few minutes to calm down again. His dragon emotions, once aroused, did not quieten as easily as his human ones. He turned his attention back to Amboise to get his mind off the late conversation; but a trickle of adrenalin in him prodded him in the wrong direction.

He suddenly found himself thinking of himself as a dragon perched here, not so much for a place of rest and security but as a vantage point for attack. A point from which he could swoop down into the town and carry off a small plump morsel of a george which he could bring back to this spire to feast on at leisure.

The shocking nature of the thought broke him out of it. He had never really considered georges as being eatable by dragons; certainly not by himself as a dragon. In fact, he was sure that he could not bring himself to eat a human being. However, as a dragon he had fed on a number of freshly slaughtered, completely raw animals, including everything but the hooves and bones, and had found them very tasty indeed. He was uncomfortably sure that a normal dragon might just find a human equally eatable. The only reason, he thought, that dragons did not go around eating georges nowadays was because of the trouble such activities would produce for them.

Above all, dragons preferred to have life as easy as possible. While they enjoyed a good fight once they were into it, it was usually too much trouble to go looking for fights. Moreover, most of them over the centuries had developed a healthy respect for what georges could do, even before the days of armed knights on horseback with lances. For one thing there were so many georges.

Jim was beginning to feel drowsy again. This also was natural dragon behavior.

Dragons liked to drink, liked to eat, and liked to sleep. In the absence of food and drink, sleep came naturally. Even as he completed the thought, Jim's eyes closed and he fell sound asleep.

The first brightening of the predawn woke him; which was not surprising, seeing that up on this piece of rock, he had a direct line of sight to the eastern horizon, beyond the city, where the coming day's illumination was beginning to brighten the sky. Again, like all healthy dragons, he woke up all at once, not feeling the least bit sleepy, nor the least bit stiff or heavy from having spent the whole night in a curled-up position.

He was both hungry and thirsty, but a dragon could ignore these things, being used to doing without food and drink for fairly long periods, sometimes, until supplies of either one became available.

He flew down to the base of the rock, changed back into his human form, dressed and headed for Amboise. Some twenty minutes later he was in position just inside the first rank of trees, a little ways off the road to the left, with his eye on the gates. The waiting crowd in front of it had grown to some thirty or forty people and at least half as many carts and draft animals.

The sun rose. It climbed higher in the sky, and the gates remained closed. Jim told himself that this was only to be expected. The guards would open the gates at their own convenience, balanced against the fact that local merchants and certain influential city dwellers might object, if potential customers or suppliers were kept from them. At some point in time the impulse not to offend their superiors would balance their natural laziness, and the gates begin to open.

They did, at last. By this time the sun was not only up, but could be seen beyond the walls above the city itself. It was a good half hour after actual sunrise.

With the first outswinging of one of the twin gates, Jim started off at a fast walk from the trees to the road, and down the road toward the gate. He need not have hurried too much. Both wings of the gate were fully open and the first of the waiting crowd were beginning to be processed through by the guards, before he reached the outer edge of those still waiting their turn.

Jim had been able to give his entrance some thought before he got to this point. The answer, he had decided, was to act as much like a typical knight as possible. How would Brian or Giles act in a similar position? Not that either one of them were exactly representative of their class. They were feisty enough, but they were not quite nasty enough. Jim had decided to add a touch of nastiness to his rendition of a footsore and unhorsed knight who had been out in the open since yesterday.

The bodies were packed fairly thickly around the gate; and a medieval bunch like this was not a crowd which someone could shove through in a twentieth-century manner, with polite murmurs of "Excuse me" and "Could I get through please?" Accordingly, he took advantage of his size and weight and hit the crowd where he thought it was thinnest, rather like a football fullback hitting a wall of opposing linemen.

"Out of my way, clods!" he roared as he plunged into them, shoulder first. There were no men anywhere near as tall as himself in the crowd, but there were a few solidly built ones, some of whom undoubtedly outweighed him. And this was a case where weight could be a factor. "You there, fellow! Attend me!"

Those he had crashed through turned swiftly to face him. But the terms of his address, naming them clods and addressing the gateman as "fellow," caused them to fall back and give him room. The guard, who had been about to accept either his tax or his bribe from a character in flour-whitened clothes and with a mule-drawn cart behind him, turned indignantly. But he changed his attitude at the sight of Jim's clothing, plus the sword and poignard depending from his sword belt.

"Let me through at once!" snapped Jim, almost running down the guard, who stepped back to one side obsequiously. "Your damned roads and fields broke the leg of a damn good horse and I've been out in the damn woods all the damn night! Here—let me through!"

With the word *here*, he thrust a coin at the gateman. It was a silver ecu, which was far too rich a tip to be handing out in a situation like this. But it was the smallest coin he had on him at the moment; and he hoped that the overrich bribe would be taken by the guard as evidence of the fact that this gentleman, whoever he might be, having lost a horse and spent a night in the woods, was thoroughly out of temper.

"Thanks m'Lord, much thanks!" said the gate guard, hastily swallowing the coin with his closed fist, so that it disappeared immediately from sight. He could have no idea whether Jim was a Lord or not, but there was no harm in using the term; and there might be a great deal of harm in failing to give Jim sufficient rank. Jim shouldered past him and a second later was in the streets of the city.

Half a minute later he had turned a corner and was out of sight of the gate completely.

He had turned into a side street which was narrow enough that he would have been able to extend his arms on either side and touch some rather unappetizing walls. It was carpeted with ordure of all kinds, animal and human, and ran between either the high sides of buildings, or walls that were solid and almost as high. Jim went down the street as far as he had to before finding a cross-street. Cross-alley would actually, he thought, have been a better term. He turned left, following the route that he believed would take him deeper into the city.

This alley, however, wandered about, so that when he took the next left turning, he found himself still with a long stretch of alley in front of him. It was some time before he blundered back into a street that was wide enough, and cared-for enough, so that it was obviously the main street from the gate. By this time, however, he was happily out of sight of the gate and everyone at it.

He would need information to find Sir Giles. The best way to get it would be to find a shop of any kind, and see if the shopkeeper could lend him or hire him a guide that would take him to the various inns about the town. Simple directions from the shop to the inn, Jim had learned by hard experience in the streets of Worcester and every other medieval town he had been in since, would only result in his getting lost again within fifty steps.

Jim therefore continued on until he found a shop that made boots. Here he struck a deal with the bootmaker to hire one of his assistants. Experience had taught him to hire one of the people working in the shop, rather than somebody they whistled off the streets for him. Very often the person brought in from the streets was someone the shopkeeper had signaled to lead Jim into some kind of a trap where he could be robbed, if not murdered. But an employee usually had some value to the shop owner, and was less likely to lead Jim to such an ambush.

Again, it was a matter of carrying off the transaction with a high hand. Jim swore luridly, pounded the counter, was rude in every way he could think of, and felt that, all-in-all, he had given a pretty good presentation of someone of gentlemanly rank who was not at all in good humor.

This behavior signaled two things to those he was talking to, he knew. One, that at the slightest provocation he would use that sword that hung at his side. Two, that he might well have influential friends within the town, who could make things even more uncomfortable for those who had to deal with Jim than Jim himself could.

The charade worked. Apparently the town was well aware of there being Englishmen within it who had arrived just recently; and that among these was one short Englishman with a luxuriant handlebar mustache. This upper lip adornment —in a time when nearly all knights were cleanshaven—was in itself an outstanding piece of identification.

Sir Giles and a number of other Englishmen seemed to have come into town just lately. They were at the biggest inn in town, and overflowing that, since they had brought along a number of what the bootmaker considered to be fierce-looking servitors. So many, in fact, that most had needed to be farmed out among various barns, and even houses, to find them quarters. The bootmaker did not know any of their names; but he knew that one of the Englishmen had a very large and savage dog with him, which he had evidently brought along to guard his room and possessions.

Not that such guarding was necessary in Amboise, the bootmaker insisted. In fact it was almost an insult to the town for the Englishman to have such a beast. On the other hand, what could you do with some great lords? Particularly great lords from—well—

At this point, the bootmaker suddenly seemed to recollect that it was another such Englishman that he was talking to, and not a fellow Frenchman. He left the sentence hanging in the air and cursed at the apprentice for standing around, delaying the gentleman instead of taking him directly to the inn as fast as possible.

The apprentice hastily led Jim off. He followed the youngster, still bemused by the thought that the bootmaker could seriously think that he, Jim, could seriously believe that there was no danger of robbery, even at the best inn in any town. On land as on sea, in this age, two laws overrode everything else. One was the law of personal survival. The second was the law of greatest possible gain—though the various classes wanted the gain for different reasons.

The peasantry, the poorest of the poor, wanted gain in order to keep themselves alive. People like the bootmaker wanted gain to climb in status among their fellows. People of the gentlemanly class, from Brian and Giles clear on up to the royal heads of kingdoms themselves, wanted gain in order that they could not merely indulge their whims, but make royal gestures from a large source of funds.

In fact the upper class, as far as Jim had been able to figure out, was to a certain extent always on stage when in public. Kings down through simple knights acted out the role that they believed God had assigned them; and, while satisfying personal desires ran a close second, the first was to appear on the world's stage as the best possible representation of what they were supposed to be.

In effect, knights were supposed to act knightly, kings were supposed to act royally, in exactly the manner in which an actor of a later date would portray a knight or a king for the benefit of an audience which had paid to see him.

But here they were, already at the inn, the entrance to which looked no different from any of the other holes-in-the-wall they had passed on the way, in which shops only betrayed their presence by having their doors ajar, as a signal that they were open for business.

The door was also ajar at the inn; and Jim pushed it open and went in, without tipping the apprentice and turning him loose until he was sure he was at the right place. But this was confirmed by the innkeeper who came forward immediately to greet him—this time a man as tall as Jim, but very thin and with a mustache. It was not a proud and up-twisted mustache like Sir Giles's, but one which hung, long, thin, black, and down-pointed on each side of his wide mouth. The innkeeper established the fact that not only was Sir Giles here but so was the other knight.

"And this other knight," demanded Jim, "what might his name and rank be?"

"Sir Brian Neville-Smythe, Your Lordship," said the innkeeper. He pronounced the title in a surprising bass voice. "They're friends it seems; and are expecting yet another friend. Would Your Lordship be the Baron James de Bois de Malencontri?"

"I am," said Jim, and almost forgot to scowl properly as he said it, so happy he was to discover that it was Brian who was here—obviously with the men he was supposed to bring—and that both he and Giles were expecting Jim himself. "Take me to them at once."

"Certainly," answered the innkeeper, turning toward the stairs, that in this, as in the previous inns of Jim's experience, led directly to the first floor above ground level.

"Oh, and tip this lad for me," snapped Jim. "Add it to my bill."

Having neatly got around the matter of having no small change with which to tip the bootmaker's assistant, Jim followed the innkeeper up the stairs, once the latter had slipped a small coin to the bootmaker's assistant and turned once more to lead Jim to his friends.

The reunion was boisterous. Giles and Brian both welcomed Jim as if he had been a long, lost brother.

Jim had originally been a little puzzled by the tendency of people of this world to make such a large matter out of greeting someone they might not have seen for merely a day or two. He finally came to understand that under the conditions of this time and place, any two people who were parted stood a fairly reasonable chance of never seeing each other again.

Death was a lot closer and a lot more possible here than it was in the twentieth century. Even a simple visit to a nearby town could mean encountering either accidental or willful destruction, so that the person going might never come back, at least alive.

Jim had finally adjusted to the practice; both in the greeting, and the inevitable celebration which such occasions seem to call for. He was consequently so occupied, in the first few minutes of the welcomings of Brian and Giles, that it was not for some moments that he noticed a very large, dark-furred, four-legged body lying comfortably on its side upon the baggage that Brian had brought with him.

Jim turned about.

"Aargh!" he said.

Aargh opened his eyes, which had been closed, and half raised his head from the stuffed saddlebag upon which he had been lying.

"Who were you expecting, James?" he growled, "some lady's lapdog?"

"Well, no," said Jim. "I'm just glad to see you. But—"

"And now you're about to ask me what I'm doing here, is that it?" said Aargh.

"As a matter of fact, yes," admitted Jim. He was about to explain further but Aargh cut in again.

"Don't," said Aargh. He closed his eyes and laid his head down again.

Jim turned back to his two friends and looked at Brian, who shrugged his shoulders slightly and shook his head. So apparently Brian did not know either. Jim put the matter aside for the moment. Meanwhile, Giles had already ordered up the inevitable pitcher of wine and wine cups. Seated around the table in their quarters, Jim began to catch up on what had been happening to the other two.

Giles, it seemed, had had an uneventful day-and-a-half's ride after leaving Jim, before he reached Amboise and put up at the inn. He had scarcely been there an hour, however, when there was a commotion outside; and he went downstairs to find Brian arriving with a number of their men.

As might have been expected, the arrival of such a force of armed individuals within the walls of the town had caused a considerable fluster there. Particularly, since the armed men happened to be English rather than French; although it was the habit of the good citizens of these towns to look askance at anyone whose trade seemed to be war and battle.

"The uproar began at the gates," Brian explained, taking over from Giles, "but since there were only four guards on the gate, and none of them had the wit to take notice of us until we were right at the gateposts themselves, we simply rode on past them. After that, it was just a matter of following the main street until we could collar somebody and get them to point out the largest and best inn in this town."

"I can imagine it," said Jim. He could, indeed.

"There was a fresh uproar at the inn here," Brian went on. "There were far too many of us for the inn to have even enough outbuildings to shelter us all. Happily our innkeeper—you've see him?"

"Yes," answered Jim. "He told me you two were here and led me up here to you."

"He's a long drink of water and may not look like much," said Brian, "but he's a tidy enough man for all that. As tidy, I wager, as anyone to be met in this city. Unless I miss my guess he's been a man-at-arms himself, when he was younger. At any rate, he, of all the rest, kept a cool head. He saw to it that the men found some kind of roof in each case, and formed a plan for getting food to everybody. Then he brought me up here to Giles."

"And glad I was to see him," said Giles, twisting his mustache happily. "We're now a good little force in case we meet with any band of Frenchmen. Also I felt that with him here, you could not be far behind. And, by St. Cuthbert, here you are."

"Yes," said Jim, "and I'm glad to be back with the two of you too."

He looked at Brian.

"To tell the truth, I'd hoped; but I really hadn't expected you this quickly, Brian," he said, "particularly with the men along with you. How many did you bring, by the way?"

"Thirty-two," answered Brian. "The rest are still behind us with John Chester and Tom Seiver. I brought only the seasoned men, including your new squire, Theoluf. As for our being able to catch up with you so quickly, it was a matter of their getting shipped shortly after you left. For that we have to thank—"

Jim held up his hand.

"Aargh," he said, looking over at the apparently sleeping wolf. "Is there anybody close enough so that they could be listening to us, through a hole in the floor or a tube in the wall, or some such thing?"

"No stink of your kind except the three of you within a good dozen lengths of my own body," answered Aargh without opening his eyes.

"Thanks, Aargh," said Jim. He turned back to Brian. "However, I think that from now on maybe we ought to avoid using certain names of people or places out loud, anyway. Perhaps there're no ears to hear; but it doesn't do any harm to play safe."

"You're right indeed, James," said Brian, and Giles murmured an admiring assent. "At any rate, we were able to move quickly and reach this town before you yourself. There you have it in a nutshell."

"I stifle in this box here," said the voice of Aargh, but when Jim looked at him he was still lying with his eyes closed and apparently unmoved. "When do we get out of here?"

"Is there any reason why we can't move out tomorrow?" Jim asked the other two.

They both shook their heads.

"There're some things we should discuss, though," said Brian. "James, you remember that our friend's advice was that I stay behind you with the men. Sitting where he was at the time, that may have seemed most sensible to him. But my own counsel now is that we leave the men under their present leaders to follow; including all those I've brought with me, save one, who should be of particular use and cannot be left behind in any case. These five of us will go on by ourselves in advance. Sir Giles and I have had some talk on this; and we can give you more of our reasons once we're out on the open road and can speak with absolute freedom."

"The five of us, that is, including Aargh," put in Sir Giles.

"Absolutely including Aargh," came the voice of Aargh himself.

"Of course, Aargh," said Jim hastily.

He looked curiously at Brian, however.

"Who is the fifth, though?"

"You passed him in the common room on the way in," answered Brian, "although he may not have been easy to see; since he likes to tuck himself into a corner and he is a quiet man in many ways. The Welsh bowman is with us."

Chapter 22

"Dafydd?" said Jim increduously.

Brian's and Giles's faces showed no expression at all. Obviously this was something that Jim would have to find out about for himself; and probably directly from Dafydd. On the other hand, if he knew Dafydd, there would be no point in asking the Welshman directly. He would get a pleasant, soft answer that told him nothing, and probably a polite hint that he should mind his own business.

Accordingly, he put everything else out of his mind for the moment and lost himself in the celebration of the occasion. It was not until the next day, when the five of them were on the road to Blois and Malvinne's castle, somewhere beyond Blois, that he thought about asking a few of those questions that were knocking around in his head.

The weather had cooled off a little bit, although it was still a warm summer day. The countryside had not had rain for a couple of weeks now; and was beginning to show the effect of it.

The road was more than a little dusty. The three knights rode first, side by side, each with a lead rein to the war-horse behind him.

Just behind them rode Dafydd, his long legs tucked up on either side of the horse that had been given him, in order to fit his feet into the stirrups at the maximum extension that their straps allowed. The Welshman's sling was gone, his bow was over his shoulder, and on the other shoulder was his quiver of arrows, neatly covered against a sudden change in weather. Behind him on his horse was a pack of his own personal supplies, including the tools he used for working on bow staves and arrows. On leads from his horse, followed three sumpter horses with all their baggage and supplies.

Aargh had vanished the minute they were beyond the city and screened by trees. Jim did not really blame the wolf. He knew how the other hated to be penned up. Several nights spent in what must have been like a wild clamor of smells and noises at the inn, would be more than enough to justify Aargh wanting to be off by himself for a while.

Jim felt sure the other would rejoin them, if not at the end of this day, when they camped for the night, then within a day or two after that. Certainly he would have reestablished connection with them once they were beyond Blois and moving directly for Malvinne's castle.

But there was another matter that could be investigated now. Jim made his excuses to Giles and Brian, and dropped back to ride level with Dafydd.

"Forgive me for not taking time to talk to you before this, Dafydd," he said. "I can't tell you how happy I am to have you with us."

"Indeed, I am happy that you are happy," replied Dafydd, in his gentle voice. "It is well that at least one of us should find my being here a good thing."

"You don't regard it as a good thing yourself, then?" Jim asked.

"I am not sure at all," said Dafydd, "whether it is a good thing, or whether I should think it so. I will not deny that I am attracted, as I always have been, to unknown places; and people who might be powerful with bow or crossbow—with any other weapon, for that matter. For I am interested, look you, in those who make an art of weapon use, no matter what that weapon might be. Still, I cannot say that I am happy to be where I am; though I am not really unhappy. It is a strange mixture of feelings that I have, Sir James, and I am not sure in truth how I feel at any moment."

"It's certainly possible to like a situation for one reason, and not to like it for another," said Jim. "I run into that myself. However, it's something that usually takes care of itself in the long run. One feeling or the other comes to the top and stays there."

"I do not think that will be the case with my feelings, indeed," said Dafydd, gazing ahead between the ears of his horse at the road. "Since both feelings in me stem from causes in that island from which we both came, I doubt that they will resolve themselves here. Yet you, Sir James, and the other two worthy knights, are both good friends and brave company to be in. So I do not regret being here."

"I'm glad to hear that," said Jim. "If there's anything I can do to help you at any time, just ask."

"I will that," said Dafydd. "In fact—"

His gaze ranged ahead to Brian and Giles, who had increased their lead somewhat, so that their dust would not be directly in the faces of both Jim and Dafydd—but most particularly in Jim's. What with the sound of the two knights' horses' hooves and their own animated conversation, they were effectively out of earshot of anything that Jim and Dafydd might say.

"Yes," said Dafydd to the horse's ears, "perhaps I will impose on your kind offer of help, Sir James. Perhaps you might favor me with some advice, so be it you have advice to give me in this matter."

"Anything I can," said Jim.

Dafydd raised his gaze from the horse's ears and looked sideways at Jim.

"We are both married men, are we not?" he said. "I do not mean to presume upon your rank, Sir James, but there is that in common between us, is there not?"

"Of course," answered Jim. "As for the matter of rank, forget it, Dafydd. We are old friends in a sense that makes rank of no importance."

"It is good indeed of you to say it," said Dafydd, "so I will ask you a question. Do you find that the Lady Angela puzzles you mightily at times?"

Jim laughed.

"Often," he said.

"I am sorely puzzled by Danielle," said Dafydd, "and, look you, for no small reason. Almost from the moment I first saw her, I gave her all my heart. And if it were possible, after that I gave her all that remained, so that for some time now I have belonged to her—heart, body, and soul. Also, I would have sworn that she had done no less to me; so that we could not be more in love, the two of us, and could not be more happy together than we were. And indeed, happy we were until just a month or two before you left England. Then came a strange time upon us, in which it seemed that in some way I could do nothing right."

He paused, and rode for a long, long moment of silence, staring at the horse's ears before him.

"Go on," Jim urged him finally. "That is, if you want to."

"I do want to," said Dafydd, "for in this I have come up against something that is beyond all I've understood of life in the years I've lived it. Always, the road was clear before me. If something was needed, then I had only to reach inside myself to find it. If it was the art of a bowyer, I reached and found it. If it was the art of a fletcher, I reached and found it. If it was marksmanship with a bow, that too I found. And when I found Danielle whom I love, what was needed, it seemed to me, was only a matter of having the courage to tell her so. And courage I brought to it; and courage, I would have sworn, had at last brought her to love me too; and all things would be well between us from then on."

Jim was tempted to say something; and then thought it would be best just to let the other go on at his own will and pace. After a while Dafydd heaved a deep sigh, and spoke again.

"I own that, at first, I may have said something about wishing I could be in France to see if there I would find men of the bow, whether it be long or cross, against whom I could truly measure myself. Because, for some time now, I have found none that can push me even a little to outdo them;" he said. "I do not exactly remember what I said or how I said it. I am not even sure I said it. But I am willing to believe that I did say something like that. But the moment Danielle seemed to find the idea unwelcome, I put it from me and said as much. I do not remember my exact words on that, either, but I am sure I told her so. That she was first and more important for me; even before the arts of the bow or anything else in my life."

Jim waited.

"So I gave no more thought about it," went on Dafydd, "until about a month before your leaving. Then—I know not how—it began to seem that all I said was said amiss, or all that I did was done at the wrong time; so that, look you, I was more of a trouble than a help to her in our lives."

"Yes," murmured Jim encouragingly.

"Then we made that visit so that Danielle might have some time with your Lady; and she stayed on at Malencontri, spending little or no time with me, but a great deal of time—in fact, it seemed she would have spent all time had it been possible—with the Lady Angela. Meanwhile, her dissatisfaction with me grew no less. I continued to say and do things wrongly; until at last she flatly told me that I should go to France and join the rest of you, if that was what I wanted. But in any case to leave her alone and not bother her again unil she sent for me."

He looked at Jim with a face that was surprisingly haggard with sorrow.

"Never had I expected to hear such from her, indeed," Dafydd said, "nor did I know the reason why. Nor do I know it now. Only one thing I know; and that is that I am not wanted where she is. Therefore, since there was nothing better for me to do, I followed the road you had taken, and caught up in Hastings with John Chester and your men-at-arms, just before they took ship."

He stopped speaking. They rode on in silence together for a while. For a long time he had gone back to staring at the ears of his horse, but finally he looked more at Jim.

"You have nothing to say to me, Sir James?" he asked. "No explanation that might help me understand what has come upon me; no advice?"

Jim felt badly torn apart inside, remembering what Angie had told him about Danielle's being fearful that, once Dayfdd had seen her swollen with her pregnancy, he would cease to love her. That was not his secret to tell Dafydd; and there was nothing else he could say to give the man comfort. Even though he would have been willing to spend a small fortune to be able to do so.

"The only comfort or hope I can give you," Jim said at last, slowly, and was surprised to hear himself speaking almost like Sir Brian or Sir Giles, in the slightly more elaborate language of this world, "is that there's always a reason in an instance like this, and soon or later a woman will tell you what it is, if she really loves you. And I give you my word that I really believe that Danielle loves you, just as she always did."

"Would I could believe that," said Dafydd.

He fell into a new silence, and this one lasted to the point where Jim understood that the other was through talking. Jim lifted his reins and rode his horse forward to rejoin Giles and Brian.

"Dafydd is very unhappy," Jim said when he rejoined the other two.

Giles looked at him, a little bewildered. Brian stared straight ahead, his jaw clamped.

"Under God," said Brian, "each of us makes his own life; and that life is like a house, where one must be invited to enter, before coming in. If I am so invited I'll do what I can. Otherwise, we each have our own houses to live in; and those houses presently are concerned not with Dafydd but with what lies ahead. It is high time we talked about that, rather than other things; now that we are on the open road, and none can possibly overhear us."

He looked at Jim suddenly.

"Unless by magic?" he asked. "James, could we be overheard by magical means?"

"I'm afraid I'm not enough of a magician yet so I can be sure about answering that," Jim said, "but I'm almost sure we can't be. That doesn't rule out the possibility. I just don't think so."

"Then let us talk!" said Sir Giles, almost explosively. "By St. Cuthbert, I have had enough of whispers and silence in this matter! We have before us an estate owned by a man, who is holding our royal Prince as prisoner. Let us to the business of discussing how he may be freed and taken safely away from there."

"It was Sir Raoul's rede, if you remember," said Brian, "that we meet one who was formerly a man of his father's, in the woods surrounding the castle of this magician; and this man would show us a means of entrance and a way to find where our Prince is being held. We all have directions to find this place of meeting, in memory."

"Er—yes," said Jim guiltily. *His* directions were written down.

"But the question arises," went on Brian, "whether the directions may not be sufficient to let us find this spot. Or, that for some reason, the former servant of his father will not be free to come and look for us there, even though we wait several nights. The longer we stand around in that wood, the more likely we are to be surprised by others of Malvinne's guardians. Therefore, it would not be an ill thing if we made plans for a case in which we must needs do without the help of this former servant."

"What plans can we make?" asked Sir Giles. "If the castle is as extensive as Sir Raoul gave us to believe, we could take weeks to simply search all around it for some safe means of entrance."

"Yes," said Jim, "that's a real problem. Right at the moment I don't see any way around it."

"It's possible I may have," said Brian. "It was for this reason I suggested that I come with you, James and Giles; and also would have it that we bring along Aargh and Dafydd. Has it struck you how apt the five of us are as a force to find its way into an unknown castle and locate someone held prisoner there?"

"I hadn't thought," said Jim honestly, "but now you mention it—"

He fell thoughtfully silent.

"With the bowman," went on Brian, "we now have the means to slay silently from a distance any guard whom we must needs pass. And with the wolf, not only have we someone who can warn us if we are approached in darkness and in silence by an enemy; but who can, if necessary, track one of the warders back to whatever doorway by which he left the castle, so that we may make our own plans for getting through it."

"But you assume something," said Giles. "That there will be more than one entrance to this castle. Few castles have more than one; and if there is an extra one, it is a privy escape route for the Lord of the castle, well hidden and probably heavily guarded."

"I am guessing," said Brian, "that in a castle such as this, that is warded as much by magic as by arms, there may be not merely more than one, but several, ways in and out."

He looked at Jim and Giles significantly. "One for large bodies of men and horses, one or more privy entrances such as you suggest, Giles; but also other ways in and out that are used by the lesser folk of the castle. It is, as I say, no more than a guess on my part; but I think it is a good guess. Moreover, the one to find out if it be true may be the wolf, who if he thinks it wise, could go in ahead of us or simply search the place while we wait at our meeting spot for the one who should meet us there, and bring us back word of any entrance we could use in case this former servitor does not show up."

Jim felt more than a little humble. As they had been descending from the boat at Brest, and heading toward the local inn there, he had thought about the fact that only his rank had caused him to be the titular head of this expedition; and that either Brian or Giles would be much better at commanding it. Certainly, Brian's thinking and what he had told them so far bore this out.

It was true that Jim was not an expert on castles. He knew Malencontri, he knew Castle Smythe and Malvern Castle, which was the home of the de Chaneys, the family of Brian's ladylove. But that was all; and, he had to admit to himself now, he

had never stopped to study any one of these castles, including his own of
Malencontri, as to its practicality for defense and its probable means of being
infiltrated by enemies from the outside.

They spent that night on the road, camping out. Aargh did not return. Late the
next afternoon, they came to Blois, and stayed overnight at an inn there; where
Aargh, of course, also did not show up. It was not until they were two days
beyond Blois that he joined them again. Meanwhile, Jim had been trying mightily
to think of some way in which he could use magic to determine what the reason
was for Aargh's presence.

He had a sneaking feeling that Carolinus could probably point him in the
direction of that reason, if the older magician wanted to. The only question was
how to contact Carolinus. There ought, Jim thought, to be some magic equivalent
of the telephone. Or at least of some form of communication that could put his
mind in touch with the mind of Carolinus.

It was not until the second night out from Blois that inspiration came to him.

Mythology was full of the kind of thing he was reaching for. Further, it had
struck him that there was a common mechanism that was used in psychology.

Mythology certainly ran along the edge of magic, in that magic was very often
involved in it. One of the very common magic happenings in mythology was that
someone dreamed something that was about to come true, or that had happened
someplace else, or was happening someplace else at that same time.

Certainly, if such dreaming was something that the magic within him could
invoke, then he ought to be able to set up a link between him and Carolinus.

That night, before he fell asleep, he carefully wrote on the inside of his
forehead:

ME/DREAM———➤DREAM/CAROLINUS

The more he thought about it—as he lay wrapped up in his sleeping cloths
under the stars and by the dying embers of the fire, beyond which the black
humps that were the shapes of his three other human companions lay—the more
he liked his idea. His mind worked it back and forth. He did his best to think of
reasons why such a clumsy formula might work, or might not. Worn out at last
with going back and forth from one possibility to the other, he slipped into
slumber.

For a while his mind hopped and slid through a series of disconnected dream
scenes that were very ordinary and customary when he was first falling asleep.
Then came a blank spell. Then, unexpectedly, he found himself outside
Carolinus's cottage at the Tinkling Water. It was just about dawn. Carolinus and
Aargh were both there, standing outside Carolinus's dwelling on the path between
the flowers. The only difficulty with his dream picture was that everything was
upside down.

"What is this?" he snapped in his dream at the Accounting Office. No sooner had he dreamed that he had spoken the words, than he was amazed at his own audacity. He had never spoken brusquely to the Accounting Office in his life. But in his dream it answered now; and its tone, far from being angry, was apologetic.

"Oh, sorry," the bass voice answered; and the scene turned right side up.

"Actually," the bass voice went on, "you were the one who was upside down."

It fell silent. Jim was left wondering how he could be upside down, when as far as he could see he was not in the scene at all. He merely seemed to be a disembodied point of view, an invisible pair of eyes. And an invisible pair of ears, also, evidently; for just then he realized he could hear Carolinus and Aargh talking.

"Well, everything's well—here at least," Carolinus was saying. "You'd be as aware of that as I would. Too bad I can't say the same thing for elsewhere. You know that James has gone to France?"

"Yes," growled Aargh. "I told him it was nonsense!"

"Nonsense is a matter of point of view, wolf," said Carolinus. "What's nonsense to you may not be nonsense to James, or Sir Brian, or a number of other people."

"All the two-legged ones—" said Aargh grumpily, and broke off. "No offense, Mage. I wasn't speaking of you. But I swear, nearly anything on two legs has about as much sense as a butterfly."

"There is more to what moves the world than simply sense; common sense, I take it you mean," said Carolinus. "This business of rescuing the Prince from France is no such thing as the Loathly Tower affair, is it? No clear-cut matter with Evil perched in a dark place, its creatures gathered below, ready to fight all comers; sending out its legions of such as the sandmirks to overcome any who might oppose it. Not at all like the affair at the Loathly Tower, is it?"

Aargh stared at the mage with hooded eyes.

"If you are trying to tell me something, say it right out, Mage," he said. "My way has ever been the straight way. I've no love for dark hints and tricky twists of words."

"Very well," said Carolinus, "then I'll tell you bluntly that this present matter is as much of a joust with the Dark Powers as was that of the Loathly Tower, of which you were a part. But this time it's cloaked about by the worldly ambitions and imaginations of men, so that it's not as visible as it was before. Nonetheless, it's the same thing all over again. There's a threat; and James, Brian, and now even Dafydd, go against it as the only hope to stop it from breaking out and doing great damage, just as it threatened to do the time before. They are all there—but you."

"No affair of mine," growled Aargh.

"You mean you won't see it as an affair of yours," said Carolinus, "and to support that blindness, you pretend that your comrades don't need you; that James and the others go up against an enemy which is no more than their equal in strength."

Aargh growled again, wordlessly but uneasily.

"You talk in large words with small sense inside them, as usual, Mage," he said. "I asked you to tell me plainly what the situation was; but you keep moving around and around it, without coming out squarely to say what it is. Why've you passed word to me to come here, now? What do you want of me; and why do you think I should give you whatever it is?"

"I tell you this way," said Carolinus, "because you're a cross-grained, hard-headed, selfish, English wolf; and you need to be able to find the answers to those questions of yours yourself—otherwise you'll never believe them. You know what a wolf cub is, I take it?"

"Do I know—" Aargh's tongue hung out in something very close to a laugh. "I not only know, there are a number of grown wolves these days who—but never mind that. My life is my life. Yes, I know what a wolf cub is and what it's like. What of it?"

"Would you send a wolf cub to fight another full-grown wolf?" demanded Carolinus.

"Your questions become slightly mad, Mage—again with respect," said Aargh. "Of course I would not. Nor would I send—not that I could send in any case, since an English wolf whatever his age is an English wolf and will do what he wants; not just what someone else tells him to do—nor would I send even a two-year-old wolf against one who has stayed alive five years, and known the fights of them. It would be like sending a sheep against my jaws."

"Then what do you think of sending a young D-class magician against a magician with a rating almost as high as mine—AAA? Would that not be rather like sending a two-year wolf against a five-year one? Or even a cub against a grown wolf?"

"You are speaking of James, and his knowledge as a sorcerer—"

"*Magician*, if you don't mind, wolf!" snapped Carolinus. "Among us whose work is with the Art, 'sorcerer' is not a pretty term. I am a magician and James is a magician. The one he goes against might justify the name you just used."

"So," said Aargh, "you're telling me that James needs me in France?"

"Yes," said Carolinus.

"Then I'll go," said Aargh, "though I've no love for traveling outside of England. And I'll do what I can to help James and my other friends, but only because they're my friends."

Aargh laughed suddenly and silently, his great jaws opening wide, deadly teeth catching the morning sunlight.

"I can help them against all but wolves," he said.

"Wolves?" snapped Carolinus. "Why not wolves as well? Are the French wolves friends of yours?"

Aargh laughed again.

"Friends? Anything but," he said. "But there are rules among wolves, too, Mage—little as you and your kind may know it. I will be on the territory of the French wolves. There I must back down from any of them; or fight all the wolves in France; and not even I believe I can beat all of the wolves in France."

He closed his jaws and cocked his head on one side, looking quizzically at Carolinus.

"And you, Mage?" he asked. "While all the rest of us are engaged with this foreign sorcerer, or magician, or whatever you wish to call him, where will what help you can give, be?"

"I've been in this before the beginning," said Carolinus harshly, "though you've not seen it, and may never see me involved in it."

His voice, for Carolinus, suddenly became unusually gentle.

"Of all the Kingdoms into which the human and nonhuman creatures of this world are divided," he said, "that Kingdom which is closest to the one that contains the Dark Powers and their creatures, is that of us magicians, Aargh. For it is a perilous study, our Art, and a hard study and a long study and one that is never done. Nor is our responsibility to help contain the Dark Powers ever done. Always we—we who call ourselves magicians—are in the forefront of any battle against those powers, and all they control, including even our fellows who have crossed over to become *sorcerers* on the other side."

"Then—" Aargh began, but Carolinus held up a hand to stop him.

"But the reasons are those which no one but a magician of my rank or near it would understand," said Carolinus. "Reasons such as why, at this moment, Jim must go up against he who calls himself Malvinne, alone; even though Malvinne towers over him as a mountain towers over a small dwelling like my own. While someone like myself, who is Malvinne's equal or more, must stand back and let what happens, happen. I cannot step forward now. But you can, Aargh; and I'm greatly relieved to hear you'll do so. Because Jim will have need of you; a need no one else could fill."

"I've always known you to be honest, Mage," said Aargh, "so we'll let it go at that. Jim's already left for the coast, and by this time may be on ship for France. If not, however, I may still catch him before he leaves, which will make my getting over the water much easier. Though I'd find a way in any case. Just do one thing for me. Don't tell Jim I do this for love of him. There's no need for him to start thinking that he need only have some difficulty and Aargh will come running. I am a free wolf; and I make up my own mind."

"I promise you," said Carolinus, "I won't say a word to him about your doing anything for love of him."

"Good," said Aargh.

He turned, and was gone in an instant.

Dreaming, Jim looked at Carolinus standing alone on the walk before his small house. For a moment Carolinus stood as if in deep thought; then he turned, and in the dream it was as if he walked directly toward a Jim who was not there. His face grew larger and larger until it blotted out nearly all of the rest of the scene.

"From here on, the real test starts, James," Carolinus said, "but don't try to reach me like this again. Malvinne dreams, also."

Jim woke up. The night was silent about him, except for a faint wind that wandered overhead between him and the stars. For some moments Jim's mind was full of what he had just seen; and then the memory of it began to fade, until he began to wonder if it really had not been a sort of wish-fulfillment dream, that he had summoned up to comfort himself.

He lay down and worked his way finally back into dreamless slumber.

Chapter **23**

When Jim and the others had approached the Loathly Tower for their final battle with its creatures, almost a year before, land, sky, and water alike—and everything enclosed by those three—had shown signs of the sort of place they were approaching. There had been a grayness, a dullness, an overall sadness—almost a deathliness—to everything.

Now, however, as they finally drew close to Malvinne's castle, there were no such signs to be seen in the day around them. It was late afternoon, but the sun still shone brightly. What clouds there were, were gathered to the eastward, so that they did not dim the sunlight in any fashion. The dryer green grass of summer was thick on the ground, the trees full with their leaves. Summer flowers bloomed in patches here and there.

Following the instructions of Sir Raoul, they had left the main road some ways back, at a point he had warned them to look for. The road to Malvinne's castle, Raoul had said, was visible only when Malvinne wanted it to be. Otherwise most traffic passed far out of sight of his estate and his territory, and never suspected he or it was there.

Their first sight of Château Malvinne was from a relatively high point of land that looked down upon the blue stream of the Loire River in the distance, just beyond the structures that made up Malvinne's castle. In some respects, in some of its architecture, it did resemble a castle, although it was spread out much farther than any castle Jim had ever seen or imagined.

All of this sparkled in the sunlight.

Only in the black wood, the black, thick wood—which must be a mile to a mile-and-a-half deep around the castle, so that it fenced the castle in completely against the waters of the Loire—was the first hint of a darkness resembling that which they had seen near the Loathly Tower.

The blackness was not merely the blackness of dark wood, but of wood that was literally black; of undergrowth literally black—bushes, small trees and perhaps even the grass itself—though there was no way to be sure of this at this distance; and it could simply be black earth underneath the trees.

The trees themselves grew thickly together, so thickly that the whole forest looked like a single bramble patch. None of the trees were tall. Jim estimated that there were hardly any of them over fifteen or twenty feet in height. But it was not necessary that they be tall. Their thick growth and intertwining limbs were sufficient to give the forest its reason and its reputation.

Yet, Jim told himself, there must be paths through it, or else those that Malvinne sent out to patrol it against intrusion would not be able to get through it. But these paths could well be like the paths of a maze—safe enough for those who knew them, but a trap for anyone who did not know them and intruded under the dark branches.

All of them stopped instinctively at the top of the green rise, including Aargh; and stood or sat silent, gazing down at their destination. Beyond the trees, the castle was bathed in the last sunlight. Only an ominous grayness of the castellated parts of it, the towers and walls and turrets, seemed at all forbidding. The sculptured gardens, arbors, small pools, and stretches of grass that lay about the foot of the castle for some distance, were attractive and inviting. But from where the castle proper started, all was as it might be around the sternest fortress; except that there was no moat.

Once Jim would have laughed at the notion—but now it occurred to him that the moat might be there after all, as invisible to their eyes as the road that Malvinne caused to appear, from his estate to the main road, when he had visitors he wished to welcome.

"We'll wait at least until twilight," said Jim, surprised to hear the note of command in his voice. "Then when the light begins to get uncertain we'll reconnoiter those woods. Meanwhile, we probably ought to find some place where we can be invisible ourselves, until the sun is down."

"Indeed, you're right, James," said Brian. "The wisest part by far is to find a place to hide ourselves, not only for the moment, but for several days if necessary. For something tells me it'll take at least several days of trying, to make contact with this thing that was once a man."

"Look down and to our left, perhaps a quarter of an English mile," said Aargh. "See where the hillside dimples. There are no trees or other growth to hide it; but unless I miss my guess that dimple turns inward, and there'll be either a small closed valley of sorts, or a cave."

The rest of them looked. Aargh's sharp sense of observation had picked it out, where the rest of them had missed it. Any casual glance would have passed over what appeared to be, as Aargh said, merely a dimple in the hillside. But now that they looked closely, there were indeed shadows in the depths of it that seemed to hint that it went back farther and to one side.

"Let's ride down to it, then," said Brian.

They went down; and Aargh was right. The dimple turned out to be an indentation in the hillside that went backward and then turned to its right; so that the bulge of its earth wall hid them from all sight of the wood and the castle below. A small stream came down the hillside, to trickle around the corner of the dimple, and on toward the trees below. It was not only a good hiding place, Jim thought, it was also a very good place to camp.

But it was a cold camp, because they were too close to the castle to risk lighting a fire. It was fortunate they were supplied with previously-cooked meat as well as bread and cheese; because these, with wine mixed with water from the stream, made their dinner.

After they had eaten, they sat around in the last light of the closing day, talking with that close camaraderie that comes to those who are about to go into danger together. The only one who had little to say was Aargh, who lay like a lion, on his belly with his head up and his forelegs projecting together before him on the ground. Although the castle and the wood were out of sight, Aargh maintained a steady gaze on the curve of the hillside that hid the view from them. Clearly, he was on watch even now.

The others compared their maps and their memories; and came to agreement on where, at the edge of the woods, they should probably find the entrance to the path that would lead them in among the trees and eventually to the spot where they might contact the one they were going to meet. They might have to search about a hundred yards of the edge of the wood, but not much farther than that.

All this settled, the talk wandered off onto other matters.

Sir Brian was not merely the eldest, but the only child of his father; so that there had never been any question about his inheriting Castle Smythe. It turned out, however—in one of those moments of openness which tend to precede a risky endeavor—that Giles was only the third son in his own family; and therefore had little expectation of any inheritance. Likewise, as a Northumbrian knight with no friends or influence in the south of England, to say nothing of friends or influence at the court itself, he stood little chance of any great advancement in life.

"Frankly, I've never hoped for any such," Giles said to Jim, Brian, and Dafydd.

None of the others commented, least of all Dafydd, whose prospects of advancement were far less even than those of Giles. For all his skill and bowmanship it was unlikely he would ever rise socially in this world. But for him, plainly, such advancement was not important. For one of the gentlemanly class, however, it was almost a duty, besides being something universally desired. The goal of everyone born to higher stations in life, where knighthood was a reasonable possibility, was to win lands and title, one way or another.

For Brian, as a matter of fact, it came close to being a necessity if he wanted to marry Geronde Isabel de Chaney. They were pledged to each other; and once upon a time, before he left on crusade, her father had approved of the pledge. But it was still possible that he could come home again with his mind changed— particularly if he had picked up wealth and power in the Holy Lands; and had developed a higher expectation of who his daughter should marry.

But Giles, who was of a gentle family, had just confessed himself relatively resigned to gaining no great name or wealth in the world.

"There's only one thing I wish," he told his companions. "It's that before I die, I have the opportunity to do one great deed, even if it is in that doing that death comes to me."

This stirred even Dafydd out of his customary silence.

"It is not for me to advise a knight how he should live—or die," said Dafydd, "but it seems to me that there is much more to be said for living and accomplishing what may be done while alive, than by dying and therefore being no more use to the world."

Jim half expected Sir Giles to flare up at this, as he normally did at any sign of a contradiction; but the Northumbrian knight was in a strangely quiet and reflective—almost melancholy—mood.

"Indeed," he said, but he said it gently, "it is not for such as yourself, Dafydd, to tell me or any other knight how to live or die. But that is the difference in our station. Consider, many knights would like to give themselves completely, even to their lives, in some great cause; but are held back by their obligations and their duties to their family, to their wives, even to their names. But chance has made me free of all such responsibilities. My father has two older sons, and two younger, so that the family holding is in no danger of falling into strange hands. Not only have I no special duty to any superior—beyond what brings us to this place now—I have even no duty to my family and my name, except to see that neither is tarnished by my actions. Therefore am I free to do one great thing at least before I die. And that is my dream and my wish."

"You're a young man to be thinking of dying, Giles," said Jim.

He knew himself to be only a few years older than the Northumbrian knight; but beyond this he felt infinitely more mature. Not only because of his marriage, but also because of his upbringing in a world far advanced beyond this one in science and society. In this moment he felt almost fatherly, if not grandfatherly, toward Giles.

"If I were older, would I be as able to give my all so well?" Giles asked him. "No, now is the time for my adventuring; and it may be that this business of bringing our prince safely out of yonder castle is the chance of it."

To Jim, who had absolutely no intention of dying, or even getting hurt if he could help it, this ambition of Giles's was shocking. It sounded like nothing so much as the terrible waste of a life. But it was clear that it was not something that Giles had thought up on the spur of the moment. It was an idea that had evidently been maturing in him for a long time; possibly even for most of his lifetime. Immediate argument would not help, and might hurt. He decided to say nothing more.

Both Brian and Dafydd seemed of the same opinion. Aargh either had no opinion, or else he felt that whatever Giles wanted to do was up to Giles and of no concern or interest to him. For all Jim knew, Aargh might approve of what Giles had in mind. That attitude would fit with this savage age that held them all.

When their dimple was in deep darkness from the sun setting behind the hill at their back, and the woods below were hardly more than blurs in the twilight, they decided to move forward. Jim had decided that Aargh should take the lead, so that the sensitive instrument of his nose would not have interference from the smell of the humans with him. Together, they moved down toward that section of the woods' edge where they thought the entrance to the path might be. The walk was easy down the treeless slope, and the footing was sure enough.

When they reached the edge of the woods they only had to search for a few yards before they came across an entrance that seemed to be the one Sir Raoul had described. It led directly into the tangle of trees before them.

The entrance fitted the minutely detailed description Raoul had given of it. There was a freshly broken twig at the end of a branch, pointing outward from the woods, that was supposed to be a sign not merely that the path was correct, but that the individual they were to meet would be looking for them.

Close up, however, the wood was even more forbidding than it had been from a distance. The trees, most of them, were as low as apple trees; but showed no sign of fruit and only little gnarled excrescences by way of leaves. Their branches were sharply angled. They ran not more than six inches in any direction before making a sharp turn to a new one; and the elbows of those turns narrowed to a spike which, while not quite a thorn, was equally sharp. The three knights instinctively drew their swords as they entered single file behind Aargh. Glancing back from the head of the line, Jim saw that even Dafydd had drawn the long knife that fitted into a sheath on the high side of his left boot.

Once within, they were in fairly complete darkness. Although as their eyes adjusted, the last light of the sky gave them some faint illumination. It was all they had until a little later on, when the nearly full moon—which had risen even before the setting of the sun—rose above the brush and sent its rays among the trees.

Aargh moved confidently ahead. Jim followed him almost by feel at first. Then it occurred to him that he could improve his own ability to see how they were doing. He wrote on the inside of his forehead:

ME———>DRAGONSIGHT, DRAGONSCENT, AND DRAGONHEARING

Immediately his vision improved to that which he would have had in his dragon form. It was not a tremendous improvement, but it was better than he had been able to see as a human. In addition, he could now use his nose to a certain extent, even as Aargh was using his to make sure he stayed on the path.

Not that there was any lack of reminders for anyone who traveled that path. It was no more than three feet wide; and any incautious movement could brush an arm or leg against one of the trees. Such casual contact almost certainly brought one up against the pointed branch-elbows, and the scratch that resulted seemed to have the ability to cut through fairly thick cloth or leather.

Still they continued; and the only thing easing their way was the fact that as the moon rose and brightened, the path itself became very much clearer. Jim switched back to his human sight, temporarily, just to check how well his two-legged companions were seeing.

He was a little shocked at what he discovered. Without his dragon sight, with its adaptability to distance and darkness, even the face of Brian right behind him was nothing more than a blur. He turned forward again, just in time to keep from blundering into a tree on his right-hand side, and reactivated his dragon sight.

The path wound amazingly. Jim had long ago lost his sense of direction. He leaned forward and whispered, knowing that the wolf's sharp ears would pick it up.

"Aargh," he asked, "do you think we're still headed toward the castle?"

"We were until a couple of turns ago." Aargh answered so softly that Jim hardly recognized the other's voice. "Since then we seem to be moving level with it through the woods. Note there's nothing but earth underfoot."

Jim had not given thought to this before; but now that Aargh had mentioned it, his own improved sense of smell confirmed the fact that there was nothing green to be scented at ground level. It would have been surprising if there had been, seeing how these trees must block out light even in the brightest daytime.

"I smell a larger patch of earth a short ways ahead," Aargh went on in the same soft voice. "Best if we stop there and decide what to do—in fact, we may have no choice but to stop there."

Jim did not understand exactly what Aargh's last few words meant. He now paid attention to what he had overlooked before, in his happiness at being able to see better with the dragon sight, and was suddenly conscious of the breathing of his three human companions.

All except Dafydd, who was last in line, were breathing heavily and uncomfortably. More than that, Brian was now muttering under his breath. With a little effort and the aid of his dragon hearing, Jim made out something of what the muttering was.

Brian was swearing steadily to himself.

". . . Bloody, damn—" Brian's voice broke off as there was a sound of something ripping through cloth. Clearly Brian had blundered against one of the sharp-pointed limb-elbows.

The near voiceless swearing picked up again. Behind Brian, however, both Giles and Dafydd were silent—Giles almost oddly so, as if he held his breath. A creeping concern for his companions began to grow in Jim.

He whispered again to Aargh.

"How close are we to that open space now?" he asked.

"Right ahead. What's the matter with your nose, James?" whispered Aargh sardonically. "You've been snuffling like a dragon for some minutes. Don't tell me you can't smell it up there yourself."

Jim sniffed forward. Sure enough, there was a strong smell of earth, naked earth up in front of them; a smell somewhat like that of the pathway under their feet at the moment, but with a tinge a little damper and more rank.

A moment later they came to the space Aargh had been talking about. Aargh moved ahead and turned around to face the rest of them; and Jim stepped aside once he was in, so that those behind him could also enter.

For a moment they stood there, in a ragged circle, and Brian, at least, was taking advantage of the opportunity to catch his breath. Now, Jim heard Giles doing the same. He breathed heavily, almost exhaustedly. Dafydd's breath still came evenly; and as far as Jim's ears could tell him, Aargh was not breathing at all, so noiseless was the breath that went in and out of him.

For a moment it crossed Jim's mind that they might have reached the point of rendezvous with the half-man, half-toad who had once been a man-at-arms under Sir Raoul's father. But this place had been reached entirely too easily and openly. Their directions from Sir Raoul had been that there would be a small, hidden entrance off the path to the right among the trees, and then back a short distance into a space that was wide enough to let them all stand together, rather than in single file. But in their present case the path had led directly to this open place.

Furthermore, looking around himself with the advantage of the full moon and his dragon sight, Jim saw at least three other ragged circles of darkness that were entrances to further paths. Clearly, this was a sort of meeting place of paths through the forest. A part of its maze-aspect. How were they to tell which one of the three other entrances would lead them toward the castle rather than away from it or deeper into the woods around them?

For the first time, with the moonlight bright upon them all, he took a good look at Brian, Giles, and Dafydd.

All were marked by the sharp, thornlike corners of the trees. Dafydd showed the fewest scratches of all on his face and hands. Brian was continuing to swear under his breath. Giles was making no sound; but his face and hands were literally dripping blood.

"Giles!" said Jim, stepping toward him. "What happened to you?"

"I see not so well at night," said Giles's voice, a little remotely. "It is something that runs in my family, some generations now. Pay no attention."

Brian had swung around by this time.

"Giles!" he said out loud, in a tone of shock. "Man, you seem to have fought the King of Cats! How did it come so badly on you, when the rest of us are only—"

There was a slight hesitation in his voice; then he went on.

"Are but slightly scratched?"

"As I was telling James," Giles began again, still in that remote voice, "it is a type of near blindness that afflicts all my family at night. I did not think it would be of any great trouble here; and indeed, it has not. These are all small scratches."

"A few more like that, and you'll bleed to death," said Brian, lowering his voice once more.

He swung on Jim.

"We must bind him up somewhat and insure that he is kept to the middle of the trail from now on."

"I absolutely agree," said Jim concernedly. "Brian, you and I can tear the bottoms off our shirts to make bandages for his hands and face."

"I protest," said Giles softly, but on a stiffer note. "It is a knight's duty to ignore such small things."

"Perhaps," said Jim grimly, "but more of this and you'll be leaving a trail of blood by which anyone can follow us."

Meanwhile, he and Brian had fished out the bottom edges of their shirts and were busy tearing off strips. Over Giles's rather weak protests, they muffled both of his hands and wrists and all of his face except his nose and eyes, tying the ends of the torn strips together to secure the bandages in place.

"From now on," said Jim, "you walk between Brian and me, Giles, with your hands holding to my belt; and Brian will hold to your belt from behind to steer you and keep you in the center of the path."

Brian turned to Aargh.

"Have you any idea where we are, Aargh," he asked, "or which of these three paths we should take?"

"The castle lies in that direction," said Aargh, pointing with his muzzle toward a solid wall of trees between two of the path entrances. "We're roughly in the middle of the wood right now. As to which trail, I know no more than you. On the other hand, were I alone, I might just go below and between the trees directly to the point where they stop at the open grounds of the castle."

Jim took a close look at the wolf for the first time. Aargh was absolutely unmarked. In spite of his four-legged friend's size, Jim realized that the other probably could do exactly what he had just said. With the protection of his body hair, he could worm his way below and between the trees in a more or less direct line until he came out on their inner side.

But that did not solve the problem for the rest of them.

Chapter 24

"**W**hich of the three do we take?" whispered Brian after a long moment. "Clearly we have to go farther, since Sir Raoul's directions were that the place would be a narrow path off to the right of the one we were following, its entrance hidden. How in God's name can an entrance to a path be hidden among this tangle?"

The question had been one that did not call for an answer. But Aargh answered almost immediately.

"When the entrance is blocked by a false tree, of course," said the wolf. "This is what comes of not taking me more fully into your confidence."

"What do you mean, Aargh?" Jim asked.

"I mean that we've already passed this secret entrance, in all likelihood," retorted Aargh. "Some small distance back, we passed a tree on our right, which had been cut through at its base and then placed back upon it, the cut being hidden with dirt from the path moistened to a mudlike consistency and patted around it. The moistening had been done with wine—either wine that was sour at the time or else, as probably, it's had plenty of time to sour since. I smelled it as we passed, but thought nothing of it; because none of you had suggested to me that such a false tree might hide the entrance you sought."

This speech was met by another silence. Jim was condemning himself inwardly, and it struck him a second later that probably the other two were doing the same thing. But he had the most reason, since his dragon nose—while not as good as Aargh's by a great deal—still should have been good enough to smell the odor of soured wine, if he had been paying attention properly.

"Let us back then to this false tree, by all means!" said Giles, breaking the silence.

"You're right," said Jim. "Dafydd, if you'll bring up the rear again?"

"I'd already expected to, look you," said Dafydd.

They started back, once more in line, down the path they had just come up. The only difference in their going was that Aargh moved a little more swiftly, with the certainty about him of someone who already knows his destination.

The rest of them followed. Jim found himself resenting the fact that he had once more to traverse the trail that had already laid its sharp marks upon him. A moment later this was followed by a sense of guilt. With the exception of Dafydd—and how Dafydd did so well baffled Jim—Jim had been less hurt by the thornlike branches than any except Aargh. This, he knew, had been because of the advantage of his dragon senses, which had allowed him to keep to the middle of the path with more certainty.

Aargh's increased pace forced them all to move faster. Since Giles was now holding onto Jim's belt from behind, and Brian was holding onto Giles from behind, the increased pace was difficult. Jim was just about to speak to Aargh and tell him to slow down when, just ahead of him, the wolf stopped abruptly.

"Here," he said over his shoulder, "this is the false tree."

With his dragon sight, Jim was able to make out the fact that the darkness of the path surface seemed to flow up the trunk of a tree no larger than the average Christmas tree. He stepped forward carefully beside Aargh, who moved over to give him room, and bent down to sniff at the trunk.

Sure enough, his nostrils caught the faint whiff of a vinegarlike smell.

Cautiously he reached in among the sharp-armed branches until he had grasped the unpleasantly rough and prickly trunk of the tree between two of the branches. He pulled it out into the path, and stepped back with it, so that the others could go around him.

Revealed, was another path, but a very narrow one. With the exception of Aargh, they would all have to go sideways. Nonetheless, with the wolf leading, they went in. Jim followed them, pulling the false tree back into place after them.

What held the tree upright on its stump was the fact that its branches intertangled with those of the trees on either side of it. Jim had a water flask at his belt, but there was no room in the narrow path for him to squat down and make a fresh mud slurry to hide the place where the tree joined the stump. They would just have to take their chances, and hope their presence would not be discovered before the one who was supposed to meet them came to this place and found them.

Jim followed, to the small space where the others were already gathered. It was perhaps half the size of the junction where the various paths had come together; and where they had stopped before to discuss their next move.

Because the space was so small, the thorn trees crowded them closely, and the higher branches knitted together overhead to break up the moonlight that came in. They could not see each other even as well as they had been able to in the moonlit open space where the paths had joined. Still, they could see each other better than they had been able to on the path.

"It would be my counsel," said Brian, "that we sit down now and drink and perhaps eat a bite. Our wait here could be long. In fact, I further suggest that, if he who's to meet us has not shown up by moonset, we leave this place and go back to our camp in the hillside for the day. Once it's daylight, we'll not want to be traveling these forest paths if we can help it."

"Indeed," said the masked and mittened Sir Giles.

"I agree, too," said Jim.

They all sat except Aargh, who lay down, again in his lionlike pose. With time, the space beneath each of them warmed a little with their body heat; and they sat in silence watching as the moon moved across the sky and down, to lose itself in the tangle of forest limbs.

Twice Aargh, almost noiselessly, warned them to silence; and a little after his warning, on both occasions, someone passed by on the main path not fifteen feet away.

But neither of those who passed stopped by the tree that hid the entrance to where they were; and finally when the moon was lost to sight, although a little of its light still reflected from the sky overhead, Brian spoke again out of the near impenetrable darkness.

"Best we go," his voice came to them. "You must lead us all now, Aargh, for I vow I cannot see my hand before my face."

In fact, even with his dragon senses, Jim was in scarcely better shape to see where they were going. They got up, holding hands, and Jim took hold of the base of Aargh's tail. They moved together until Aargh stopped suddenly, and Jim, reaching past and over him, closed his hand on the false tree, though it cost him several scratches to get a grasp on the trunk, and set it aside. They moved out into the main pathway and turned left.

Jim replaced the tree on its stump. Then, using water from his water bottle and with the guidance of Aargh's nose, plus feel, he managed once more to coat the jointure between stump and tree with the clayish earth of the path. They all turned left, back down the path they had originally used to enter the woods.

The first brightening of the sky in the east had begun by the time they emerged from the woods. It was not much improvement in light, but after the brooding presence of the woods, it felt almost as if they had emerged into broad daylight. They found their way back up to their camp. There they all lay down, wrapped themselves in their bedding materials, and prepared to fall asleep.

"Where's the wolf gone?" asked Giles groggily, propping himself up on one elbow just as they were all about ready to fall asleep.

"Probably hunting for something to eat," answered Jim. "Remember, there was no food or drink for him inside the woods; but he waited there with us just the same."

"He did indeed lap at this stream a little before leaving. I saw him," said Brian's voice, "but he'll take care of himself, Giles. Let us rest now; for I vow I, at least, need it."

Evidently, they all did. Because they slept through the day until the sun rounded the shoulder of their dimple and beamed directly in their eyes; and they woke sweating.

The next three nights, they made the same pilgrimage to the hidden place. Still, no one came. Giles was ready to give up waiting and try adventuring down some of the other paths. He said as much.

"Let's be a little more patient," said Jim. "Whoever was to meet us did not even know what week we would be coming, let alone what day. Also, it could easily be that whoever it is can only check that spot once in awhile. They may have him on guard days, instead of nights, for a week at a time."

They put in another three nights without result. By this time even Brian was beginning to incline to the idea that they should give up hope of waiting for the half-man, half-toad.

"Look," said Jim, as they once more approached twilight, "let's try it one more night. There's nothing else we can do tonight anyway; and we've got no plan for deciding which of those other paths to take if we do go beyond our hiding place. Let's give this once-upon-a-time man-at-arms one more chance to make contact with us."

The others gave in; although Jim could not help feeling secretely that it was more because of their acknowledgement of his leadership than because he had convinced them.

As soon as it had grown dark they went back down into the wood and took the path once more to the secret waiting place.

They had made it securely into that hiding place, and the moon was barely beginning to rise, when Aargh once more alerted them to the fact that someone was coming. Hands at their swords and Dafydd's on his long knife, they got to their feet, holding the weapons ready.

They all heard the steps approach. This time, they stopped. Just at this moment, also, the moon broke through a tangle of particularly close limbs and shone down almost brightly upon them.

To Jim's tense mind, it was as if a spotlight had been turned upon them.

They heard the false tree taken and put aside. Then a low, croaking voice spoke—it seemed as if from only an arm's length in front of them.

"Sir Raoul sent me to watch for you."

The men relaxed, but not completely. Jim was conscious that he had been gripping the hilt of his sword so tightly that his fingers ached. He loosened his grip a little, but continued to hold the sword ready.

"If you're the one we were to meet here," he answered in as low a voice as he thought would carry to the other, "come forward—but with no weapons in your hands."

"My hands are empty," croaked the voice.

There was the faintest sound of movement, and a moment later a dark figure joined them in the hiding place. It was so tight there with the addition of one more body that they were all almost breathing in each other's faces. But the figure was in the moonlight now, and he held up purely human hands to be visible in that light; and those hands were empty.

At the same time a shiver ran down Jim's back. For in spite of the human-shaped hands and arms and the humanlike legs, what faced them was badly misshapen. The upper body seemed almost bloated and the head was unnaturally large and flat.

"Name yourself," whispered Jim.

"I am Bernard," answered the other in his soft croak, "who once was a man like yourself, Sir Knight—for knight I judge you to be, since Sir Raoul would send no one less to meet me on this errand. I've been as you see me for years now—and I thank God in his Heaven that it's in the dark you look at me and not in the daylight, for I can scarcely look at myself in a pool of still water and bear what I see."

"That's all right," said Jim, stirred to pity by the grotesque shape before him. "Just take us to someplace where we can get inside the castle and point us to where we can find our prince. That's what you're here to do, isn't it?"

"Aye!" answered the shape. "Twelve years have I pretended to be a good servant in this place, waiting my chance to do something to pay back Malvinne for what he did to my Lord and my Lord's family. Now that chance has come and I would trade whatever hope I have of Heaven for it. I'll take you to the castle and inside—just inside, for in truth, I'm not one of those permitted to be within. Then I'll tell you as best I can how you may find the young man you speak of. From then on it's up to you. I ask only one thing."

"What's that?" asked Jim.

"You will none of you try to look at me directly, while I act as your guide," said the figure. "Promise me that alone, for love of Mary."

"We promise," said Jim.

Brian, Giles, and Dafydd all murmured affirmative responses.

"There, you have our promise," said Jim. "But are they likely to suspect you, if we find our Prince and get away with him? Wouldn't you do better to wait and join us as we leave; and leave this place behind you?"

There was a hoarse, bitter chuckle from the figure.

"Where in this world would I go?" the thing that was once Bernard answered. "Even the holy monks of the monastery would shut their doors against me. Even the lepers would turn aside and hide from me. No, what has been done to me has been done. I'll stay here and hope that perhaps another chance will come, to strike one more blow against Malvinne."

"But if you are suspected, just even suspected," said Jim, "it may go very hard with you indeed."

"I care not," croaked Bernard. "There is nothing they can do to me compared to what has been done to me already. Now let us go, for it's still some distance, and we may have to stop and hide along the way. Were I alone I could go directly to the castle. But this many together in company would be sure to attract attention."

His voice rose impatiently.

"Let us go, now! For the love of all things, let us go!"

He turned without waiting for an answer and sidled out through the narrow passageway into the wider path beyond. The rest of them followed. Once in the path, he put back the tree; and using what was clearly water, this time, from a flask at his belt, plastered mud around the jointure where it had been cut off. Having done this he straightened up, but did not immediately lead off. Instead he spoke to them again.

"The way I'll take you," he said, "is not the most direct one to the castle, but it's the surest one for you through this forest maze. You'll note as we go that we bear always to our right. If we do so it will bring us out eventually into the gardens of the palace grounds. Similarly, if you manage to secure your prince and are escaping, enter the woods by the same place by which you left, and bear always to your left. So, eventually, you'll come out beyond the trees on the hillside. From then on, God speed you; for I cannot."

It was some little distance to the inner edge of the forest. But Bernard led them with enough speed and confidence so that they covered it swiftly.

They emerged at last into the gardens of Malvinne's castle. The difference from the trees, come upon suddenly this way, was shocking.

All at once it was a warm and lovely night. The moon, only several days old from full, shed a good light over the various arbors, lawns, and plantings and the carefully graveled paths that they followed toward the dark bulk of the castle ahead.

The moisture from the various fountains and little artificial lakes seemed to soften the air and cause the odor of night-blooming flowers filling the gardens to hang at head level, rather than be stirred away by the small breezes that wandered through from time to time.

Now they moved swiftly over the paths. In no more than ten minutes they were up against the stone wall of the castle. A door scarcely larger than the front door to the homes Jim had been used to back in his own world was in front of them.

Bernard opened it and led them into a room empty of people, then stopped.

"Here, I leave you," he said.

Jim looked around. The walls were of stone and the ceilings were heavy timbers set close together. The floor was bare flagstone rather than strewn with the medieval carpet of rushes or grasses, or covered by the actual woven cloth carpets of Jim's world.

The room was wide and long, but the ceiling was no more than a foot above their heads. Altogether, it was not an unpleasant place, but it was a far cry from the attractiveness of the garden they had just left.

"From here," went on Bernard, "go openly. There are many fully human people in this castle serving Malvinne; and some of them of gentle rank. The dog might make them remember you, though. It's too bad I didn't think of that sooner. You could have left him back in the woods."

"On no account," said Aargh.

Bernard jumped. It had to be called a jump because it was more than a simple jerk of startlement. The room they had stepped into was lit with cressets burning open flames in holders along the walls. They illuminated the room well, but left deep pools of shadow, here and there. Bernard had stopped in one such pool, so that his shape and appearance were still hidden from their eyes.

"Is that a wolf?" he asked.

"None other," said Aargh, "and I go with these others; and you ask no questions—any more than we ask of you."

"Well enough," said Bernard after a second. The angle of his head in the shadow betrayed that he was still staring at Aargh. "It will be that all others take him for a dog, as I did. At any rate, to get back to my directions. The wolf has a sense of direction, I take it?"

"Else would I have gone hungry many days over the past years," said Aargh, "seeing how I may travel fifteen miles from the place of a kill to someplace else, and not return until the next day by another route. Give us our directions."

"Then, you see that farther wall there," said Bernard, pointing to the wall farthest from them and the door in it. "You go through its door and take the left doorway out of that room. Turn immediately right and keep generally in that line through a number of apartments like this one. Some will be empty. Some will be places where food is being prepared, or other work is being done. You are obviously, as I said, gentlemen—"

He glanced briefly at Dafydd.

"At least the three of you. It will be only natural that you ignore the others and continue on your own way. Move surely, as if you not only knew your way, but were on some important errand for Malvinne. If you keep to this line despite the offset of doorways, through the next nine such rooms you pass"—he hesitated— "you'll have reached the base of the tower where your Prince is being kept. At this point comes the greatest danger."

He paused.

"Yes, yes, man! Go on!" said Brian impatiently.

"You'll pass through a door that is plain on this side but is of highly carved and polished wood on the other. It will let you into a place of carpets and of much larger and taller rooms. Bear right, and you'll come to the base of the staircase that leads up the tower. You'll know it for what it is, because the steps are stone, with no cloth or carpeting or other covering upon them."

"How wide are these steps?" demanded Brian. "Wide enough so that all four of us can go up abreast?"

"It has been some time since I saw them," answered Bernard. "Some years, in fact; for I went up those steps a man and came down what I am now, never suspecting as I climbed what was in wait for me. Questioning, torture, and death I half-expected; nor was I disturbed by it. Such things must be considered part of the life of anyone who chooses to be a man-at-arms. But this—this I had not expected. However, to answer you: No."

"How wide then?" persisted Brian.

"Wide enough perhaps for three, if you crowd closely together," said Bernard, "but I suggest that if you want your sword arms free, you go no more than two, side by side, up the steps. You'll notice one end of them touches against a wall. That end will continue against the wall; for the steps wind up the inner surface of the tower. After you've passed several levels, there'll be only the naked steps and the walls of the tower going up and up before you, with a drop off the open end of the steps that becomes deeper as you climb, and is interrupted only as you reach the top of the tower. In one of those top levels your Prince is held."

He paused as if so much talking was beginning to hurt his hoarse voice. "Also in one of those top levels," he went on, "is the secret working place of Malvinne himself. So you can see that he's kept his prisoner close to his most secret secrets all the time; and therefore no doubt warded not only with locks and bolts—for no one is welcome up there except by special order—but by magic, as well."

He paused and stepped backward to the door.

"Go, then," he said, "and luck with you. I would wish you Godspeed, but I doubt that God hears from such as I nowadays. And if you should chance to slay Malvinne in your rescue attempt, you may command me for the rest of my days."

He opened the door behind him, but hesitated before stepping through.

"I will try to be somewhere outside the outer door when you come down," he said finally, "but the odds are against it, since I am not free most of the time to do what I wish. But when I am free, I will be close. Don't count on me, then; but go swiftly to the opening of that path from which we came out, and which I had you look at so closely. Once in that, you stand half a chance of getting free; so be it that the creatures of Malvinne are not close behind you."

He went out and the door closed behind him.

"Let us be moving," said Giles eagerly. "I could swear I feel his royal self waiting above us."

They moved out together. There had been no one in the first room they had stepped into, and the second had only a few people, some entirely human, some half animal, stacking sacks, which Jim guessed were filled with grains or other food, so that the room was a sort of warehouse or storage locker.

No one spoke to them and they spoke to no one, going quickly the length of the room and through the left door.

They entered a kitchen that seemed to be given over to the preparation of fowl; and beyond that were more rooms in which more things were being stored or being taken from the walls against which they were piled. All in all, it was only a short length of time until they stood before what should be the final door.

Here they stopped for a moment. The rest looked at Jim.

Jim looked at the door, wishing there was some way he could see through it. He was positive that somewhere inside of him was some sort of enabling magic that would allow him to do so. But his mind could not envision any that would make it possible.

"We'll just have to take our chances on what's beyond," he said at last; and, leading the way, he opened the door and pushed his way through the opening into the area beyond.

Bernard had not exaggerated the difference. The room they stepped into was almost as large as all the others they had passed, put together. Its walls soared to a ceiling that must have been between thirty and fifty feet high; and the floor itself was covered, not with a single stretch of carpeting, but with innumerable small rugs that had the same effect. Some ornate furniture stood, as the furniture had stood in the various inns they had stopped at—and as, Jim had learned, was medieval custom—against the walls.

This room was thronged with people, all of them human, young, and good-looking and all of them dressed in expensive, if sometimes fanciful, costumes. They were standing around in groups, gossiping it seemed; but unlike the people that they had come across before, these did pay attention to them, breaking off their conversations and frankly staring at the four men and Aargh.

Chapter 25

"K eep moving!" commanded Jim under his breath; and the five swept forward, ignoring the stares, comments, and a few small burblings of laughter from those around them—driving forward, as if they were in the grip of some very strict duty, to the foot of the stairs, against the wall on their right.

The minute it became obvious that they were going up the stairs, the attention of those in the room left them. It was as if knowledge of their destination had made them, not only no longer of interest, but something into which it probably would be better not to inquire.

In silence they mounted the stairs, the only sound being that of their boots upon the stone surface of the steps. Aargh, as usual, moved noiselessly.

After a large number of steps, they passed through an opening in the ceiling; and their staircase, which spiraled around the wall of the tower, carried them beyond the sight of those below. They looked down now on a different room, this one equally lavish in its furnishings—even to a small pool and a fountain tucked in a corner of the room—but with no living creature in it.

They went on up.

Jim had discovered when he was very young that he was almost completely free of the fear of heights that bothered so many other people. As a boy he had taken advantage of this to show off to his friends, by going where they dared not follow.

He had stopped this only when one friend, obviously terrified but determined to do what Jim had done, tried to follow him along a ledge that was barely a couple of inches wide, panicked, and almost fell to his death.

Sobered by the knowledge that his freak ability was not to be played with, Jim stopped using it to show off. In the years between, he had all but forgotten it. It only came back to mind in situations where he realized he was with somebody else who might be bothered by heights.

Because of all this, he had unthinkingly taken the outside of the steps, where his feet trod inches from the edge of the gray stone; that had no guardrail above it and fell away to the ceiling of the last floor they had passed.

Between the lower floors it had not been bad. But then these lower floors ceased; and they began the long climb toward the circular ceiling far above them that signaled the floor at the top of the tower. Now the empty space beyond the edge of his right boot deepened and deepened. He congratulated himself on having started in this position; so as to save his friends the vertigo they might have experienced there.

Glancing at his companions, he saw that his self-congratulation was justified. Beside him, Brian was hugging the wall against which each step anchored. Below them, Giles and Dafydd had instinctively crowded together, also near the wall. One step below them even Aargh was much closer to the wall than to the outside of the steps.

They continued to mount, however; and while Jim's fearlessness of heights continued to hold good, as the distance of empty space by his right boot increased, he found himself glancing upward at the narrowing spiral of steps that went up and up and up toward the top floor of the tower. For the first time it struck him what a fragile route this was, with the steps cantilevered out from the wall.

Their farther ends would be buried deep in the wall to counterbalance them and anyone who might walk up them; but still, there was a possibility of a block cracking and giving way, precipitating anyone on it to the depths below, where death would be certain.

With this thought in mind, he felt a slight touch of vertigo himself, as he looked up at what seemed to be the endless spiral of the stairway upward on the now-naked walls of the tower. However, as he looked, he began to alter his attitude about the fragility of the steps. He noted that, all the way up, the stairs were supported underneath by a thick triangular spine that projected from the wall; a spine that must be at least six or eight feet deep at the wall and curved outward to where it was even a couple of feet in thickness under the outward end of the step.

The stairs might look fragile, seen from his perspective looking up the tower, but obviously they were not. They had been built most solidly.

It was at this point in his thinking that he was interrupted by Brian.

"We have been climbing at a fast pace," said Brian breathlessly. "Maybe it would not be amiss to rest for a moment or two, then go on more slowly, since there seem to be so many more steps above us?"

"Of course," said Jim, and stopped, hearing those behind him stop as well.

To his surprise, his own voice had been breathless. Immersed in his thoughts, he had not realized how the climb had been getting to them; and that he was probably responsible. As his thoughts had taken hold of him, he had increased his climbing speed unconsciously. There was no need to race up these stairs. If Brian had not called his attention to it, his own body would have forced him to acknowledge that it was getting breathless and tired, within a few more minutes.

Brian leaned against the wall to his left and breathed heavily. Below him, Giles was leaning against the interior wall the same way and Dafydd, in lieu of leaning up against Giles, had reached one long arm past the knight and was supporting himself on that. Below, Aargh was leaning against nothing, but his jaws were open and his tongue was out as he panted.

Jim was a little surprised that he had been able to exhaust those with him, all of whom he knew to be in much better shape than himself. It just went to show how mental occupation could block out physical discomfort to a certain extent— unless, somehow, his ability to work magic had entered into it, so that he had unconsciously and magically ordered his lungs to supply him with more oxygen.

The final thought struck him as farfetched. But at the same time, it started him to thinking. And he cursed himself silently for not having thought in that vein before. Malvinne obviously kept no guards on this stair. It could be he trusted completely to the fear of those who served him, to keep them from mounting the stairway without proper permission. But was it likely that such a magician would trust to that alone?

Not likely, Jim concluded.

Somewhere up ahead, Malvinne must have laid some magic traps for any foolish or unwanted intruder. At first, the notion filled Jim with despair; for he knew very well that Malvinne was capable of setting traps that would be far beyond his own magical ability to comprehend. Unless . . . Malvinne was trusting to the lack of suspicion and experience of those who might try to climb as Jim and his friends were doing now.

At the same time, Jim, with his little knowledge of magic, could not imagine what kind of traps Malvinne, with his much greater knowledge, might choose to set.

That was the sticker. He had learned the hard way that in order to create any magical change he had to be able to envision both whatever he started with and whatever the result was to be. Since he had no idea what kind of traps Malvinne would lay, he had no way of doing that with them.

He found himself pinched between a need and a lack of knowledge. There had to be some way around it. . . .

Abruptly, something occurred to him. Hastily he wrote on the inside of his forehead:

ME/SEE———>MAGICWORKSABOVEINRED

As usual, there was no particular feeling to tell him if one of his attempts at magic had worked. So far, he had been able to confirm success only when a change occurred to show him that his attempt had worked, as when he turned into a dragon; or when he had made himself able to breathe in Melusine's lake. So now he was left wondering whether his latest attempt at magic had actually worked or not. He looked up the inside of the tower; but could see no difference.

"We should get on," said Brian.

The knight had got his breath back, and behind him Jim could hear that Giles and Dafydd also were breathing less obviously. He glanced back and saw that Aargh had also stopped panting.

"You're right," he said, "let's go."

They resumed their climb, this time more slowly. Brian had been quite right about the speed with which they had been mounting the steps. It was very easy to exhaust yourself going up steps like these in a hurry. If they had been the kind of steps that Jim had been used to in buildings back in the twentieth century, it would not have been so bad. But these steps, while only about eighteen inches wide, each rose a good two feet above the one before, so that climbing them, particularly at speed, was not all that easy.

Now, at a slow and steady pace, they climbed without too much difficulty. They had covered about half the distance between them and the bottom of the first of the tower's upper stories, when Jim saw something that brought him to an abrupt halt. Brian stopped beside him, and the ones behind also stopped.

"What is it, James?" asked Brian.

"I thought I just saw something," answered Jim. "Let me go back down a couple of steps."

He went back down Aargh's step and looked up. Even here, the angle was bad, so he went another half dozen steps down the stairs. Above him, the rest were staring at him—all except Aargh, who seemed to be grinning slightly, as if at a secret joke.

From the step on which he finally stopped, Jim was not only further underneath what he was viewing, but was partway around the tower from it, so that he looked at it more directly. What had caught his eye was the color red. He made it out clearly now. The final step before the stairs reached the top landing shone red all the way through, including the buttressing underneath it. In fact, the whole structure glowed in a subdued way, as if it had been carved in one piece from a dull ruby.

"I've just tried a little magic to look for traps that Malvinne might have set for anyone coming up," Jim told the rest as he rejoined them, "and I've spotted one. It's the step just before the landing."

They started up the stairs once more, Jim's mind busy with the business of that final step. His first assumption was that the whole step and buttress were hinged inside the wall, so the moment anyone stepped upon it the added weight would cause it to pivot, throwing the unfortunate person out and down for the long, fatal fall to the ceiling of the level far below.

He thought no more about it until they were right at the very top of the stairs; then he discovered an additional complication. The step that he still saw marked in red was not like the steps below it. It was a good eight feet in width. That meant that a standing broad jump from the step below was not likely to carry anyone across. The trap had been a little more complex than he had figured.

Jim called a halt while they all considered this.

"It looks like we're well and truly blocked," said Jim grimly. "Any touch against that step may send whoever touches it into a fall. Does anybody have any ideas?"

There was a dead silence from his companions. Brian and Giles were staring at what to them must appear to be an ordinary step, except for its unusual width. Dafydd was also considering it, but with a more thoughtful look on his face. Aargh was merely looking at it intently, his head a little forward, his ears up, his mouth closed.

"Shame to us if we go back!" said Giles, after a long moment.

"Yes," said Brian.

But still, neither of them made any suggestions on how the gap might be bridged.

It was to Jim at last that an idea came. It was not an idea he particularly liked; but it seemed the only possible way that any of them could think of. He cleared his throat to draw the attention of all the others.

"I've got a plan," he said. "It's not one I particularly like; and I doubt that the rest of you are going to enjoy it either."

"Liking has little enough to do with duty," said Sir Brian; and Giles murmured assent. Dafydd merely nodded; and Aargh looked at him with yellow eyes.

"I can turn myself into a dragon and fly over this step, myself," said Jim. "The problem is to get the rest of you over. Now you all weigh too much for me to simply pick you up and fly off with you—"

"Can this be so?" asked Giles. "Remember, you're a very large dragon, James. Also, it seems to me I've heard many times of dragons snatching people up and carrying them off to—er—uh—dine upon them at their leisure."

"I think you'll find most stories like that have little substance in fact," answered Jim grimly, "or if they have, it was actually a small child or something weighing not more than a hundred pounds that the dragon picked up and carried off. Believe me, I know what I can do as a dragon; and there's no way I can carry a full-grown human being any distance and stay aloft."

He turned to Brian.

"But let me tell you the rest of what I plan," he said. "There isn't room here on the steps for me to change into a dragon. So what I'll do is jump off into the air and make the change as I'm falling."

Aargh grinned. Brian frowned. Giles's eyes got as large as saucers.

"James," said Giles, "does it work that way for you? Do you turn into a dragon automatically when you get into the air?"

"Well, not quite," said Jim, "but I think I'll have plenty of time to change into a dragon and fly back up before I fall the whole way down, or hurt myself."

He paused for a moment, thinking that the phrase "before I hurt myself" was rather an understatement.

"Then once I'm a dragon I'll swoop by and take you up, one by one, over that step," said Jim. "Now, all of you but Aargh will have to do one thing. Take off your belt and wrap its ends around your fists so that it can't come loose; and hold the rest of the belt up over your head, so that I've got something to grab with the claws on my hind legs. You've got that?"

"If you mean do we understand you, James," said Brian, "indeed we do. And then I can imagine the rest. You want us each, one by one to hold on as you carry us to the landing? Am I right?"

"Exactly right," said Jim.

"Yes," said Brian, "I've not been hawking since I was twelve years old without knowing something about what might be necessary in a case like this."

"Now there's one more thing I want you to do for me," Jim went on. "The one who is going to be lifted by me should stand on the step by himself, with everybody else at least three steps below, so that I'll have plenty of room to come in. Please stand as close to the outer edge of the step as you can bring yourself to do. I'll need room for my wing that's closest to the wall. Stand crouched with your legs bent, ready to jump. And when you feel me take hold of the belt over your head, *jump!* Jump as if you're going to cover that whole step ahead of you by yourself, without my help. That's understood?"

All three men nodded.

"Now, there's one other thing," said Jim. "I'm going to have to take my clothes off to turn into a dragon—otherwise I'd burst them apart. So I'll do that right now."

As a matter of fact, he had already begun to strip off the things he was wearing.

"Take my belt here," said Jim, handing it to Dafydd, "and make a loose loop around Aargh's back and stomach with the buckle on top, and just behind his shoulders. That'll give me some way to grab hold of him and lift and carry him over the step. Also, Aargh, you can help me by jumping upward and forward at the same time."

"That I can do," said Aargh sardonically. "In fact, if it came down to it, I might be able to make the leap myself, even without your help—though it would be a close thing, a very close thing. But I think you've forgotten something, James. That belt of your is going to do you little good if it's lying flat on my shoulders. Better you sink your talons right into me to lift me; as you may do anyway, if you try to take hold of the leather strap lying on my shoulders."

"Two of us could crouch each side of Aargh," said Brian, "low enough so that we would be below the level of his back, but pushing up the leather on each side so that it stood up and bowed above his back and gave you some room to catch it. What of that, James?"

"That sounds good," answered Jim. He was nearly naked now; and conscious that the tower was uncomfortably cold. The goose bumps on his skin, and the thought of jumping off the steps and changing form in midair, were leaving him feeling a little queasy inside. Heights, he was not afraid of—but courting possible suicide was something that not even his indifference to heights could ignore.

Nonetheless, he stood at last completely naked. He tied all his clothes in his shirt and threw the shirt beyond the magic step safely onto the landing. Then he turned to the edge of the step he was on and hesitated there. The granite of the steps was cold under the naked soles of his feet.

He found himself beginning to hesitate a little bit too long. He was conscious of the eyes of the others on him. Dafydd had already buckled Jim's belt around Aargh's chest, just behind the shoulders. Luckily it was a belt that had once belonged to Sir Hugh, and a great deal larger than Jim needed. There was a fair amount of loop above Aargh's shoulders.

There was no putting it off any longer. Jim jumped. He had tried to tell himself, in the split second before jumping, that he was doing no more than a free-fall, as someone might do with a parachute on his back. But the thought was somehow not convincing. He found himself suddenly in midair, with the roof far below rushing up at him. Almost in a panic he wrote the change command on the inside of his forehead.

There was a shock as his wings opened with a flap; and automatically, he began to fly. He checked himself just as he flashed past the others still standing on the steps of the stairway—just in time to keep himself from smashing into the roof barely ten feet above the landing toward which they were all headed. Once again he had forgotten the tremendous surge of lifting power that a dragon could generate in his wings for a short time.

But as the last of his panic left him, he spiraled down within the confines of the tower, which made for very tight turning indeed, then commenced a climb up again.

It was necessary to take Aargh either first or second, since two of the other three had to crouch beside him and hold the loop of leather up. He climbed up, turned in at an angle to the stairway, tilted himself so that his left wing would not brush the stone, and snatched at the leather.

He missed. He went down, gathered himself, came up, and tried it again.

Again he missed, and again. Then, as he was beginning to get desperate, his claws clutched tight on the leather of the belt. Aargh sprang beneath him; and together they lifted over the magic step and onto the landing.

Jim let go of the strap just in time to keep from dashing himself against a wall in which was set a dark wood door.

He angled sharply away, dropped the equivalent of perhaps fifty steps, and came up again. Practice was paying off for him. He needed only two tries to pick up Dafydd and carry him to the landing, and only one try apiece to bring up the two knights.

He almost flew into the wall beside the dark door, after lifting Giles to safety—Giles being the last one up.

Jim banked away just in time and circled outward into the tower. Even the full width of the tower was narrow quarters for a flying creature as large as himself. He turned, dropped a little, climbed again, and made a short swoop to the open space of the landing. For a moment he had toyed with the idea of changing into his human body just as he landed; and then decided that the timing was too tricky.

He pulled up and landed, accordingly, with a thump.

It was a louder thump than he had intended; and clearly his companions thought the same. The two swords and the long knife were out immediately; and Aargh's teeth were bared. All four were clustered around the dark door, like tigers at a gate behind which some prey had taken refuge.

Hastily, Jim changed himself back into a human being. Shivering, he redressed himself, regained his belt from around Aargh, and strapped his sword and poignard on again. For once, strangely, he had felt more vulnerable as a dragon than as a man; and now felt much more confident and able to protect himself in his human shape and with his human weapons. He drew his own sword and joined the group about the door.

"Time to let ourselves in," he said.

Chapter 26

J im led the way, his eyes open for anything colored red. They had stepped into a sort of lobby, from which four entrances opened into further, separate rooms, which filled the rest of the space at this level of the tower. The rooms were smaller than the ones below, because the tower was smaller toward its top, and the ceiling was no more than fifteen feet above the innumerable carpets that were laid down.

The furniture, though still sparse by twentieth-century standards, was opulent and plentiful by fourteenth-century ones. Heavy tapestries hung from ceiling to floor over every inch of the walls except that space where the window slits occurred.

These were slightly wider than ordinary window slits and at least six feet in height. Each one was rimmed with red; and on glancing at them Jim saw why. With the help of magic, in daylight they would be able to admit much more light than something equally tall and wide should; and give a correspondingly larger view of the countryside from their high elevation in the tower. So that the effect would be almost that of a penthouse with picture windows, from Jim's own world, placed at the same height.

Cautiously, with weapons ready, they investigated all the rooms; but, as Aargh had announced almost immediately, there was no one there.

"There's someone above, though," Aargh said. "Human—I can scent whoever it is."

There was a curving staircase nearly as wide as the one they had just come up, leading to the floor directly above. They went up it and discovered another series of rooms off a much smaller central chamber. There were four of these rooms and each one had a solidly closed door that blazed red to Jim's vision.

"The doors are warded with magic," Jim told his friends. "If we can find out without touching them which one might have the Prince behind it, we'd be ahead of the game. Aargh, can you tell?"

Aargh went close to each of the doors in turn—only close, for he stopped a good six or eight feet away—sniffing, and cocking his head to listen.

"There's someone beyond this door," said Aargh, after he had investigated them all and come back to the third one. "A single man, I think, for I can hear him breathing. He seems to be asleep."

"It must be our Prince!" said Sir Giles, moving forward. "Let us in and have him out of there—"

"Stop, Giles!" snapped Jim quickly.

Giles checked and turned to Jim with a wondering, almost injured expression on his face.

"Remember I said it's warded by magic?" Jim reminded him. "Any attempt to open it is undoubtedly going to sound an alarm to Malvinne—if not worse!"

Giles drew back. Jim stood staring at the door. The others waited, staring at him.

"Can't you magic them open, some way, James?" asked Brian after a long moment.

"That's what I'm trying to do!" said Jim; and then felt guilty at having snapped at Brian. "Forgive me Brian. I'm busy concentrating on how to get past that magic."

"It's quite all right, James," said Brian earnestly. "You know I'm well acquainted with Carolinus. One expects such from a mage."

It had never struck Jim before that a necessary concentration of this sort might be some excuse for Carolinus's asperity. But he had no time to think about that now. His mind was galloping.

The more he thought about it, the more certain he became that whatever protected the door would be, aside from anything else, an alarm that would alert Malvinne himself, personally, that someone was trying to get into one of his protected rooms. It was hardly likely he would trust an underling to respond to anything as important as an intrusion into what were obviously his private apartments.

Whatever else the magic might be supposed to do—like burn the would-be entrant to a crisp—it would be set up so that Malvinne himself would not be either warned, or harmed by it, himself, when entering the room. Jim could not possibly understand the magic protecting the door. But it was a safe bet that if he could switch the magic protection from Malvinne to himself, he might be able to keep knowledge of the switch from Malvinne; and at the same time avoid the traps set for anyone who tried to get into one of the rooms.

He thought a moment and then wrote on the inside of his forehead:

ME/NOT MALVINNE———➤MAGIC WARNINGETC./IF THISDOOR OPENED

As usual when he created a magic command in his head, he also made an attempt to envision what the command embodied. In this case the vision he produced was of something like a ray of light being redirected from wherever Malvinne was to himself.

Also, as usual, he heard and saw no difference in anything about him, and felt no specific change.

Still, he found himself staring at the door and doorway and hesitating over what to do next. Theoretically, the door had been disarmed. Now he should be the one who would be warned; and anything dangerous about the door should not operate against him if he tried to open it.

He would not know this until he actually tried to enter the room.

The door, of course, had no knob, twentieth-century fashion. Instead, there was a small bar about where a knob should be—a bar just big enough for the hand to enclose nicely and push. The minute he touched that bar, he would know whether the magic had worked or not.

"All right," he said on a deep intake of breath to the others, without looking around at them. "All of you, stand back. I'm going to try to go in through the door. If I can go in safely, probably the rest of you can. Are you standing back?"

The voices from behind him assured him that they were.

He let out the breath he had been holding, took another, then reached out, grasped the bar and pushed. As he did so, he suddenly realized there might be something as ordinary and mundane as a bolt that was also securing it. But by that time he was already putting his weight against the door to push it open.

No lightning bolt of lethal magic struck him. Only, a deep, gong-type note sounded three times in his head, followed by a voice that said, *"The blue-painted chamber has been opened. The blue-painted chamber has been opened. The blue-painted chamber has been opened. . . ."*

It continued to repeat itself; and he was beginning to think it would go on forever, when it stopped abruptly. He looked about the room and saw a young man just waking up in one of the little beds pushed into a corner, that had been so common everywhere he had gone.

So far, so good. The only question remaining was whether Malvinne had been alerted by some side-element of the magic. If that was so, if he had been alerted after all, then there would be people after them in a hurry. The faster they moved the better.

Jim went into the room. The young man—youth was a better word for him—was sitting up on the edge of the bed and rubbing his eyes. He looked younger than he had at first glance. Somewhere between sixteen and nineteen Jim guessed; although it was sometimes impossible to tell with these fresh English faces, which were youthful until time and weather or scars had left their indelible marks upon them. There was something of the innocence of John Chester about this lad, too. But at the same time, there was something sophisticated. Something that was a result of either training, or a self-control that overlay the visible innocence.

He was dressed simply enough; but his clothes were rich. He had been sleeping, as many people in this world did, in the same clothes in which he lived during the day. Above his hose he was wearing a dark blue *cote-hardie* (or jacket), with tiny jewels, or at least, tiny, refractive bits of jewellike glass sewn into it at certain points, so that they caught the light and flashed as he moved. His hair was an auburn brown, cut short, and there was a gold chain around his neck, from which hung a medallion. The figure on it was unrecognizable to Jim. A pair of ankle-high, soft leather boots stood by the bed; and he paused to pull them on now before speaking to Jim.

It was in that moment that Jim realized that since he was safely inside, perhaps the others could come too. He turned to tell them so, only to discover that they were already there.

The two knights were each down upon one knee, facing the young man on the bed. Dafydd was still on his feet, as was Aargh; but the bowman had taken off his steel cap, which he had been wearing ever since Jim had met him in Blois. It was a man-at-arms cap; very different from the soft, almost beretlike cap that he usually wore.

Jim had obviously been a little too late in warning the others that it might be dangerous to follow him. He put that whole matter aside, now; caught on a rather embarrassing question of etiquette. Theoretically, he should be kneeling too. After all, he was directly in fief to the King who was this youngster's father. But a lifetime of habit got in his way.

"To hell with it!" he told himself under his breath, and remained standing.

"And who might you gentlemen be?" asked the young man, looking at Jim, Brian, and Giles, now that he had pulled on the second of his boots. He gave a wave of his hand. "Rise. By all means, rise. This is no place for ceremony. If you're enemies, I expect none. If you're friends, you're granted permission."

"We are friends, Your Highness," answered Brian, standing up and stepping forward. "And Englishmen—that is, the three of us are English. The one closest to you is Sir James Eckert, Baron de Bois de Malencontri, by gift of your royal father within the last year; and Sir Giles de Mer, a loyal knight of Northumberland. Also, myself, who am Sir Brian Neville-Smythe, a cadet branch of the Nevilles of Raby, if it please Your Highness. The others are also friends, though not English. The tall man with us is a Welshman named Dafydd ap Hywel; and with him is Aargh, an English wolf."

The Prince smiled.

"It sounds to me as if at least four of you are English," he said, "if the wolf so qualifies, also."

"I was born an English wolf and will die an English wolf," said Aargh, "though not of your kingdom, since I'm a free wolf and my people have always been a free people. Still, I'm a friend; and will remain such to you since you come from my own country. Only don't expect human ways from me. That has never been a practice of us wolves."

The Prince yawned involuntarily for a second.

"You are excused from any such manners, Sir Wolf," he said. "I am in no case to look askance at the ways of any friends who reach me here. In fact, I would have never dreamed that anyone, Englishman or otherwise, could find me in this place where Malvinne has me prisoner."

He smiled up at them from the bed.

"And now that you've reached me," he said, "what?"

"We get you out of here, Your Highness," said Jim, "as fast as we can."

"But how are we to do that, James?" Brian asked. "The moment we reach the bottom of the stairs with His Highness here in company, all those down below there will recognize who he is. If they don't attack us then, immediately, they will scatter and spread the warning. And we are in the very heart of Malvinne's castle."

"You are speaking of the stairs that circle the inside of the tower?" asked the Prince, getting to his feet.

"Yes, Your Highness," said Brian.

"I'm not sure," said the Prince, frowning a little, "but I think that Malvinne had another way out of here, a secret way, one known only to himself. He has more or less spoken of it from time to time when we've been together."

"You see him often?" asked Jim.

"He takes meals with me, every other day or so," said the Prince. "In fact, his face is the only one I have ever seen up here in this accursed place that has been my prison."

Jim did a quick calculation in his head. It had been early dark of an evening when Bernard had found them and taken them to the castle. From then until now could not be more than a couple of hours—three at most. There was no danger of Malvinne showing up for lunch right in the middle of their escape.

"He is a curst, overprideful dining companion," went on the Prince, "let alone that he drinks nothing but water with his food. But I must admit the wine he gives me, as well as the food we both eat, is good enough. But most of the time is given over to his telling me of his great powers and abilities; and one of the things that has come up in his conversation from time to time, have been words to the effect that he has his own secret ways about his château."

"But how can there be one from here?" asked Sir Giles. "Begging Your Highness's pardon, I do not mean to seem to doubt what you've heard, but this tower is completely bare, except for the stairs that circle its inside. For myself I can see no way even a flea might escape from here by any other way than the stairway itself."

"No more do I, my good knight of Northumberland," said the Prince. "Nonetheless he has hinted at such—or alluded to it, I should perhaps say. For he never said it out straightly that he had a secret path to and from here."

"It would be a road of magic, no doubt," put in Brian.

"Perhaps . . ." said Jim.

He was thinking deeply and swiftly. Certainly, immediate transference by magical means, from wherever Malvinne might be to this high tower, would be a much more comfortable way of getting here than climbing that long series of steps. On the other hand . . .

There had been something that niggled at the back of Jim's mind ever since Carolinus had mentioned Malvinne's lavish way of life in comparison to the humble one that Carolinus himself followed.

Carolinus had impressed upon him from almost the very first moment of meeting Jim, when Jim was in the body of the dragon Gorbash, that the First Law of Magic was the Law of Payment.

Any kind of magic required payment in equal amount. Moreover, the Accounting Office was there to keep the accounts and make sure that payments balanced income. Income came by doing approved work that produced a credit to a magician's magical balance, in addition to whatever ordinary way it might pay him. Ordinary payment and magical payment had no connection with each other.

For example, Carolinus, on Jim's first meeting with him, had ended up dickering like a tinker at a county fair with Gorbash's granduncle Smrgol. It was only, finally, for what seemed to Jim a rather tremendous price in gold and gems that he agreed to help Jim recover Angie.

Later he had said that if he had realized that the rescue was in a good cause they could have had his help for nothing. Not that he had ever given back the gold and gems, come to think of it. But what that episode had pointed up was the fact that a magician needed ordinary income in order to live in the ordinary world. At the same time he needed a healthy magical balance with the Accounting Office in order to do his magic.

Apparently the magic that was done at Carolinus's level of AAA+ competence, just as at Malvinne's level of AAA, was an expensive process—in terms of that magical balance, if nothing else.

What all this boiled down to was that Malvinne might have a good source of ordinary human income; but he might at the same time be living close to the wire as far as his magical balance went. The Accounting Office would undoubtedly know what his balance was; but Jim was quite sure without asking that they would not tell a class D magician like himself what the balance of a class AAA magician was. But, just assume that Malvinne was in a position where, in order to keep up the way he wanted to live, he had to expend his magical balance close to its available limits.

In that case, he might occasionally, or even routinely, look for ways to do things by ordinary means, so as to avoid doing them by magic and depleting his magical balance any more than necessary.

In that case, if he had a secret way up here, it might well *not* be a magical route. It might be a perfectly ordinary one, but very cleverly hidden from ordinary eyes, to conserve Malvinne's magic balance.

The question was, as Giles had mentioned, where could any other route—from the levels far below up to here—be hidden in this open shell of a tower?

Jim came to a sudden decision.

"How such a way could be is beside the point," he said. "Let's first find the entrance to it, if there is one. Once we've found it we'll automatically find out how it could be hidden."

The faces of the others lit up, but Jim had already turned and headed out, completely forgetting the business about needing the permission of royalty before leaving a room where a royal personage happened to be.

He did remember it, the minute he was outside the door. But then, on second thought, decided that it was a good idea that he had ignored it this time; because with the difficulties they were undoubtedly going to have getting the Prince back to his army of Englishmen, there would be no time for such protocol. Just as well they should start now.

The others had followed him out, by the time he stood facing the three remaining doors. He intended to use the same warning signal transference on each door to let him into the other rooms safely, so that these could be searched. For a moment he played with the idea of some kind of all-purpose command that would open all the doors up to him at once. But he decided to play it safe. He approached the first door on his left, and wrote on his forehead the magical command to switch the warning from Malvinne to him if the door was open.

He went in this time without hesitation. The room within was completely bare. The others had followed him in; and he left them to search it while he went to try the next room. This also was completely bare. There was a stone outer wall with its window slits—the curving wall of the tower itself—and the three flanking walls, also of stone. Nowhere was there any red coloring to suggest magic had been used to guard anything like a secret entrance.

He left it and went on to try the fourth room and found that to be about triple the size of the other three rooms, including the one in which the Prince had been held.

This room was clearly the fourteenth-century equivalent of a laboratory. A number of odd-looking instruments and vessels, almost entirely of glass, were scattered around on tables and on shelves against the wall. Most of these containers had cryptic marks on them. It occurred to Jim that there was probably some magical way to make those marks readable; but there was really no time for that sort of thing now. Whatever was in them would probably not help them escape in any case.

Beyond this equipment and the tables on which it was set out, the jumble in the room held nothing living, except for something that looked rather like a large yellow birdcage, which contained six rather ordinary looking house mice.

Jim opened the cage door, on the principle that it would at least give the mice a chance at freedom away from Malvinne. But the mice cowered in a corner and made no attempt to go out through the doorway. Jim simply left them in the cage with the door ajar. Soon or later, he guessed, they would summon up the courage to stick their heads outside and shortly after that they would find themselves free. After that it would be up to them.

He went back to the open lobby space of the second floor outside the entrance to the four rooms. The others gathered around him, waiting for further commands.

It surprised Jim that the Prince had not been full of questions or demands. Part of him had been braced for that. However, in this society, whoever led at any time was the leader. His leadership could be challenged, of course; and probably often was. But until that happened, everybody else seemed to fall into line and follow automatically, ready to obey.

"Sir James is a Mage, Your Highness," he heard Brian explaining to the Prince. "That's how he was able to open the doors safely. Otherwise Magic probably would have destroyed us and warned Malvinne.

"Indeed!" said the Prince, looking at Jim with a freshened respect.

"A magician of a much lower class and ability than that of Malvinne, I'm afraid, Your Highness," said Jim. It would not do to let the Prince get any false ideas about what Jim could accomplish. "Look, there's obviously no entrance up here. We'll examine things down below, in what seem to be Malvinne's private quarters."

He hurried down the stairs with the others after him, telling himself that he should have looked downstairs in the first place. It would be much more likely that any private entrance would be in Malvinne's own rooms, rather than in his laboratory, or in the other rooms he kept—either as cells or for whatever purpose might be needed.

On the floor below, he was struck again by the richness of the furnishings. What furniture there was, was carefully built, carved, and finished. Moreover, outside of a few low tables and some piles of cushions that gave the place almost an oriental look, there were none of the ordinary stools or tables that had been constructed for service only.

The layers of rugs were thick on the floor and the heavy tapestries hung still on the walls, not even stirred by the occasional drafts that came up the hollow tower from below.

"I think all of us should search, so as to cover as much ground as quickly as possible," said Jim, "including yourself, Your Highness, if you'll be so good? You, more than any of us, might have heard something from him that you don't recall right away, but which could suggest something to you when you look at it down here. For the rest of you, look for anything that resembles a door, or could be a door in disguise—a panel, a chest, anything of that sort."

They scattered to do as he said. Meanwhile, Jim himself went hunting, not for any particular signs of a doorway, but for anything that showed the color red about it. If there was a secret entrance to the way they had imagined, it would almost certainly be guarded by magic. While the others went over each room closely and Aargh used his nose in various places, Jim searched the walls and even the floor for any glimpse of red.

The total space covered by the rooms down here was only slightly larger than that of the rooms they had looked at upstairs, because of the way the tower narrowed from its base upward to its top. There would be a roof above the floor above, or else an open space protected with breast-high walls, so that the tower could be defended in normal medieval fashion from any who might try to storm it.

Jim did not think there was any point in looking up there. Any entrance that they might find there would have to pass through both floors below to provide passage downward; and while a passage might be hidden somewhere on this level, certainly there had been none hidden on the one above. Putting all the rooms together, it had been possible to see the bare wall of the tower all around.

It took them only about half an hour to make their search. It would not have taken that long if it had not been for the extra furniture and some cabinets or cupboards that needed to be investigated. None of these were warded by magic; so Jim let the others look into them. Aargh in particular stuck his head into each one to see what his nose could tell him. In each case the result was negative. In fact, the result was negative as far as the whole floor was concerned. They met together once more, outside the rooms of the floor, clustered next to the stairway and baffled.

"I fear me, Sir James," said the Prince, "that whatever road Malvinne traveled other than the stairway must have been a magic one. Certainly, we have searched this area high and low and found nothing."

Curiously, their very lack of success was making Jim stubborn. The more he thought of it the more he became convinced that there had to be a secret and purely physical route from here down to the floors below. Suddenly, an idea exploded in his head.

"Look again!" he said, suddenly. "Look behind the tapestries. Look for anything red—but if you do see red, whatever you do, don't touch it."

"Red, James?" asked Brian.

Jim swore at himself internally. Of course, he was the only one who was able to see the warning color he had picked. Hastily, he wrote a new magic command on the inside of his forehead:

ALL SEE———>MAGICWARNING RED, HERE

"Yes," Jim said. "I've just now done a bit of small magic that should make any such doorway shine with the color red. If you see anything like that, call me at once. Again, don't touch it. Don't even get close to it if you can avoid it. Anything that is red-colored may be deadly."

They scattered once more to their searching and Jim himself began feverishly working down one of the walls, lifting the edge of the tapestries away from the stone.

This time their search took a little longer, perhaps something over an hour; but it also turned up nothing in the way of what they sought.

When they were all back together Jim noticed that Aargh, instead of standing with the rest, was apparently asleep against a pile of cushions on the floor. He looked as if he had been there for some time.

"Aargh!" called Jim. "Didn't you search like the rest?"

Aargh opened one eye and then the other, then got to his feet and shook himself.

"No," he answered.

They all stared at him.

"Why not?" demanded Jim.

"I should have thought one like yourself would know, James," said Aargh. "We wolves are unable to see what you on two legs call colors. To us, such differences are merely part of a straightforward world of black and white and gray. Indeed I have only the word of humans for it that there's anything beyond those shades I see.

"Nor, probably, would I have been that useful if I had been able to see this red coloring," went on Aargh, with a yawn. "My eyes are not good for that kind of seeing; though in other ways I often notice things that you others will not. Of course if this 'red' had a scent, the rest of you would probably be far behind me in discovering any of it."

"Of course! I've been a fool!" said Jim. "Aargh, prepare to use that nose of yours!"

"You are not going to magic me?" demanded Aargh swiftly.

"No, no!" said Jim. "I'm going to magic what we hunt for. So that in addition to having color it'll have scent. How about the scent of garlic?"

"That," said Aargh, and his jaws opened as if he was laughing, "is one that I think even you humans might find in time. By all means let it be garlic."

Jim wrote a new magical command on the inside of his forehead:

MAGIC———>RED TO SMELL LIKE GARLIC

The words were barely written before Aargh's ears pricked up and he trotted over to the landing just above the magic stair which they had gone to such difficulty to surmount. He sniffed at some rugs there. Then he shoved the end of his muzzle down under the edge of one of the top rugs; and took what seemed to be a deep and highly enjoyable sniff. He took the edge of the rug between his teeth and pulled it aside.

"Well, James," he said, dropping the rug he had pulled aside and going back to attack the one underneath it, "what are you waiting for? I've found it."

There was a concerted rush to the spot and they all began hauling aside the many layers of rug.

As they drew them clear, a glint of color began to be visible. A glint of red.

"Stand back, stand back all of you!" said Jim. "I'll do the last of the uncovering, here."

He waited until the others had backed off, then he bent down and began pulling the last few rugs clear. They came back to reveal a trapdoor in the floor; and it was glowing solidly red. Once more the magical warning rang in Jim's head.

He waited until it had cleared, and then turned to the others.

"I'm going to try opening this trapdoor," he told them. "I ought to be able to do it as safely as I opened the doors upstairs; but in case I don't, and anything happens to me, try making some kind of a rope, attaching a weight to it, and letting the weight fall off this landing into the open air in such a way that the weight of it pulls back and up on the trapdoor to open it. Then one of you try it and see if it's safe. If it is, the rest can follow after."

"You fear for your life if you lift that trapdoor, James?" said Brian.

"There's some risk," admitted Jim.

"In that case," said Brian, "let me do it. You are more useful to His Highness in helping him clear of this damnable place than any of the rest of us. So if there be risk, let me take it first."

"Thanks, Brian," said Jim. He was touched; for he read more in Brian's words than just a concern for the safety of the Prince. He knew Brian too well. The other was also concerned about him, James; and as usual was offering to put himself between danger and his friend. "But I'm afraid the magic that should protect me won't protect the rest of you. So there's no choice about it. I have to be the one who tries to lift the door first. Stand back."

He turned to the trapdoor again without looking to see whether they did as he had said. Reaching out, he took a firm hold of the handle of the trapdoor, which was not really different from the handles of the doors upstairs; except that it was set into the surface of the trapdoor, which must be of some considerable thickness.

He took hold of it, therefore, expecting to lift a heavy weight. But the trapdoor must have been counterweighted in some way, because it tilted up easily at the first effort he put into lifting it, revealing an open hole and steps leading down. The red did not touch the underpart of the trapdoor, or anything below the floor in which it was inset. Looking more closely, he saw the red coloring around the trapdoor had disappeared, as it probably did whenever that which it identified as Malvinne's hand lifted it.

"So," said Jim, "there's our solution. See where it leads?"

He pointed. The steps led down into the buttressing below the regular staircase. The space was so narrow they would have to go single file, and both Dafydd and Jim would have to duck their heads as well because there was not much space between the steps they trod on and the underside of the steps above their heads. But it was clearly and plainly their passage out and away from here.

"Follow me," Jim said to the others. "Your Highness had better be the one directly behind me. All of you be careful so that you step from a rug directly onto the first step below the surface of this floor. I don't think the edge of the hole is still dangerous to you, but it might be."

"You've done well, Sir James," said the Prince, looking at him with a touch of awe, "as did Sir Wolf. I will remember this in both your cases."

He looked around himself generally.

"As I will remember all of you, my rescuers," he said.

"We aren't out of it yet," said Jim, "but at least we have a chance."

In spite of his words, his heart had lightened. He had the feeling that if Malvinne had gone to the trouble to make a secret passage like this, it could well lead by secret ways clear outside the castle. At least, it might be a good bet. But he hesitated to mention this to the others yet, for fear that this guess of his should turn sour.

He headed down the steps and the others followed. Jim carefully closed the trapdoor, with rugs atop it, behind them.

Chapter 27

The steps and walls about them
glowed with what was unmistakably a magic form of lighting. As they got about
ten or fifteen feet below the level of the landing, the headroom increased so that
Jim and Dafydd could walk upright. Jim had feared that they would have to make
their trip in darkness, feeling their way down the stairs. That Malvinne had set up
lighting was only to be expected, and Jim was inwardly embarrassed he had not
expected it.

Still, there was reason for self-congratulation. It was still a long, slow climb
down the secret stairway to the inhabited regions where the other stairway above
them had begun to wind upward. Jim discovered a bonus in their descent,
however. Little cracks had been allowed between the steps and the risers, in
places.

These were apparently accidental cracks. But they occurred at fairly regular
intervals; and by looking out through them he was able to get a limited, but very
useful, view of how close they were getting to the level from which they had
originally begun their upward climb.

Finally, they were almost back to that original level. Jim led the way down the
last of the stairs; and they came to a place where the secret passage ended. Where
it stopped, it was crossed by another passage leading two ways.

To the left, it led up steep stairs and around a corner, as if it would climb to the height of another tower. To their right, a smooth-floored, narrow passage tilted slightly downward, as if by gentle degrees it would descend to a somewhat lower level.

Jim moved out to the right on this smooth floor to give the others room to descend, so that they could all stand together. The stairway to their left had cracks through which light filtered, and there were a few such cracks in the ceiling of the smooth passage, although the height of the ceiling there made them impossible to look through. Nevertheless, they relieved the gloom with light from outside; enough so that the passage below was visible.

"Now where, Sir James?" asked the voice of the Prince in Jim's ear.

Jim turned from inspecting the dimly lit, smooth-floored passage to look at the stairs again and then at his companions.

"I've no sure way of knowing which way to take, right or left," he told them. "Does anybody else have reason to think one might be better for us than the other?"

There was a complete silence from the rest of them. Even Aargh did not make a suggestion.

"Aargh," said Jim, "doesn't your nose tell you anything about what might lie either up those stairs or along this passage?"

"It's the same smells everywhere," answered the voice of Aargh. "Two legs, food, and all the smells of the places where you people live."

Jim drew a deep breath.

"All right, then," he said. "In that case, it seems to me that we want to go anywhere but up. The passage to the right slants down a little, as if it might come out at ground level outside the castle, or even underneath it for some distance. That might mean that if we go to the right, we'll be on a secret escape-way that Malvinne's had made for himself in case his castle should be attacked and overrun. I think we should turn right."

There was another short moment of silence and then the voice of the Prince answered.

"In this situation, you lead, Sir James," said the Prince. "I don't see a better course for us than following you."

"Thank you, Your Highness," answered Jim. "Here we go, then."

He turned and led off along the downward sloping tunnel. He could hear the others following.

Things seemed quite ordinary and straightforward—until, without warning, the path beneath him suddenly pitched steeply downward and his feet slid out from under him as if the floor had been greased. He tumbled to the ground and began sliding downward with increasing speed. Behind him, he could hear the others also falling and sliding after him, under the cover of the Prince's wordless shout of alarm, and the rich cursing of Brian and.Giles.

The speed of their fall increased to incredible proportions, so that they seemed to be going down at the rate of a bobsled on a bobsled run. It became apparent that the path was circling downwards in a spiral, as the stairs had spiraled up the inside of the tower. Jim suddenly saw a flash of red behind his eyes—not in reality, but in his mind.

As his senses began to swim from the incredibly rapid swirling, he found time to rage at himself over a mistake that had been purely his own.

Going up the staircase, he had written on the inside of his forehead the magic command that enabled him to see anything magical higher up than where he was, any trap, in red. But he had applied this specifically to traps up and ahead of him.

He had not stopped to think that they might encounter magic at a lower level in the castle. Now, clearly, they had. Some kind of magical trap had been laid at the point where the secret stairway reached the cross-path. And he, idiot that he was, had phrased his command so badly that, going down like this, the trap had not shown itself in warning color the way the ones above had done. Now it was too late and they were caught in this slippery, spinning chute that was carrying them into the bowels of the earth.

How long their fall lasted, was impossible to say. Jim later thought that he must have passed out at some stage, either from dizziness or from some other, magical reason. At any rate he came to, abruptly, lying hard up against something vertical and unyielding; with the bodies of the others piled up against him, so that he felt crushed to the point of suffocation.

He opened his mouth to ask the others to get off him; but they were already doing so. A second later, he was able to climb to his own feet.

They stood in total darkness.

"Where are we?" came the voice of Giles. "My memory fails me. I remember only just a moment ago waking to find we were here."

The voices of Brian and the Prince agreed.

"But where are we? Sir James?" went on the voice of the Prince. "Are you there, Sir James?"

"I'm touching Your Highness," said Jim. He moved his arm against the body next to him, to prove the point.

"What do we now then, Sir James?" demanded the Prince. "I'm still dizzy, but I think I can keep on my feet. Where are we?"

"I don't know, Highness," answered Jim. "I'm right next to some kind of wall. Wait a minute. Let me see if there's some kind of opening in it, or if it opens itself."

He turned to face the vertical surface against which he had been pressed and began running the palms of his hands over it. It felt like wood, rather than stone or anything else; and the suspicion came to his mind that it might be some kind of door. He searched across it at a level at which a handle might be; and, sure enough, he came across one of the small handles that he had found on other doors in Malvinne's castle.

He pushed on it. But it did not move. He tried pulling, and it gave easily.

Almost without intending to, he flung the door wide, and light flooded in, blinding them all for a moment. Jim, who had been leaning forward, half-fell, half-stumbled out, and heard the others coming after him. Gradually, his sight cleared.

They stood on what seemed to be a tightly fenced-in landing, barely large enough to accommodate all of them. From the landing to the right of the doorway, a short flight of steps led downward to the floor of what seemed to be an enormous stone cavern. At least, the floor was stone, the nearer wall was stone, and the farther wall, some thirty yards away, looked to be stone also. But the walls went up vertically until they were lost in a place to which the light around them, for which there seemed no particular source, failed to reach. There was no way to be sure whether it was a true cavern in the sense that the stone walls finally arched together to completely close it in, or not.

Reason said that there had to be a roof up there somewhere. They had fallen so far that a good deal of the earth's crust must lie between them and the surface above. Also, the light was neither the light of the sun nor of the moon or stars. It was a strange, unnatural light, such as might be found underground.

They stood all together, like prisoners in a three-sided cage, looking down at the floor of the cavern. It was thronged with people, men and women, in what seemed to be black uniforms, wearing strange hiltless knives almost the length of a sword, and carrying round, targetlike shields. They were all perfectly visible in the strange light, with one exception.

As Jim looked directly at their faces, he recognized none of them, but as his gaze shifted around, it seemed to him that out of the corner of his eye, a face he had looked at just a moment before altered and became the face of someone he had once known and liked, if not loved. But all these faces seemed frozen, distorted into an expression mixed of almost insane hate, fear, and terror.

The one space clear of this multitude was thirty yards directly ahead of their landing; and twenty yards ahead of the foremost of the blackclad figures below; and this space was clear except for two enormous thrones on which sat two equally enormous figures.

One was male, one female. They wore loose robes that covered them from the upper chest to just below the knees. Their arms were extended along the arms of their thrones. Their most marked difference from the humans, outside of their size—for they must be, Jim thought, at least twenty feet tall—were their abnormally long necks, which accounted for a good four or five feet of their height.

Above his neck, the head of the man was a handsome one, with dark hair and piercing eyes, the hair clinging tightly to his round head. The woman's hair was also black and clung closely to her head; and she was darkly beautiful.

Both faces were expressionless. It was not, however, until Jim's gaze shifted from them back to the blackclad horde below, that he recognized the real peculiarity about the two on the thrones.

Just as the faces of those in black had seemed to shift and change just before they moved out of the range of his vision, so the faces of the enthroned man and woman—if that was what they could be called—seemed to shift; her face to that of a serpent, his to that resembling a jackal. But this animal aspect of them could not be seen when Jim focused directly on them. It was only just as he glimpsed them peripherally that he could see the snake head and the jackal head.

Whatever else this was, it was not a place for Jim and the rest. Jim turned swiftly to the door behind him, took hold of the handle on this side, and tried to pull the door open. But it was now as solid and immovable as the surrounding rock. Swiftly, he wrote on the inside of his forehead:

ALL LOCKS, LATCHES——→RETREAT

He concentrated on the image of bolts and latches withdrawing into their recesses and leaving the door free from the frame in which it stood.

It did not give. But his attempt produced a response from one of the mighty figures.

"So!" A great voice rolled toward them. The male of the two enthroned figures was speaking. "Violation upon violation! One of you is a magician. Having already sinned in Our eyes by coming here alive—all of you—one of you is sealed to forbidden arts. Your kind has always been prohibited from this place, magician— and, as you see, your magic will not work here. Here, nothing rules but Our laws."

"God save us all!" said Giles.

"Your God can do nothing for you here, either." Again the great voice rolled from the huge figure like thunder between the stone walls. "Six of you. A beast from above, four living humans, and a magician. All an offense in this place. And armed as well. Let their weapons fly from them!"

None of the black horde below moved; but the poignards and swords beside each knight stirred in their sheaths. That was all. Brian and Giles both had their hands already upon the hilts of their weapons. Brian whipped his sword from its sheath and held it point-up before him.

"You cannot take this!" he shouted in a voice burning with fury. "It is a *cross*; and, for all your boasting, it is not for you to take it from a Christian knight! Pull it from my hand if you can!"

On the throne both the man and woman were frowning like thunderclouds. The sword in Brian's fist stirred again; but did not leave his grasp.

"Indeed," said Dafydd, as controlled as always, "but there is no hilt to my knife, and yet that has not been taken. Ah, I see now, the board with which I tie it down makes a cross upon the hilt, and holds it to its sheath. As do the cords upon the casings of my bow and quiver."

Jim's heart, which had sunk clear out of sight, stirred and began to rise again with a faint hope.

"This is the Kingdom of the Dead; and we are King and Queen of it!" thundered the huge male figure. "Though some small things may not answer to us, that will not save you! You will be dealt with. Oh yes, you will be dealt with!"

Aargh snarled.

"You are Ours," the King of the Dead went on, unheeding, "and we will deal with you in such a manner as the lesson will be remembered for thousands of years by those who might once again violate our place with living bodies. The dead we receive down here; but the living, never! Offensive, offensive, *offensive*—you are all offensive in Our eyes!"

Jim's mind was racing. The return of hope within him had started the engine of his brain working again. There had to be a magical way out of here that would get all of them away from this pair of long-necked monsters and their blackclad crew. He felt a sort of recklessness in him. He had realized since he had come to France, that he was digging into his own account, using up its magical balance on this and that; and that there was no telling whether he had enough of a balance left to do anything as large and dramatic as that which was now tickling at the edge of his mind.

The shape of the plan that stirred in him, he could not quite define. It fled before his mind could grasp it. But he could feel it there, tickling away all the same. Whatever it was, it was big; and it would dig deeply into what was left of his account—if indeed there was enough left to do it. But the only way to find that out would be to try doing it.

Only, first he had to get clearly in mind what he wanted to do; and time was running out. There had to be a way, using things he could envision, to simply move them magically and instantaneously from this place to somewhere safe.

Up on his throne, the King of the Dead was still thundering, his unbelievably powerful voice rolling through the cavern.

"Look at those below you." His tones battered them and tumbled over them, as they stood at the top of the short flight of stairs. "Those you see below you are those I have raised again from the Dead to be our bodyguard. They will bring you to me, now—"

He broke off. There was a stir below. He looked down and raised one finger from the arm of the massive throne on which he sat. The blackclad figures between the landing and the thrones parted. Jim, with sudden shock, saw Giles advancing at a determined walk toward the thrones and the two gigantic Gods upon them. He stopped and looked up at the King of the Dead, slowly stripping off his left glove with his gloved right hand.

He took the glove off and held it in his right hand. He advanced one foot a little and put the other hand on his hip. He stared up at the huge male figure.

"I have been honored," shouted Sir Giles—although his voice was strong, it was like the piping of a bird, after the great sound that had come from the long throat of the creature before him—"to be entrusted as one of those who hath in momentary guardianship Edward, Crown Prince to our throne of England. In his name, I defy you; and I challenge you, here and now, to single combat to prove your rights upon me, if so be it you are able!"

And he flung the thick leather glove in the direction of the huge figure.

It flew through the air to within six feet of the other's face; then checked suddenly—and wafted like a feather, slowly and softly and silently, down to the stone floor only a dozen feet in front of the God.

"Giles, you idiot!" Jim shouted, leaping forward down the steps; but his voice was drowned by the earsplitting rumble of the voice of the King of the Dead.

"Take him!" the King of the Dead extended his finger, pointing toward Giles. At once, the blackclad ranks closed around Giles; and he wheeled to face them, drawing his sword.

They would have overwhelmed him, like a black wave on a sand figure built by some child on a beach; but Dafydd's arrows were already taking their toll among them, and Brian and Jim were upon them. The black-furred shape of Aargh was ahead of all the others, savaging them and throwing them aside with a twist of his neck as if they were toys.

They fought their way to Giles, surrounded him, and, fighting madly, retreated with him, to the foot of the steps, back up the steps, and onto their platform.

The black tide surged after them, but was checked.

"Halt!" thundered the King. "We will do this as it should be done. You will go up there and take away the one I name first, the most offensive; then the next I shall name; then the next, no matter what the cost to yourselves."

Back up on the landing, panting and disheveled among his panting and disheveled friends and companions, Jim's mind was finally working at full speed. What Giles had done had been stupid, but also magnificent and *bold!*

That was what was called for from Jim now, in the way of magic. If he was going to get them all out of here, he must think *boldly!*

No sooner had he told himself this, than his mind finally came up with a wild scenario that just might be turned into a magical way to save them all. There was no time to test it out.

On the inside of his forehead he wrote:

ALLOFUS———>HOLOGRAPHS———>HIGHPOINT

Wonder of wonders—it worked!

Jim saw his friends flickering and fading and becoming transparent around him. He could feel nothing himself, but looking down, saw that his own legs had become semitransparent. His mind had seized on a high point at random, the first thing that came to mind; which in this case was the main room in Malvinne's private quarters, which they had left with such relief some time before—just how long ago he had no idea, because of that timeless period of vertigo and disorientation. It could have been seconds or could have been hours, sliding down the spiral chute in darkness.

Suddenly, they were there again, in Malvinne's private main room. The transparent figures of Brian, Giles, the Prince, Dafydd, and Aargh took on solidity, resolving out of the air around him—

HOLOGRAPHS———>BODIES

He wrote hastily on the inside of his forehead. They were saved. They were here.

The only trouble, Jim suddenly recognized, was that Malvinne was now here also.

Chapter 28

Malvinne had evidently been eating a midnight meal, or a very early breakfast, by himself. He had clearly not checked to see if he still held his princely prisoner.

He was seated at a small table which was—surprisingly—covered with a cloth; and on that cloth were the remains of what seemed a rather sparse meal, and a glass carafe of what appeared to be water. The carafe looked as if it could hold about a liter of water, but now had only perhaps a glassful left in it.

He had risen to his feet, staring as their transparent figures appeared and then shifted into solidity.

Jim had never seen him before, nor had him described. But that the man before them was Malvinne, he had absolutely no doubt.

Just as longtime teachers, physicians, and people in other specialized occupations can be recognized toward the end of their career as practitioners of their specialty, Malvinne—to Jim's eyes—could never be mistaken for anything but a master magician.

This had nothing to do with his general appearance or the clothes he wore. He looked about fifty years younger than Carolinus, whom Jim had understood to be Malvinne's contemporary. His hair was auburn without the slightest tinge of gray in it. Auburn, also, was the neat mustache on his upper lip. He was a small, brown-eyed, sparrowlike man, beautifully dressed, not in any kind of robes that would suggest the magician, but rather in the richest sort of garments—a red velvet *cote-hardie* above soft blue hose that a courtier might sigh for at the court of a monarch. A narrow sword, too light to be a broadsword, and too long to be a dress sword, hung by his side—almost as if he had anticipated the rapier, even down to its basket hilt.

To the untutored or casual eye, he might have seemed anything but a magician. But Jim, from his long acquaintance with Carolinus, responded to elements that Malvinne clearly shared with Jim's friend of the cottage at the Tinkling Water.

There was the same quick, bright gaze, the same indefinable air of authority and power, an air that went beyond the richness of his clothing. Added to this was an air of competence—almost arrogance—that he radiated. Even here, in his surprise at this unexpected appearance, everything about him seemed to indicate that he expected to dominate this situation, as he would any other.

And dominate he did, with a single word.

"*Still!*" he snapped.

Instantly, Jim and the others stopped and stood without moving. Jim struggled against whatever was holding him, but he was paralyzed. Malvinne's gaze, dismissing the others, fastened on him.

"By Bleys, the Master of Merlin!" he said, "an apprentice, a cubling, a bungling semi-amateur throwing his magic around in my château! Where would you get the impertinence—"

He broke off, his eyes narrowing.

"Are you that cubling of Skinny's—of Carolinus's? Only something like that could give you the overwhelming gall to be here at all! Is he behind this? Answer me! I give you back use of your vocal cords in order to answer."

"Carolinus has nothing to do with this," said Jim, suddenly repossessed of a voice that would work. "We're on a mission to rescue our Prince from you, that's all; and—Aargh! Help!"

Almost in the same second, Malvinne was on his back on the carpeting, Aargh's front paws pinning his shoulders down, Aargh's jaws parted in front of his face, and the hot breath of the wolf fanning the little, auburn mustache.

"I was waiting to see how this pretty play came out, James," snarled Aargh. "Couldn't you have let it go on a little longer?"

"You young devil!" choked Malvinne, helpless on the rug. "Where did you learn that the wolf wouldn't be affected?"

"A very large gentleman, quite some distance beneath us, said something that gave me that idea," answered Jim. "Now, how about freeing us?"

"I'll see you in the fires of Beelzebub first!" snarled Malvinne.

"Release," Aargh almost whispered at the fallen man, "or die."

Jim felt the constraint fall from him. He was free to move; and he saw out of the corners of his eyes that his companions were free also.

"What's this about someone beneath us?" snapped Malvinne. Flat on his back on the carpeting, he still retained the attitude he had had on his feet. "Only Carolinus could have told you my commands might not work on an—an animal."

"I didn't learn it from Carolinus," said Jim. "In fact, Carolinus simply turned me loose to learn by myself."

All the time he was talking, his mind had been racing. Malvinne, as long as he was anything short of dead, was essentially a stick of dynamite that could go off the minute Aargh released him. There had to be a way of immobilizing him. But the ordinary ways would not work. It stood to reason that simply tying him up would do no good. Jim had a fair idea that the other could release himself from any kind of bonds in a second.

The same uselessness would apply to locking Malvinne in the cupboard, or any such thing as that. Jim was willing to bet, in fact, that Malvinne could free himself from a situation in which his body had been cast in lead and dropped in the deepest part of the sea.

Abruptly, another touch of memory came to his rescue. It had been the King of the Dead's mention of Kingdoms between peoples that had made him gamble on the fact that perhaps the animal kingdom had some immunity to what a human magician could do. Humans—and this was the reason Jim had been granted arms that showed red upon them to warn anyone of his abilities—had to take their chances against those of their own kind who chose to go in for magical studies.

The most that could be done for ordinary men and women was to give them warning that the one facing them had such powers. But animals were in a different situation. They would have no means of defending themselves simply because they were warned that the human who had trapped or cornered them was able to handle magic. Therefore they must be largely untouchable by it. So, at least, Jim had reasoned. On it he had gambled; and the gamble had paid off.

Just at that moment, the other memory that had been tickling at his mind came brightly back to life. It was of Melusine throwing herself into his arms, exclaiming about how lonely she was—and passing out. Hastily he wrote on the inside of his forehead:

WATER/MALVINNE'S STOMACH——————>COGNAC

He had gambled again. This time the gamble was that Malvinne could not directly read the spells another magician made inside his head; although he might be aware of their making. It developed that he had gambled correctly.

On the rugs, Malvinne laughed.

"Do you think to place a charm upon me, cubling?" said Malvinne. "Whatever it is, let me assure you it was wasted. The minute I become aware of the nature of it, it will be as air, rendered null and void."

"It may be," answered Jim. "We'll wait and see. Meanwhile, maybe you'd be good enough to tell us the most direct and secret route out of your castle."

Malvinne laughed again, wildly.

"Why the child is insane," he said, "to think I would tell him what he wants!"

"Perhaps you'd rather die, after all," said Aargh.

"No, no," said Malvinne sneeringly, "that won't work twice. Kill me because I don't give you an answer to that question and you, youngster, will be in very deep trouble indeed. Trouble from which even your teacher won't be able to rescue you. The most you can gain from this wolf who is crushing my shoulderbones to powder with his weight, is to keep me from taking further action against you. The wolf has the right of defense, and you're connected with the wolf; at least for the moment. So for now, at least, you're safe from me. But that'll change."

"You really think so?" said Jim interestedly. "Perhaps you'll tell me how."

"I?" Malvinne laughed again. "Carolinus is the one charged with your education, not I. Figure it out for yourself if you can."

He laughed yet again from where he lay.

"Actually," he said—and Jim's ear heard that the word came out a trifle blurred, as "achuallsy." Malvinne was obviously a teetotaler, and the enchanted water already in his stomach was apparently beginning to work. The only question was whether Malvinne had drunk enough. But the size of the carafe and the lowness of the water now in it made it probable that he had most of the original liter's-worth of water in him, now in the form of cognac.

The thing was to keep him talking.

"Maybe you'll explain why you're so confident," said Jim.

"How could I be anything else?" said Malvinne. "Your wolf can't stand over me forever; and once his touch is removed from me, I can so ward myself with materials he can't get through that I'll be able to do what I wish. And believe me, I *will* do what I wish then."

Jim felt that he had to keep the man talking. He was afraid Malvinne would become aware of the fact that the water in his stomach had been turned to an alcoholic liquor. So far he did not seem to have noticed it; and also, possibly because he ordinarily was a drinker of water only, he had not identified the feelings of incipient drunkenness that must be even now beginning to overcome him—judging by that blurred word of a moment ago.

"What would you do?" said Jim, trying to sound uncertain.

Malvinne laughed raucously. He was, in fact, doing a lot of laughing, which in itself seemed another indication that the alcohol was having its effect on him.

"Didn't Carolinus teach you the laws—I mean all the laws—I mean all lahws, of maggishk?"

His speech was really beginning to give him away; but he still seemed entirely too full of energy and purpose to be trusted with Aargh's paws off his shoulder.

"How y'like to be speci-speciminnines, pinned to a board?" said Malvinne, somewhat slowly and unclearly. "How'd you like that? Onna board, like bu'rfly specimennines. Eh?"

His attention and his eyes wandered for a moment; then his gaze came back to Jim's face. "But I asked you question. I asked f'you knew the Laws. You don' know Laws, do you?"

"Actually," said Jim, "as I say, Carolinus hasn't really been teaching me; he's been letting me learn by myself; and—"

"And so you donno," said Malvinne triumphantly. "Well lemme tell you one'f them. There's a Law says when there's a group got a magician 'mong them, like you, then they're fur-fair game for 'ny other magician. And your rating with the Counting Office's nothing t'do with it!"

"Well, well," said Jim, trying to sound unconcerned. Actually, inside, he was in sudden turmoil. It struck him that Carolinus might have told him at least about this Law. "That does make it rather uncomfortable, doesn't it?"

"That's right," slurred Malvinne, "uncomfortab-tab- . . ."

His eyes closed; and for a moment Jim's optimism began to come back. Then the eyes opened again.

"So don' think . . . don' think . . . don' think . . ."

Malvinne's voice trailed off. His eyes closed again. They waited, all of them, tensely, but the eyes did not open again.

"I hear him breathing like a man asleep," said Aargh at last.

"All right," said Jim, "maybe it's safe to let him go. Try stepping off him; but be ready to jump back on if he shows any sign of coming to. Remember you have to be touching him to control him."

Slowly Aargh stepped back, taking his paws off Malvinne's shoulders. Malvinne began to snore lightly.

"I think the sooner and the faster we get out of here, the better," said Jim to the others. He explained to them what he had done to the magician.

"Should we not gag and tie him, first?" asked the Prince.

"Nothing we could do that way would really hold him, Highness," said Jim.

"And then what?" asked Sir Brian. "When he wakes up, he'll be after us with everything and every creature and every man and woman he controls, will he not?"

"He might," said Jim. "On the other hand, you heard him. The man drinks only water, according to His Highness. So he can't be used to being drunk. He may not wake up until tomorrow morning; and then he may wake up so sick as not to be able to arrange a hunt for us for hours, if not a full day. The one thing we can do, though, is make him as comfortable as possible; to encourage him to sleep as long as he can."

"Strange thing to do to an enemy," growled Aargh, "tuck him into bed."

Nonetheless, they picked him up and carried him into the room that held his own sumptuous bed, took off his boots, loosened the neck of his shirt, and left him with his head on a pillow and a light cover over him. Then they headed once more for the secret staircase down to ground level.

They went as rapidly as they could. Still, it was a long climb down the secret stairs for a second time.

As they got close to the bottom, Jim suddenly remembered something.

Abruptly, he used the inside of his forehead again to correct the earlier spell that had led him astray at the foot of these stairs.

ME/SEE———➤ALL MAGICWORKS EVERYWHERE INRED

He envisioned this.

It was what he should have done in the first place; but he at least had remembered it now, before they got to the foot of the stairs and faced the problem itself. They went on down to the foot of the stairs. Once there, they stopped as they had before; but this time, to Jim's eyes, both stairway and pathway shone an unmistakable, dusky red.

"Why are we stopping, Sir James?" came the voice of the Prince from behind him. "Surely we take the stairs to the left, this time?"

Jim glanced again at the stairs to his left. There was no doubt that they, like the path to the right, were an unbroken red in color.

"I'm afraid, Your Highness," he answered, "that both ways are part of a magical trap that Malvinne has set. At the present moment, I'm seeing magical signs that tell me both ways are dangerous."

"Both ways?" echoed the Prince, then fell silent. The others were silent also.

Jim was busy thinking. There must be a way around this. But the only way he could imagine would be for him somehow to be able to nullify the trap—cause it to cease to exist, by preference.

"At the moment," he told the others, "I'm still trying to find some way of handling this. Let me study it a while longer."

The others responded to him with courteous silence.

The more Jim thought of it, the more likely it seemed to him that either way would lead them to some undesirable end. Possibly, both would lead them right back into the Kingdom of the Dead; and that was the last place they would want to be again.

A wistful wish passed through his mind that he could pass this problem over to Sir Brian, and have the other find a simple, practical, everyday solution to it.

The thought was like a catalyst. He almost struck his forehead with the heel of his hand, in annoyance at his own stupidity. It was a good thing, he thought, that Carolinus could not see him in this present situation. Carolinus had sent him out to learn; and one of the things he had already learned was that a magical command could be put to use in more than one way, to deal with different situations. For example, he had effectively immobilized Malvinne, a master magician, with exactly the same bit of enchantment he had used to immobilize Melusine.

He had also, he remembered now, come up with a command to open doors that were supposed to open only to Malvinne. There was no reason why a small variation on that command could not solve the present problem, also.

He wrote on the inside of his forehead:

ME=MALVINNE——➤REMOVE/REPLACE THIS MAGIC

Nothing happened. Then, it occurred to him that he had not completed the full, necessary, magical process. He added a further command:

REMOVE——➤THISENCHANTMENT

The red color vanished; but that was the least of what happened. The stairway suddenly smoothed out into a level passage leading off to their left; and where the path to their right had been, there was now nothing but a stone wall.

"All right, everyone," said Jim, turning into the new passage that had replaced the staircase, "the enchantment's been lifted. Here we go."

He led them down the passage a little way, then stopped.

"Wait," he said.

He turned and went back a short distance, but stopped well short of the foot of the staircase they had just come down and wrote another command on his inner forehead:

REPLACE——➤ENCHANTMENT

Immediately, all sight of the staircase and what had been at the foot of it was blocked out by the underside of stone steps that led up into the roof of the passage and glowed an unmistakable red. The appearance of things as usual would not fool Malvinne for long. He might even be able to make the cross-passage speak, and tell him what had happened. But the appearance of everything being unchanged might slow the pursuit by the master magician down a bit.

Jim turned back, rejoined the others, and moved up in front of them.

"Now we can go on," he said.

Chapter **29**

The new passage they were in jigged and jogged, turning at an abrupt right or left angle every so often.

Clearly, it was built within the interior walls of Malvinne's castle; and at least one reason for this became apparent as they went along.

After the first twenty paces or so, the magic illumination of the secret staircase was no longer with them. But now it did not matter. Sufficient light for them to travel by came in through what amounted to peepholes in the walls on either side of them.

Evidently, Malvinne believed in keeping an eye on his household without their knowing it. Also, his household was clearly used to being active until all hours of the night. What could only be described as a general, castlewide party seemed to be going on, lit by sconces in the wall and large torches. As a result, the air coming through the peepholes was hotter than an August day in broad sunlight.

From Jim's point of view, the light these peepholes gave was their greatest recommendation. But his human companions seemed to find themselves attracted to the point of fascination by the idea of looking through the peepholes at what was happening on the other side of the wall.

Jim could really not blame them. Under different circumstances, he himself would have been interested in the behavior of Malvinne's household—if only for the purpose of gathering information about Malvinne himself. But there was no real problem until all of those with him, except Aargh, stopped at apertures at one particular section of the wall, at once. Brian and Giles, in particular, were not only peering, but commenting about what they saw in tones of admiration.

Jim gave in to the general pressure and found a hole through which he could look, too. What he found himself looking at was a room filled only with women, in various stages of dress and undress. It seemed to be a sort of combination robing and gossip center for those within it.

"Damme!" Brian was saying. "Will you look at the one with the green thing about her, there, Giles—"

"Gentlemen," said Jim, standing back from his eyehole, "interesting as this may be, I think perhaps—"

"I mind me two years ago," the Prince had started speaking at exactly the same time, "that my Uncle John, Earl of Cornwell, took me—Sir James, you interrupted me!"

He stood back from his peephole and looked haughtily at Jim.

"My deepest apologies Your Highness," said Jim. "It was inadvertent, I assure you. But every moment's precious, if we're to make good our escape before Malvinne wakes up and is in good enough shape to put pursuit on track after us. I think it unwise to waste our time looking through these viewing holes."

The high lift of the Prince's head lowered; and his haughty expression was replaced with a frown.

"No doubt you are right, Sir James," he said. "I should have thought of that myself. But, seeing these gentlemen looking led me to do the same."

"A couple of the gentlemen already have ladies of their own," said Jim severely, looking at Brian, Dafydd, and Giles, who had now also withdrawn their gaze from what was beyond the wall. "Possibly they would be better engaged in thinking of those ladies than looking at others now."

"Indeed—I stand rebuked!" said Sir Brian. "You're quite right James. I've not given the Lady Geronde Isabel de Chaney anywhere near the thought a man should give his love, when in foreign parts."

"And I," said Dafydd, his face solemn with sadness. "In truth I want nothing but my golden bird. As Sir Brian says, Sir James, you are right. We should think on our own, only."

"Sorrowfully," said Giles—and he did indeed sound sorrowful—"I have no lady. No lady would look twice at me, with this great lump of a nose I have. Nor do I blame them."

"Why, Giles," said Brian, "your nose is none that large. I have seen larger. I would not call it a large nose so much as a *strong* nose."

"Assuredly, Sir Giles," said the Prince, "you have my royal word that I have seen gentlemen at court with noses more prominent than your own, veritably surrounded by the ladies."

"You think so, Sire?" asked Sir Giles, doubtfully, fondling his fierce beak. "It might have some attraction then, rather than repulsing a lady?"

They all assured him that this was so; and he cheered up remarkably.

"But, as the good Sir James has just said," said the Prince, "we must on with all haste. Let us have no more of peeping through holes."

"I think so, too. By Saint Cuthbert I swear it!" said Sir Giles enthusiastically; and the others chimed in with assurances weighed down with the names of their own favorite saints.

"Humans!" snarled Aargh disgustedly. "Like dogs. No male wolf will force his attentions on a female one unless she is willing."

"Here's an impertinent wolf!" said the Prince angrily.

Aargh rolled a wicked yellow eye at the young man.

"Remember, I am of a different kingdom," he said. "I am not your subject, young Prince and I say what I please. I have, and always will. But, unlike others, you can believe whatever I say because I do not lie."

"It is true you're not an Englishman," said the Prince, suddenly thoughtful, "nor yet one of whom a gentleman's manner should be expected. As to your truth, that is a great thing, if indeed it is so. I have had many about me, even in my few years, and almost none I could trust to say as much and not be lying."

"Your Highness, the rest of you," said Jim, "remember, I mentioned time was slipping away from us. Let's move quickly."

Move quickly they did; and it was not more than fifteen minutes later when they came at last to a point where the passage proper ended in a solid stone wall. A flight of stairs led off to their left alongside that wall to continue their route if they wished to go that way.

"Could this be another magic trap?" asked the Prince, looking at the steps distressfully. It was dark down where the stairs led; and a smell like that of damp earth came up from it.

"It is not, Highness," said Jim, with some certainty, for the stairway was nothing but plain stone in color. There was no sign of red anywhere. He went on.

"I think we've come to the outer wall of the castle," Jim said. "These steps may well lead down alongside it to the foundations; and then possibly underneath to some sort of escape passage or tunnel; or I miss my guess. Certainly, Malvinne would not want to be without some way of escape in emergencies."

"In that you are right, James," said Brian. "I know of no castle whose holder has not made himself some sort of secret way out, in case of necessity."

"Here we go, then," said Jim.

He created by magic a bundle of twigs, which Brian lit with flint and steel from his purse. They went down. This was no descent like that into the wild spiraling chute that had shot them downwards into the realm of the King and Queen of the Dead. It was more like going down into someone's long-unused cellar. They came out at last in a tunnel leading off at right angles, that soon ran beyond the walls. It was braced with timbers against both of its sidewalls and paved with stones. For all that, there was plenty of dirt about them, and their way smelled earthy.

They hurried along its dark length, the flames from the torch bent backward in their passage, and the shadows cast by those flames flickering amongst the timbers and on the stony floor. It seemed they went a considerable distance; and even Jim was beginning to wonder whether they might be heading into some trap, after all; when they came at last to a solid wooden door that ended the passage.

The door was secured by a heavy bar which rested in two L-shaped metal supports. The bar did not look difficult to lift, but Jim, still in the lead, hesitated. There was no color of red about the door, but he was still suspicious.

He turned to Aargh, behind him.

"Aargh," he said, "do you smell anything we ought to be careful about, either with this door or whatever may be beyond it?"

Aargh pushed forward to the door and sniffed it over thoroughly, snuffling particularly at the side and bottom cracks of it.

"There's nothing beyond, but dirt and growing things," he said at last.

"All right then," said Jim, "let's go through."

He took hold of the bar to lift it. It was not unusually heavy, but had been in its sockets long enough to become somewhat fixed there. Brian moved forward to help him; and together they took it out of its holding place. The moment it was removed, the door swung inward of its own weight.

At the top of a slanted earthen hole, above them, they saw a section of night sky, studded with stars and framed by the tendrils of either grass or bushes.

"I'll go up and take a look first," said Jim. "Brian, you and the rest stay back here to guard His Highness."

"You're a fool in some things, James," snapped Aargh. "Let one go who knows more about such looking than you'll ever learn."

In a second, Aargh was past them and up the earthy slope. At the top of it, he occulted the stars for a moment; then he was gone.

They waited.

"Do you think he might have found trouble, or else decided to leave us for good?" the Prince whispered uneasily in Jim's ear, after some few minutes had passed without Aargh's return.

"No Your Highness. Neither," Jim whispered back. "What he said was right. If anyone of us can go up there safely, look around, and return, it'll be him. What's keeping him, I don't know. But I've no doubt he'll be back. We just have to wait."

They continued to wait, uneasily. As they waited, the restlessness, even inside

Jim, increased. Suppose some accident had happened to Aargh? He dared not voice the thought aloud for fear of taking the heart out of those with him. But he thought it.

Then suddenly Aargh was coming down the slope back to them, and another figure blocked out the stars, standing upright at the top of it.

"All is well," growled Aargh. "One was even waiting for us. You see him up there."

"Who is it?" asked Jim, straining his eyes through the darkness to get some clear idea of who waited at the top of the slope.

"A friend," said Aargh. Jim could not see Aargh's jaws in the darkness, but from the tone of the other's voice, he imagined them open in laughter, that silent laughter that marked his own wolvish brand of humor. "Come then."

Jim, leading the way, with sword drawn just in case, climbed the steep slope. But there turned out to be no use for the sword; except as something to drive into the earth to help him up the vegetation-covered earthen angle he had to climb. At the top a familiar voice spoke to him.

"It's good to see you," said the voice. "You are here, as I was told you would be."

The voice belonged to Bernard. Jim wiped his sword on some leaves and put it back in its sheath.

"Who told you?" he asked. "And why are you waiting for us here? How did you know this was where we would come out?"

"Those questions will all be answered in due time," said Bernard, as Jim stood aside to let the others up onto the level ground. "There is someone who can do a better job of answering them than I can. My job is only to bring you to him as quickly as possible."

"Sir Raoul?" asked Jim, at a venture.

"He is with the other," answered the voice of Bernard. As before, he had his back to what moonlight there was, so that his upper body was hidden in darkness. "But I will answer no more questions. If you are all up beside me now, follow me."

They followed him. They were in one of the garden areas of Malvinne's estate. He led them almost at a trot through this, with the black wall of the enclosing forest at their right, until he suddenly turned and led the way into one of the path openings that broke its solid wall of limbs and tree trunks.

Along this path, still at a jog, he led the way through perhaps another two miles of winding, beaten-earth path with a handful of stars showing through the interlocked branches above their heads, until, just as suddenly, they emerged onto the open hillside.

"Here, for a moment, we can rest," said Bernard.

He was careful still to stand so that no light illuminated his face or upper body directly, except for the feeble starlight, which was not able to resolve anything out of the dark gloom that was his upper shape.

As soon as they had rested, he led them on, into a cleft in the hills, very much like that dimple in which they had set up their temporary camp before entering the forest. But this cleft wound on back. There was no water flowing through it, as there had been in the dimple, but there must have been at one time, for underfoot in the base of the cleft there was no earth or grass, only rocks.

Their feet grated on these rocks for some distance: Jim tried to estimate how far it might be, but what with all the twistings and turnings of the cleft, he had by this time completely lost, not only his sense of direction, but a clear idea of when they had entered it.

They came out at last onto another hillside, enclosed by rises of sparsely treed grassland, where a fire was burning, illuminating the shape of a horse that cropped the grass nearby, and two figures—no, three—at the fire itself.

Jim stared at the third. For it overtopped the other two, even though he could see it only in silhouette from where he stood. It was the shape of a small dragon.

Jim and those with him came closer, circling around the fire so that they could see the three who sat there, who until now had their backs to the group led by Bernard. Jim's group rounded the fire and Jim stared at the three.

One was Sir Raoul, all right, his lean face sardonic in the shifting light from the leaping flames. The other, as Jim had guessed from the general shape seen in silhouette from behind, was Carolinus. That was a surprise, but not as much of a surprise as it might have been if someone else had sat there. Carolinus was capable of magically transporting himself from place to place. He had not only done this himself, but after their final victory over the Dark Powers at the Loathly Tower, he had moved them all to the inn where they later had their victory dinner.

But the third was a shock.

"Secoh!" cried Jim.

"Surprised, James?" Secoh preened himself. "Perhaps you'd have recognized me if I'd spoken first and in a voice like this—

"—*I'm a French dragon.*"

The words rang an immediate chord of memory in Jim's mind. They brought back the moment in which he had been bedded down for the night on top of a spine of rock and a small dragon, hidden in darkness, had clung to the rock a dozen or so feet below him and asked him questions about where he was going and what he was doing.

But the voice, to Jim's human ear, was unmistakably Secoh's.

"*I lowered my voice and misled you completely,*" said Secoh.

Perhaps the voice had been lower, but to Jim's ear it was unmistakably Secoh's still. He tried to imagine it with his dragon hearing; but he still could not remember it as being that much deeper than the way Secoh ordinarily spoke.

The truth of the matter was, Secoh probably was not capable of lowering or raising the pitch of his voice very much. Perhaps no dragons were—including Jim. Jim made a mental note to try this out himself sometime when he was in his dragon body and in a private place where he could experiment without anyone else hearing him. This was beside the fact that, not expecting Secoh under any possible circumstances, he had simply taken it for granted that the dragon he had dimly seen on the rock was someone he did not know. So that, when that other dragon identified himself as being French, Jim had believed him.

But there was no point in hurting Secoh's feelings by puncturing his belief in his ability to disguise his voice.

"I guess you're right. I didn't recognize you at all," said Jim, "but what were you doing calling yourself a French dragon and asking me questions like that?"

"Well," said Secoh, settling down in a comfortable position, like any dragon about to recite a long tale, either about himself or some other dragon.

"Not now, Secoh," said Carolinus sharply.

"But Mage, I've got to tell him I'm an ambassador from the English dragons."

"Later," said Carolinus, in a tone of voice that effectively shut Secoh up completely. In contrast to Sir Raoul and Secoh, Carolinus was seated in something like a pillow-chair. A soft structure, that yet had a back and armrests. His quick, faded blue eyes caught Jim's gaze upon it.

"Old bones!" he snapped. "Get to my age and you can have one also, James. Meanwhile, the rest of you sit down on the other side of the fire there; and we'll get matters straightened out."

Jim, Brian, Giles, Dafydd, and the Prince all seated themselves. But Bernard still stood, back out of the circle of firelight.

"You too, man!" said Carolinus irritably to Bernard. "When I hold a meeting, rank doesn't count."

"I am not a man," answered the dark, shadow-hidden shape of Bernard, "and it is not rank that stops me from sitting; though it well might be, for at your fire sits the son of my former Lord. But I choose not to show myself; and that is my right, is it not?"

"Of course," said Jim quickly, before Carolinus could answer. "Although you might think about the fact that possibly Carolinus here can reverse what Malvinne did to you, and turn you back into a whole man again."

"What's that?" demanded Carolinus of Jim.

"He's half-man, half-toad, because Malvinne changed him that way from being a man-at-arms in my father's service," Sir Raoul answered for Jim. "Could you indeed turn him back into a full man?"

Carolinus stared at the shadowy figure beyond the firelight.

"It could be done, of course. . . ." he began slowly.

"I thank you, no," interrupted the voice of Bernard. "If I stay as I am, I can stay close to Malvinne and maybe one day these hands of mine will let the life out of him. For that alone I live. I would not take my whole self back again if you gave it to me as a gift."

There was a moment of uneasy silence around the fire.

"It seems we are answered," said Carolinus, then. "You there—"

"His name is Bernard," put in Sir Raoul.

"You there, Bernard," said Carolinus, "you are not to be moved from that decision?"

"No."

"Then we are indeed answered," said Carolinus. He returned his gaze to those others seated around the fire. "Let's talk about the situation. First—you, Raoul, bring James and the rest here up to date in the matter of the English and French forces."

"It's no more than to be expected," said Raoul. His voice was slightly bitter. "Your English knights could not sit still long. Soon they grew tired of drinking and wenching and would march on our French King without waiting for the rest of your army, namely most of their men-at-arms and archers. Shortly after you left Brest, Sir Brian, they had begun to burn and pillage their way east through our fair France toward Tours, Orléans and Paris."

"In what force?" The words shot from Brian's lips.

"Four thousand horse and some four thousand archers and men-at-arms. So I was told," replied Sir Raoul.

"And how many of archers alone?" asked the soft voice of Dafydd.

Sir Raoul waved the question aside.

"I heard no exact numbers," he said. "Somewhere between one and two thousand, I believe. Of the total army"—his voice sounded as if he was going to spit in the middle of the sentence—"over half were Gascons, of course!"

In the silence that greeted this remark, Sir Raoul went on.

"But our good King John has gathered his own army of loyal Frenchmen, over ten thousand in number, and is proceeding southward even now to meet and give battle to your English intruders. He will have passed Châteaudun already; and may possibly have reached Vendôme. If you wish to get your Prince back to the English army before French and English meet, you will have to move swiftly."

"And the French forces?" asked Brian again. "Have they archers or crossbowmen in any number among them?"

"I know not the number," said Sir Raoul, once more with a dismissive wave of his hand. "A sufficiency of Genoese crossbowmen, I understand. We French do not depend upon footmen like you English."

"To their great loss, particularly in the matter of archers." Dafydd's voice intruded gently once again.

"We will not talk of that," said Sir Raoul. "Let me remind you that I would be with that army were it not for this matter of Malvinne. It is that, and that alone, that leagues me with a race I do not love against my proper King and people. Malvinne must be stopped for the greater betterment of France, no matter what else; or France as we know it will cease to be."

"That is a strange statement indeed, Sir Raoul," said Brian. "I do not see how one magician could make that much difference."

"That is because you do not understand!" flared Sir Raoul. "If you but knew—"

"I think it best that I explain matters from here on." Carolinus's old but authoritative voice broke in on the words of the French knight. "There are things involved here that all of you should better understand. As I once told James, here, perhaps it is time for one of my lectures. I charge you all sit still and listen—and remember. Particularly you, Edward. For all of you have things to learn from this."

His words had a strange solemnity, spoken above the flickering flames of the fire. A stillness fell upon the rest of them, that Jim at least felt was not completely of their own doing. Carolinus had not merely asked them to listen, he was compelling them to listen.

Carolinus was silent for a moment. He picked up a small length of wood and prodded the fire, so that sparks flew upward to be lost in the darkness.

"There are matters about Magic, the Art of it, and those who practice it," he said slowly, "that those of you who do not know it will never completely understand; and in the ordinary course of events would never need to understand. But now time has brought you to a point where you need to be made acquainted with some part of it."

Jim felt a shiver run down his back. Carolinus's eyes were on the fire, and his voice was abstracted, but his words had a strange power about them that seemed to draw them all more tightly together.

Chapter 30

A little cold wind sprang up from nowhere and circulated around them. The dark sky with its stars seemed to move down and draw in more closely about them.

"There are many kingdoms," Carolinus's eyes were on the fire and his voice, although low-pitched, sounded clearly in their ears, "and you've been made acquainted with at least a couple of them just recently. The Kingdom of the Dead, and the Kingdom of Wolves, with its freedom from the powers of human magicians such as even myself and Malvinne. The law is that whoever rules any such kingdom—if any does—may have direct power over only those in it. Those outside he or she may touch and control only by that part of magic that has ceased to be magic and become a part of ordinary life and ordinary ways."

"But, Mage," blurted Giles, "how can you know this about Aargh and the Kingdom of the Dead? It was but hours since that we had to do with both things."

"How I know is not for you to know," said Carolinus, raising his eyes briefly to Giles. "There are laws beyond laws that none of you, even James as yet, have discovered. I will not tell you how I know. I couldn't, and I wouldn't. All that need concern you is that I do know. And all that need concern all of us now is that you know that there is this separation of places and kingdoms; and that each one has its own laws and its own rights and its own powers—but nothing beyond that."

He prodded the fire again; and there was a little space of silence before he went on, his eyes once more on the flames.

"There is the Kingdom of the Dead," he said, "and there is the Kingdom of the Animals. But within many of these kingdoms there are other kingdoms. Within the Kingdom of the Animals there are smaller kingdoms where different laws apply. Among the animals this is true of both the Kingdom of Wolves and the Kingdom of Dragons, because they are something more than simple animals. They are peoples. Over the simple animals themselves—you have seen me with a watchbeetle, James, so you'll remember—a human magician may have some power. But not over wolves or dragons, or some others which I will not name now."

He paused again.

"Some of these kingdoms," he went on, "hold entities—the rest of you will not know that word, but James will—that are not like the rest of us. Not like humans or wolves nor dragons, nor naturals like the fairy Melusine—"

He lifted his eyes briefly to Jim.

"Who still pursues you, by the way, James," he said. "You have made an impression on her as no other man has, and she has been tracking you ever since she lost you. She may not have you because you are a magician, though a small one. But she doesn't know that yet."

He looked back at the fire.

"But to return to what I was saying," he said, "among those kingdoms in which what rules is not alive as we know the meaning of life, is that of the Accounting Office, and also that of the Dark Powers.

"The Dark Powers," he went on, "can do nothing directly to humans, who are not of their kingdom. They can only attack what is human with their servants—the Ogres, the Worms, the Sandmirks. . . ."

His voice trailed off for a second, then picked up again.

"But this does not mean we are safe from them," Carolinus continued. "They are always at work to find those among us who may be turned against others of our own kind. As Bryagh, the dragon, was turned against his own fellow dragons and stole away the Lady Angela."

"He was not a bad dragon, before he turned rogue," said Secoh, almost dreamily.

"Perhaps. Nevertheless, he turned rogue under the influence of the Dark Powers," said Carolinus. "But it is not that specifically that concerns us now. Even as there are kingdoms within kingdoms among the animals and others, so there are kingdoms within kingdoms among humankind. Those humans who have given themselves completely to God are beyond anything the Dark Powers can touch. Even the servants of the Dark Powers fall helpless before those who have committed themselves fully to something else.

"The danger lies," he went on, "in the rogues, those the Dark Powers can suborn and turn against us. But to understand what this means I will have to make you understand something else. Something few people do."

He had been poking the fire again, but now he laid the stick down and looked around at all their faces.

"When the ordinary person thinks of a mage," he said, "they think of something that has very little to do with the reality of being one. They conceive of the Master Magician as someone who can, with the wave of his hand, produce anything he wants—without effort and without cost. Even if this were true, which it is not, they never stop to count what it cost him to become a Master Magician in the first place.

"Those great in magic," he went on, "those who are remembered, as Merlin and his master Bleys are remembered, did not involve themselves in the great art that is Magic for the sake of the personal rewards it would bring them. It was not the wealth nor the power that summoned them down that long path to what they finally ended up being. It was the work itself, the glorious thing that is Magic, itself, standing apart and alone as an Art and a Science."

He sighed slightly, and a little wind came from somewhere out of the darkness to stir for a moment the wispy, white hairs of his beard. His voice did not change to their ears. But suddenly, within them, they seemed to hear it, still clearly but as if from very far away, down some long and dimly-seen passage.

"It is necessary now that you—all of you—gain some understanding of the price one must pay, man or woman, to become a Master of Magic."

He paused and lifted his head to look about at all of their faces again.

"Basically," he said, "that price is all—everything that he or she has in him to pay is the cost of that he would learn."

His gaze paused for a moment on Aargh.

"Of all of you," he went on, "it is Aargh who will appreciate the loneliness of that long road best. You all know loneliness, for it is laid upon the human race that each of us, close as we may come to our fellow men and women, yet must live alone within ourselves. This loneliness for the Master magician becomes even greater. He is like a hermit who withdraws into a desert, that he may be alone with nothing—nothing—but that which concerns him. Have you ever stopped to ask yourself why a hermit would do that?"

None of them answered except with the silence that is itself a "no."

"It is for love," said Carolinus. "It is for that great love of that which has picked him up and carried his mind and soul off, so that its need now overrides all other things. We all do it, but in different ways, we who give our life to magic and are known by the title of *Mage*. That which we are in love with leaves us no room for other things. So we find different places, in the world but apart from it—most of us, at least."

He looked down at the fire again, picked up his stick and poked it once more to send the sparks flying wildly upward.

"And there comes a time," he went on almost gently, "when the best of us asks himself or herself—was it worth it? Was it fair that I should have to deprive myself of all the ordinary pleasures of living, in order to learn what I have learned and understand what I now understand? And always the answer comes back—*yes, it was worth it.* But, nonetheless, because we were human beings to begin with and we will be human beings until we die, the ache of what we have lost or never had, never leaves us. It is such a lingering wish and hunger as that, that the Dark Powers search to exploit. It is like the dragon's hunger for an ever-greater hoard and thirst for unlimited wine."

He looked up at Secoh.

"You know that hunger and thirst, Secoh," he said; and Secoh hung his head. His eyes shifted to Jim. "Even you, James, know what such desires are, from the times when you have been a dragon."

Jim also found himself looking away from those faded blue eyes in the firelight.

"It was the promise of the Dark Powers that Bryagh should have a greater hoard and all the wine he could ever call for, that turned him rogue," said Carolinus. "Even within our greatest Masters, this longing for what we have given up as the price for what we have won, lingers, and is a crack wherein a tendril of evil may enter. It can happen to the best of us. Never have the Dark Powers succeeded with our truly great magicians, except for the minor success of Nivene who cozened Merlin of the spell that would lock him in a tree trunk—Until he gave in and she used it on him; and set more evil loose in the world.

"But those close to being great, those who already possess tremendous power and wisdom—to them the temptation comes most strongly, for that they already have so much they can conceive of even more to own."

His gaze went to Jim and his tone softened again.

"That is why James, here, will never make a truly great magician," Carolinus said. "He is already bound too tightly to the world outside of magic by the loves that exist in him, and which in some part existed before he ever became acquainted with Magic."

His voice became hard again.

"But that is beside the point," he continued. "The interesting fact is that, because James comes from another place—of which he knows much, and the least of which the rest of you could never comprehend—his connection with this world and Magic has made him a particularly troublesome opponent for the Dark Powers. It is not something he is trained to be; it is only something that has come upon him by the workings of Chance and Circumstance in this our world." He paused to look directly for a moment again at Jim. "I shall speak to you privately at another time, James," he went on, "more on that subject. What I have just said will be enough for now. What all the rest of you need to know is that James, and therefore those of you who are his Companions, are critical to this moment in which the Dark Powers are once more on the march and very close to winning a massive victory, after which it will be hard to wrest from them what they will have fully gained by it."

One more time, he looked down at the fire, and hesitated a long time before going on.

"It is a shame to me that I have to say it," he said at last, "but it is one of my own kind, of my own kingdom; it is a fellow magician of great strength and wisdom, who has been touched and gained by the Dark Powers. You will have long since guessed who he is—Malvinne."

He looked up at them and his voice strengthened.

"For reasons which I can't now explain to you," he said, "we true workers of the Art of Magic would be putting matters at far too great a risk, if someone like myself—of equal or greater credit than Malvinne—set out to stop him from the course on which the Dark Powers have put him. On the other hand, any lesser magician would normally stand no chance against him. Only one who is different from all of us, not strong yet in magic, but in other things, that not even the Dark Powers can conceive of, might possibly be able to defeat him and block them. So it has fallen to me, as his friend, teacher, and a Master in this Art to which we are both sealed, to volunteer him for the perilous attempt of going against Malvinne."

He paused briefly.

"And so I did," he said. He looked directly at Jim. "Blame me alone, James, if you will. It was my decision alone to take; and I took it, without consulting you, or giving you a chance to refuse—such was the necessity of the matter. It had to be done and I did."

"D-d-do the Dark Powers know this about James?" stammered Secoh. "Does Malvinne know?"

"The Dark Powers knew the moment I made the decision to volunteer him," said Carolinus.

He had not taken his eyes off Jim.

"That attack on your castle, Brian, was their first move against him. It was not the castle that was the goal, it was the chance to kill James in combat for which he was still largely untrained—and he came closer to death then than you may have realized."

"James, if I'd only known—" Brian was beginning in a conscience-stricken voice, when Carolinus interrupted him.

"Even if you had known, Brian," he said, "it would have made no difference. It was an attempt that James alone had to meet and frustrate. Since then, there have been a number of times in which he has come close to death, because of the efforts of the Dark Powers. Only the guardianship of you, his friends and Companions, has helped save him. It was hoped that you would kill him at the inn, Giles, over that matter of the room."

"'Fore God, James!" burst out Giles. "It was that cursed temper of mine, only that! How can you trust me now, knowing this?"

"I will always trust you, Giles," said Jim.

"Blame not yourself, Giles," said Carolinus. "The dice were loaded against you that day, in ways you could not see or even suspect. Remember also, later, when you had become a friend and a Companion, how you, by being a silkie, saved James and the ship and all else aboard it, when it became caught on a rock that a master mariner like the one commanding that ship should never have run his vessel upon, in waters he knew well."

"It's true, Giles," said Jim. "You saved us all that day."

Firelight was not all that excellent an illumination; but it was possible to see that Giles flushed, and looked down at the fire himself.

"It was something of hauling on a rope, merely," he mumbled to the fire.

"I command you that you forget it," said Carolinus and Giles's head came up, his eyes looking a little bewildered and astray. "There was nothing more of blame in that than there would have been for Melusine, if Jim had not changed out of his dragon form before he came upon her lake, as the two rogue dragons that took his passport had directed him to travel."

He turned to Jim.

"Didn't you wonder, James," he asked, "that dragons seemed so hard to find in France until you ran across those two?"

"It did puzzle me," answered Jim, "but I thought it might have something to do with the way the land had been devastated by rival armies in recent years. Or perhaps it might have been simply because the dragons in France were sparse in certain areas."

"It was neither," said Carolinus. "It was the Dark Powers blocking your perception of those true dragons you passed, until you came to that husband and wife pair to whom you gave your passport. But enough of this. Let me merely say that Malvinne was not a corrupted magician for many years; not until the Dark Powers touched him in the vulnerable spot I've described. Then he began to yearn for the worldly elements of wealth and power. He dared not run down his balance with the Accounting Office to get most of these things; therefore he became adept at using human tools to rob the humans around him."

"Such as my father and my family, by the Lord!" said Sir Raoul fiercely. "That same appetite in him has ruined dozens of great French families, bringing them first falsely into disrepute with our good King, then attacking them with military forces of his own. My two elder brothers died, sword in hand, resisting the intaking of our castle. My father was taken prisoner and later cruelly done to death."

"So it was," said Carolinus. "However, that is in the past. We are now most desperately concerned with the future; and the near future at that. The French and English armies are marching toward each other. In only a matter of days they will meet. And the English forces are badly undermanned of the archers that helped bring them to victory at the battles of Crécy and Nouaille-Maupertuis in 1365—more commonly known as the Battle of Poitiers."

"As I thought," murmured Dafydd to the fire.

"Yes," said Carolinus, glancing at him, "but more importantly, the French army will shortly be joined by Malvinne, who has with him a false Prince Edward—"

"A false—an impostor, you mean?" exploded the Prince.

"Not such an impostor as you imagine, Edward." Carolinus turned on him. "The false Prince is a creature made by magic. I may not tell even James how he was done without disturbing the Pattern of Chance—but it is the exact image of yourself, Edward, right down to the clothes you are now wearing. Also, the rumor has already been put about that you have come to terms with King Jean; and will be fighting with him against your own English forces."

He paused a moment to let that information sink in.

"If either side should win," he said slowly and impressively, "*either* side, mark you—then the result will be a bloody and endless war that will tear France apart; and out of which Malvinne will gain more and more temporal power; until *he* rules, rather than King Jean, and, together with his forces and his magic, throws out the English entirely, once and for all."

He turned to look at Sir Raoul.

"Raoul," he said, "you may think that you would welcome this driving out of the English, even at this cost. But I tell you this is neither the time nor the proper way of it. Moreover the land under Malvinne will not be the France you have always known; but a running sore upon the face of Europe, from which all sorts of evil things will come, in an attempt to take over not only the territories adjoining your country, but eventually England and the world. Also, the longer that state should exist, the more powerful it will be, until there will be no stopping it."

"You need not tell me this," said Sir Raoul. "I know—well I know—that where the way of Malvinne goes nothing good can follow. But what can we do about it?"

"There is only one hope," said Carolinus. He looked back at Jim. "And I am barred from even counseling you in ways to go about it, James. Somehow, you must reach the battlefield in time to stop the war with neither side having won, unmask the false Prince, and have the real Edward here with us recognized in his place. It is just past dawn now; and even though you have been up all night I counsel you start immediately. I have told Raoul where the meeting place will be—which is not too far from the location of that earlier Battle of Poitiers, the English having gotten word of the French advance and turned south to look for better defensive position."

What he said about the dawn was true, Jim suddenly realized. It hardly seemed that a whole night could have gone past, what with their escape from the castle and Carolinus's talk; but the light of the coming day was already brightening the sky to the east, paling the last flames of the fire, which had sunk down and burned itself out to the point of being little more than embers.

"I have horses for all of us," said Raoul.

"We have our own horses and gear back at our camp," said Brian. "We cannot be far from it, even now."

"You aren't," said Bernard. "I can go fetch them in moments."

"Their gear only, Bernard," ordered Raoul. He smiled sardonically at them. "It would be a strange thing if a French knight, in France, could not supply you with better mounts than those you have procured. And I have."

Chapter 31

"Horses for all of us" referred to horses on which the humans could ride, and these were very good animals indeed, furnished with saddles, bridles, and all necessary gear. But they were, necessarily, for the humans alone. Secoh and Aargh were left with no option but to travel under their own power.

This was no problem for Secoh, who could fly. As for Aargh, he traveled along with the horses quite easily, clearly deriving a certain amount of evil enjoyment from the fact that he made them nervous if he moved close to them. In fact, his deliberate scaring of the horses this way pushed things to the point where Jim had to ask him to stop it.

Aargh made no pretense of not understanding what he was talking about.

"I have to admit it's good entertainment," Aargh said. "However, under the circumstances and considering the fact we've work before us, I'll do as you say, James, and keep off a little ways. That is, unless the road happens to crowd us together—then, if these big, four-legged clodhoppers of yours get upset because I'm close, don't blame me for it."

"In that case," said Jim, "I won't."

Secoh was not so well able to keep up with them on foot. A dragon walking on his hind legs, although it might be work for him, could keep up well enough with horses at a walk. However, Raoul took advantage of open stretches to trot the horses. This was a little hard on Jim; who had not yet, in spite of a year in this world, become a real horseman. But it was even harder on Secoh. A dragon could run on his hind legs, but it was an energy-expensive exercise and not one that he was built for. And Secoh's presence alongside had a tendency to spook the horses even more than Aargh's did.

A solution was found by Secoh being directed to a place later on where he could meet them, and taking off to get there by wing and await their arrival. This worked quite well, with Secoh flying anywhere from fifteen minutes to half an hour ahead of them, and then joining them when they stopped to breathe the horses, or to eat and drink.

The weather was still sunny, and warm without being too warm. They made excellent time and soon crossed the trail of the French army. They saw evidence and heard eye-witness accounts from local people whom Sir Raoul was able to approach and question—although these same individuals would have run from Jim or any of his other Companions—that confirmed that the army was at least a good two days ahead of them. The path of the French host seemed to be curving westward. They all took this to mean that the French had learned that the British forces were moving off in that direction and were now in active pursuit of them.

"You never did get to tell me how you come to be here. You're an *Ambassador*, you said?" Jim asked Secoh at one of their meal stops.

They were stopping more frequently now, on the excuse of resting the horses, or of eating or drinking something themselves, or just about any reason that one of them could dream up. The truth of the matter was that all of them, except Secoh and Sir Raoul, were dead for want of sleep; and no one wanted to be the first to fall asleep in the saddle.

"I never got to tell it right," said Secoh sulkily. "Carolinus stopped me before I could."

"I know," said Jim sympathetically, "but there're so many important things going on. . . ."

He let the words trail off. Secoh brightened up a little and shed his sulkiness.

"Oh, well," he said, "what happened was that Carolinus told me about you and the Dark Powers; and how they were steering you to those two rogue dragons in the old château. So I went to the Cliffside Dragons again and suggested that they send me as an Ambassador to let you know what your rights were with the French dragons; in a case like this where two of them who had turned rogue had gotten hold of a valuable passport—for which they would all be held responsible. Well, to make a long story short, after not too much talk at all they agreed to let me go; even though it meant that they had to pony up a few extra jewels to accredit me as an Ambassador."

"That was good of them," Jim said. "I didn't think they were that concerned about me, actually."

"Well, truthfully," said Secoh, "they were really more concerned about the jewels they'd given you for the passport. Their jewels.

"In fact, the truth is," went on Secoh in a sudden burst of candor, "I was a little concerned about the jewel I'd put into the passport collection myself. You see, it was the only jewel I had left of my family hoard. It had first been acquired by my great-grandfather, eleven times removed; and each father swore his son never to part with it. My father swore me, and I never did let go of it, no matter how hungry I got out on the meres."

A single tear formed in one of his eyes and rolled down his long, bony muzzle.

"Now, maybe," he said, "it's lost forever."

"Secoh, that was wonderfully generous of you!" said Jim. "To put something that meant that much to you in, just to start the collection of jewels for my passport."

The tear now reached the end of Secoh's muzzle and his right nostril. He snuffled it up.

"Oh well," he said, "what are friends for? Besides, it wasn't actually like giving it away. I was sure I'd get it back."

"You will, Secoh, you will," said Jim grimly. "Either that or something just as good. I'll find those two dragons I dealt with and make them hand the passport back! And if I don't, I'll find some way—I don't know just how yet, but I'll find some way—of replacing it with one just as good."

"It's not easy," Secoh snuffled. "We dragons don't gamble, you know—not for anything as valuable as jewels, anyway."

"I'll still get it for you or replace it," said Jim. "First I'll try confronting those two dragons."

"If you can find them," said Secoh. "Remember, this is France, and they're French. They could know places to hide where you'd never be able to locate them."

"Anyway I'll do it—" Jim was beginning, when Secoh cut him off.

"Actually," Secoh said, "Carolinus thought, and I agreed with him, that it would be much better for you to put pressure on the community of French dragons in general. If they let a passport like that be stolen by one of their own dragons, and word of it gets out, no other community or nation of dragons anywhere is going to trust them, no matter what they bring as passports. Either that, or else all the other communities will feel free to help themselves to any passport they're offered. The French dragons have a lot to lose if you put pressure on them, James. Also, they'd be much better than you or I would, at finding those two rogue dragons and making them give up the passport."

"How would I put pressure on them?" Jim asked.

"Well, that's the point of my being an Ambassador," said Secoh. "You see, I can speak for you. I can contact the French dragons, get a hearing with the responsible ones among them and explain the situation. I can convey any demand you want. You can authorize me to ask for anything you can think of as a penalty, including the return of the passport. The penalty can be something that's worth so much more than the passport, that they won't be able to wait to give it back to you instead of meeting your demand."

"Is that so?" asked Jim, suddenly very interested.

"Time to mount up and get going again." Sir Raoul's voice overrode the various conversations that were going on.

More than a little saddle-sore, Jim climbed back into the high cantled medieval saddle that had been his prison for the last seven or eight hours, groaning silently as the inside of his legs, where it felt as if the skin had been rubbed off, came once more in contact with the saddle leathers. The pain was only momentary; and his mind was once more wide awake. What Secoh had just told him had started him thinking.

As they set off again, his thoughts were busy. His first concern was what kind of price he could ask for the missing passport. There had to be some kind of opportunity there. At first he seemed to be able to think of nothing that could match the tremendous value of those oversized gems he had brought into France. If his guess was right, there was probably enough value in them to buy up half the land in France. He continued to think, however; and at last an idea came to him. At the next rest stop, about half an hour later, he took up the conversation with Secoh again.

"Tell me something," he asked the mere-dragon. "The French dragons don't like the French georges any better than the English dragons like the English georges, do they?"

"I should say not," answered Secoh promptly. "Oh, I don't mean that certain georges aren't likable—like yourself and Sir Brian, whom I've gotten to know now; and maybe this Sir Giles, since evidently he's half-seal, him being a silkie and not like other georges. But nearly all the georges, English and French both, are just like Sir Hugh—you remember Sir Hugh de Bois de Malencontri, who had your castle before you? *He* captured me and promised me my life if I'd call you down so they could capture you when you were headed out toward the Loathly Tower. You recall that? And then, after I'd done it and they'd captured you, he only laughed when I asked to be turned loose, and said he wanted my head for his wall."

"Then I've got an idea," said Jim. "I've been doing some thinking and it seems to me the thing to do is to ask a price of them that they can't refuse to pay, but that they will not, *dare not* pay; for one reason or another."

"I don't understand, James," said Secoh. "How can you come up with a price like that?"

"I'll tell you," said Jim.

It had occurred to him that he might be able to kill two birds with one stone—or rather shoot two birds with one arrow, to put it in the language of this world and period. "Suppose you tell them for me that I demand they show up with the jewels in three days. Also, every dragon in France of fighting age and condition has to turn up at the battlefield between the English and the French, to form a formation to fight on the English side against the French."

Secoh stared at him.

"I don't . . . Yes I do!" said Secoh suddenly. "They don't like individual georges, but they've got to live in France with them; and if all the georges here set out to make a job of getting rid of all the dragons, their lives won't be worth living. And that's exactly what would happen if they started fighting on the English side. They'll *have* to produce the passport—or if they can't, a bag of gems just as valuable! James, you must be the smartest george in the world!"

"I doubt that," said Jim, "and anyway, it doesn't matter. Will you carry that message to them then? Remember, use just the words I gave you. *They are to show up in a formation to fight on the English side.*"

"Why are the particular words so important?" asked Secoh, looking at him oddly.

"Just take my word for it," Jim said. "As Carolinus said, this is something I can't explain. I couldn't and I wouldn't. It's critical you tell them exactly the words I just gave you."

"Oh I'll do that all right," said Secoh. "You want them to show up in formation ready to fight with the English, and with the passport, in three days. That's not much time."

"No, it isn't," said Jim. "Maybe you'd better start looking for them right now. Right away."

"I'll go right now!" said Secoh.

He waddled off to one side to get some wingroom, crouched a little, and extended his wings to their full length in the *up* position. There was a terrific clap of air from his initial downbeat as he sprang into the air and began quickly to mount into the sky. The tethered horses whinnied, screamed, and reared in alarm.

"What's going on?" shouted Sir Raoul from a little distance away. "Sir James, what is this?"

Jim decided it was time that Sir Raoul understood very clearly who was in charge of their party.

He walked over to where the others stood.

"Sir Raoul," he said, "none of us know your rank."

Sir Raoul frowned darkly.

"My family name and my rank are my secret, Sir James," he said, "and you still have not answered my question of a moment ago."

"I'm in the process of answering it right now," said Jim. "We respect your wish to keep your real rank and name a secret. But there is no secret about something else. That something else is that I am a magician. Are you a magician, Sir Raoul?"

Sir Raoul's frown became a scowl.

"What nonsense is this?" he said. "You know I am not!"

"Nor is anyone else here, I believe?" said Jim.

"Of course not," said Sir Raoul.

"Then perhaps you'll understand that there can only be one leader here," Jim said. "That is the knight who is also a magician. Myself. You are entrusted with showing us the way to the place that Carolinus told you of because none of the rest of us can find it as easily as you can. But I am in command. Do you have any disagreement with that?"

For a moment they stood with their gazes locked together. Then Sir Raoul looked down.

"No, Sir James," he said in a lower voice. "Indeed you are right. There can be only one leader; and that leader can only be yourself."

"Good. I am glad we're agreed," said Jim. "Now I'll tell you this once, but in the future I'll not explain things. I've sent Secoh off on a special mission. I'm sorry it disturbed the horses and perhaps yourself. But that's all you need to know about it, and all you will know."

Sir Raoul nodded slowly, and looked up at him.

Jim turned to look at the others, who had come alert at the sound of the two men's voices. Jim looked them over. They were all obviously out on their feet—all except perhaps Aargh, who may just have been better at hiding his reactions. Aargh lay on his belly with his paws stretched out before him, his head on his forepaws and his yellow eyes looking up at Jim.

It was remarkable, thought Jim, that Aargh showed no sign of weariness at all. He must be as tired as the rest of them. Or was he? Jim had a sudden memory of finding Aargh napping after they had all spent some time searching Malvinne's rooms for any sign of the color red. For a second Jim felt a slight twinge of jealousy; then he put it from him. That small nap could have made some difference, but it could not make much. Essentially, Aargh had been as awake and busy as the rest of them since they had left their camp the night before their rendezvous in the woods with Bernard.

He looked again at Brian, Giles, Dafydd, and the Prince. They all looked exhausted.

Brian and Giles, he knew, would fall out of their saddles rather than admit to being weary before somebody else did. The Prince, obviously, had been brought up in a comparable school. He was royal, therefore he should be able to do better than any other man there in anything—even if it came to staying awake. Nonetheless, it was time to put a stop to this. Jim turned back to Sir Raoul.

"I know it's only midafternoon," he said to the French knight, "but I think we've reached the point where we should rest. We'll find the closest protected place and catch up on our sleep. Better to start out at dawn with a full night behind us, than ride half-stupid with tiredness directly into some situation we might otherwise avoid. Do you know of any place close to here where we could put up for the night?"

"I have friends," said Sir Raoul simply. "If you will mount and follow me."

He led them less than three miles before they came to a small castle. It was as he had said; he was recognized immediately not merely by the owners of the place but by the guard at the gate. Gratefully and wearily, they accepted the quarters that their host offered them—all except Aargh, who as usual preferred to stay out from under a roof if he possibly could.

"I will do my sleeping in the woods," he said; and left them before there could be any argument.

Jim woke automatically in the gray dawnlight coming through the single window slit of the chamber in which he, Brian, Giles, and Dafydd—all except Sir Raoul and the Prince, whom Jim suspected of having been offered slightly better quarters of their own—were sleeping on pallets.

Jim found himself feeling remarkably refreshed and full of energy. It was not until he tried to get to his feet and discovered how stiff he was from riding, that anything marred this good physical feeling.

The castle was small enough that they had no trouble making their way to the Great Hall and finding a servant, whom Jim sent in search of Sir Raoul. When the other arrived, he arranged for breakfast; and shortly after that they were in the saddle once more, joined by Aargh.

The second day's riding, Jim discovered, was not as hard as the first. To a certain extent, as the morning brightened, he rode off his soreness. Also, he had taken advantage of his overnight stay to pad his legs under his hose in the area where they had rubbed against the leathers. That day, the signs that they were on the trail of the French army began to become very fresh, in the way of wagon tracks and horse droppings. Accordingly, they swung wide to bypass the army and continue safely toward the destination Carolinus had given.

They made good time; and before noon they came upon evidence that they were on the track of the English forces. The two armies were closer to each other than anyone had guessed. They had been traveling with fewer rest stops than on the day before, but with the sun high above them, they stopped for a midday meal. While they were stopped, Jim talked to Brian.

"How are we going to make contact with our men?" he asked. "They're probably still waiting for us back somewhere near Malvinne's castle. I thought of sending Sir Giles or yourself back to get them; but with the armies this close, time is plainly too short for either of you to go back there and bring them up before these two armies fight."

"Not so, James," answered Brian. "They should already be with the English forces. The word I left with John Chester was to hold the men near Malvinne's castle for two days only. Then if he hadn't had word of us, to go on to join up with whatever English forces, wherever they might be—that at least they might strike a few blows against the French."

Sir Brian's face was momentarily grim. "But needs we must come up with them," he went on. "Have you forgotten, James? Our armor and all our gear are with them. We're none of us ready to take part in a battle, unarmored and armed only as we are. To say nothing of lacking my good war-horse, Blanchard, without which I would not like to get into anything resembling a battle with full-armored knights."

"I hadn't forgotten that," said Jim, "but I may have another, special use for our men. We'll see. Assuming they are with the English forces, do you think we could find them?"

"Assuredly, James," said Brian. "All of us know John Chester and our own men-at-arms by sight. And they'd know us. But we would not find them in a moment, you understand. It might take as much as a quarter- or half-day of searching to find them in a host even of this size."

"Well, that's what I think we'll plan to do," said Jim, "and while we're searching, the rest of us will hold back a little ways and try to find some safe place to keep the Prince. If what Carolinus said was correct, the English have accepted the fact that the Prince has gone over to the French. They will take anyone dressing and looking like him as the impostor; not the one with Malvinne. On the other hand, if any of the French forces should happen to discover the true Prince, they'll be even quicker to try to take him. They may not know that the Prince with Malvinne is a piece of magic, but they'll know that there can't be two Princes; and the chances are they'll try to capture Edward and take him back to the French leaders to find out what's going on."

"You're right, James," said Brian seriously, "that's exactly what would happen. If you like, I can ride ahead now so as to start searching our army for our own men before you get there."

"No, I don't think that's wise," said Jim. "We should stay together, if possible. Also, the armies won't immediately ride at each other the minute they see each other, will they?"

"Usually, with large forces like these," Brian said thoughtfully, "getting into any kind of battle order takes time. Also, nearly always there are some parleys between them—invitations to surrender, and so forth. You're right. We should have the better part of a day, at least, after the French army comes in sight, before they line up in battle positions and actually begin an advance against us. That is, if it's they who are the attackers."

"Would you expect us to be the attackers, with a very inferior force; and, as we've been told, a lack of the usual complement of archers?" Jim asked.

"No," said Brian slowly, "I would not expect it. However, you never can tell what'll happen."

"Let me find out what I can about what the French are likely to do," said Jim; and went over to talk to Raoul.

The French knight, while with them all the way, had been maintaining a sort of distance between himself and them. It was not as if he had any actual dislike for them, or a reluctance to be closely in their company. It was almost as if duty required him to show that he was not one of them.

"Sir Raoul," said Jim, coming up to him.

Raoul, who was seated cross-legged on the ground, eating some of the meat and bread that their late host had sent them out with, got to his feet.

"Yes, Sir James," answered Sir Raoul.

"You'd have a better idea than any of us about how fast the French forces can move," Jim said. "I was just talking to Sir Brian; and the indications are that the English forces are less than a day away. How soon do you think it'll be before the French forces come up with them?"

"Not much more than that one day, Sir James," answered Raoul. "King Jean will be eager to come to battle with these intruders. And his knights will be no less eager. It's true, that once they sight the English forces they will have to arrange their own in battle array. That may take half a day or so."

"So you think that possibly tomorrow by this time, about noon," said James, "we might see a battle starting?"

Sir Raoul's lean face broke into a harsh smile.

"I would not doubt it at all, Sir James," he said.

"Then I'll tell the others," said Jim. "We'll need to push on as fast as we can. Today we're more rested; and so, today we ride!"

Indeed, they rode. Thanks to the padding and to two more days' experience in the saddle, Jim found in himself more strength than he had expected. He assumed it was the same with the others. They neither complained, nor showed the outward signs of tiredness they had shown the day before. They covered ground.

Soon after nightfall they came to the fringes of the English army and set up headquarters for the night in a thoroughly ruined stone chapel some distance behind the English campfires. The chapel was so small that it was hard to believe that so much work had gone into building something that could house so few worshipers.

Chapter 32

Jim woke before dawn to the sound of voices and horses moving by where he had been sleeping. He peered out of the rubble of the chapel, amongst which they had all found places to bed down, and saw about a dozen lightly armed men-at-arms on horseback riding by. They had all the earmarks of a foraging party starting out early to see what they could sweep up from the countryside by way of food and drink for the English army.

They paid no attention to the chapel. From this Jim judged, much to his relief, that it had been investigated long since and dismissed as having nothing of interest about it. Their lack of interest was particularly fortunate because the horses Jim and the others had used were tethered in the woods behind the chapel, and if the foraging party had happened to have been going in a slightly different direction, it might have stumbled across them. As it was, they and the horses were safe—for the moment.

Jim threw off the saddle blanket in which he had rolled himself to sleep; and got up shivering from the morning chill, to go outside the chapel and look around in the beginning light of day.

A short path through the trees in front of the chapel brought him out into the open space where the English expedition was camped. It was on a small rise and

from there he could look out some distance. There was light enough to see clear
to the horizon, and the new day brought a new shock.

The French army was already here. It might not yet be in position. But it, too,
was camped—perhaps half a mile distant across the open meadowland between
the English army and itself.

There was no time to lose. Jim went back in and roused the others.

"Breakfast!" croaked Brian, on being awoken—as automatically, Jim found
himself thinking, as a nestling squeaking with open mouth as its parent landed on
the edge of the nest with a juicy worm in its beak.

"Cold food only," said Jim. "We can't risk lighting a fire, with foragers moving
around us."

Eventually he had them all assembled outside, both Giles and Brian champing
on the last of the bread and meat.

"Giles, Brian, Dafydd," said Jim, "all of you will have to go out, as I will, and
search through the English lines until we find John Chester and our men. Once we
find them, we want them to slip away quietly, by twos and threes, from the rest of
the line, attracting as little attention as possible and gathering here at the chapel."

"And I, Sir James," demanded Edward. "Would it not be better if I simply rode
forward openly and announced myself to my own people?"

"We don't dare let anyone see you, Your Highness," said Jim. "Not while,
according to Carolinus, most of them believe you've joined the French king. You'd
be surrounded immediately, and possibly treated as an enemy. In any case, you'd
be mobbed; and the English forces would be thrown into a tangle of dispute
between those who believed in you and those who did not; at the very time when
they ought to be getting ready to face an assault from the French. Let's get our
men here first. Then I may be able to arrange a situation in which you can be put
into sight with the least danger to yourself; as well as confronted with this
magically-made impostor of Malvinne's."

"Indeed," said the Prince, his eyes narrowing and his hand clasping almost
convulsively, "I can't wait to meet such an impostor, weapon in hand."

"If all goes well, you shall, Highness," said Jim, "but for now, until we have our
men about us, any attempt to bring you forth will be too risky."

"What do you suggest I do then, Sir James?" demanded the Prince.

"Stay hidden here, Highness," Jim answered. "I've had a good look at the
chapel. There's one way in that's at all clear, though it's only wide enough for one
man at a time. It's a former aisle of this place, and ends in a pile of stone that goes
up to a still-standing part of the roof. It looks as if there's no way out beyond it.
But actually, one of the lower stones is easily moved by one person and you'll find
behind it a hole in what was formerly the back wall of the chapel. If you stay at the
inner end of that aisle, you can easily slip out through the back wall, pulling the
stone back into place behind you, if anyone tries to enter the chapel. Or stay

where you are, if others are outside, and not be seen. Aargh, who'd better not go out among these humans in any case, and Sir Raoul, can stay with you, as guardians."

"I think I can put myself to better use than that, Sir James," came the voice of Sir Raoul.

Jim turned to look at the French knight, as did all the rest.

"I can make a circuit and penetrate among those of the French forces who don't know me personally," said Raoul. "That way I can learn a good deal about what King Jean and his troops intend. You may need that knowledge."

"I don't know, Sir Raoul," said Jim doubtfully. "The Prince needs protection; and while Aargh is more than a match for several ordinary light-armed humans like the ones I saw earlier, an archer or a crossbowman presents a real threat to him."

"I'll survive," said Aargh. "If not, then death merely comes to me here rather than elsewhere."

"Let Sir Raoul go," said the Prince, with a tinge of contempt in his voice. "Only, in any case, one of you give me your sword belt and sword. It is unseemly that one of royal blood and a Plantagenet should go unarmed."

This demand sent a wave of uneasiness through the group. No one of them there, particularly the knights, liked the idea of being parted from his primary weapon. On the other hand, it was hard to deny the Prince—particularly hard for Brian and Giles. Neither of them was wearing their golden spurs of knighthood; and, aside from those spurs, it was the sword and sword belt that marked them as men of rank. For Raoul—even if he would give his sword to an English Prince—to go among the French forces with nothing but a poignard would be to put himself at a tremendous disadvantage, as far as learning the information he had promised to try to get for them. For Brian and Giles—and, for that matter, Jim—to be without their swords was less critical, but only slightly less so. The hard fact was that they had no extra sword to spare for the Prince; although his request was not something that could ordinarily be denied.

"I think I can be of some help in this situation," came the soft voice of Dafydd. "I will go to my gear and be back in a moment."

He was gone before any of them could ask him what he meant. He returned a moment later with a long bundle, which he unwrapped to reveal before them not only a knight's sword, but a sword belt studded with jewels.

"Indeed, it is a belt and sword such as a knight of consequence would wear," said the Prince suspiciously. "But how did such as you come by this?"

"One of your royal father's wardens of the Welsh marches," answered Dafydd, "—I will not name the name of that particular Lord, that no one may suffer for this—decided to hold a tourney. And it came to him that as part of the entertainment it might be amusing to his English audience, as well as instructive to the Welsh among them, to see three English knights, with lances and in full armor, ride down a certain Welsh bowman of whom they had all heard, who was supposed to be deadly even to knights in plate."

"The archer was yourself?" asked the Prince.

"It was that," said Dafydd, "and little say was I given as to whether I would play my part in this entertainment. Nonetheless, I went with them; and when the time came, stood at one end of the lists with my bow and quiver of arrows while the three knights rode down upon me."

"And then?"

"I had no choice," said Dafydd. "I slew them all, each with a shaft through his heart."

"Through plate armor?" said the Prince incredulously. "At what distance?"

"The full length of the lists," said Dafydd, "and for all that they had specially armored themselves as well, underneath their regular suit of plate, so that they wore chain-mail shirts below the solid metal. I had asked one thing only of that Warden before the tourney: that, since when two knights encountered in tournament, the loser gave up horse, weapons, and armor to the victor, I might have the arms and weapons of those I overcame—and, laughing, he said it should be so."

For a moment silence held them all.

"I do think that he was ready to change his mind and not make good on his promise, after he saw his three knights lie dead on the ground," went on Dafydd with no change of tone, "but there were too many watching, both English and Welsh. His word had to carry some weight of honesty for a man in his position. He let me take what I wanted; and I chose only one thing, this, the best of the swords and belts; for I had no use for armor, look you, nor for war-horses ordinarily. I had but asked for all to make my point."

He stopped speaking, but still no one else seemed ready to speak. They all merely stared at him.

"It is a strange thing." His voice became thoughtful. "You will remember, Sir James. Back in the matter of the Dark Powers and the Loathly Tower, when for a moment you turned your back on the duty of rescuing the Lady Angela as we were at banquet in the hall of Castle de Chaney? In that moment of your decision, the flames of all the candles there leaned as if in a wind, but there was no wind. You will recall I remarked on this at the time, though the rest of you had not noticed? I mind me I mentioned then, that in my family, from father to son, and mother to daughter, for many generations, there had been eyes to see warnings, good and bad. So it was with this sword. I was sadly gathering my gear together to go with you; and I had no thought of taking it. But strangely, that morning, when my golden bird, Danielle, had as much as ordered me out of her sight, it seemed that everything I touched and would take with me felt cold to my touch. However, when by chance I touched this sword and sword belt, they felt warm. And the old feeling came upon me. So I brought it—I knew not then why. Perhaps the reason for my bringing it is now."

He laid it on a stone before the Prince.

The Prince reached a hesitant hand toward it, then drew the hand back.

"It is a knight's sword, certainly," the young man said slowly, "but I do not wish to wear it."

There was another moment of silence. Then the silence was broken by Giles's voice.

"If His Highness would deign to wear the sword and belt of a small but honest knight," said Giles, unbuckling his sword belt, "I would be proud to give him mine; and wear this one that Dafydd has brought, in its place."

He held it out to the Prince, who took it almost eagerly.

"I will accept this with thanks, Sir Giles," said the Prince, "and consider it an honor to wear the sword of a man who has used it in combat, when I have never."

Edward buckled on Sir Giles's sword belt and sword, while Giles took up the one that Dafydd had brought and put it on. The jewels in its belt flashed in the morning light, so that belt and sword together seemed strangely out of place on this small, fierce man with his hooked nose and large pale mustache.

"That's settled then," said Jim. "Aargh will stay with you, Highness—and you will keep yourself well hidden until we return?"

"I shall take no chances on being seen, Sir James," said Edward with a touch of humor. "You may count on me for that."

"And you may count on me to guard him while I live," growled Aargh.

"It is a good wolf," said the Prince.

"It is neither good, nor impertinent," answered Aargh. "It is a wolf—few can say that. Further, it is Aargh; and only I can say that."

So, with a touch of embarrassment on the part of the listening knights, the gathering broke up. The Prince retreated into the security of the ruined chapel, Aargh vanished into the woods as was his habit; while the rest of them went to their horses and, once astride them, headed off in their different directions.

They fanned out as they approached the British lines from the rear. Jim had chosen to take the far end of the line from the chapel, which happened to be situated behind the right-hand side of the line near its outer edge. But he wanted to begin his present examination of the archers and men-at-arms on the left wing of the English forces, for that was the common position of the archers—out on the wings in what was known as the harrow formation—when they lined up for battle. Before a battle, therefore, the English archers were normally to be found at the ends of a camp, in preparation for movement into their combat positions.

Jim reached the far end of the camp line—or what he assumed to be the end of the line, because it was impossible to tell exactly where the English army stopped in that direction. People straggled in and out of the lines at all times. He turned back, riding along the line toward the center of it.

He passed over the archers fairly quickly, for none of the men he was seeking had been archers and it was unlikely that he would recognize a familiar face among them. Dafydd would be on the other end of the British lines, going through the archers there more slowly, and looking for any who might be recruited to help.

Beyond the archers Jim came to the men-at-arms. These were scattered in small groups around individual fires, seated, sharpening their weapons, and doing other small maintenance duties; or simply lounging and gossiping.

There was little if no eating or drinking going on, since the foraging parties had not been sent out as a routine measure but simply because the British, as they had been at the Battle of Poitiers in the history of Jim's own world, had literally been caught with their supplies down. Jim noticed a great number of wagons loaded with plunder, but the lack of food and drink would be of more serious concern.

The plan had been that both he and Brian would only glance at the archers at opposite ends of the line, and then work more slowly down the line of lightly armed men-at-arms until they met at the middle. Meanwhile, Dafydd might well have even dismounted from his horse and be mingling and talking with the bowmen, looking for recruits.

If he found none at the right end of the line, he would try the left end of the line. If he had relatively good success at the right end, he was to return to the chapel as quickly as possible; and aid Aargh in being ready to defend the Prince against any who might stumble over that royal personage.

Jim went slowly along past the seated men, earning hardly a glance from any of them. He was a typical knight, effectively in undress uniform—without his armor, heavy weapons and war-horse. Unhappily, he recognized nobody; not John Chester, not those few men-at-arms of Brian's whom he knew by sight, and none of his own. Eventually he saw Sir Brian riding slowly toward him, and assumed that the other had had no luck either.

Jim's hopes took a downward plunge. He wondered what had happened. Most likely, John Chester and the men had either lost their way, failed to find the English forces, or blundered into the hands of the French. Any of these mishaps would make them unavailable. If that happened, it would create more than a small problem, because such hazy plans as Jim had in his mind at the moment all depended upon having their full complement of men-at-arms with them and ready to fight.

He came together at last with Brian; and spoke to him in a voice too low for any of those near to hear.

"No luck for you either?" he said.

"No, no luck— Hah!" replied Brian in the same low voice; and then Jim saw a smile breaking out at the corners of the other's mouth and Brian's right hand twitching on the pommel of his saddle. Only then, Jim realized that the other was longing to make a fist out of that hand and punch Jim exuberantly upon the shoulder. "Of course I had luck! I found them not fifteen minutes ago. One of the men even knew where the chapel was, so he has gone first with John Chester to guide him to it. Then he'll return and direct the others as they go off, by twos and threes. Theoluf will stay to the last, to make sure that all get off all right, and without causing a stir. I kept on riding down to meet you, so as not to attract any unusual attention."

He raised his voice.

"Come," he said, loud enough for his voice to carry to those nearby. "We may be out of meat but I still have a flask of wine left. Come with me, old friend!"

He dropped his hand on Jim's shoulder and turned his horse away from the lines. Jim followed his lead, and they rode away from the line, not in the direction of the chapel, but back into the woods. Once within the trees, however, they turned and galloped swiftly toward the chapel itself.

By the time they got there, some dozen men had already arrived. John Chester met them with large smiles.

"Well done, John!" said Brian exuberantly, swinging his right leg over the saddle, freeing his left toe from the stirrup, and sliding off his horse's back. Jim, who had never learned that particular trick of dismounting, got off more sedately; and Brian gestured at one of the men-at-arms to take their horses. "Well done all the way along, John. We'll make a knight of you, yet!"

"I thank you for the compliment, Sir Brian," said John Chester, "but it can be no secret to you that, if it had been left to me, I would have been a poor leader indeed. It was Theoluf and the more practiced men-at-arms who kept the company in order and saw it got where it should."

"But you learned, John? Hah?" Brian cuffed him in a manner that Jim thought a little too rough to be friendly, but which John Chester did not seem to object to. "That is the main thing. You learned. Just keep on learning, and what I said will come true. Knighthoods are not won on the battlefield, alone—though you'll have your chance at that, too, before the sun is twice more down, or I'm badly mistaken!

"Let us, you and I, James," he said, turning to Jim, "inside, and see how His Highness has put up with this waiting."

They entered the ruin together. But when they came to the narrow stone-choked alley that had been an aisle, they had to go single file, Jim first. At the end of the aisle, the Prince was seated more or less comfortably upon some of his belongings, to pad the surface of a stone block. Aargh was lying before him. They were deep in talk.

Jim was surprised, for it was Aargh who was doing most of the talking, in a steady, low, growl of a voice. He broke off as Jim and Brian came up; and both he and the Prince looked at them.

"Sir Wolf is very wise," said Edward. "He would make a good teacher. I have been learning much."

Aargh opened his jaws in his silent laughter.

"From 'pert' to 'good' and now to 'wise,'" said Aargh. "I'm improving in this human's estimation."

"Truly, I have much to learn," said Edward seriously, "and being still young I often ignore the gold of wisdom when it is scattered on the ground before me. That, at least, I am not doing at this moment. When I am King, I will have responsibilities. Then knowledge and wisdom will be called for. For this is a new age, mark you, gentlemen; and a new time coming in my generation."

"It will little please me if it does," growled Aargh. "I am all for the old ways and no change in the land as I know it. But I am willing to talk to one who will listen."

"And I have been willing to listen," said Edward. "It is a new thing for me to hearken to one who neither fears nor even very much respects me. One, in fact, to whom even one of *my* blood is somewhat less in some ways."

"All of us can learn from others at some time or other, I think, Highness," said Jim. "However, the rest of us have been up to the English lines and found our own men. They're coming in, two and three at a time; and soon we'll have thirty to fifty good men here, plus any archers that Dafydd may have been able find and bring to our help."

"It is a scant enough force," said the Prince, "but I have not asked for any defense at all, even a small one."

"Forgive me, Highness," said Jim, "but it is not your defense I have in mind directly for these men. Some I'll leave with you for that purpose; but there are other things to be done. I hope to use them to reach the false Prince, and eventually bring you face-to-face with him."

"God send the hour!" said the Prince. His eyes glittered and his fingers played with the hilt of Sir Giles's sword.

Giles returned, and they were all gathered now except Sir Raoul, Dafydd, and anyone whom Dafydd might have been able to find. Sir Raoul was the next to arrive. Jim and Brian, the Prince and Aargh had moved back outside and had been joined by John Chester at Brian's orders. Sir Raoul rode up and dismounted with a thin smile.

"I see you found your men," he said, as one of the men-at-arms took his horse at the wave of Theoluf's finger, and began to lead it back behind the chapel to join the other horses there. "Well, I too have been successful, as far as information goes. There is to be a truce and a parley while the French and English discuss terms that good King Jean has offered them."

"I heard nothing of a truce on the English side," said John Chester. It was doubtful whether he would have spoken up so freely to Brian or any of the other English knights, but the fact that Sir Raoul was French had evidently made him feel he had a certain amount of license.

"Possibly you English do not talk as much between yourselves as Frenchmen." Raoul dismissed the objection with a wave of his hand, not even looking at John Chester. "No battle will take place until tomorrow. They will use the night on either side to discuss things, and send envoys back and forth, for it is already too late in the day to get forces into position and begin a battle, which if started now, must end in darkness and confusion."

"Then tomorrow?" asked Brian. The smile vanished from Sir Raoul's face.

"I should expect battle shortly after dawn," he said, "for King Jean and those with him will not yield in their terms; and certainly the Duke of Cumberland, who commands on this English side, is too pigheaded to back down from his position."

"Do you know in what part of the line the King himself and his bodyguards will be fighting?" asked Jim.

Raoul looked at him.

"I know you particularly charged me to find an answer to that question if I could," he said. "It is my understanding that the King himself will command in the third division, or the furthest back of the three battle lines of the French troops. This is uncertain information, since it may well be changed on the morning; but I think you can pretty well count on it, in this instance. Because of that position, it may well be that he and his division will not need to enter the fight at all. For certainly the first two divisions alone are enough to ride down the English."

"We are not entirely without archers on our side," said Brian, "and you French found it none too easy to ride us down, either at Crécy or Poitiers. If it had not been for the wisdom of your King Jean then in resting his Genoese bowmen and sending them out secretly to fire into the English right flank, at a time when the battle might have gone either way, you would not have won the field that day."

"But he did, and we did win!" Sir Raoul's eyes flashed.

"Let's not fight past battles now," said Jim. "Remember, we're gathered here for one purpose only. That's to unmask the false Prince Malvinne created, while my own special charge from Carolinus is that neither side win. That can only be done if battle is prevented completely."

"And you've a plan for this?" Sir Raoul asked him.

"No solid plan, yet." Jim shook his head. "But I've got the makings of a plan, and I have hopes. We may have more help coming than we imagine."

"What help would that be, James?" asked Giles.

"That, I won't tell you now," answered Jim. "Best none of you count on it. Because I'm going to endeavor to set things up so that, if nothing else, Malvinne's falseness will be demonstrated even to the French King. If that alone is done, much will have been accomplished."

"I do not see, in any case, how battle can be prevented—" Raoul was beginning to object; when a babble of voices among the men-at-arms, and a parting of their ranks some short distance away, revealed Dafydd coming toward them, followed by three men, all with bows over their shoulders and full quivers of arrows at their belts.

"Only three bowmen?" said Sir Raoul, almost sneeringly. "Here's reinforcements!"

Chapter 33

Dafydd came up to the group in conference. The three with him, while not as tall as Dafydd, nonetheless could no more have been mistaken for anything but bowmen, than Malvinne to Jim's eye could have been anything but a magician. They were all lean, tanned individuals, with faces brown and set with premature lines from long exposure to the sun, though none of them seemed to be older than their mid-thirties. They walked with their bows cased behind their shoulders as if the weapons had grown there.

Dafydd brought them up to the waiting group before he stopped with them; and when he spoke he addressed himself directly to Jim.

"I bring you," he said in his soft voice, "Wat of Easdale, Will o'the Howe, and Clym Tyler. All are master bowmen, whom I have shot against in contests of archery over more than a few past years; and I have found them among the best in the world with the long bow."

An awkward silence threatened, but Jim rushed to break it with at least some words of welcome.

"We're glad to have such men with us, Dafydd," he said. "If some of us do not seem as overjoyed as we might, it is only because we rather expected that you would stay longer among the archers, and return with more men than just three."

"So could I have done," answered Dafydd, "but I think that, look you, you will find these three and myself more than ample for the purpose that I have in mind; and that I think you will welcome. Important indeed it is that they be master bowmen, not merely as to skill with the long shaft; but men who have stood in line of battle before, and can be counted on even in the thick of things to do what they have been set to do."

"By Saint Dunstan!" said Brian. "I do not remember you being asked to plan our fighting for us!"

"I was sent to find archers; and archers are used to a particular purpose, or they are wasted," said Dafydd. "Being the only archer here myself among us, it seemed to me that I must take upon myself the planning of what the archers should do, for none of the rest of you are trained to do so. Am I wrong in that? Or was I wrong?"

"No, Dafydd," Jim answered for all the rest, "you were not wrong and are not wrong. Let's at least hear what you have in mind."

"It is not ordinary for an archer to tell belted knights how fighting should go, I know," said Dafydd, "but an archer, look you, is like a tool to the hand. No two tools are exactly alike; and some are better fitted to a particular job than any others, even though others look so like to them that those not used to tools cannot tell the difference. I have here three bowmen specially fitted to a certain use. Whatever else you plan to do, Sir James," he said, now addressing Jim directly, "it is your plan to bring yourself, these gentlemen with you, and in particular your Prince, close to King Jean and Malvinne. Is it not?"

"That's true," said Jim.

"And your only hope of approaching him is during the battle, am I not right?" went on Dafydd.

"You're right," said Jim.

"And am I further right that in a battle, the King of France will be surrounded as thick as they can ride, by at least fifty picked knights, who will be ready to die in place rather than let any possible enemy close to him?"

"That is no whit less than the truth," said Sir Raoul, "and by the Lilies and Leopards themselves, I have from the beginning imagined no way by which a small group like this can penetrate such defense. If you have come up with a method, archer, I freely give you my apologies for any opinion less than favorable of you I have had in the past."

"What I suggest," said Dafydd, as calmly and quietly as always, "must needs depend upon myself and these three being carried safely within a certain range of King Jean and his bodyguards. From that point, however, they may become the tool to open up that steel shield that surrounds not only the French king and Malvinne but the false Prince, for he is sure to be there also as a sign to both armies that he is on the French side."

"I think there is much sense in what the archer says," said the Prince unexpectedly.

"Indeed, Your Highness is probably right," said Brian. "But, Dafydd, just how did you plan that we were to carry you that close?"

"Ah, that," said Dafydd with a slow smile. "I leave to you gentlemen of metal weapons and dress. Think you, that whomsoever leads the approach against these knights cannot be naked men such as myself and these three archers, but must be armored in steel as they are. You know that in such battles as these, your men of the bow are of great power from a distance; and so long as they can retire behind armed and armored men when the enemy comes to close blows. At close range, we are so much cold meat to be sliced."

"True enough, Dafydd," said Jim, as much to end the discussion as to give Dafydd his due. "The making of plans to get us close is within my province. Even our men-at-arms must follow we leaders who're in full armor; or else they, too, could not face the clash with those armed and clad as we. In fact, they'd stand the shock only a little better than you and your bowmen. As it happens, I've got some ideas on that."

"It would be of a great benefit," said Brian wistfully, "if you could go before us in your dragon guise; and at least throw their horses into dismay and excitement. So that they will be less free to oppose us, for needing to control their steeds. But such would not be a gentleman's way, James, as I'm sure you know. Magic should only compete with magic; otherwise it is a case as Dafydd has said, of naked men against those better weaponed and prepared."

"You can indeed turn into a dragon at will, Sir James?" asked the Prince, fascinated.

"Yes, Highness," answered Jim, "although I'm not much of a magician in other ways."

"He is overmodest, Your Highness," said Brian. "He got us into the inner parts of the castle of Malvinne and brought us safely out. That latter part in particular you know, yourself."

"That is very true," said the Prince. "But I'd greatly like to see you change into a dragon someday, Sir James."

"As well wish to see me venture into the castle of a magician to rescue a Prince," snapped Aargh. "It can be done; but it is not something to be done except for special and very strong reasons."

The knights around the Prince all drew back slightly, as if instinctively expecting an outburst of royal temper at this rebuke. Instead, to the surprise of all those there, including Jim, the Prince merely looked thoughtful.

"That also is true, Sir Wolf," he said. "Once again you teach me to think before I speak. I am indebted to you all; and I am sure that great reasons as well as great courage impelled you to come to my rescue where I was held."

There was the beginnings of another awkward silence, but it was Brian this time who hurried to fill the gap.

"James, you said you had some thought about how we could approach King Jean and those with him?" he said. "Remember, Raoul has just told us that the King will be in the third division, with the bulk of the French army before him."

"Exactly," said Jim. "That is why I've planned all along to make a large circuit with all our people and approach from the rear, or from some angle behind them where they are least likely to expect an attack."

Brian looked dubious. So did Sir Raoul.

"Easier said than done, Sir James," said Raoul. "Behind the third line will be the baggage wagons, the retainers, the horse-holders; all the rabble that follows an army. If you plan to charge through that, both horses and men will be worn out before they ever strike the body around the King; and also those with him will be fully alerted that an attack is coming from behind."

"No doubt," answered Jim, "but while I wouldn't use magic directly in battle against anyone, I think it's a legitimate use of it to help us approach to a distance from where a charge will do some good."

Looking around, he saw no disbelief on the faces watching him. The irony of it struck him then; for he was nowhere near as sure as they seemed to be that he could manage what he had just said he would do. But from the standpoint of those around him, magic could do anything; and a magician could work any magic.

He had expected them at least to ask him how he was going to use magic to make their close approach to the King and his bodyguard possible. But none of them asked; and he was content not to have to explain. They must have some hope of success no matter how flimsy. It was best none of them knew that, of all the several possibilities to get them at the false Prince that he was still juggling in his mind, none of them might work. They might be killed to no purpose, all of them. But let the disappointment from that come, if it had to come, tomorrow, after they had all tried their best.

"So much for that, then," said Brian. "However, let us all—you too, Dafydd—move a little apart from these others so that we may speak in freer voices without a thought of being overheard, even by our own men. But before that—Theoluf! Tom Seiver!"

Jim's new squire and Brian's senior man-at-arms detached themselves from the group of the others, from whom the three archers were still standing a little apart, and came up to Brian.

"Yes, Sir Brian?" they said.

"See to it that these three good archers are welcomed among our men. You understand me, Tom, Theoluf? They are one of us now, and to be treated as such."

"It will be so, Sir Brian," said Theoluf.

They went to the archers, spoke to them, and led them over to the men-at-arms. Brian was already leading the others around the corner of the ruined chapel to a small grassy spot.

Once there, Brian turned his attention to Dafydd.

"Dafydd," he said, "now that we're apart, not only from our men-at-arms but from your bowmen, tell us frankly how you think the four of you might open a way for us through that wall of knights surrounding King Jean."

"It was my thought," answered Dafydd, "that the long bow cannot be fired from horseback after the manner of some eastern archers with shorter bows, of whom I have heard, and who shoot even at a gallop. Still, horses might bring myself and my three bowmen close enough to the bodyguard of the King, so that we could work great destruction with our arrows, even against their plate armor, if so they are all dressed in it. To this end you will have to supply us with horses. One reason there are only three with me, is that I wanted not only master archers, but archers who knew how to ride—and all three do so, having been accustomed to horseback since boyhood, for various reasons."

"I can see how this might be a help to us," said Brian, "but I see no special use for it. We will still face a solid wall of steel and whatever lances or weapons have been turned to meet us at the sound of our approach."

"You underestimate what the bow can do, as most of those who are not bowmen tend to do," said Dafydd. "Particularly bows in the hands of such men as these three I brought with me. Think you for a moment, Sir Brian, our arrows can empty the saddles of those directly before you, therefore breaking the solid wall of defenders against which you charge; so that you may be in among them before they are solidly set to face you with horse and weapon."

"Hmm," said Brian, suddenly thoughtful, "there are indeed possibilities in that."

"Indeed," went on Dafydd. "Further, if we are able to place ourselves at the angle to your assault that I hope, perhaps we can continue shooting those ahead of you for some distance in; and, close-packed as those knights must be, if any have a dead knight ahead of them, or a riderless horse, they will have difficulty coming at you until that obstruction is out of their way—which is not likely to be brought about easily or quickly, since all the other knights of the bodyguard will be attempting to get close to you at the same time."

"I see," said Brian. "A very pretty, if hardly chivalrous, way of attacking. But, since we are largely outnumbered, and with the odds much against us, I think it should be justified. It comes to me also that your arrows could help protect the more lightly armed men-at-arms who will follow us forward knights in our full armor."

"I had that in mind too," said Dafydd.

"What do you think of this, James?" asked Brian, swinging on Jim.

"It fits in excellently with what I had in mind myself," said Jim. "It means, of course, getting horses for these three extra bowmen and of course one for His Highness, as well as weapons."

"And armor," put in the Prince swiftly, "nor do you forget a lance, Sir James."

There was the beginning of another awkward silence. Jim took it on himself to break it.

"I am afraid," he said to Edward, "Your Highness forgets how difficult it might be to have the luck to find a suit of armor that would exactly fit Your Highness. We'll do what we can to armor you, but it'll probably run more to a helmet, and mail shirt, with plates that can be strapped on the upper legs and arms. You can count on a shield as well. As for the lance—"

"I'll have you know, Sir James!" broke in Edward hotly, "I have been under instruction by the best teachers in Europe for all kinds of weapons. I doubt not I am the match of anyone here or anyone I am likely to encounter on our way to the King tomorrow!"

"None of us doubts that, Highness," said Jim, "but—"

"Then you will find me armor and a lance, plus all other necessary knightly weapons!" said the Prince haughtily. "I so command it!"

Jim felt a little weary. These gentlemen, lords, and kings were always on stage to a certain extent. Their first concern was not only how they wanted to act, but how they thought one of their rank would be expected to act under given conditions.

One who had rank was expected to show not merely courage, but a temper to match. Being royal, Edward was now demonstrating a royal wrath at the possibility of not being obeyed without question.

It was one of the ridiculous, but deadly, conventions of this society. He sighed and opened his lips to answer.

This time it was Brian who challenged the royal wrath.

"Forgive, Highness," he said, "but I very much fear me that Sir James is right. It is no reflection upon your skill with weapons; but consider that in this clash with close-packed mounted men, the lance would be effective only in the initial shock, if at that. I am beginning to think that if Dafydd can clear saddles for us in the outer ring, then we are better off without the lances entirely, and depending entirely upon our swords. Indeed, in such a close-packed melee as this, it may well be even that our swords will be less effective than our poignards. In fact, I wish myself that I had my small axe with me. It would be ideal for such a situation as this."

"We will look for armor for you, Highness," said Jim, "in what time we have to spare to search for it. But in all honesty, I do not expect that we shall find anything to fit you. Yet we shall try. That is all we can promise."

The Prince's anger, having proved mistimed, was as quick to dissipate as it was to kindle.

"Forgive me, Sir James, Sir Brian, and all the rest of you," he said, "but I had never seen a pitched battle before Poitiers, and I was forced to surrender there, without a blow being struck in my vicinity from the beginning of the fight until my capture. Who am I to advise those who know what it is like in the thick of the encounter? I will abide by what you can do for me, gentlemen, and dress myself accordingly, both as to armor and weapons."

"Thank you, Highness," said Jim, "you are indeed Princely, to listen to as well as command those who will fight for you."

The Prince flushed.

"It is a lesson I am learning," he said somewhat shortly. He gave a wave of his hand. "But on with your discussion, and I will listen."

"Thank you, Highness," said Jim. He turned to the others. "As far as the actual assault is concerned, the charge into them—I have an idea on that. There is a formation—"

"Formation?" asked Giles.

"It is a way of grouping men for an assault," explained Jim. "I know it is more normal for all of you simply to charge in line-abreast. But inevitably that line becomes ragged, as one horse outdistances the others; and it's only when the full body of horse on both sides is committed, that the weight of the attack is felt one way or another."

He paused for objections, but there were none so far.

"There's a different way of riding into an enemy line," he went on. "It's called the Wedge formation; and is shaped like one of the broad arrowpoints on the war shafts shot by a long bow."

He paused to see if they had followed his description of the formation. Apparently they had.

"Its great value is that all ride closely together and strike the enemy line with the point of their wedge and all their weight behind it, so that the momentum of all the horses together helps to drive it through."

He paused again.

"I thought that while some daylight remained we could practice riding to attack the bodyguard in that manner. If we can find a place back behind these trees where no one will see us, we can try riding a short distance in that formation, concentrating on staying together, as we will do tomorrow, with our heavily armored men at the point and our lighter-armed, behind."

He expected to have to talk these essentially conservative companions of his into trying out the new method of attack. But he found instead that, far from holding back on it, they were all eagerness to try it out. The only difficulties came later, after they had gone half a mile beyond the trees that surrounded the ruined chapel, and found a clear area of meadow in which they could get up speed and pretend to be hitting an enemy concentration.

The objections came when Jim broke the news that he wanted them to practice without their armor—for fear of attracting undue curiosity in anyone who might see them so riding—and also carrying lengths of tree limbs in their hands instead of weapons and shields, for the same reason.

This latter suggestion, took most of the fun out of it for a great many of them. The knights in particular had a tendency to feel foolish, galloping their horses in close formation while holding what they disgustedly referred to as sticks. Nonetheless, Jim insisted; and finally they agreed.

As he had expected, the main trouble was getting them to hold together in the formation. Again, half the excitement of the battle charge for these men was the race to see who could be first to come to blows with the enemy. Jim finally fell back on faking some magic, to impress them.

He made them get on their horses in wedge formation, then he himself, on foot, walked slowly about them muttering and waving his hands.

He explained that he was casting a magic web over them that would bind them together; because the only way to victory would be the holding power of the web that kept them in arrow shape. The magic would not only hold them together, he promised, but would triple the strength of each of them, by its tight, if invisible, bonds that held them close to each other. So that the only way the wedge could fail would be if somebody happened to lose touch with those next to him, and lose the extra strength the web would give.

They accepted this explanation so wholeheartedly that Jim was secretly ashamed. But he consoled himself with the fact that nothing less would make them hold together the way they should; and that it was vital they do so.

Much to his surprise, the magic was so firmly believed in, by all, that on the next mock charge they clung together like veterans of fifty such charges; and afterwards they were busy commenting to each other on how they could each feel his strength tripled under the influence of the magic.

"It's because you're sharing each other's strength in the magic," Jim explained with a straight face.

This satisfied them so completely that, for safety's sake, he added that this was something that worked only during such a wedge-shaped charge. They should not attempt to get the extra strength by staying close together under ordinary battle conditions. Too ready a belief, Jim had already discovered, could be as dangerous as too much skepticism.

"Now," he said, when he finally brought the exercises to a halt, "we should be thinking about getting those extra horses."

By the time he said this, the wedge had already separated, as its human parts normally did, into three parties: one consisting of Jim, his Companions, the Prince, and Sir Raoul; another consisting of the men-at-arms; and a third of Dafydd's three archers. In fact, since the archers had no horses, they had stood to one side and watched the exercises, clearly more than a little put out at not being able to join the rest—although their interest in what was going on tended to override this.

It was time to stifle this sort of division among the men; and that had prompted Jim's decision to mention that it was high time that they saw about getting extra horses, not only for the three bowmen, but for the Prince. Horses of any serviceable kind would do for the bowmen. Unfortunately, a fairly good horse would be required for the Prince—in short, a knight's horse. It seemed to Jim that the only way of providing these horses would be to sneak around the back of the French lines and steal them from the French. Sir Raoul would be able to show them the way. The real problem would be to find men capable of doing the stealing.

Jim rode his horse over to where the men-at-arms sat theirs. He noted with a touch of annoyance that Theoluf was still among them.

Jim beckoned Theoluf aside.

"Theoluf!" he said in a low voice. "You're my squire now. You should be over with the rest of us who are leaders in this."

"Thank you m'Lord," said Theoluf. "I own I'm not brave about mixing with those above my station. Also, there's still the matter of getting the bowmen accepted by the men-at-arms, who've a tendency to look down on archers in general. I was still seeing about that."

"Well, that's fine," said Jim, "but, start joining our war councils across the way, simply so you know what's going on. If you stay with the men-at-arms, you learn only what's issued as orders to them. There's more to your new rank than that."

"I stand corrected, m'Lord," said Theoluf. "I'll be beside you from now on."

"Fine," said Jim. "Now—I want the attention of all the men-at-arms."

Theoluf turned his horse back to face the other men-at-arms and shouted at them.

"Pay heed now!" His voice rang out. "M'Lord James has something to say to you all!"

Jim and he rode back to the group. Jim looked at the faces of his own men and Brian's. As Brian had mentioned, he had brought only those who were veterans. The faces that looked back at Jim, consequently, were hard, experienced faces, none of which gave anything away by their expression.

"Men!" said Jim, raising his voice. "We've reached the point where we have to get horses not only for these new archers but for Prince Edward. Who among you has some experience in stealing horses?"

There was a dead silence from the assemblage before him. No one spoke. No one changed expression.

Jim waited a few moments. Then it became obvious none of them were going to speak up. He raised his voice again.

"Is there any among you who have known horse thieves, then? Or perhaps heard of some of the ways they go about their stealing?" he asked.

Once more he met the same poker-faced silence. Evidently, it was no use. He turned briefly to Theoluf.

"Join me when you can," he said in lower tones to his new squire. Turning his horse about he rode back to join the group of those belonging to the upper class.

As he joined them, his mind was busy with the problem that had just erupted. He had been sure that of the men-at-arms one, at least, since they were all old soldiers, might have some idea on how to provide themselves with riding horses under conditions like these. But, evidently not.

The question was now, what should he do? Sir Raoul would show him the way to the back lines of the French, and soon twilight and approaching darkness would make thievery possible. But he, himself, had not the slightest idea of how to go about getting the horses he needed. Furthermore, he was quite sure that none of the men of rank around him would know any such thing.

He was roused from his thoughts by Brian's hand plucking at his elbow. When he looked up, Brian caught his eye and inclined his head a little to the side. They rode off together a short distance, enough to give them privacy from both groups.

"I heard you there," said Brian. "James, James! What did you think to gain by speaking to the men that way?"

"Why, I hoped to come across at least one who had some experience in stealing horses," said Jim. "Exactly what I asked them."

"Exactly," said Brian. He shook his head, "James, James! Sometimes I think you are the wisest man on earth, wiser even than Carolinus. At other times, you seem to know as little about the ordinary things of life as someone from the depths of the sea or the other side of the world."

"I don't understand." Jim stared at him.

"Why," said Brian, "you asked these men, standing all together, each overhearing your words and in a position to overhear the words of any who answered you, which of them were horse thieves. How could you expect them to answer? If any had said you yes, from this day on if they happened to be anywhere nearby when a horse was stolen, and there was one of these others around who remembered that one identified himself as skillful at stealing such, they would immediately be mentioned as one who had experience at that thievish trade."

"I see," answered Jim slowly. He had lived in this world long enough to know that, here, an accusation was tantamount to a universal certainty that the person was guilty of whatever he was accused of. "But how am I supposed to find out who among them does know something about picking up horses for our archers and the Prince?"

Brian turned without giving him a direct answer and shouted in the direction of the men-at-arms.

"Tom Seiver!"

Tom detached himself from the group and came over.

"Tom," said Brian, "we need at least two men who know something about stealing horses. Go find us some. We'll wait here."

"Aye, Sir Brian," said Tom Seiver, turning back toward the men-at-arms.

"Is Theoluf still there with you?" Brian called after him.

Tom stopped and turned back.

"Yes, Sir Brian," he answered.

"Perhaps Theoluf can be of advice and assistance. In any case, see to it. Bring us two such, right away," said Brian.

"Right away, Sir Brian," said Tom, as matter-of-factly as if he was starting off to fetch a couple of flasks of wine. He strode back to the group.

"You understand now, James?" Brian asked. "This is what such men as Tom are for, set up to be captain among the other men-at-arms. They already know if any of the others have horse-stealing skills. There will be no public asking or answering aloud, but merely understanding and an order."

"Yes," said Jim wearily. It seemed that he would forever be learning about this new world that he and Angie had decided to live in. All that its inhabitants knew from birth, almost without knowing how they learned it, he needed to learn by trial and error.

Chapter 34

Tom was back within five minutes with two men. One was a small, brisk-looking youngster with a brush of red hair above an open, guileless face. The other was a taller, leaner, and older man with thinning black hair. Both moved and wore their weapons like the experienced men-at-arms they were.

"This of the red hair is Jem Wattle," said Tom. "With him is Hal Lackerby. Sir Brian knows them well, Sir James, but I thought you might wish to be told their names if you had not known them before." A hard smile crossed Tom Seiver's face. "They're just the men you need to spy out the French lines after dark."

"Thank you, Tom," answered Jim.

"Jem—Hal!" said Brian. "Attend Sir James until he sends you back to your usual duties." He turned to Jim. "Shall I stay with you James, or—"

"If you would, Brian," said Jim. "I'm going to be talking to Sir Raoul. It'll do no harm to have someone back here who knows what we're busy about."

"Come then," said Brian.

He turned his horse, leading the way. James rode with him, and the two men-at-arms silently brought up on foot behind them as they rode over to where Sir Raoul was standing beside his own horse.

"Sir Raoul," said Jim, as the other knight looked up at him, "we would like to speak to you—a little aside if you don't mind."

Sir Raoul swung up into the saddle of his own horse and the five of them moved off across the grass of the meadow into the lengthening shadow of the trees. Out of earshot of the others, Jim halted his horse and turned it back to face Sir Raoul's and incidentally that of Brian, as well as the two men-at-arms.

"Sir Raoul," said Jim, "you know we need horses for the archers, and another horse, of some value, for the Prince. I've found two men who might be useful in helping us get such horses. Will you guide us to the rear of the French lines again?"

"Not the English lines, of course, for that," said Sir Raoul sardonically. "Oh well; I expected it would be the French lines. Come with me, then, all of you."

It was full dark when they reached the rear of the French lines. They had been reduced to going slowly, for the trees were still about them and, while the sun was all the way down, the moon had not yet risen. However as they reached the rearmost wagons of the French baggage train, the thin moon began to rise. With the aid of its increasing glow, they found their way up into the main baggage area of the French.

"We are now in the center of the baggage area behind the French lines," said Sir Raoul. "There'll be horses, both alone and herded together, picketed to the right and left of us. Whatever you want to do from here on is up to you. I'm simply in attendance until the time comes to guide you back to our people."

Brian had been talking in a low voice to his two men-at-arms.

"Away with you then, lads," he concluded. "You know what's needed. Horses, saddle gear, armor, and weapons for His Highness. See that you find it all."

The two men vanished among the baggage carts and other paraphernalia. Brian turned back to Jim.

"Now, James," he said, "we simply wait."

"I think I'll take advantage of the situation by examining the area myself, while we're waiting," said Jim. "Would you stay here, Brian, in case Jem and Hal return before we do? That way we can all regather on you."

"I'll hold this spot," he said grimly.

"Thanks Brian," Jim said gratefully. "I won't be long."

He turned to Sir Raoul.

"Raoul?" he said. "Will you show me where you think the most likely place might be for the King and his bodyguard to stand while the battle takes place? I'd like to have an idea of the ground over which we might need to charge."

"I can only guess, Sir James," said Raoul, a little stiffly, "but if that is what you wish . . ."

"It is what I wish," said Jim.

Sir Raoul rode off. Jim caught up with him and they rode their horses around and through the baggage carts, toward the first line of what looked like a small row of hillocks. As they got closer, the hillocks turned out to be medieval versions of tents. Most of these were lighted from inside; and from within them came the sound of men enjoying themselves, most undoubtedly with the help of food and drink, probably mostly the latter.

Sir Raoul rode through this line of tents and led Jim on to a point where the ground rose a little bit and became freer of trees. They were at the very edge of the open area in which the two armies confronted each other.

"I think this is the most likely place for His Majesty to want to place himself so that he can view the battle," said Sir Raoul. "Again, remember this is only a guess on my part. I promise nothing. But if I were in command of this army, this is the place I would choose."

Jim rode about, examining the land in several different directions. If this was indeed to be the place that the King would choose, then it was ideal for Jim's purposes. There were a number of directions that gave enough open space for his group to get up to charging speed, even after emerging from the tree line, which surrounded this open area as if holding it in a cup.

"If the King picks this spot, we've a good chance," he told Raoul, who only grunted in answer. "Now tell me. Is there any place not too far from here where we might put the Prince with some guards, and where those guards could defend him in case anyone stumbles across him? He'll need to be close, if we win through to the King and Malvinne; but not too close, in case he gets seen and taken before we've had a chance to do our work."

Sir Raoul's head bowed for a minute toward his breast as if he was thinking.

"There's another stone ruin," Raoul said, after a few seconds, "not too far from here, back in the woods. It's not so large as the place which we have made our headquarters so far. This may have been just a wayside chapel at some time. Nonetheless, it's also of stone; and it may be that in its ruin there's a defensive position. I'll take you there."

He lifted his reins and led off. Jim followed. In not more than a matter of minutes they came to a mound of darkness rising above the level of the forest floor. It was, as Raoul had said, of stone, and possibly looted many times.

"If you'll hold my horse, Raoul," Jim said, "I will investigate this on foot."

He got down and began feeling his way around the pile of stone in the gloom. As Raoul had said, it was much smaller than the ruined chapel, and if anything, was in a worse ruin. Still, he found a way in among some of the blocks for a distance of about eight feet. It could only be traveled by one person at a time. With the Prince at the inner end of this, and one or more people standing guard before him, whoever wished to get at the royal individual would literally have to get there over the body of the guard. Jim backed out, brushing the stone dust and dirt from his hands, and remounted his horse.

"Good," he said briefly to Sir Raoul. "Now, let's get back to Brian."

When they reached Brian, Jem Wattle and Hal Lackerby had already returned with not merely four, but five horses. One was larger and healthier looking than the rest—at least as far as Jim could tell in the darkness—and laden with what must be the armor.

They had, indeed, managed to steal a knight's horse, or at least a horse a knight would be willing to ride, for the young man.

"All set?" Jim said to Brian. When the other nodded, he turned his horse's head away.

The ride back went swiftly. By this time the moon was well up, and by its light, the three archers were allowed to try out their horses and show that—as Dafydd had said—sure enough, they could ride well.

"Everybody turn in and get what rest you can," said Jim. "We'll have to mount a guard through the night. And the last guard is to start rousing the rest of us at moonset, which should be a good hour or more before sunrise. I want us on our way to the rear of the French camp before full daybreak."

A hand on Jim's shoulder, shaking it—Jim never found out whose hand—woke him in the early morning. He got creakily to his feet, stiff from the cold in spite of having wrapped himself in a saddle blanket and chosen what he thought was a wind-protected niche among the fallen stones of the chapel. The stiffness, cold, and a hunger for more sleep almost conquered him. But he told himself that if he got up and moved around, all of this would improve.

He left the protection of the chapel, and began trying to check on whether all the rest were up.

They certainly seemed to be, although it was still too dark to count heads. Most of them could be seen moving about much more briskly than he. Jim had come to envy the people around him ever since he had become a denizen of this world. Nearly all of them seemed able to sleep in any position, under any conditions, wake up at a moment's touch, and ignore any of the feelings that were bothering Jim now. Practice, begun in infancy, he supposed.

He bumped into several people in the darkness before he was able to discover Brian.

"Is everybody up?" he asked Brian, more to have something to say than anything else.

"Yes, yes," said Brian, with that slight testiness that had a tendency to afflict him on the morning of any action. "Of your love, Jim, give me room. I must get into my armor now. So should you. Where is your Theoluf? A squire should be with his master at all times such as this. Ho! John Chester!"

"Here, Sir Brian," spoke up a voice out of the darkness near Jim's elbow.

"Where's my breast plate? Go find Theoluf and have him fetch Sir James's armor and bring it here and start to help him dress!" said Brian. "Where have you been all this time?"

"Right here, Sir Brian," answered the voice of John Chester. "I was but waiting for Sir James to finish speaking to you and stand aside."

Jim hastily moved off to the left and bumped into somebody else, which must have been one of the men-at-arms, for with an apologetic, "sorry, m'Lord," the other figure disappeared into the gloom.

"As soon as there is any light in the sky at all so that we can see each other," said Jim, "I want you to go off with me a little ways. I need your help in trying out something."

"Certainly, James. Certainly. John Chester, the breast plate goes over the breast, not the stomach!" said Brian.

"Sorry, Sir Brian," said John.

"Indeed you'll be sorrier, if you don't learn how to dress me properly and with more dispatch!" said Brian. "Yes. Certainly, Jim. As soon as I'm dressed. Just come get me. John Chester—"

But Jim was already moving off in the darkness.

He cannoned into another body.

There was a rattle of something metallic falling to the earth.

"Sorry, m'Lord," said the voice of Theoluf. "I was just bringing your armor. . . ."

"Oh," said Jim. He stood still. "Well then, if you can see well enough to do it, you'd better start getting me into it."

How Theoluf had recognized him in the darkness, or how that other man-at-arms had done so, Jim had no idea. It could be he still smelled differently to these other people. He and Angie took regular baths, but over the months they had gotten used to the smells of the unbathed people who lived in their clothes around them; particularly those of the servants. On the other hand, he had not had a bath since leaving home, which was a matter of some weeks now. Still, perhaps a difference remained. He stood as quietly as he could, enduring Theoluf fastening the pieces of plate armor around his legs and arms and body. It went on over a sort of padded jacket and leggings, which were supposed to take up some of the shock that the metal passed on when a weapon struck it. Jim had never noticed that they did any good; and invariably when he had to wear full armor, it turned out to be a broiling hot day with a bright sun beaming down, and the heat from that weight of clothes upon him was almost more than he could take.

But everyone else took it for granted; so he had learned to grit his teeth, say nothing and put up with it. Finally, he was fitted with all of his armor, right down to the spurs on his heels. The only piece of equipment Theoluf did not put on him was his helmet, which would be left off until the last moment, not only because of the discomfort of being enclosed by it, but because it limited eyesight with its small, hinged visor.

Theoluf tucked the helmet solictiously under his arm.

"Shall I bring up m'Lord's horse?" he said, standing back.

There was now enough light to pale the stars in the eastern half of the sky and allow them all to make out the shapes of those around them.

"Not just yet," said Jim. "Bring me Sir Brian first. Then bring both our horses."

"Yes m'Lord."

Theoluf went off, disappeared in fact into the grayness about them that was scarcely better than the absolute blackness to which Jim had wakened. The new squire was back in a few moments, just behind a fully armored Brian, also carrying his helmet. Theoluf had both their horses saddled and bridled and was leading them forward by the bridles.

In the armor, it was much easier to ride than walk. Jim climbed heavily and clumsily into his saddle, with Theoluf's help, while Brian vaulted into his own saddle without help. He hung his helmet on the front point of his high saddle, and Jim did the same.

"Where to, James?" asked Brian.

"Just off from the rest far enough so that we can't be seen," said Jim.

They rode off a small distance; and at Jim's direction they both dismounted once more. Jim searched around and found a bush, from which he broke a twig bearing several leaves. He tucked this in the niche between the visor and the helmet proper of Brian, making sure that the twig was firmly in place.

"What's afoot?" asked Brian, clearly mystified.

"Nothing too important," said Jim. "I just want to check out a piece of magic with your help. Put the helmet on your head, would you?"

Brian did so, automatically whipping up his visor once the helmet was on. The twig, Jim was glad to see, stayed in place.

"Now, just stand there a moment, if you don't mind," said Jim, "while I work this magic."

He had given what he was about to do considerable thought. Invisibility was something that Jim's twentieth-century mind could not believe in; and that therefore he could not envision. But someone who looked straight at something, but refused to admit that he saw it—that he could believe in. It was a common hypnotic trick.

Even as he thought this, he was writing on the inside of his forehead:

ANYONE WITHOUTLEAVES———>WON'TSEE ANYONE WITHLEAVES

To Jim's eyes Brian vanished.

"When are you going to do the magic?" Brian's voice boomed hollowly out of the vacancy before him.

Jim tucked the other twig into the hinge of his own helmet and put it on. Brian was suddenly visible again, directly in front of him.

"I said when are you going to do this magic?" Brian asked. "I don't wish to complain, James, but there are orders to be given, and we should be getting people together if we're going to move."

"It's more or less been done," he said. "Just one thing more. Stand still while I walk around behind you."

Brian did so. Jim walked around behind him, took the twig out of Brian's helmet as well as his own, and tossed them away.

"I don't understand this at all," said Brian as Jim came back around in front of him. "What is this business with the twigs? When are you going to do the magic? As I say, we should be getting back."

"We can go now," said Jim, "it's all been taken care of. Would you give me a hand up onto my horse before getting on your own?"

"Now I am to play squire to you," grumbled Sir Brian, helping Jim onto his horse. Jim let the grumble pass. Brian's temper was, if anything, a little worse than usual this battle morning. He would cheer up instantly once they had reached a point of going into action.

With Jim safely on his horse, Brian mounted his own, and the two of them rode back to the waiting men. In spite of Brian's insistence that he was urgently required back at the chapel, to Jim's eye everything was pretty well taken care of. The men-at-arms had armed and armored themselves, taken their light lances, and were all on horseback. So also, were the archers and the other knights. Apparently they had only been waiting for Jim and Brian to get back.

However, as Jim returned, a slim figure without armor and wearing the same clothes the Prince had worn since they had first picked him up, rode up to him. The figure had a helmet on and a heavy lance in one hand. The visor was down.

"Sir James." The figure put the visor up to reveal the Prince's face; and the horse was reined in beside Jim's. "The armor would not fit."

"I was afraid of that, Highness," said Jim. "However, I think we can contrive things so that you won't miss your share of action, even though you may have to stand aloof from some of the early parts of it."

"I was counting on charging with the rest of you!" complained the Prince.

"So was I, Highness," lied Jim, "but of course, without armor, we don't want you in the wedge. I'll tell you what; we'll arrange a safe place for you, close enough so that you can come out as soon as we have broken up the bodyguard and opened a way to King Jean, Malvinne, and the false impostor."

"Good!" said the Prince. "But I shall still hold it a shame and a fault that I was not among the rest of you in the charge. But we of royal blood must learn to accustom ourselves to things that would probably bother lesser men."

He rode off to join the group of knights, who were waiting to move out, and who had already been joined by Brian.

"All right!" said Jim, raising his voice. "Sir Raoul, will you ride in front and guide us? Good! Then, let's move!"

Chapter 35

The sun had not yet risen by the time they reached the rear of the French lines. But there was enough light reflected from the sky now, so that things were as visible as they might have been on a thickly clouded day. Jim halted them all some three hundred yards behind the baggage lines. Sitting his horse, facing them in a little open space between the trees, he had two men-at-arms dismount and search for two twigs apiece for every person there. At his direction they brought these twigs back to him.

They had necessarily done the twig-gathering on foot. He leaned down from his saddle to take two of the small leafy ends, and held them up so the rest could see them.

"Now," he said, "I want you all to watch me and my horse carefully."

He waited until he was sure all eyes were on him, then leaned forward and threaded the small woody stem firmly into the headstrap of the bridle, so that there was no danger of it falling out. He leaned back then, sitting upright in his saddle, and looked at them, still holding the other twig visibly in the air in his hands.

"What do you see?"

There was a murmur of wonderment from those before him. No one, it seemed, wanted to take it upon himself to give a direct answer.

"Sir Brian," said Jim, "what do you see?"

"Why, you are but sitting in thin air above the ground!" said Brian.

"Exactly," said Jim. "Now watch this."

He tucked the other twig firmly into the hinge of his helmet visor, so that it could not possibly come out.

"Now what do you see?" he challenged his audience again. "Brian?"

"James," said Brian, "are you still there? We can see neither you nor your horse, if you are."

"I'm here, all right," said Jim, "and you'll see me again in a minute."

He turned to look down again at the men-at-arms with the rest of the twigs in their hands, both now staring open-mouthed at apparently empty space.

"You two," he ordered, "take the rest of those twigs and pass them out, two to each man here. Each of you, as you get your two twigs, put one first firmly into your bridle, around the head, where it can easily be seen from a distance. Then put the other securely in your helmet or some other place, that again you can be sure it won't fall out by accident. Do it now."

The men-at-arms jerked to life as the voice came at them from the empty air, and moved out among the assemblage before him, passing out the twigs. As each man took his pair of twigs, he did what Jim had said; and a new murmur of voices arose. They stared at those around them who got their twigs in first and disappeared, then reappeared, once the person staring had put his own twigs in place.

"Let's not raise our voices," said Jim. "We should be far enough from the baggage lines to be safe but I don't want to be overheard. Now, have you all got your twigs in place? If so, can you all see each other and me, again?"

A murmur of agreement arose.

"A wondrous thing, Sir James!" came the voice of the Prince clearly.

"Thank you, Your Highness," said Jim, keeping his own voice down, "but, by your favor, please remember what I said about not speaking loudly. Now, to anyone else who does not have twigs attached to their clothing or stuck in their hair, or some other such place, you'll all appear to be invisible. See that you don't spoil that invisibility by making any noise that would make them think there's someone there—but invisible."

He paused to make sure all got the message. Then he went on. "Bear in mind, this is a different magic from plain invisibility. You haven't really been made invisible. You've only been changed so that anyone who looks at you will convince himself he *doesn't* see you. If you speak, the sound may fight with that conviction and they may end up seeing you, after all. This applies to the horses as well. Let's ride them as quietly as possible, at a walk."

He turned to look at Raoul.

"Sir Raoul," he said, "will you first take His Highness and the knights to the

place we picked out yesterday and leave them just inside the trees? Then return
here and guide another party of ten of our men to that position, and so forth, until
they're all there. I'll wait, to go with the last group."

They went as Jim had directed. He came in with the last group to find the rest
of them already seated among the trees at the edge of the little rise open land
between the armies.

The knights, as was to be expected, had picked the choicest spot. This was a
clump of trees against which they could lean their backs, on the very edge of a
small stream that ran through the wood, but not out into the open battle area
itself. Descending from his horse, Jim emptied his saddle flask, which held a good
quart, so that he could refill it with water from the stream.

"James!" called Brian from where he was sitting. "What's this? You're pouring out
good wine on the ground just so you can fill your flask with water?"

He got up in his concern and came over to Jim; who, having emptied the flask,
was now holding it below the level of the stream and letting it fill, while bubbles
from its empty interior floated down the surface of the stream.

"I want water in this flask," he answered Brian, squinting up at the other from
where he squatted.

"But plain water's not good for you," said Brian concernedly. "I've had reason to
give you that warning before, James. In especial, French water will give you the
flux."

"We shall see," answered Jim. The flask was now full. He took it up out of the
stream and stoppered it. "In any case I can protect myself against the flux by
magic."

"Oh. Of course. I forgot," said Brian.

"Perfectly understandable," said Jim, rising to his feet again, and carrying the
flask back to where he could strap it onto the saddle of his horse. He just wished
he could be sure that his magic would protect him from the flux—by which Brian
undoubtedly meant diarrhea. He tied his horse's reins close to where the horses of
the other knights and the Prince were tethered, Brian accompanying him.

"Raoul has been telling us about your reasons for picking this place," Brian said
as he tied the horse. "I take it that now, we simply wait to see if the King and his
bodyguard place themselves on that space about seventy-five yards out there?"

"Yes, that's right," answered Jim. "If he hasn't moved there with his knights by
the time both armies are in formation, we may have to seek him out, wherever he
is. It'll be important that the men stay quiet; and that none of them lose the twigs
they're wearing."

"Some of these lads were amusing themselves after they got here, by pulling the
twigs secretly from the helmet or clothing of their friends, and leaving them with
no means to see the rest who surrounded them. A bit of a change in blind man's
bluff. I put a stop to it."

"Good," said Jim. "Now, it would be helpful if we had a couple of lookouts up in the taller trees to advise us how quickly the two armies form up as the sun rises—which I see it's starting to do now. Do we have a man with particularly good sight for distance?"

"I have, unless Theoluf knows a better among your men," said Brian. They had now reached the rest of the seated knights. John Chester and Theoluf were standing close, leaning back against some trees, but not daring to sit in the presence of their superiors. "John Chester! Theoluf! To us!"

The two squires came over.

"John Chester, who is that particularly sharp-sighted lad of mine among the men-at-arms? Luke Allbye? Fetch him over. And you, Theoluf, do you have anyone among Sir James's men who could compare with Luke for seeing at a distance?"

"There is myself, Sir Brian," answered Theoluf. "I would think I can outsee your Luke on any fair day; although he may see a little better when things are misty, or in the twilight; but it is six of one and half a dozen of another."

"Then let him be—don't you think so, James?" Brian turned to Jim. "It is just as well not to have a squire scrambling up trees in contest with a man-at-arms. We will send Luke up and see what he can tell us about the gathering of both French and English into formation."

More than a few moments passed before Luke, a tall, thin, sad-looking man-at-arms in his early thirties, put in an appearance. Meanwhile, Dafydd had just come up with the gray-haired one of the three archers he had brought.

"What's this, Dafydd?" asked Sir Brian.

"As I heard Sir James say just now," answered Dafydd quietly—he had been seated not exactly among but close to the knights, "he needed the sharpest pair of eyes possible to read the forming of the French and English battle lines. This, you will remember, is Wat of Easdale, whom I do believe has eyesight better than any of us here, if not in all England and Wales, for that matter."

Luke Allbye and John Chester looked sour. Brian frowned.

"An archer must needs have better sight than most men, look you, for the proper striking of his target," went on Dafydd, "and a master archer such as Wat here is far above ordinary men in his ability to see what he shoots at. Is it not so, Wat?"

"Indeed, by your leave, sirs," said Wat of Easdale, "it is God's truth!"

"Well, there's a simple solution to all this," said Jim. "Let's have them both climb trees and come back and tell us what they see. Aside from deciding which one is better than the other, our main interest here is to learn as much as we can. So, if either one can tell us more than the other about what he looks at, we're ahead of the game."

"Right enough, James," said Brian, although the thin line of his mouth showed that he too had been touched by the challenge of someone else claiming to be able to see better than the best pair of eyes in his household. "Both of you, up a tree and study what you see. Then return and tell us what you can."

Jim, Brian, and Dafydd sat down once more to await results. Meanwhile, as the morning sun rose in the sky, the air began to warm, and on its warmth came a fresh scent of the grasses and trees around them. They had had good weather almost every day since they had landed in France, and today evidently intended to live up to the mark. It would be magnificent—though perhaps a little hot for those in full armor. Jim was already wriggling a little, secretly but uncomfortably, under the padding beneath his metal breast armor.

The woods around them resounded to the songs of birds. To all appearances, things could hardly be more peaceful. It seemed almost unthinkable to Jim that within a few hours, barring some kind of miracle, men would be busy maiming and killing each other with edged and pointed weapons.

He remembered Carolinus had told him that the battle must be won by neither side, if the Dark Powers were to be frustrated. Jim had no idea—or at least only a vague idea—about how this might be managed. Carolinus was evidently depending upon him to do it; but so far he had not thought much beyond the point of getting through to the false Prince, and getting King Jean to recognize the real Prince.

His thoughts drifted off at a tangent, trying to think of ways in which they could go about finding where the King was to make his stand, if he decided not to make it here. The invisibility was all very well, but it would be difficult to move a body of men this large safely along a busy line of warriors getting ready to fight. Yet, to break them up into individual groups was also very risky.

He would have to trust them to find each other again, wherever the site for King Jean's observation of the battle would be. It would be taking a very large risk of not being able to get an effective number of them back together again in time to be useful.

His thoughts were interrupted by the return of Luke Allbye and Wat of Easdale. They came back, along with John Chester and Dafydd, who had evidently gone with them and stayed with them, probably at the foot of the tree each one's particular lookout had climbed.

"About time," said Brian, as the two came up. "Luke, what have you to tell us?"

Luke took off his helmet respectfully before answering, and Wat—clearly suddenly reminded of this—also took off the helmet with which he had replaced his customary archer's flat cap.

"Sir James, m'Lord," replied Luke, "both armies are all but in ready position. The French are in three divisions, as expected, one line behind the other, with the back line almost up against the tents of the Lords and Knights here today. The English, so far as I could make out, are in a single line, in harrow formation, as they were at Crécy and Poitiers, with the men-at-arms aligned facing front, toward the French, and the archers in two, close, forward-running lines at each end. The lines lean inward toward their forward ends, so that one bowman can shoot past another safely."

He had delivered the first batch of information all in one breath and paused for a second to gulp air before going on.

"At my best guess, Sir Brian and m'Lord," he said, "there are six thousand men-at-arms of the English, perhaps a third of the number of that in the French three lines. The French have also Genoese bowmen in ranks before their first line of men-at-arms, forward a little so that they can shoot over each other's heads. My guess is three thousand of the crossbowmen. On the English side, contrary to what we heard earlier, there seem to be somewhere between four and six thousand archers, instead of the two thousand that was spoken of."

"Thank you, Luke," said Sir Brian. He looked at Jim. "Have you anything to ask him, James?"

Jim shook his head.

"And you—" Brian's eyes went to the archer, Wat of Easdale. "What, if anything, do you have to add to what Luke has told us?"

"Only that there are not six thousand archers, but merely two thousand at best," replied Wat dryly.

Not only Brian and Jim, but the other knights who were listening, stared at the archer, who bore their scrutiny with complete composure.

"How can you tell us something like that?" said Brian. "The archers were surely too far off to see individually; and I know Luke to be a good judge of numbers."

"Surely," said Wat of Easdale levelly, "it must have seemed quite clear to Luke that the harrow ends must contain at least six thousand archers, in the two lines of men he saw extending from the main division of men-at-arms. But this can only be a trick of our English, to deceive the French. Of those lines of what appeared to be bowmen, two or more out of every three men, are not archers at all, but men-at-arms—or for all I know, cooks and bakers from the among the baggage servants—holding a staff of the length of a bow stave and standing as they believe an archer stands."

"Sirs, they were all archers!" broke in Luke hotly. "I swear it."

"Then you put your soul in peril by so swearing," said Wat calmly, without turning his head to look at the other man. "They may stand a man in formation, and put a stave in his hand, but only the lifetime of training that makes a bowman, will cause him to stand with it as a bowman stands. It was plain to me, who am a man of the bow, and have grown up and lived with others who are also of the bow, that more than two out of three of those in the archer lines were no true archers."

"Even if what you say is true—yes Dafydd, I believe he knows a bowman from a man-at-arms." Brian interrupted himself, seeing that Dafydd was just about to object to the word *if*. "Still, these lines of archers were at such a distance, how could any man see such small differences in the way they stood and held whatever they held?"

"I could," said Wat, "and did. With respect, Sir Brian, if you had looked over the point of your arrow at a mark three hundred yards off, at which you were shooting, as often as I have, you would learn to notice small differences, even at that distance. I tell you flatly that the English have only two thousand archers at most, and that the others are false, set there to make the French cautious."

"Cautious, it may make some few, rare Frenchmen," said Sir Raoul angrily, "but do you think it will frighten any of them into not charging when the time comes? And once they get close, will they not see the deception and charge all the harder?"

"Indeed, I'm sure that's what'll happen, Sir Raoul," said Wat, "and therein lies the use of it from the English side, if they have as few as another five hundred bowmen on each side lying hidden in the grass, or behind hedges, out beyond the flanks of the harrow. When the French discover what they think to be merely a trick and increase their charge, their line will be spread out more unevenly than usual, with the faster horses pulling far ahead of the slower ones. At that moment, the bowmen hidden on either side can rise up and begin shooting; and if they do not wipe out half the French horse in that first charge, before a single Frenchman reaches the first false English archer to cut him down, I will eat my bow and quiver to boot!"

"And if they wipe out half the horsemen in that charge, what matters it?" said Sir Raoul, almost savagely. "There are five times as many French behind, just waiting to take their place."

"I think the advantage of it is pretty plain," said Jim. They all looked at him, because he had been quiet up until now. "Such an unexpected reversal, and the possibility that there might be other such traps waiting for those who will charge after, may be enough to make the French, and even King Jean himself, lose his temper. And you know yourself, Sir Raoul, that when your countrymen get outraged they have only one thought in their minds. That is to get to close quarters with the enemy as soon as possible. So whatever battle plan the French may have can fall into confusion and be lost."

Sir Raoul glared at Jim, opened his mouth, closed it again, and ended by saying nothing. Whatever further argument might have developed was cut short, however, by Tom Seiver running up to them.

"Sirs, a large group of knights moving this way! They move all together, in a body; and if I mistake not they carry the royal banner of the Leopard and Lilies in their midst."

"It will be the French King then!" cried Sir Giles joyfully. "He is coming here, after all!"

All around them the men-at-arms were on their feet; as were the knights, who had already started to head for their horses.

"Not yet!" Jim's voice stopped them. "Let them get into position and settled first. Keep everyone well back in the woods. Your Highness, the time has come for me to speak to you about something. Will you step aside with me?"

"Very well then, Sir James," said the Prince, coming toward him.

"And will you attend us, too, Sir Giles," said Jim.

The Prince raised his eyebrows at this but said nothing. Giles did not question the matter, but simply came toward them. Together, the three went off into the woods.

"Where are we headed, Sir James?" asked the Prince, after a few moments. "I thought you meant merely a step or two aside, out of earshot of the rest. But you seem to be taking me somewhere."

"I am, Highness," answered Jim. "Bear with me, if you will. It is only a little farther on."

He and the Prince continued side by side a little farther, with Giles bringing up the rear. Then they had passed through the trees, and the tumbled ruins that Jim had found the night before came in sight. Jim led the Prince to the edge of it, then stopped.

"Your Highness," he said, "I know you had rather be with us in the charge, or at least nearby when we charge. But consider, if anything should happen to you, if by any chance we should lose you, we lose everything. The English forces here lose everything. England loses everything. There is a small niche in these stones you can move into for something more than the length of a man. It's only wide enough for one person to pass along at a time. With you inside there, and Sir Giles between you and the entrance, no one can get at you. You're not only protected, you're hidden."

The Prince blushed.

"Sir James, you are presumptuous!" he said. "I am not a child or a servant, to be hidden away when a war is being fought. Nor do I choose to be so hidden. I shall return to the others right now and pick the place from which I will watch the charge!"

He turned his back on the tumbled pile of chiseled stones.

"Highness! Stop!" said Jim, not moving. "Consider your duty! Consider your obligation to your father and to England. Stop at least long enough to think over what I just said to you!"

The Prince was already walking away, but his steps slowed until at last he stopped. Slowly, he turned and slowly, he came back. He halted in front of Jim.

"I do not consider the danger anywhere near as great as you seem to think, Sir James," he said in a level voice. "You forget that I am a Prince of England. I am worth infinitely more alive than dead. Even if the French should find me, and surround me, so that there was no hope of my escaping or fighting my way out from them; still the most they could do would be to capture me. And in due time my father would ransom me. It could not be otherwise."

"No. Think!" said Jim. "Malvinne has made and set up a false Prince Edward, which he controls utterly. And it is Malvinne who effectively rules in France now, rather than King Jean. The power is the King's, there is no doubt of that. But the will behind that power is the will of Malvinne. No Frenchman would want to kill you. As you say their aim would be to capture you instead. No Frenchman—but one. That one is Malvinne. As long as you're alive, you're a threat to the false Prince he made. Surely, from the time we first escaped with you from his castle, Malvinne's been hunting you, not to get you back, not to capture and hold you for ransom, but to destroy you—secretly and utterly—so that there'll be no one else to dispute the reality of the thing he's made."

Jim stopped talking. He stood, waiting to see how the Prince would react. On his part, the Prince merely stood, too, looking away past Jim. Finally he sighed. His shoulders slumped. He looked back at Jim.

"Once more, Sir James," he said, "I find myself listening to you against my own wishes. You're right, I do have a duty. Whether that duty is just as you say I don't know. But I can think right now of no other way it could be. So I'll do as you say. Where is this swamp hole of yours I must creep into?"

"You won't have to creep, Your Highness," said Jim. "You can walk in. And it should only be for an hour or two. If the King and his knights are on their way here, we only need to wait until they're settled in position and have turned all their attention on the battle, so that they're careless about what might be behind them. Then we'll charge; and we'll either win through within minutes, or else we'll lose utterly within minutes. You should hear the clash of arms even from here. If it ceases, and I or someone else doesn't come to bring you face-to-face with the false Prince within half an hour at the outside, then be sure we've lost and think about your own safety."

He paused.

"Sir Giles," he went on, "will stay with you; and if things should go badly for the rest of us, the two of you should try to make for Brest and the protection of what English are still there, having arrived since the ones in this army left. If Malvinne can't risk leaving you alive, he also can't alert the countryside that he's hunting for someone who looks just like the captive Prince of England. It'd raise too many questions. With any luck you should make it safely to Brest."

As he had been talking, Jim had been leading the Prince around the circumference of the wrecked building, searching for the opening he had found before. He had located the hiding place originally in near darkness and the place looked different in daylight. He found the niche at last and pointed out its entrance to the Prince.

"About six feet inside," he said, "and listen for the sound of arms."

"Very well, Sir James," said the Prince. "Reluctantly, I do what you say."

He turned and went in.

Giles had begun to follow him automatically, when Jim caught his arm, just at the entrance to the niche. The short knight turned and looked inquiringly at Jim.

"I didn't even ask you first if you'd take on this duty," said Jim. "Forgive me, my friend."

"For what?" answered Sir Giles, also in a low voice, but smiling. "This is a great honor, James! And I've you to thank for it!"

Jim let go of his arm and saw him disappear. He heard the sound of voices from within, as the Prince and Giles arranged their relative positions for the hours of waiting, then turned to make his way hastily back to where the other knights and the rest of the men were waiting.

When he got back there, he found knights and men alike instinctively standing silently in cover, behind trees or bushes; and King Jean, with Malvinne, the false Prince, his royal flags and knights, just coming into the area and up onto the little rise.

Chapter 36

"They make a brave sight," said Brian, as they watched the King with his knights move into position on a little rise of land ahead of them.

"Do they not!" said Sir Raoul, a little wistfully, standing on the other side of Jim, who was between the French knight and Sir Brian.

They stood slightly inside the woods, but quite in the open, in order to get a good view. If they had not been invisible—*unseeable* might have been a better word for the effect of the magic Jim had used—to the King and his bodyguard, they could not have failed to have been observed where they were.

The King reined in his horse on the rise of land, the knights with him stopped, and they all sat facing outward toward the open space and at the line of the English army, some five hundred yards off. The great flag above the King's head snapped in the brisk little breeze that had come up, following the stillness of air just at dawn, and before the sun's heat could begin to make itself felt.

"I counsel," said Brian, shading his eyes to look, not at the King or his knights, but down the French line that was already being formed to their left and right, "that we wait until the first French division makes its charge. If possible. If Wat of Easdale says true, it would be even best to wait until the business of the false archers and the hidden bowmen puts itself into play on the English side, so that the attention of the King's party will be thoroughly fixed on the field before them. That will be some little waiting, but it could be the time will be well spent."

"A good suggestion, Brian," said Jim.

Jim felt a pull on his right elbow. He turned, expecting to find that Dafydd, who was standing just behind him with his three bowmen, wanted his attention. But it was neither Dafydd, the bowmen, nor anyone else he had expected. It was Carolinus.

"They cannot see or hear me, these here with you," said Carolinus. "Make some excuse and come aside with me, so that I can talk to you."

Jim looked back to his front. He wet his lips, took a breath, and spoke suddenly.

"Hah!" he said. "And I was going to attend to that earlier! The rest of you stay here and keep watch. I'll be back in just a little bit."

"We will, that," said Brian, still shading his eyes against the morning sun. "I do believe the first division of the French are ready to ride out."

"They will be eager," murmured Sir Raoul.

Jim turned about, and saw nobody watching him. Even Dafydd and the bowman behind him had their eyes fixed only on the field and the two armies on it. Carolinus was standing a couple of steps off, and he beckoned. Jim went toward him.

Carolinus led him off until they had passed among trees that hid the field, as well as the rest of their own men, from his sight. Then he turned and faced Jim. Coming close, Jim was surprised to see that Carolinus's face was drawn and tired; touched with the grayness that older faces show when they have been exhausted almost beyond their strength.

"James," said Carolinus, "you do not know this world, even yet. So you must forgive me for what I've done."

"Forgive you?" said Jim. "I've never known you to do anything without a reason, Mage. Not only that, but the reason was usually as much to the benefit of others like myself as to your own purposes. Didn't you tell me once that, when the Dark Powers move, we must all stir ourselves to push them back?"

"Did I tell you that?" said Carolinus. "Well, it's true enough. But what I'm referring to, James, is that you still have not fully grasped how an inferior is owned by his superior. Brian, for example could hang one of his men-at-arms simply because he decided to, and no law could bring him to book for it. It's true that if he did such a thing without acceptable reason, he might well lose most of the rest of his men; and certainly the best men among them. Therefore he would not normally do it. But nonetheless, if he needed to, or had cause to, he could and would."

"I think you underestimate me," said Jim soberly. "I believe I've already come to understand that."

"Have you?" said Carolinus. "Did you ever stop to think of it as far as it applies to the relationship between you and I?"

Jim stared at him.

"Us?" echoed Jim. "You and I?"

"Exactly," said Carolinus. "In our relationship as teacher and pupil. When I took you on as my student in Magic, you became effectively my property. I would teach you, but at the same time I was free to use you or destroy you as I would. That is the way, at this time, in this world."

"No," said Jim slowly, "I hadn't thought of that."

He looked into Carolinus's faded blue eyes.

"But in any case, I'd expect you to have a reason for doing anything of that nature," he said, "and like Brian—"

Carolinus interrupted him.

"There's a difference, James," he said. "In your case, outside causes could force me to deal with you beyond the limits of what you'd expect. Unfortunately, in this particular contest with the Dark Powers you've become like a pawn in a chess game, pushed forward to achieve an end, or be sacrificed. I could help you only to the extent of sending Aargh, and aiding in the sending of Dafydd. Also, there've been other little things; but nothing I could do directly. I should congratulate you. It was a clever way you had of making a magic that made your men and you so that other people would not see you."

"The truth is," said Jim, "I couldn't imagine any other way of doing it. And I find that what I can't imagine, I can't work as magic. Maybe that's a law of magic?"

"I wouldn't put it in just those words," said Carolinus, "but it is very close to the truth. However, I was congratulating you, not just for finding a magic, but for finding one that drew on resources from your past in another world. Therefore they drew the more lightly on your magical balance here. Did it never strike you, that you had been doing a great deal of magic for someone with only a D rating?"

"I never thought of it," said Jim.

"Well, think of it now," said Carolinus grimly. "The fact is, you used up the last of the energy which permits you to make magic some time ago."

"Then why have I been able to go on doing it?" asked Jim. "Did you lend me some energy from your account?"

"That is strictly forbidden," said Carolinus, "and with good reason. Otherwise a teacher could make his pupil stronger than he should be, according to his rating with the Accounting Office, by giving him the use of loaned energy from a superior and much better filled account. No, I could not lend you anything. What I did, was allow you for some days now, to draw on my account. Strictly speaking, this also is something I should not do; and I will undoubtedly be fined from the Accounting Office when all is over; unless we win strongly in this encounter with the Dark Powers, and therefore find our accounts replenished at their expense."

"That's something else I don't understand," said Jim. "Where does the Accounting Office get what it puts into our account? Does it have its own supply of it, unused, or—"

"Do not ask!" said Carolinus so fiercely that Jim was checked into silence. For a moment neither of them said anything.

"You will find," said Carolinus in a kinder voice, when he finally broke this silence, "that the more you learn about Magic the more you'll realize is impossible, forbidden, or otherwise fenced away from you. You'll also learn how much there is yet to learn."

He checked himself.

"But enough of that now," he went on. "There's little I can do for you further. But that little I am going to do. One is, to warn you of things that you may need to know. One of these is the fact that your account is empty. This means that, until it fills again to some extent, your education as a magician is at a standstill. You're essentially like an ambassador without portfolio. You do not lose the fact that you are to become a magician—for which you should be grateful."

He looked at Jim with unusual grimness.

"For one thing," he went on, "the King of the Dead has made strong complaint to the Accounting Office about a magician showing up in his kingdom. Those with you did not matter. They are humans. If they wander into his territory they legitimately belong to him, unless and until they can escape from it again, as you and your friends did. Unfortunately, you used magic to escape. The use of magic in his kingdom, where all magic is controlled by him—it is not really magic but magic compares to it to the point where it is forbidden—is an even greater crime than your appearing within that territory. You face being called to account on this."

"But we were only there because Malvinne's magic tricked us into going there!" protested Jim.

"True," said Carolinus, "and the Accounting Office will take that into account; but only if you defeat both Malvinne and the Dark Powers. Then, it will be Malvinne who will be brought to account. But only then."

"It doesn't seem fair," said Jim.

"Who said it had to be fair?" demanded Carolinus fiercely. "But listen to me. Another problem that you may not be aware of, is that Melusine is here, close by. She wants you back. The further point is, she can't have you back."

"She can't?" said Jim, brightening up. "Why?"

"Because, as I've already said," said Carolinus, with a touch of his usual testiness, "you remain a magician, even without a balance in the Accounting Office. The law is, that there be no trafficking between kingdoms. That's why the King of the Dead has no power outside his own kingdom. That is why he can't acquire even the dead that die in the human church. These go elsewhere—and this is something to which he and his consort, whom you saw down there, have never been reconciled. It makes him doubly fierce at pursuing such cases as this, when a human who is a magician intrudes upon the grounds of his kingdom and then escapes by forbidden magic."

"But what's all this got to do with me and Melusine?" Jim asked. "Something about kingdoms is involved with the fact that she can't have me because I'm a Magician?"

"That's right," said Carolinus. "Melusine is an elemental; and the kingdom of the elementals is separate—well, almost separate. Your friend Giles is a mixture of elemental and human; although I suspect that since he has been a very young child, he has been ashamed of the elemental part, and done his best to deny it and all that goes with it. Melusine is a full elemental."

"I know," said Jim. "I've seen her using her own magic."

"What the elementals have and use is not really magic," said Carolinus. "Only humans use true magic. Though most elementals and others will tell you that what they use is magic. But actually, what elementals have is a sort of instinctive power to shape their environment; the space around them. For example, do you know how Melusine drowns dragons who wander at all close to her lake?"

"No," said Jim.

"She causes the lake to extend itself so that it is deep water underneath the point where the dragon is then standing or walking. The dragons flounder about, drown, and she draws them down to that part of her lake bed where she wants them; and leaves them for the fish to strip."

"Why does she hate dragons so much, anyway?" asked Jim. "I asked her once and she gave me some answer about the fact that they were like bats and were up in the air and so on and so forth. It didn't make a great deal of sense."

"In any case, it doesn't matter," said Carolinus, and this time he was definitely his old, testy self. "Something about dragons, sometime, possibly something some dragon did, rubbed her the wrong way. She will probably even have forgotten what it was by this time. I told you elementals operate by instinct. They don't use thought as we humans do. Basically, as I say, they have this power to shape their environment. To a certain extent that allows her to shape her environment toward you, no matter where you are. It isn't quite as simple as I'm making it sound; but what it means is that Melusine herself instinctively travels toward you, no matter where you are. You have been moving, and so stayed ahead of her until now. But now you're fixed, here at this battle site, and she'll inevitably find you."

"But if she can't have me, what difference does it make?" asked Jim.

"All the difference in the world, you numbskull!" said Carolinus. "Didn't I just finish telling you that unless Malvinne can be brought to book for your being in the Kingdom of the Dead, you'll be held responsible for that? Similarly, with Melusine. Any damage she causes outside her own personal kingdom in the process of hunting for you and finding you, or in her upset at discovering, as she will, that she can't have you, will also be held to your account. You'll be the responsible party. Do you understand?"

"You make it sound like part of a legal matter," said Jim, his head whirling.

"It *is* a legal matter. A matter of law—even if that law is different from the law you're used to!" said Carolinus. "I've warned you. That's all I can do now, except for one more thing. This, too, I will be called to account for; but like the business of letting you use my account to do magic, it'll only involve me in your violations to the point where I'll have to pay a fine. By your standards—a very heavy fine. By mine—well, it will be something I can live with. Similarly, with what I'm going to do now. Theoretically, I should do nothing for you magically, as long as you have no account and, while technically a magician, are not considered practicing. But I'm going to do it anyway; and incur another possibly heavy fine. For the next twenty-four hours, therefore, I hereby protect you against any magic that Malvinne may direct at you."

"That's—very good of you indeed!" stammered Jim, "but if it's going to cost you more than you can afford, then perhaps I should try to muddle through without it—"

"You wouldn't have a chance, boy!" said Carolinus. "Don't you understand that? The minute you corner Malvinne, he'll begin to use magic against you. What little you know about the Art will stand no more chance in the face of that, than a sparrow would, trying to fly into the teeth of a hurricane."

"Tell me one more small thing, then," said Jim. "You've already said that somehow I have to prevent either army on this field from winning the battle; and I don't have the slightest idea of how to go about it. If you could give me just a hint—"

"*I can hint you nothing!*" said Carolinus in a hard voice. "I've done all I can do; and more than I should do, already. You know what needs to be done. Do it if you can."

His voice softened suddenly.

"And my love and good wishes go with you, James," he said gently. "Forgive me, but that's all that I have to give you now. Come, you should be getting back to your men. The first division of the French horse has already begun its charge down the field at the English line."

Chapter **37**

"H ell! Already?" said Jim, and started out at a run through the trees back to where the rest of his men were.

He ran, however, for only a few heavy, thudding yards, before it became obvious that, dressed in armor, he could not keep up this pace. He dropped then to a walk, and strode out as fast as he could. Just as he reached the point where the trees stopped and the field began, so that he could see what was going on beyond, he saw Brian and the other knights, standing rapt at the sight of the first slightly ragged but thick line of French armored horsemen moving their heavy war-horses from a walk into a trot, as they approached the midpoint of the field.

There was a single, many-throated shout from the Genoese bowmen just before them. No shout in answer came back from the English line. The Genoese fired their crossbows, so that their bolts rose like a wide band of black pencil marks against the blue sky, and then scattered, to be out of the way of the knights riding up behind them.

The crossbow bolts fell into the English ranks, but it was too far away for Jim to see what happened, even though he was panting up now to join Brian and the others. However, arrows now began to arc through the air from the two ends of the English formation, where the archer lines stood, and the French horse began to stumble and go down.

But those who fell did not slow the advance of the line, which was now moving from a trot into a canter, making the ground thunder with the weight of its advance. Pennons and banners streamed bravely in the sun, and lances began to be moved into fighting position. It made an awesome sight, and it was hard to believe that the ponderous weight of that rank of iron could not sweep aside anything that stood in front of it, particularly the thin English line.

"Brian!" gasped Jim, at last reaching his Companions. "What are you standing here for? It'll be any moment now that the hidden bowmen show themselves, if there are any hidden bowmen. Right now the King and his knights are as caught up in what they see on the field as the rest of you are. Get them to horse! Get them in wedge position, back in the woods, ready to go. No man is to take the leaves from his horse or his clothing until I give the word!"

Brian and the others started as if they had just been turned from statues into living humans. Brian leading, they ran back into the woods, signaling the men-at-arms to move back with them to the horses.

Jim was left, still fighting for breath, with only one person before him. Dafydd.

"Didn't you hear what I said, Dafydd?" croaked Jim. "Get your men ready—your archers. Get them in position!"

"It's in position they've been, the past half hour," answered Dafydd without moving. "Wat and young Clym Tyler are out on the right flank of where your wedge will ride. Will o'the Howe is on the left flank, waiting for me; and I go to join him now. I wait for only one word from you. On what signal shall we archers take the leaves from us and become visible?"

"We—" Jim still had to stop to snort in air. "We want to wait to the last moment. I'll have the knights take their greenery off before they charge. There's too much danger of one of them forgetting, if I wait. But I'd like your archers to stay unseen as late as possible. What if they stand up now, ready to shoot, then throw their leaves aside just at the moment that our wedge passes you? Or is that cutting it too fine?"

"It is not," said Dafydd. "If we notch our arrows at the moment when the wedge passes, we will have time and to spare for picking our targets. So we will do, then."

He turned and strode off to Jim's left on his long legs. Neither the King nor any of those with him looked back and saw the parting of the grass, as Dafydd's invisible shape moved to position. Once at the point from which he would shoot, Dafydd stayed erect. Will o'the Howe rose from the grass to stand with him; and, seeing this across the little distance between them, the other two archers also rose and stood ready.

Jim turned and hurried back to join the rest of those in the wedge. To his relief, they were all armored, mounted, and ready, although the wedge itself was not yet formed. Theoluf was standing, holding his horse for him. Jim climbed into his saddle, took the lance that Theoluf handed him, and watched his squire mount his own horse.

Then he rode into the knot of men and horses at the front of the wedge, where the knights were.

"Everyone ready?" he asked of them all. "Now, I'll take the point of the wedge—"

"The Goddamn bloody hell you will!" exploded Brian. He checked himself, breathed deeply for a moment and then went on in a voice only slightly lowered. "Forgive me, if I seem to ill-say you before these gentlemen, James. But well you know I'm aware of how you are with weapons. And I tell you frankly to your face that you are not such a lance as is needed to lead at the point of this wedge. I will ride point in the wedge. Sir Raoul, I take you for a man who has seen battle before. Will you ride half a horse length back and at my right? John Chester, the same position on my left. Behind John Chester, Theoluf—and well you remember, Theoluf, that your shield is to guard two men; not merely yourself but Sir James!"

"Fear not, Sir Brian," said Theoluf harshly. "That is the last thing I will forget."

"James, do you take the middle position, with your horse directly behind mine, and your spear leveled out to the left across the withers of John Chester's horse," went on Brian. "Tom Seiver, you will ride on Sir James's right, likewise remembering that you guard not merely yourself but him; and direct your lance to the right across the withers of Sir Raoul's horse, when the shock comes—"

"Just a minute!" snapped Jim. "What are you trying to do with me, Brian? Guard me, as the King of France is guarded? I'm here to fight along with the rest of you; because every lance we have is going to be needed!"

"Every lance but yours, James," said Brian, his mouth a thin line. *"But yours, James!* Consider, that if we lose you we lose everything. What boots us to win our way to the French King, Malvinne and the false Prince, unless we have you alive with us to deal with Malvinne and expose the magic that makes the false Prince seem what he is? The whole purpose of our charge would go for naught, if you should be killed along the way. As it is, I doubt not you will find work enough, even surrounded by the rest of us, as you are!"

Jim winced internally. It was no more than the same argument he had used with Prince Edward only a short time before. He could not argue against it now. Moreover, he thought, facing the truth within himself, this was the moment in which Brian should be the field leader and should be making the decisions. If Giles were here, Giles would also be riding ahead of him or on one side of him—and correctly so—according to what Brian had said. Jim had to admit that all of it was the truth. He bit his tongue against any further argument.

"The rest of you know your positions as we practiced them," Brian was saying. "Into them now, immediately. Follow my signal forward, but be ready for Sir James's order that you throw away all twigs about both you and your horse. Let not one of you fail to do that, for I will hang any man who does. James, when the time comes, you had probably best shout. We will be making more than a little noise with our horses' hooves and armor. I doubt not that, even interested in the field as they are, the King and those with him will hear our approach and do their best to turn and face us."

Jim cast a quick eye back over the wedge and saw them all in place behind him, as they were in place before.

"Now!" he shouted. "Throw any twigs and leaves you've got away now!"

Sir Brian smiled back over his shoulder at him, a brief, grim smile. Then his head turned forward again.

"Ride!" he cried. "And keep together!"

They started out, as the French first line had done, at a walk, but much more quickly accelerated to a trot, a canter, and a gallop. As they emerged from the trees there was a cry before them from the men around the King. Off to the near side, which was the only side he could see well at all, Jim now saw at each end of the harrow, a new line of men stretching forward toward the French, on their feet and holding bow staves in their arms. A fresh flight of arrows marred the blue of the sky.

For a moment the King and those with him had no eyes, except for what was in front of them. Then someone's ears must have picked up the thunder of hooves behind them; for a voice shouted over the babble of talk that was going on.

"We're attacked!"

It was impossible for Jim to see the King and his knights clearly, because of the bodies rising and falling with the galloping of the horses, ahead of him. They were going all out toward their target and it seemed to him as if they had been taking an unreasonable length of time to reach the group around the French King. Then, without warning, they reached it.

Jim had had the experience of his battle with the Ogre, when he had been in the body of Gorbash the dragon; and he had also felt the impact when, with his own men-at-arms and Brian's, he had ridden into the rabble besieging Castle Smythe. But nothing had prepared him for this terrific shock, in which heavily armored individuals on heavy horses slammed into equally armored men and horses at a speed that must be close to twenty miles an hour.

The impact was unbelievable. Jim literally felt himself thrown against the hard interior surface of his own armor. Horses were forced up on their hind legs by the forces of their coming together, screaming and lashing out with their hooves. A shock he could not believe traveled up the lance he was holding, and he stared dumbfounded at the half of its splintered length that remained in his grasp.

They were deep among the body of French knights, but the crash of coming together had forced the wedge apart. He found himself facing an unfamiliar figure in armor with slanting black lines painted across the upper part of its visor and helmet. Jim's sword—he was not even conscious of having drawn it—was in his hand and it jarred against the other's sword in midair. He remembered to bring up his shield, as he disengaged his sword, so that a second blow hammered on the shield, driving him backwards in the saddle.

Jim struck back with his own sword, but met only empty air. The knight with the black bars painted on his helmet was falling out of his saddle, face forward, with the feathered end of an arrow sticking out of the center of his armor's back plate. For a moment there was no one in front of Jim. He saw two more enemy knights drop from their saddles as if by magic, and knew that the arrows of the bowmen were doing exactly what Dafydd had promised, clearing a way for them. Brian was still ahead of him. Brian rode forward and he followed.

Suddenly they were in an open space, with none but their own men around them.

His horse, Brian's, and Raoul's were roughly level; and then in the little space before them stood a knight of slightly less than ordinary size, in armor richly inlaid with gold, apparently already unhorsed. He held his sword in hand, but had no shield. The staff of the French flag, driven into the ground behind him, still held the Leopards and Lilies aloft, curling slowly as it rippled in the light breeze.

By some miracle Brian's spear was unbroken. He leveled it now at the knight in the rich armor.

"Yield!" he said.

But Sir Raoul was already off his horse, down on his feet, and kneeling before the very man at whom Jim's spear was pointed, trying to pick up one of the knight's gauntleted hands that was free and bring it to his lips that he had exposed by throwing back his visor.

"My liege!" said Sir Raoul. "Forgive me! It was never against Your Majesty, but against Malvinne, I acted!"

"And who are you?" asked the knight in the rich armor, putting up his visor and looking down at Raoul.

"I am the son of he who was the Comte d'Avronne; who was a true and loyal servant of Your Majesty, even after the arch-sorcerer Malvinne falsely attainted him of treason, and had him stripped of his title and his lands—to Malvinne's benefit. While he lived he served Your Highness, nonetheless; as have I. My only object is to rid you of that incubus I just mentioned. All my enmity has been against him! Forgive me, if that enmity has made me seem to league against you, my King!"

"Yield, Your Majesty!" said Brian again. "You are surrounded. You have no way of escape."

"I yield me then—" The French King looked down at Raoul, and passed him the sword he still held. "But to this gentleman who kneels to me now, and who is a good Frenchman rather than an English. I yield on one condition. Call off those devil archers. I would have no more of my good Lords and knights slain by their wicked shafts."

"Dafydd!" shouted Jim over his shoulder. "Tell the archers to stop shooting!" The whistling of the arrows ceased.

King Jean raised his voice, in turn.

"I have yielded!" he shouted. "All knights of mine, lay down your arms and surrender as I have done."

Brian was off his horse now, and he knelt on one knee also, before the French King. Jim dismounted clumsily and followed his example, wondering a little at himself. He remembered he had not been able to bring himself to kneel before his own, English Prince. But here he was kneeling before the French King. Perhaps practice was making it possible.

"Forgive us also, Highness," said Brian. "We do not rejoice in your capture. But it is a duty to our own King that brings us to it."

He rose to his feet again, and Jim felt he was therefore at liberty to do likewise. King Jean took Sir Raoul's hand and raised him to his feet as well.

"And now you have conquered me, gentlemen," said the King, taking off his helmet. He was a pleasant looking man of middle age, going bald, and with what hair he had left already turned to gray. "What do you propose to do with me?"

He looked at Brian.

"I assume you command this band of English ruffians?"

Brian took half a step backward.

"Not I, Highness," said Brian bluntly, "but Sir James Eckert, here beside me. His fame may not have reached to your land, but in our own country he is known for his deeds by the name of the Dragon Knight."

"Yes," said the King, his eyes shifting to Jim and running him up and down. Jim felt that he should take off his own helmet, and did so. "Some rumor of you, sir, has reached even our ears. I was also aware of the red upon your shield. So, you are another magician, are you not?"

"A minor magician, Highness," answered Jim. "But it is in that capacity I am here; since my concern also is Malvinne, your minister."

"A minor magician to deal with Malvinne?" said the King. "What sense is this? Malvinne is a mighty sorcerer and wizard. Otherwise I would not have raised him to the exalted position he now holds as my counselor. To send a minor English magician to deal with him in any capacity is not only ridiculous, but comes close to being an affront to our royal self as well. By the way, where is Malvinne and the English Prince?"

The King looked around him.

"Right here," answered half a dozen voices that Jim found familiar, interrupted by another, waspish voice that Jim had heard before in the castle where he and the others had rescued the young Prince.

"And keep your hands off me, unless you want them turned into leper's claws!"

Malvinne walked out from among the horses, with the Prince beside him. Jim's breath checked for a moment. It was almost impossible to believe that what he was looking at was not the young man he had left to hide among the stones only a short time past. What he saw now not only looked like Prince Edward; but *was* Prince Edward, in every detail down to the clothes, the manner of walking, and the expression on his face.

"I stood back to see just what was going on before I showed myself," said Malvinne, marching forward to stand by the King and being followed by the Prince. He pointed a finger at Jim. *"Still!"*

Jim found himself under no compulsion to keep from moving. To prove this, he pulled off his gauntlets and hooked one thumb in his sword belt. He stared at Malvinne.

"Still I said!" snapped Malvinne again, his finger holding in midair. His eyes widened. "What have you learned to keep that command from touching you?"

"I have made him proof against all your powers," said the dry voice of Carolinus. He stepped around from behind Jim to stand beside him, to a murmur of amazement from the men behind Jim.

"But a second past he was not there. . . ." Jim heard muttered behind him.

"You!" said Malvinne, glaring at Carolinus. "What's he to you?"

"My pupil, Stinky," said Carolinus conversationally. "Remember how we used to play our little tricks on each other when we were at school together? I haven't seen you in a long time, Stinky."

"Keep your schoolboy slang to yourself!" said Malvinne. "A plus does not make that much difference between us."

"I beg to differ," said Carolinus. "That plus can destroy you."

He turned to Jim.

"Didn't you want the real Prince here to see this?" he asked.

"What is this of a real Prince?" asked King Jean. But before the question could be answered he had another. He stared at Carolinus. "Are you indeed that Carolinus of whom so much is said? There are those who claim you are of the same age as Merlin. What do you do here, this far from your magic isles in the western ocean?"

"You've been misled, John," said Carolinus. "Merlin was lost to the world many generations before I was born. And I live in no magic western isles, but in England."

"In England!" King Jean's eyebrows went up and he looked haughty. "What would bring a magician of your repute to dwell in England?"

"The fact that I was an Englishman before I was a magician," answered Carolinus. "But that's beside the point."

He turned once more to Jim. "The Prince?" he asked.

"Yes," said Jim. He wheeled about and scanned those behind him. His eyes lighted on Theoluf, who was still on his horse. "Theoluf, ride to the west of where we waited for His Majesty, here, a hundred yards; and then turn right and go directly back. You will come to a pile of stone, which is all that's left of a small wayside shrine, within which you will find Sir Giles and His Highness waiting. Take two extra horses and bring them both back here—as soon as possible!"

"At once, m'Lord," answered Theoluf. He turned his horse around, unceremoniously ordered off their horses two men-at-arms close to him, and snatching up the reins of the horses, headed off through the crowd that made way for him. The space that opened among those standing or sitting and watching the drama taking place beneath the great flag, closed quickly again.

"What's this about a Prince?" asked King Jean.

"Edward, Crown Prince of England," said Brian harshly.

"Edward?" The King looked from Brian to the Prince at Malvinne's elbow and back again at Brian and then back again at the Prince.

"What nonsense is afoot here?" he asked Carolinus. "Yourself—this young magician—a talk of Princes?"

"You must ask any questions of Sir James Eckert," said Carolinus.

King Jean stared at him for a long moment, but Carolinus's face did not change nor did he move. He might have been a carved wooden statue of himself.

"What is this?" demanded the King, turning to Malvinne.

"Your Highness," said Malvinne, "this is all a plot against me. I cannot explain it to you because it is magical in nature."

"You, Sir!" said the King, rounding upon Jim. "Will you give me a straightforward answer? What is afoot here? I insist on knowing!"

"You will know shortly, Majesty," said Jim. "It is something that must be shown rather than told."

"I expect," said Malvinne, with a wicked twist to his mouth and a wicked tone in his voice, "they will produce some impostor and claim he is Prince Edward instead of this young man with us here, whom we both know and honor."

"Something like that," agreed Jim, "but not just like that."

"Sir James!" It was the voice of Theoluf calling at a little distance. A moment later the circle of watchers around the flag split apart and let through a horse so suddenly and strongly reined to a halt, that it danced and had to be tightly held. "Sir James, I found the stones and if the Prince is there he is being attacked! The attackers are knights like those here with the black stripes across the helm—there must be a dozen of them! I think I glimpsed Sir Giles fighting at the entrance of a little hole in the stones, but he will be overwhelmed shortly, unless help reaches him immediately!"

Chapter 38

"**B**lack-striped helms?" cried Sir Raoul, leaping for the saddle on his horse. "They are some of Malvinne's own knights, sent to slay the Prince, the real Prince, before he can be shown here! Haste, before Sir Giles is overwhelmed!"

There was a general scramble for horses. Giles was liked not merely by the members of his own class, but by the men-at-arms. Underneath his fierce surface there was an innocence that drew them all.

Brian, for all the weight of his armor, made a running vault to place one foot in a stirrup and swing his other leg over the back of his horse. He started to rein it around, then recollected himself.

"Take twenty men, Theoluf!" he shouted. "Only twenty. All the rest stay here to guard these knights who have surrendered!"

Slowly, he began to dismount again.

"So, there is such an impostor," said King Jean to Malvinne.

"Assuredly, Majesty," said Malvinne, "though my knights have orders to capture him only, not to slay him. If they found him. I kept word of this from you because I did not wish to concern Your Majesty with what is after all a petty detail. Once brought here, it will be seen that he is totally unlike our Prince."

"I think he'll prove exactly the opposite," said Jim. Almost to his own surprise, he felt a fury against Malvinne building inside him. "As for your knights being told to capture him only, that's a lie. They could have been hunting him for only one purpose: to slay him, and hide all knowledge of him from King Jean."

"You call what I say a lie?" Malvinne swung rapidly toward him, raising his finger again. Then, as if realizing the uselessness of it, let the hand and finger drop again to his side. "We shall see."

They waited for perhaps fifteen or twenty uneasy minutes, during which the wounded on both sides were attended to with as much skill as one fourteenth-century soldier could give another. The King, Brian, and everyone else not occupied had turned their attention back to the field of battle.

The first division of the French, caught by the hidden bowmen, had been shot to pieces. In the past year Jim had seen the bow used many times, and was aware of the devastating effect of the arrows it could throw. But never before had he seen the concentrated effect of the shooting of hundreds of bowmen at once. Lines and bodies of armored knights at full charge were simply wiped out, their saddles emptied, their horses shot from under them. What had begun as an almost invincible sweep down the field turned into a tangle of untidy clumps of still surviving horsemen.

As the English had expected, the sight of this had been too much for the French knights waiting in the second division. The knights and horsed men-at-arms had begun a charge toward the other end of the field without waiting for an order; so that it was not so much a line as an untidy gang that swept down, into the same deadly fire. Now the third line was attacking, and had been met head-on by a charge of the horse from the English side, so that the field had now disintegrated into innumerable knots of struggling and fighting men, in individual contests.

It was at this moment that a shout went up from those near the outside of the group around the King, and a moment later a lane opened among the English there, and Theoluf rode through, followed by the Prince, without armor, the sword scabbarded at his side, and his head uncovered. He reached King Jean and the others beneath the flag and leaped from the saddle.

"Cousin—" he said, advancing with both arms outheld toward the King, addressing him as monarchs usually addressed one another.

King Jean recoiled and folded his arms on his chest, so that the Prince stopped and his own arms fell to his side.

"And who, sir, are you?" demanded the King.

"I?" The young man's head came up haughtily. "Who else could I be? I am Edward Plantagenet, Crown Prince of all England, firstborn son of Edward, King of England. Who are you, sir?"

The King ignored the final question.

"Certainly," he said, turning to Malvinne beside him, "he greatly resembles our Prince."

"Say rather, your Prince greatly resembles our Royal Edward, here," said Brian harshly.

"Let us see," said Malvinne.

He darted forward and jabbed out with a pointing forefinger that almost touched young Edward's nose.

"*Still!*" he said.

Instantly there was an immobility about the Prince, that left no doubt in anyone's mind that Malvinne's magic had worked. Malvinne laughed and threw a glance at Carolinus.

"I thought not!" he said. "You would not have been able to throw the cloak of your protection over all these here. Now I have this one you call the Prince!"

Carolinus did not answer. He was as still as the Prince, although something about him gave the appearance of being free to move if he wished. But he did not. It was as if he stood and watched all that went on, but Malvinne did not exist.

"Meanwhile," said Jim, going to his horse and detaching his saddle flask, "let's establish now which is which."

"Stop him!" cried Malvinne. "What he carries in that flask is a magic potion! Don't let him approach the true Prince!"

"It's only water," said Jim. He stepped to King Jean, removed the top of the flask and poured some of the flask's contents into the palm of his hand. He held it up for the King to sniff.

"Do you smell anything, Your Majesty?" he asked. "As I say, it's only water."

"It is enchanted water!" shouted Malvinne.

Jim ignored him, as Carolinus was ignoring him. He walked over to the real Prince.

"Forgive me, Your Highness," he said, "but it is absolutely necessary!"

He threw the palmful of water into Edward's face.

Edward was not able to stir, and no muscle about him moved. But his eyes blazed with fury, and something between a moan and a growl arose from the other English present. There was a general move, on horseback and on foot, in Jim's direction. But then it stopped.

"Forgive me again, Your Highness." Jim bowed. "If there had been any other way I'd have taken it."

He turned and went toward the other Prince, who now stood between the King and Malvinne. Malvinne tried to get in his way but Brian took one quick step forward and jerked the magician clear. Before Malvinne could turn upon Brian and immobilize him, and before the King, who had begun to stir, could interpose himself between Jim and the Prince at his elbow, Jim threw the second palmful of the water into the face of Malvinne's Prince.

A cry arose from everyone there, even King Jean, who stepped back with a startled oath.

The face of the Prince that had been splashed with water, was changing. There was a slight hissing, sizzling noise from it; and although the features of the Prince's face did not distort, they shrank. The mouth became shorter, the nose smaller, and the eyes closer together.

All of this, the Prince who had just been splashed did not seem to be aware of. He continued to stare at Jim with the stare of one who does not understand what is going on.

Jim took the open bottle and generously splashed as much of its contents as he could slosh with a couple of quick jerks of his arm into the face before him.

The hissing and sizzling noise increased. The face shrank rapidly. The figure itself lost stature and dwindled inside its clothing, so that same clothing now hung loose upon it. Within the garments, the Prince himself continued to dwindle, even though the water had disappeared.

Jim stood back. Before the view of all of them, the Prince who had stood between Malvinne and the King grew smaller and smaller until he dwindled away completely; and there was nothing but a pile of the clothes on the ground.

Carolinus moved, turning about sharply on his heel.

"Accounting Office!" he snapped.

"I am here," responded the startling deep bass voice out of thin air about four feet above the ground.

"Take special note," said Carolinus, "of the questions and answers you're about to hear. James?"

Jim looked up from the pile of clothing at Carolinus. In spite of the fact that he had known what would happen as a result of what he did, he was shaken by it. He could not help feeling as if he had committed a murder.

His eyes met Carolinus's.

"James," said Carolinus, "was that water you used literally nothing more than water?"

"Plain water," answered Jim. "I got it from a stream a few hours ago. Sir Brian saw me empty out the wine that was in this flask and replace it with the water."

"By Heaven's Hand, I did," said Brian, in a shaken voice.

"Why did you splash the water on the false Prince?" asked Carolinus.

"Because—" Jim had to swallow. "Because I knew it would make him melt. I knew that such simulacra always had to be made by magic out of snow fresh from the mountaintop."

"And who told you that simulacra had to be made of snow?" demanded Carolinus. "Who told you that anything made that way would melt if you poured water on it, as snow itself does, when water is poured on it?"

"It's mentioned," said Jim, "a number of times in the fairy tales in my—in the place where I come from."

"You heard all that, Accounting Office?" said Carolinus.

"I heard," responded the bass voice.

Carolinus's own voice relaxed. It was almost gentle.

"That's all for now then," he said. "Jim, step aside with me so I can talk to you."

He turned without looking at Malvinne, and Jim did not have the heart to look at the other master magician himself. He was about to follow Carolinus when there was a stir among the men in front of him. Seven men-at-arms appeared, carrying someone on a battered shield, which was being used as an impromptu stretcher. At one end, one man supported a helmetless head; at the other, two held up the legs that reached beyond the further end of the shield. They brought their burden up into the open space not far from the flag, and laid it gently down.

"Giles!" cried Jim. And at that, two things happened at once.

"You are released," said the invisible bass voice just above the ground, and a slight blue-jerkined body pushed past Jim and fell on its knees beside the man on the shield.

"My brave Sir Giles!" It was the true Prince, and he was weeping. "How can I thank thee for this, and for all that thou has done to save me, my life, and my honor?"

On the stretcher, Giles's face was bloodless. His lips moved; but Jim could not hear what he said. The Prince took up Giles's limp hand and pressed it to his lips. The armor still on Giles's body had been hacked almost to pieces, and there seemed to be none of it that was not smeared with blood. Theoluf dropped to his knees on the other side of Giles and began with damp cloths to clean and stop the bleeding of Giles's wounds.

At this moment, a commotion among the thick circle of armed men diverted their attention. The body of men parted almost as if a battering ram had come through it. Coming down the open lane were four knights on horseback. The leader, a large, burly man, rode his horse almost to the foot of the flag. There, he dismounted and took off his helmet, to reveal a round, graying head and a short-cropped, graying beard on a square, heavy-boned face. He went down on one knee before King Jean.

"Your Majesty," he said, completely ignoring Jim, Brian, and the rest. "Forgive me for not being here sooner; but word of your yielding personally to an Englishman just reached my ears. I am, with your favor, Robert de Clifford, Earl of Cumberland and Commander of the English forces here. It was our sorrow that such a Monarch and knight as yourself should be forced to so yield; but it brings upon us a question that must be answered. Since you yourself are now an English prisoner, are you prepared—as you should be by right of arms—to yield the field by all the French force to our Englishmen as victors hereon?"

"Rise, Earl Robert," said King Jean dryly. "But you are under a misapprehension. I yielded myself, not to one of your English, but to a Frenchman—the Comte d'Avronne here—and ordered only the personal knights of my bodyguard about me to lay down their arms. I see no reason why I should yield the field while the battle is still in doubt."

He looked out again, over the field, as they all did. Indeed, the battle was still in doubt. Struggles were still going on as far as the eye could see, between individuals and small groups. But there was no cohesiveness to the fighting, and no clear line of battle on either side. It was impossible to say who was winning, except in the cases of combats between individuals.

The Earl of Cumberland, who had risen, scowled.

"Surely Your Majesty can see no benefit in this continuing," he said, "since it can only end in the death of many of your Frenchmen."

"And many of your Englishmen, Earl Robert," said King Jean. "At this moment, who can say who shall lose the more? Or in which way the fighting will eventually go? In the end one side or the other must drive its opponents from the field. So far that has not happened; and I know not about you English, but we French are not likely to give up a field where the issue is still in doubt."

"But Your Majesty—" Earl Robert was continuing, when there was a second, unexpected interruption.

It came in the shape of a very attractive young lady dressed in a light and flimsy robe of green; who ran lightly down the way opened for the Earl of Cumberland through the surrounding soldiers, to the group by the flag. Unfortunately, as Jim recognized at once, the lady's beauty was balanced for him by the fact that her name happened to be Melusine; and she was headed directly for him.

He would have dodged her, but she caught him and clasped her arms around him.

"Oh, my beloved!" she cried. "I have found you at last. How could you think that I should let such a beautiful one as you escape from me! We'll go back to my lake at once! You are mine!"

"No, he isn't," said Carolinus. "You can't have him."

She whirled toward the sound of the spoken voice, her eyes ablaze with anger—then immediately softened at seeing who she was face-to-face with. She dropped a curtsy.

"Mage," she said, almost cooing, "I'm so honored to see you. You are beautiful, yourself. But I know you are far beyond my reach. Why should I not have my James, here?"

"For the same reason you couldn't have me," said Carolinus. "He also is a magician."

"A *magician!*"

Melusine's eyes grew wide, her arms dropped from around Jim's waist, and she stood back, staring at him. "All this time, James; and you never told me! How could you do this to me?"

"Well—" Jim began, not really knowing what to say.

Melusine began to cry daintily into a flimsy green handkerchief that she produced from somewhere about her gown.

"To lead me on so, only to have me face this cruel disappointment!" she said. "How could you, James!"

"Well—" began Jim again, helplessly.

"Oh, well." Melusine dried her eyes almost briskly and the handkerchief disappeared. "It is the way I have always suffered. I must look for a new love, it seems—ah, what a beautiful little man. I'll have you. And I'll never let you go!"

She had darted forward and clasped King Jean around his breast plate.

"You can't have him either," said Carolinus.

"Why not?" pouted Melusine, still keeping a death grip on the King.

"Because I am a King, Death of God!" spluttered Jean. "As a King, I am destined; and beyond all magic and the ways of all such unnaturals as you!"

"Truly?"

Tears formed again in Melusine's eyes. Her hands dropped from the King. The handkerchief reappeared.

"To be twice so disappointed!" She wept into it. "And you are even more beautiful than James. I will always love you, my King. But—since you, too, are beyond me—"

She looked around, and her eyes fell on Giles, with Theoluf kneeling on the far side of him, trying to staunch Giles's many wounds with sections of cloth donated from the shirts of the men-at-arms around him.

"Oh, the poor one!" she said, running over and dropping on her knees on the other side of Giles. "He is hurt. I will mend him!"

"Can you make blood, lady?" said Theoluf bluntly. "He has no one wound enough to slay him. But so many are his lesser wounds that he has lost nearly all the blood in him; and is fast losing what little remains, for I cannot stop the bleeding."

"Make human blood?" said Melusine, dismayed. "Alas, that is one thing no one but a human may do for himself."

"It is not to be surprised he should bleed so," said Theoluf gruffly. "I counted six dead knights with black-marked visors before the hole wherein he hid the Prince."

"Could you not at least move him to the shade?" Melusine asked.

"That, at least, I can do," said Theoluf. "It was well thought of, my Lady."

He got up and began picking men-at-arms from the ones behind him, for stretcher-bearers, as she leaned toward Giles.

"Oh, it is so sad," she crooned. "You are so young and beautiful. And I have this strange feeling that we are like to one another."

Giles lips moved. No one else there could hear if he actually answered, but Melusine had evidently heard him.

"But your nose is *beautiful!*" she said. "Never have I seen such a magnificent nose!

It was the first thing I noticed when I looked at you. Oh, it is delicious. I could bite it right off you!"

She bent over, covering the nose with kisses.

"Pick him up gently, now!" said Theoluf, returning with the men he had picked. "We'll carry him into the shade of that tree right over there."

Gently, they did as he said. With Melusine following, they went off into the shade of the tree, while the rest of the men-at-arms there made room for them.

Meanwhile, Jim had been standing by, listening to the Earl of Cumberland negotiating with King Jean. Surprisingly, for all his burly physical appearance, the Earl turned out to be an astute negotiator. His arguments had reached the point of bringing the King finally to recognize that there was nothing to be gained by letting the battle go on; and, while the cost of surrender might be high, that too, was something that might be negotiated to better terms at a later time. Meanwhile, it made only common sense to preserve the veteran French warriors from death—and the kind of serious wounds that in this early time might bring them to death eventually—for future use against the English.

It was just then, however, that Jim noticed the Prince standing to one side of the Earl, with his gaze fixed steadily upon the nobleman. The Prince's face was more and more resembling a thundercloud that was about to spawn a tornado. Jim moved hastily to do what he could to avert a full-sized explosion.

He interrupted the Earl.

"Forgive me, my Lord," he said, "but I believe our Royal Prince might wish to have a word with you."

The Earl turned his head slowly to look at Edward, of whom he clearly could not have been unaware all this time.

"Yes, Highness?" he asked coldly.

"So you *do* know who I am, sirrah?" snapped the Prince.

"I know you as my Royal Prince," replied the Earl, still coldly, "though I have been informed you had lately turned from the English and the land of your birth, to lend your support to the French against all things English; and mayhap you had acquired a different title in the process."

"Insolence!" snarled the Prince. "Down on your knee before me, my Lord, or I'll have your head off in punishment for not doing it sooner. And I have the men with me who'll perform that task for me if I order it." He looked behind him. "Have I not?"

There was a sudden chesty shout from the men-at-arms behind him. There was nothing that would have suited their temper better at this moment, Jim realized, than to cut off a head of an Earl at the legitimate order of their Prince.

The Earl had come with only three companions. He sank down on one knee immediately.

"Look to your right, my Lord," went on the Prince in a steely voice. "You see that pile of clothes that somewhat resembles what I wear myself? Within those clothes until a short while ago was an impostor made out of snow by the magic of the evil sorcerer who stands behind you—and behind the King of France, as I now notice. He, it was, who gave substance to the false tale that I had joined the French. How could I leave England when England is myself? Will you tell me that you believed such a lie?"

"I will not say I believed it in my heart, Your Highness," answered the Earl. His face had paled, but his voice was firm enough. "Yet there was not only the tale, but the witness of men of good repute who had seen you, if from a distance, riding comfortably in French company, armed, and to all intents one of them. I could not easily find it in me to credit such a thing. But, being human, I wondered. Sire, I freely admit that wonder, which afflicted many English in this expedition. If that is a fault for which I should lose my head, then my head is yours to take."

"True," said the Prince, a little more calmly. "Still, you were probably no less bemused than others. And in fact it might be said that the magical impostor was such a complete copy of myself, I had difficulty believing I was not looking into a reflecting glass and seeing myself therein. Well, how do you feel now? Shall I prove myself further to you, my Lord? Shall I take horse and ride against the French on yon field? If so, there are at least some men behind me who will follow me." He turned his head back over his shoulder. "Are there not?" He challenged the knights and men-at-arms behind him.

"Are there not?" he repeated.

A shout, deeper and stronger than the one earlier, answered him fiercely.

"And this being so," said the Prince, "do you doubt, my Lord, that if I ride forth with these men at my back crying *'Saint George-Guienne'* and attacking the first French I see, that all Englishmen there who see me will not in the end rally about me? I ask you."

"Your Highness," said the Earl with deep sincerity. "I myself would be among the first to follow you!"

The Prince stared at him for a long moment. Then he relaxed.

"Rise, my Lord," he said. "I do accept you to be a loyal and trusty Lord of mine and of my Father the King. But never again give me reason to doubt you."

"That I will not, Highness," said the Earl, "while I live."

He rose to his feet again.

"Well pleased am I to hear it," said the Prince. "That matter being settled, you may continue discussing the terms of surrender with our cousin the King of France. I will listen and leave the discussion to you, because you have more experience in this, my Lord, and I admit it. Secondly, because it will the more ensure that the fighting yonder be brought to a conclusion as swiftly as possible."

"I am afraid you are in error, cousin," said King Jean. "At no point in our discussion have I agreed that we French should surrender. We will either continue the battle as men of honor should, or offer the English such light terms, that there will be no shame in their accepting them. I see the frown gathering dark upon your brows, young cousin. You are about to remind me that I am your personal prisoner. Let me dispose of that now, once and for all. You may cut off my head, instead of that of this the Earl of Cumberland, before I will give commands to my Frenchmen to yield a fight they have not yet lost."

"In that case," said the Prince, "I have no choice. A horse for me! A horse! Ho!"

The nearest horseman among the men-at-arms slipped from his saddle and led the beast up to the Prince, dropping on one knee and offering up the reins in his hand. The Prince took the reins and swung himself up into the saddle.

"You give me no choice then, cousin," the Prince said to King Jean. "For some time now it has looked to me as if the battle were very equal. Mayhap it may turn to the favor of the English, if I ride out on that battlefield. So ride out, I will—and your French will have their chance to see if they can win the day!"

He looked back over his shoulder again at the other mounted men.

"Follow me, all!" he said, pulling his sword from its sheath, raising it in the air, and turning his horse's head toward the field.

Chapter 39

"W ait!" shouted King Jean. His
face had not changed, but as close to him as Jim stood, he thought he could see a
slight sheen on the royal brow, that could indicate a hint of perspiration there.
"Wait, young cousin! I honor your desire to lead your English to victory. However,
think you a moment. There are good knights on both sides that will die
if you carry this through; for surely both Englishmen and Frenchmen will
fight to the death once they see you on the field and in the midst of the
battle—"

The fact that these were the very arguments that the Earl had been using on the
King did not seem to inhibit the King from using them on the Prince.

"Consider, cousin," went on King Jean. "This day has gone awry in many ways.
Let us not run the risk of piling error upon error. Certainly the matter should be
discussed. If it is enough to keep you from the field, I am willing to discuss, not
only the surrender of the English to the French, but the *possible* surrender of the
French to you English—though I advance this merely as a matter for discussion,
you understand."

"Highness?" said the Earl of Cumberland, swiftly and hopefully.

The Prince sat his horse for a moment in silence, apparently thinking deeply.
Then he looked directly at the Earl.

"My Lord," he said, "you are experienced in these things. Would you counsel that I delay my going out to the field while you talk awhile longer?"

"I would, Your Highness," replied the Earl swiftly. "I most earnestly would. I see no dishonor in it; and I think of your value to England, not only now but in the future, should some accident befall you out on the field of battle."

"I would not hold back from going out because of fear for myself!" scowled the Prince.

"No, no, I'm sure Your Highness would not," said the Earl hastily. "Still, I would strongly advise and counsel that we talk further with His Majesty of France."

Edward swung down from his horse.

"Very well," he said, "I will be guided by your advice. Continue your talk, then. I shall listen closely."

He stepped over to stand as a third in the group of two that had originally contained only the Earl and the King.

To Jim, also listening, the discussions now took an entirely new turn. It became obvious immediately that now both the Earl and the King were trying to work out some kind of no-win, no-lose decision for both sides. The apparent problem with this was in finding the proper language in which to fit it, since all discussions of this sort had been very strictly win-lose, with one side only doing the winning and the other doing the losing.

It looked almost as if the problem Carolinus had set Jim was solving itself for him. It was unexpected; for Jim had never stopped to think what the psychological effect would have been of the young Prince on the field leading the English into their fight with the relatively equal number of French who remained. The English, of course, would be tremendously heartened to find the Prince definitely on their side. And the French, inevitably, would have felt remarkably let down by the fact that their ace-in-the-hole, which the Prince's supposed adherence to France had implied, was no longer there.

It was exactly the kind of emotional factor that could sway the outcome of a battle such as this; and clearly not merely the Prince and the Earl, but King Jean himself realized this.

Meanwhile the discussion struggled to find the proper words into which to fit its solution to the present situation. It was difficult merely to call a truce, since the usual conditions under which a truce were called—namely, that the two armies had not tested each other's strength—was not there to hinge the agreement on. At the present moment the testing was literally going on.

The final solution agreed on was an immediate temporary truce. This, in theory, was to be followed by discussions, and a decision about who had actually won the battle would be put off and put off until it became ancient history. This was certainly a solution that was agreeable to both King Jean and the Earl; and it did not seem disagreeable to the Prince.

It was therefore agreed on. Unfortunately, the agreement brought up a very knotty question indeed.

How to proclaim the truce and get the armies to stop fighting.

The procedure was obvious. It would be to send Royal heralds about the field, with trumpets and proclamations; both French and English heralds proclaiming that an immediate truce had been called because the young Crown Prince of England was now restored to the English side; and diplomatic details needed to be ironed out before the matter could be put to the test of battle again. The fact that there was no intention of putting the matter to the test of battle again—at least in the minds of those making the agreement right at the moment—was left unsaid.

The problem came from the fact, and it was a fact that was foreseen by everybody but Jim, that this was easier said than done.

"But what's the problem?" asked Jim quietly in Brian's ear, so that no one else could catch the question.

Brian turned his head to him so that his answer should go likewise unheard.

"Knights do not always stop fighting, just because they're told to," he said. "A command may stop them from starting to fight until it is time; but once started, they do not stop easily. Particularly, they do not stop, if one side or another feels it is winning; and that only a little more effort will bring victory into its grasp."

. Jim was forced to believe this as he stood and watched, after both King Jean and the Earl had sent messengers to the Royal heralds on both sides to spread the word of a truce on the field. It began to dawn on him what Brian had meant.

What Brian had said turned out to be only too true. The heralds galloped from one end of the field to the other, blowing their trumpets and shouting their proclamations both in English and in French. But there was a remarkable lack of response by those still hotly engaged in battle.

Slowly, Jim began to understand. Your medieval knight did not go to war to stop fighting. He went to war to win battles and kill people. Possibly, also—just possibly—to be killed himself. It was possible, if luck went against him, to lose a battle. But he never went to war to suddenly stop going to war. The truth was that these knights unabashedly *liked* fighting. He had heard their complaints all winter, even at the round of parties that he attended, that were given by anyone of the gentry who had a castle or a hall big enough to entertain. Winter was a period for passing the time impatiently until spring made it possible to do the one thing that made life worthwhile—fight.

As he had heard any number of the males in the gentlemanly class say on occasion, there were only so many meals you could eat, so much wine you could drink, and so many women worth being interested in. You went through these rather quickly, and after that it was a matter of twiddling your thumbs until the snow was off the ground, and the real business of a knight's life could take up again.

"James."

Jim turned to face Carolinus, with a sudden guilty feeling. He remembered that Carolinus had spoken to him some moments ago about wanting to talk to him aside; and in the rush of events he had forgotten all about it.

"Come with me," said Carolinus. "No one else will notice you're going—except Malvinne. And he'll be expecting us to go off and talk."

Carolinus turned without waiting for an answer, and threaded his way among the men-at-arms. Jim followed him. He was interested to see that, although none of the men-at-arms seemed aware of them or deliberately shifted out of their way, there were little movements aside on the parts of many of them, to widen the space through which Carolinus might pass. They reached the outer ring and walked off a short distance, far enough into the trees so that they could not see the people behind them, and the sound of talk back there could not be heard.

At the foot of a large tree that shadowed them from the midday brightness of the sun, Carolinus stopped and turned back to face Jim. Jim stopped also; and their eyes met.

"You're going to have to make up your mind what to do about Malvinne, James," Carolinus said. "It's time now to make your decisions."

"Do?" Jim said. "Matters seem to have taken care of him pretty well. His false Prince is gone and an agreement has been reached between the Earl and King Jean. It's just a matter of stopping the soldiers on the field from fighting."

"As you noticed," said Carolinus dryly, "that part of things hasn't taken care of itself too well."

"No," admitted Jim, "but it does seem to me that Malvinne is now pretty effectively out of the picture."

"Out of the ordinary temporal picture, yes," said Carolinus. "The question remains what to do about him as far as the Kingdom of Magic is concerned."

"But deciding what to do with him isn't my responsibility, is it?" asked Jim, abruptly very uncomfortable. "Certainly there are other people, or other rules, or something like that that will deal with him."

"There are, in a sense," said Carolinus. "Primarily the Accounting Office. However, what the Accounting Office does, depends upon the action you decide to take."

"Why? What action should I take?" asked Jim.

"That, as I say," answered Carolinus, "is something that has to be your own decision. I can no more help you now with this, than I could help you earlier. It was necessary Malvinne be stopped and brought to book; not by a magician like myself, but by someone like you, of much inferior rank. That is part of the rules that govern all who deal in magic. It has its roots in the need to set up a system that would keep strong magicians from fighting each other; with possible resultant danger to the other Kingdoms that inhabit this world, the space above, and the space below, its surface. I may have explained some of this to you. What I brought you out here for is to tell you exactly what your position is, right now."

"Tell me, then," said Jim.

"Very well," said Carolinus. "First, you should understand that of all the magicians in this world, you are the only member of our craft and art who was in a position to do anything about Malvinne. It was necessary, as I say, that he be brought down by an inferior. But by definition, no inferior could succeed in doing so. The exception to this rule was an inferior who had had training that no other magician in this world has had—primarily, the training in something you call by another name, but which has totally shaped your future world in the place you come from."

Understanding woke in Jim.

"You mean, technology?" said Jim.

"If that's the name for it, yes," said Carolinus. "This was necessary, because in no way was I allowed to assist you—and that included teaching you the things you would need to know to survive what Malvinne might strike at you with in the way of magic. Moreover, I did not know what he might strike at you with, and to protect you against all possibilities, I would have had to teach you enough to bring you up to a rank equivalent to his. Even if this had been allowed, we wouldn't have had the time. The teaching alone would take years."

"But how does technology come into this?" asked Jim.

"Because, with this particular background of yours, you were able to teach yourself, in a way that no student of magic from this world could," Carolinus said, with a strangely patient note in his voice. "To begin with, you are not bound by the unconscious habits and reactions that people growing up in this world acquire without realizing they have them. Habits and reactions it takes many years of the study of magic to unlearn, before you can proceed to its higher orders. For example, one of the things that takes years for a young magician usually to unlearn, is the sense of unquestioning awe where the effects of magic and other things are concerned—such as the ability of elementals like Melusine, or the powers of the King and Queen of the Dead within their Kingdom."

"I didn't realize that," Jim said. "Why am I specially free of that?"

"Because," answered Carolinus, "you, because of your acquaintance with this thing you call *technology*, are used to having to do with situations or devices, where remarkable things are made available to you, or experienced by you, the actual workings of which you do not directly understand. There will be other humans in your world who *do* understand why such things work, and can even explain them; but you are quite content to take their workings on faith. In fact your attitude to them is a very everyday one. You regard them, in spite of their wonder-working, as no more remarkable than a spade or an axe."

"You think so?" said Jim. He found it hard to believe. Then he thought of cars and television sets.

"I'll give you an example," said Carolinus. "When you were leaving the two dragons to which you had been steered, one of them deliberately sent you by Melusine's lake, so that you should be trapped and drowned by her."

"Yes," said Jim, "but why is that an example of me being different?"

"Because," said Carolinus, "of a number of factors dependent on early conditioning in this world, being once in the dragon body, a young magician like yourself would never have changed out of it simply because it was uncomfortable. From your standpoint, however, it was the natural thing to do. As a result, you were human when you came by the lake; and Melusine reacted quite differently than if you had been still a dragon. Similarly, when you led your Companions into the castle of Malvinne, it never occurred to you that the magical traps he had set could not have some findable solution. At no point did you say to yourself, 'Whatever traps are here must have been set by a greater magician than myself, so there can be no hope of my trying to discover how they may be defeated or overcome.'"

"Well, no," said Jim, "but what's that got to do with my situation with regard to Malvinne right now?"

"At the present moment," said Carolinus, "Malvinne is facing the need to answer a charge by the King of the Dead as to being an accessory in allowing a Magician to enter his Kingdom. This is a charge he can dispose of by admitting merely collateral responsibility; and simply paying from his account with the Accounting Office to the King of the Dead a fairly respectable percentage of what he has, but nothing at all crippling. Outside of that, the Accounting Office has no charges against him."

"What about the simulacra, the false Prince?" said Jim, astonished.

"You are under a rather natural misapprehension," said Carolinus dryly. "You think the Accounting Office is concerned with either morals or ethics. It is concerned with neither. It is concerned only with the balance of the energy for which it is responsible. The complaint of the King of the Dead is therefore of importance to it, because it implies a disturbance of the balance of that energy between the Kingdom of the Dead and the human world to which Malvinne, even though a magician, still belongs. Malvinne's snow-Prince, however, is something that was an effect merely within the human world, and does not affect that balance of energy—just because it happened."

Carolinus placed a particular emphasis on the last words that made Jim look narrowly at him.

"You're suggesting there's something else there that could be of interest to them?" he said.

"There could be," said Carolinus. "If another magician should point out that this was done to aid the Dark Powers to alter the shape of things to come. Things to come are forbidden even for the Accounting Office to anticipate. Magicians are strictly enjoined from stimulating any disturbance within them. That, by the way, is a very serious charge. If proved, it could strip Malvinne not only of all of his account with the Accounting Office, but with any status that his AAA rating might otherwise entitle him to. This last is highly important within the ranks of the Kingdom of Magicians, themselves. It means he will be stripped to only his temporal powers—against which you should remain on guard, for with his temporal wealth alone, he is still dangerous."

"But if he's still dangerous," protested Jim, "what's the use of his powers being stripped from him? What's the point of all we've done?"

"It robs him of being of any further use to the Dark Powers—for they never use the same tool twice. Unstripped, however, they will put him to use anew."

"Well then, why don't you—" Jim broke off, staring at Carolinus. "You mean I should bring that charge to the attention of the Accounting Office and against Malvinne?"

"I mean nothing," said Carolinus. "I may not enter this situation in any regard, because of the law that forbids me to help you in any way, and which I violated only to the minor extent of making you impervious to Malvinne's personal magic this day. When the twenty-four hours of protection I gave you earlier is over, by the way, you will lose that imperviousness. Then Malvinne may use the powers still in his account to even things up with you."

Jim stared at Carolinus. Carolinus's eyes met his with a great deal of meaning in them.

"You're telling me, then, that I have less than twenty-four hours to make my charge against Malvinne?"

"I repeat," said Carolinus, "that I am *telling* you nothing. What deductions you care to make from the statements I have made—statements about things as they are—are yours to make, alone."

"Can you answer one question for me?" asked Jim.

"Possibly," said Carolinus briefly.

"If I don't make these charges, and the twenty-four hours get used up and Malvinne is released from what you put upon him—"

"And for which I shall have to pay a fine, as I explained," said Carolinus, interrupting. He winced. "It will still be costly. What makes up an account at the Accounting Office is not gathered easily, you know."

"Yes, yes," said Jim, "I know. The point is if I wait until after sunup and do nothing, how much of what Malvinne lost will he be able to recover?"

"I'm not in a position to pronounce on what a fellow magician might do," said Carolinus. "In the case of such a hypothetical situation, a magician such as the one you're talking about could possibly recover everything he had lost, and more, to boot!"

"In other words, if he's about to be stopped, he has to be stopped now," said Jim.

"If that is a deduction from my hypothetical situation, I'd have to agree with it," said Carolinus. "Note, a lesser magician bringing such a charge against an elder mage of AAA rank, can expect, if his charge did not carry, to be stripped of all his powers and possibly even turned completely outside the Kingdom of Magicians. Not even Malvinne faces that, at worst."

"But I'm not even sure of the sort of charges I could bring!" said Jim desperately.

"In the way of giving instructions to a pupil, I might advise you," said Carolinus, "that the charge that could be brought in such a hypothetical case would be one of creating a situation that could ultimately result in the amount of energy controlled by the Accounting Office being permanently decreased. So, degrading the power of the Accounting Office itself and lessening its ability to act as a ruling control over the Kingdom of Magicians."

Jim stared at the slight figure before him, with its wispy mustache and beard.

"You mean," he said at last, "that could actually be a result of what Malvinne's done?"

"In this same hypothetical case. It would be, of course, a matter for the Accounting Office to decide. My own opinion, which is unimportant, is that the charge is absolutely irrefutable. Action would have to be taken against the hypothetical magician we are speaking of—I mean, of whom we are speaking!"

Carolinus ended on an angry note, correcting himself.

"My grammar gets more atrocious with the years," he grumbled. "However, all that aside, you now should have a general grasp of what's involved in the situation we've just been talking about. My duty ends. The decision to enter charges with the Accounting Office or not, is up to you."

"And there's no middle ground?" asked Jim. "If I enter the charges, this hypothetical magician you're talking about will be completely ruined?"

"Yes," said Carolinus, "and speaking off the record for a moment, I can't think of another hypothetical magician to whom it could better happen! Particularly to one who has abused the great Art and craft of magic for years. Also, one who has on the purely human level caused a great deal of misery."

There was a long moment of silence between them.

"Well," said Carolinus, "we had better be getting back to the others. I have told you what I wanted to tell you."

He turned and strode off. Jim followed. As the two of them reached the ring of men, Theoluf hurried up to Jim.

"Sir James!" he said. "I couldn't find you. Sir Giles is very close to his end now and he has asked for you!"

Chapter 40

As Jim approached the tree where Sir Giles lay in the shade, he could see that the other had been made at least a little more comfortable. Some man-at-arms' wadded-up jacket had been made into a pillow for his head; and his helm and those parts of his armor that could be taken off without disturbing him too much had been taken off. Melusine still knelt beside him, holding one limp, white hand and talking to him, although Giles seemed incapable of answering.

As Jim came up, Melusine stopped talking to Giles and looked up at Jim.

"Good!" she said. "Quickly, quickly! He needs to speak to you and barely has the strength to do it. You must put your ear right to his mouth!"

Jim knelt beside Giles, taking Giles's other hand, which felt cold and strange in his grasp, with all the blood drained out of it.

"I'd rather have lost almost anything than you, Giles," he said.

He saw the other man's eyes focus on him and a little life came into them.

"I'll listen to what you have to tell me now," said Jim. "I'll put my ear right at your lips."

He bent over from the kneeling position he was in, and put his ear against the cold lips for a moment before withdrawing it a fraction of an inch to give Giles freedom to speak. He listened intently.

"Sea . . ." Giles whispered with great effort. ". . . bury . . ."

"I give you my word, Giles," said Jim, squeezing his hand. "Rest easy. You will be buried at sea. I promise it!"

Giles may have sighed, or it may have been that for a moment the breath coming through his lips made a slight sound. But his eyes closed and his face relaxed.

"Oh, the poor one," said Melusine, still holding his hand.

Giles was not quite dead yet. His chest still moved slightly with his breathing.

"It is the water," said Melusine, staring down at him. "Like me, it is the water he wants at the end. . . ."

Jim got to his feet and found himself surrounded by a semicircle of the men-at-arms, just behind the Prince, who had been standing throughout this, watching Jim with Giles. Like the men-at-arms, there was hope in his eyes as those eyes fastened on Jim, hope that he could do something to keep Giles from dying.

Jim shook his head slowly.

"He wanted to tell me he should be buried at sea," Jim told them. "I promised he would be."

Moved more than he would have thought possible, Jim turned away from Giles. Clearing his throat, he pushed his way through the men and came back to the place before the flag, where the Earl of Cumberland and King Jean of France still discussed the terms of a truce that, judging by the sight of the scattered, still embroiled warriors in the field, was anything but assured. As Jim came up, they were talking about the burial of the dead.

"Yes," King Jean was saying, "I like that idea, my Lord Earl. I myself will build and endow a Chantry, where prayers shall be said for those Frenchmen fallen on this field on this day."

"And King Edward will do the same, without a doubt," said the Earl, "for those English also fallen here. The field itself shall be consecrated, and all the Englishmen who fell today will be buried together."

"In a single grave. Yes, it shall be so for our French dead, also," said King Jean. "It will be a fitting marker for the occasion; and—in line with our further purpose—it will draw the attention of all the world on the place, rather than the fact that the truce is left unresolved. Our dead, sleeping together but in two separate great graves, will set a seal on the occasion that shall silence questions."

"We must scour the field, to make sure that no body of an English knight escapes us. The lesser ranks—those who are not gentlemen"—he waved his hand—"can be buried off in the woods, so as not to detract from the solemnity of the fact that our gentlemen lie here."

"Also with our French gentlemen," said King Jean. "The lesser sort and particularly such as the Genoese must be placed off the field and apart. That will be no matter—"

"Forgive me—" said Jim.

For a moment it seemed as if the two had either not heard him, or would ignore him completely. Then both turned their heads slowly to stare at him.

"He is one of your English, I think, my Lord," murmured King Jean.

"To my shame I own it!" snapped the Earl, his eyes still on Jim. "Sir, were you taught no manners at all, wherever it is you come from? The King of France and I are speaking—to each other."

The Earl's tone put Jim's teeth somewhat on edge, but he kept his own voice as calm and polite as he could.

"I know," he said. "Forgive me for intruding, my Lord and Your Majesty. I would not have spoken up at all, but I chanced to overhear your plans for a common grave for the knights of each side and Chantries to pray for their souls. It is an excellent idea. I only wish to point out, that one of the English knights that fell here today, has a need to be buried elsewhere."

The Earl of Cumberland stared at him and both the close-cropped gray beard and gray mustache bristled.

"What's this of his need, whoever he is?" snapped the Earl. "He shall lie with the rest, of course! Otherwise, there is no point in the whole matter of setting up a Chantry Guild and telling the world that all the English dead lie here."

"I'm afraid," said Jim, with an effort still keeping his voice calm and appeasing, "that won't be possible—"

"Hell's Hounds!" exploded the Earl. "Do you talk of necessity to me? Where got you this impertinence? I tell you he shall lie with the rest and the matter is done! Now leave us!"

"You don't understand," said Jim desperately. "It is Sir Giles de Mer I'm referring to. The knight that kept the Prince safe when Malvinne's knights would have killed him while we talked up here. Certainly, he's earned the right to be buried when, where, and how he pleases."

"He shall lie with the others!" snarled the Earl. "Go! Before I have you dragged away!"

"You'll have me dragged away, my Lord?" For the first time, a little of Jim's hard held but growing inner anger crept into his voice. "You have four men with you."

He left unsaid the fact that he had fifty men; but the point was not lost on the Earl.

"Go!" said that Lord.

Jim had a stubborn streak that was seldom roused; but at this moment it was becoming very much alive within him.

"I'll leave after it's perfectly understood that Sir Giles will be buried at sea, as he asked just now," said Jim. "I gave him my word it would be so."

"And what is your word to me?" snarled the Earl. "Do you think to frighten me with the red on your shield, or anything else about you? Do you think to force me with a handful of men because I am alone? These matters are not decided by such as you. They are decided by such as myself and His Royal Majesty here. He will lie with the others and nothing will change that. I have said it!"

Jim's stubborn streak was now fully in command of him.

"Then you've wasted breath on something that won't happen, my Lord," he said. "I will go. But I leave, saying to you flatly that Sir Giles will not be buried here at this field. He will be buried where he asked to be buried—in the sea."

The Earl's face was brick red with rage.

"Never have I encountered such pertness!" he shouted. "By all the Hosts of Heaven, you may say that this hedge-knight friend of yours will be buried in the sea. You may even try to take his body hence. But the moment the truce is settled, which will surely be within twenty-four hours if not before, I will set such force upon your track as will hunt you down like a rabbit and will return his bones and what stinking flesh remains upon them to this place where they belong!"

"Your Lordship will not have to wait beyond the twenty-four hours, itself," came the venomous voice of Malvinne from a little behind King Jean. "I, a Minister of France, promise it."

"Try it, then!" snapped Jim; and turned to go, to get Giles—if he was already dead—and start taking him toward the distant sea of the English Channel across which the two of them had sailed to this land.

"A moment—" said the voice of Carolinus.

Jim saw that the elderly magician had appeared again, almost as if from nowhere. But it was not Jim at whom Carolinus was looking, nor Jim to whom he spoke. He spoke to the Earl instead.

"If Your Lordship would listen to a word from me—"

"Out on you, sorcerers all!" raved the Earl. "I will listen to no one on this subject. It is closed. You hear me! Closed. I have the authority here, and I say what will be. That is all any of you need to know."

He turned back to the King, as if to continue their conversation. Carolinus put out a hand to catch Jim's arm.

"Wait here," said Carolinus, looking sternly at Jim.

Jim stayed where he was. Carolinus went off with surprisingly long strides toward the knot of people around where Sir Giles lay. He disappeared among them. Jim waited; but when nothing seemed to be happening, he turned back to the Earl and the King, who were back to discussing the Chantries that were to be built so that prayers could be said for those in the two mass graves.

They continued to ignore him, and he had nothing to say. So he simply stood and listened with only a part of his attention. He was paying little attention because his mind was as thoroughly made up as it ever had been. He would get

Giles's body to the sea no matter what happened. It was no longer a desire, it was a fact.

There was suddenly a flash of blue *cote-hardie* and Jim looked about to see Prince Edward beside him. The young Prince's face was flushed.

"What is this I hear, my Lord?" he said to the Earl of Cumberland. "My brave Sir Giles is not to be allowed the resting place of his choice?"

With an obvious effort, the Earl of Cumberland mastered the emotions that Jim had evoked in him. He tried to speak reasonably to the Prince.

"It is merely a matter of the necessary arrangements for the truce I am arranging between us English and King Jean," he said. "To help make the truce effective and satisfying to both French and English, we decided that two Chantries shall be built in this place and two great graves dug; one for all those French gentlemen who have fallen on this field and one for all those English gentlemen who have done likewise. It will be a great honor to be buried so; to say nothing of the fact that their souls will benefit from the prayers of those in the Chantries."

The Prince's eyes flashed.

"You are avoiding my question, Lord Earl! I asked whether Sir Giles is to be buried where he wished, or not?"

"Necessarily, Highness," said the Earl, "he must lie with the other English knights who will have died here."

"In spite of his wishes?"

"I regret, Highness," said the Earl solemnly, "but yes."

"In spite of *my* wishes?"

The Earl was obviously nothing if not a brave man. But he risked one quick glance at King Jean at this point. However, the King of France was observing the field, and pointedly staying out of the discussion. Cumberland turned back to face his questioner. As he did so, the dusky color of anger began to creep once more into his face, and Jim saw that the Earl's own stubbornness was being aroused.

"I would not in anything ordinarily go against your wishes, Highness," he said, "but—forgive me—you are still a young man, and while you know something of the world, there are elements of politics between nations, which—"

"I said, *of mine?*" snapped the Prince.

"Well, Highness," said the Earl, turning a shade darker in the face, "if you must have it! I am commander here of the English forces; and an army can have but one commander. As that commander, I must judge what is best for all, on my honor and on my responsibility to your Royal father. I regret, but Sir Giles must be buried here. It is a matter of necessity. Surely you must see that."

"I see a hot Earl, who is determined to thwart his Prince!" The Prince's voice soared upward in volume. "You ignore the fact that Sir Giles was not one of your command, not from among your forces. He was one of another group, including this good knight beside me, sent to rescue me from a most sad capture; and well did they perform that task! He is under my command, not yours. I say he shall be buried where he wishes to be buried, in the sea and nowhere else!"

"With infinite regrets, Highness," said the Earl stubbornly, "I cannot admit that he is not under my command. All Englishmen who fought and died here are under my command. He must lie with the others."

Standing beside the Prince, Jim winced, but did not know what to do about the situation. It was this same matter of being on stage that he had remarked among the gentlemanly class in this world. The Earl was acting the part that he felt life had called him to act. He was acting as an Earl should. He was insisting on his authority in the face of what must surely be the lethal enmity of a member of the Royal Family next in line for the English throne.

If the Prince lived to succeed his father, the Earl could look forward only to ruin. And possibly the Prince might even be able to ruin, if not execute him, even before he had ascended to the throne. But, being a knight and an Earl, he could not back down.

Similarly, the Prince was feeling himself challenged. It was unthinkable that a mere Earl should stand against the Crown Prince of England in anything. Neither man was in a position now where they could back down. Jim's mind was searching desperately for some excuse to interrupt the dialogue, when the Prince solved that matter for himself.

"Very well, proud Earl!" snapped the Prince. "You make up my mind for me! I was right in the first place. I will to horse and out on the field to rally what English I can around me and see if we cannot win this day after all!"

"Young cousin—" said King Jean, starting forward and holding out his hand to stop the young man.

But the Prince had already whirled on one heel.

"My horse!" he shouted. "And make ready to follow me out onto the field—"

His voice broke off. Everyone behind him was staring skyward. He too turned and stared toward the sky in the west, up over the English lines. Jim joined him.

Coming into view rapidly, was a wide band of black specks, the closer of which resolved themselves into dragon shapes.

It was an unnerving sight. Jim, who had a better measure of such things from his experience of being a dragon himself, checked his wild imagination after its first gasp of astonishment, and told himself that there could not be more than a couple of hundred dragons at most in the air, high up, coming toward them. But at first glance it had looked—and to every other human there it must also look—as if the sky was being filled with dragons. As if there were literally thousands of them.

As the front line of the great bodies in flight approached above the English lines, some arrows flew into the air toward them. But the dragons were flying far too high for the arrows to do any damage. They came on, beginning to overshadow the field; and on the field itself, all combat had ceased. Opponents, who a moment before had been hacking away at each other, now sat on their horses, swords still in their hands, staring upward together at the oncoming of the dragons.

Jim let a slow sigh of relief escape him. No one else was close enough to hear.

"Well," he thought, almost ready to smile in his relief, "better late than never."

The dragons came on. As they began to come over the actual field itself, they stopped their forward travel, caught thermals, and circled individually above it. There were not enough of them, to actually get in the way of the sunlight, but it seemed as if that the mass of them would overshadow all the earth below.

Out on the field, the heralds were at last being heard. Weapons were being sheathed or hung back upon the saddle from which they had originally been taken. Shields were being lowered. Below the darkness of the dragons, it seemed almost as if French and English had become one company. Now, at last they were all listening to word of the truce that was being proclaimed by the French and English heralds.

"What brings them?" said the stricken voice of King Jean, behind him. "Why are they here?"

Jim turned back to face the King and the Earl.

"They are here to aid the English cause, Highness," he said harshly. "In my capacity as Dragon Knight I made that agreement with them sometime since. They are a little later in arrival than I had hoped. But they are here now."

The King stared at him. The Earl stared at him. The Earl was the quicker of the two to recover.

Turning back to the King, he spoke directly at him.

"Perhaps you would care to discuss the terms of a surrender, after all, Your Highness?" he said.

"No!" said Jim sharply.

The Earl turned as sharply upon him. Then, suddenly realizing that the situation had changed, choked back whatever angry words had been about to come from his lips.

"May I ask why, Sir Dragon Knight?" he said finally, in a voice that he struggled to keep level and polite.

"Because it is in a truce that this day is destined to end," said Jim, "for the greater good and the greater glory not only of England, but of France as well. You must trust me in this, my Lord and Your Majesty. It must be so."

Once more the Earl and the King exchanged glances, then looked back at Jim. They were wordless. And, indeed, that was not surprising. For there was now nothing left for them to say.

Chapter 41

For the waters of the English Channel, it was a calm day; and the sailing vessel that carried Jim, Brian, Dafydd, and Aargh, as well as all their men and horses, was a much larger vessel than the one in which Jim and Brian, with Giles, had gone originally from England to France.

Nevertheless, hove to for the ceremony of burying Sir Giles, the vessel pitched uneasily; and there were not a few of the men-at-arms and the several archers that had somehow become added to their company, whom Jim suspected of wanting to see matters over with as soon as possible, and the vessel back on its way. Not that the motion of the vessel was much better on queasy stomachs when it was sailing, but they would be that much closer to dry land again and England.

Nonetheless, Jim, Brian, and Dafydd had no intention of cutting short the consigning of Giles's body to the ocean waters. They had been unable to ship a priest along with them for the final ceremony, so Jim recited as much of the burial service as he could remember, trusting to the lack of understanding of Latin among those about him to keep them from noticing his omissions and errors.

The day was without rain, although the sky was heavy. The gray clouds and the gray sea seemed to enclose them as they stood by the section of open railing where the body of Sir Giles, complete in arms and armor, lay on a couple of planks that could be tipped to slide him off to his final resting place.

Jim reached the end of the service. He turned to nod to Tom Seiver and the other men-at-arms who were standing by to lift the ends of the planks.

The men lifted, Sir Giles slid down the boards and into the sea that was only a few feet away. The rest had averted their eyes at the last moment, but Jim, Brian, and Dafydd leaned over the rail, to see the last of their Companion.

And it was well they did.

As Sir Giles slipped into the water, a thing happened that most of those watching would have been highly alarmed to see; but which the three friends found the happiest sight they could imagine.

As the armored figure slid into the water, a miracle seemed to happen. The armor burst outward, as once Jim's armor had burst when he had turned into a dragon on the way to Carolinus's place. But this time what emerged was a gray harbor seal, which turned one lively eye on them for a moment, before diving and being lost to sight permanently beneath the gray waters of the Channel. The three drew back from the side of the boat.

"You knew this was to happen?" Brian asked Jim, awed.

Jim shook his head and smiled.

"No," he answered in a low voice that carried only to Brian and Dafydd, "but I'm not surprised."

"Will he be a seal forever more, now?" asked Dafydd, in similar hushed tones.

"I don't know," said Jim. "Perhaps. Still . . ."

He turned away from the rail, shaking his head, and the question was left unanswered. He had been unaccountably depressed since the evening following the battle, when he had called up the Accounting Office and submitted his charges against Malvinne. Until this moment, he had not been sure that what he had done was for the best for everyone concerned. Now, the bright, brief gleam of the eye of that seal had somehow reassured him.

"Ho, now, shipmaster!" Brian hailed the ship's master, "we are done. Away to England!"

About a week and a half had passed, before the three of them, with their mounted men-at-arms and archers—the total number of which had somehow grown on their way back from France—strung out along the forest trail behind them, once more approached the castle of Malencontri.

They were finally less than a mile away from Jim's home; and the weather this time was in tune with their homecoming. It was a bright, hot day in late August; and the forest shade was welcome upon those who wore armor, or even the heavy protective jackets of boiled leather which the archers, and some of the men-at-arms favored.

Jim, Brian, and Dafydd rode abreast at the head of the line of men. Aargh had left them almost upon landing, saying he had no intention of being held up by their slow travel. Meanwhile, all difference of rank between the three had now vanished, not only worn away by what they had been through, but by the death and sea change of Sir Giles.

Brian's grief at the death of the other knight had been more than Jim had expected; but then he was always underestimating the suddenness and the depth of emotion that could crop up in these people with whom he now lived. But finally, it seemed to have vanished entirely, exorcised partially by Giles's sea change and by another attitude Jim had come to recognize as part of this world; that things done and over with were to be accepted and forgotten.

Now Brian's concern was all for Malencontri; and whether he might find his ladylove still visiting there. Dafydd had said nothing; but Jim suspected that the Welsh archer's thoughts were likewise concentrated on the hope that his wife would also be at Malencontri when they got there. However, apparently to keep his mind off questioning the aforesaid hope, Dafydd was chatting of other things.

"You have heard or felt—not even in a way in which only a magician might—" he was now asking Jim, "anymore of Malvinne, did you mark that apparently he disappeared at just about the time the dragons showed up? You should have told me sooner that Carolinus had warned you that after twenty-four hours Carolinus's power to protect you against that French sorcerer would be gone."

"It didn't matter," said Jim almost absently. "By that time I'd made my charges to the Accounting Office."

"Charges?" asked Brian.

Jim caught himself. This was business private to the Kingdom of Magicians.

"It's too difficult to explain," he said. "Just take my word for it Malvinne won't be able to harm anyone with magic for a long, long time, if he ever is able again."

"You are troubled," said Dafydd, riding on the other side of him.

Jim glanced at the archer. Above the fine straight nose, the dark brown eyes were concerned.

"Somewhat," he admitted.

"Troubled?" echoed Brian alertly. "About what James?"

"He does not know, I think," said Dafydd, "but there is still a black shadow over everything. It is darkest wherever Malvinne is. I can feel it too, but I can no more understand it than he can."

Jim chewed his lower lip for a moment, wondering whether to try to explain. He decided against it. It was too mixed up.

"Dafydd's right," said Jim. "There's a dark shadow—and I don't understand it. Don't ask me about it, please, Brian. When I can understand it to any extent, I'll tell you about it."

"As you wish, James," said Brian, "but in case of need—you will not forget me?"

Jim had to smile at him.

"In case of need, Brian," he said, "you are the last person I would forget."

"Well then, let trouble come," said Brian. "Troubles are as common in this world as fleas. And it is as impossible to clean them all out. There is nothing to do but wait till one comes close to the fingers; and then deal with it."

For some reason, this lighthearted bit of philosophy was comforting to Jim. But it did not lift from him that shadow sensed by Dafydd's sensitiveness to things beyond the normal. Something was still wrong. He was forgetting something.

In his own mind he examined the situation for the several hundredth time. Theoretically, things could not be better. He had succeeded in following Carolinus's directions. England and France were restive now beneath a truce that neither one of them was really happy with, but which neither could think of any good reason to break.

King Jean had been released from his capture back to his proper position on the throne of France as a quiet codicil to the truce. Jim himself had recovered his passport.

It had been brought to him by a positively beaming Secoh, who had descended from among the horde of dragons circling above the battlefield—and who had come very close to having not merely one, but a number of arrows, through him from the three archers Dafydd had recruited.

It had only been Jim's voice and Dafydd's speaking out just in time, that kept Secoh from becoming very dead indeed, as he planed in for a landing. As a matter of fact, he would have been no more safe on the ground than in the air. Every armed man there—which meant all of them—was ready to repel his attack by attacking him first. In this latter case, it was Jim and Brian's interposition that saved Secoh's life.

With Edward's threat, the battle was ended without either side winning; and Jim had the passport back inside him. He had had a little trouble remembering exactly what the procedure was for shrinking it down so that he could swallow it again; but he had recaptured the proper spell words at last, and since gotten over the extreme feeling of fullness that having it inside him had once more produced. He looked forward to returning it to the Cliffside Dragons; and never having to do with anything like it again.

He still felt an uneasiness that he could not pin down, a premonition of danger. But he could think of no corridor from which the danger could come at him. Even if it did, he was extremely well backed up by the men-at-arms and archers that rode behind him. Brian was right. It was best to simply wait for trouble to show itself, before becoming overly concerned with it.

Brian was in the midst of asking a question of Dafydd, who rode on Jim's other side, so that he was effectively talking across Jim as the three rode forward.

"Something I'd been meaning to ask," Brian was saying to the archer. "I by no means account myself good-looking. Nor, with all truth can I say whether another man is good-looking or not to female eyes, though insofar as ladies and even ordinary women are concerned I am no bad judge of looks, I flatter myself. But it was my own Lady that pointed out to me that you, Dafydd, are considered to have an appearance highly attractive to practically any woman. It wondered me at the time, and since, that when Melusine was pouncing upon people on whom to visit her fancy after being deprived of Jim and King Jean, that she did not light upon you, who was with us at the time, since you are accounted so desirable by the gentle sex."

"I do not think it of great likeliness," answered Dafydd, "though, in truth I have been myself told that I have some small attraction for some women. Yet I would not for the world that even the least thing be said of me that might creep, as slander does, back to the ears of my golden bird, about an interest supposedly between me and some other lady. Therefore, once I recognized Melusine's tendency to respond to men, I plucked up again a bit of twig with some leaves upon it and stuck it in my cap. Whether that made me invisible or not, I do not know, but certainly her eyes did not light upon me, nor her effect—"

He broke off speaking with unexpected suddenness, and spurred forward, reining in his horse almost immediately about five yards ahead of them.

"Hold!" he cried, holding up a hand in the air.

This command, from one who ordinarily never commanded, produced a sudden halting of the column. As Jim and Brian watched, Dafydd leaned far down from his saddle to pluck from among a bunch of weeds by the wayside what proved to be an arrow.

Once upright in his saddle, he sat staring at it and examining it.

Jim and Brian rode forward together to him.

"What ails you?" demanded Brian. "It is only an arrow, such as may have been lost by any bowman out hunting game."

Dafydd turned a face on him that was so grim, that Brian stiffened in his saddle.

"It is a shaft of my golden bird's!" said Dafydd, "and it can only be here as a message that she is in difficulties, and we should be warned!"

"Why, how do you read all that from a simple arrow?" asked Brian.

"Do I not know my golden bird's shafts as well as I know my own?" Dafydd snapped at him. "More than that, it would not be here except to send me a message. That message concerns us all, but requires the proper eyes to read it."

"Lord knows," said Brian, "I have no eye for reading arrow shafts. Read us this message then, if it has things we should hear."

"I fear me it does," said Dafydd. "Look you, to begin with we are right now at the farthest Danielle might be able to send a shaft from high in Malencontri's tower. It was also at about the farthest turn of the road that can be seen from such a high point, through the trees. If you will look about us here, you will notice there are no tall trees close to our road. She knows the road well, therefore she knew this spot along it. She has aimed the arrow with all her strength in this direction."

"And you're sure of this?" asked Jim. "How can you tell that it isn't a shaft that she may have lost even some weeks ago, when out hunting?"

"Look you," said Dafydd still grimly, turning his eyes on Jim, "it was almost straight up and down in the earth, therefore it had been shot high in the air to get the greatest possible distance. The shaft has not been subject to weather for more than a day or two at most—I could tell if it had. Further, if it were needed, my golden bird does not lose her arrows. Like all good users of the bow, when she aims at a target, she also looks beyond it to someplace where it may lodge, so that she can find it again, if she should miss her mark—and well you know she does not often miss her mark. In fact, I can never remember of her missing; though it is true she has not shot at such distance and such marks as I myself have shot."

"All right. I see what you mean," said Jim. "The arrow was shot high—but how do you know from the castle?"

"Why else would Danielle shoot an arrow at random into the air?" said Dafydd. "No, no, to think of her shooting without a purpose is to think wildly. If she did not shoot without purpose, then the only likely place from which such an arrow should come would be from the castle. Also, the only reason for it being shot at all, would be for us to find it on our way to the castle. Clearly, it is a message and a warning."

"But you might just as easily have missed it as we rode by," said Brian. "For myself, I vow I did not even see it until you had pulled it clear of the grass and weeds."

"I not see it, a shaft from the bow of the one I love?" Dafydd answered him. "Would you fail to see a torn piece of cloth from a dress that you knew well your Lady often wore, caught on a bramble bush in the forest?"

"Well, no," said Brian, "but is there not a difference—"

"There is no difference. I will not say it again," said Dafydd. "In fact, enough of this talk about how and why the shaft got here. Take my word that it was shot of purpose to warn us, and that it carries a message. It is that message that is important."

"What read you in it then?" asked Brian.

"That she—and therefore probably all others in the castle—are prisoners there, now," said Dafydd. "It would have been shot either at early dawn or late twilight—which would account for her missing the path itself. Otherwise we would have found it squarely in our way. She is held, they are all held, by those who are enemies of ours. This shaft was to warn us against riding unprepared into an ambush that they had set up for us."

"But we have no enemies," said Brian. "Aside from that raiding band we drove off before leaving for France, all our neighbors are good friends. Nor is it likely that sea-raiders would come this far inland again, so soon."

"Think again," said Dafydd, studying the arrow, and not bothering to lift his head to answer the knight. "They are held prisoner by those who are marked in black—marked four times in black."

"How read you that?" asked Brian.

"Four of the feather spines have been touched with ink, deep in, close to the wood of the shaft itself, so that the marking will not be obvious. Who do we know who marks himself and those with him four times in black?"

"Malvinne," said Jim.

He had said the word aloud, but it was obvious that the association had been made as quickly by Brian, and had already been in Dafydd's mind.

"But I can't believe it," Jim went on, half to himself. "Malvinne here? And enough ahead of us to take my castle, and lay an ambush in for us?"

"You are a fool if you make that a question, James," said a harsh voice; and suddenly Aargh was beside them.

They looked down from their saddles at him.

"Aargh," said Jim, "how long have you been here? Is Dafydd right about all this?"

"He could not be more right," retorted Aargh, "and if you did not expect something like this, James, I have even less respect for your wits. Malvinne may be, as you told us, the day after we left the battlefield, now without magic. But didn't you notice that he left before anyone else—that he was gone before the day was out, and a full night and half a day before we ourselves left that field?"

"That's true," said Jim glumly. "You're right Aargh. I should've been thinking."

"It would become you, James," said Aargh. "I highly recommend it. Clearly he rode as fast and as hard as he could toward the coast, somehow gathering up money and men of his own on the way; so that he could take ship long before us. So he could be here in plenty of time to reach Malencontri, take it from the small handful that now holds it—if he did not trick himself into possession of it—and has since been waiting for us. He will also have had someone waiting in Hastings and all the other of the Cinque Ports, with orders to ride to him with all haste if you are seen disembarking on English soil. So warned, it'd be a small thing to figure the time it would take you to get here; and start setting up a daily ambush well before the expected time of your arrival. You did not think of any of this?"

"No. I'm ashamed of myself, but I didn't," said Jim, caught between chagrin and fury. "I only felt danger looming, from some quarter or another."

"Of what nature and how many men of what sorts and weapons are involved in this that Malvinne has laid for us at Malencontri?" asked Brian, practically.

"It was known that you had to come by this path, if you came suspecting nothing," answered Aargh. "There are eighty men with horses behind the castle, in two groups, out of sight and waiting for you. But they are not like your men-at-arms, light-armed and light-weaponed. All are heavily armed and armored, ready to sally around each end of the castle at you once you've cleared the trees and are in the open. These wait only a signal from the castle. As soon as anyone on the battlements up there sees you coming, he'll pass words to those below and behind the castle, who are there now, already dressed and armed. Then each group will mount and charge together at you, around the castle ends."

"How many bowmen, either long, cross, or both?" demanded Dafydd.

"I counted eighteen," answered Aargh. "Say twenty to twenty-five for a good guess."

Dafydd slowly scrubbed the heel of his left hand across his eyes and forehead. When he took his hand down, his eyes were closed. He opened them again and turned back to face the men behind him, raising his voice.

"Who knows every place within twenty miles of here?"

Several voices answered; but only one man pushed himself forward. He was a man-at-arms, showing untidy tufts of gray hair from under the front edge of his helmet, and a touch of gray stubble upon his chin and cheeks.

"I grew up here," he said to Dafydd, when he reached the tall Welshman.

"A guide is needed," said Dafydd. He turned in the other direction, saw Wat of Easdale, Clym Tyler, and Will o'the Howe standing together not too far from him. He beckoned Wat forward. "How many archers have we now?"

"Six," answered Wat. There was no expression on his face. "Counting yourself."

"And there are twenty to twenty-five in the castle—how many of them longbowmen, and how many of the crossbow, I don't know," Dafydd said. "This man-at-arms here with me—what is your name?"

"Rob Aleward," answered the man-at-arms.

"Rob Aleward will be your guide, Wat," said Dafydd. "I want you to scour the vicinity, going first to those places that are closest, and bring back every man who ever pulled a longbow. It matters not what skill they claim to have, or have not. They are to come and they are to shoot for Lord James. They should come willingly, but if not they are to come anyway. I can trust you to do this?"

"You can trust me," said Wat. He turned to Aleward. "Lead me to the nearest place where there is a bowman."

They went off together.

Dafydd turned back to face Jim and Brian.

"That's the most I can do, look you," he said. "Gladly would I storm the castle single-handed, if it would do any good; but it would not. The rest is up to you, Sir Brian and my Lord."

Dafydd's return to the use of their titles emphasized the seriousness of the moment. It was not an hour for friendship, courtesy, or anything at all but who could lead best in what situation. Jim felt it as much as Dafydd obviously did. He turned to Brian.

"Brian," he said, "you've more experience with something like this than I'll probably ever have. What do you suggest?"

Chapter **42**

Brian scowled in deep thought.

"The one thing we don't want to do," he said, "is ride on out there and let them catch us like a fish snapping up at a fly. They have the better of us in numbers. By rights we should be ambushing them, not the other way around, to make things even. That, James—"

He looked at Jim.

"Is the answer, if you wish one," he said. "Ambush them. But damme, if I know how to go about it. James, you'll have to exercise your wits on the means."

Brian was right enough, Jim thought. This was not a military situation that offered its own, immediately obvious answer. It was unfair of him to shove it all off on Brian, and expect the other to provide him with a neat little package of what to do.

"Well, let's see," he said. "There's eighty men out there behind the castle, sitting and no doubt lying about all day long, waiting for word that will put them on horseback and send them charging around the castle at us. . . ."

He was thinking out loud, but it was the only thing that occurred to him to do at the moment.

"Come to think of it, they can't stay there all night," he went on. "They must go out in the morning and come in at evening. Now, when are they most vulnerable?

Early in the morning, when they've just woken up and are coming out? Or at the end of the day, after they've gotten thoroughly worn out and bored and hot from sitting around in their armor all day waiting for something that hasn't happened?"

"End of the day, I should think," said Brian. "A man may be a bit stiff and cold in the morning; but he warms up quickly enough when action starts. On the other hand, later in the day—after a meal, say—they'll be tired out from doing nothing. Most likely, they'll be at small odds, one with the other over small disagreements. A dozen different little things will have put them out of the mood to go instantly and eagerly into battle together. Add to that a sudden reverse of some kind, which disheartens them and also scrambles their wits, so that things seem to have gone much awry; and we might well have a group in some confusion, and that much more likely to be overridden and conquered."

"You know," said Jim, "you're right, Brian. You've put your finger on it. What's most needed will be something happening that's the last thing they expect. We need to attack them; not them us. And we ought to not only do it at a time when they least expect, but contrive something that will really throw them into disorder."

He thought of the cleared area behind his own castle. Like the cleared area before, it had been essentially a matter of taking out the trees down to a few stump-ends, at most, and letting the grass and normal ground cover grow back now that it was out of the shade. This time of year, the grass would be going dormant again, and the ground would be hard. Good conditions—aside from those few stumps—for a cavalry charge at a stationary enemy. His mind began to work, as if it had newly woken up.

"There's another angle to this," he said, thinking aloud once more. "Why is Malvinne doing this?"

"Revenge," grunted Brian, "on you, James. What other reason could he have?"

"That's reason enough, I suppose," said Jim. "I've cost him everything he had; and had a hand in upsetting his best-laid plan as well as forcing him to disappoint the Dark Powers. But it seems to me that someone like Malvinne would go for more than just revenge. He'd try to get his revenge, yes; but also with it some advantage that would help him climb back to the power and position he had originally."

"Of course," said Brian, "if he captured you alive, he could take you back to France, either to hold for ransom, or even to be tried for some crime under French law. Something that would lose you all that you had gained in the eyes of French and English alike by ending the battle on a truce. Perhaps he hopes to reconcile himself with King Jean."

"Yes," said Jim thoughtfully, "this arrangement has to be set up to take me, and perhaps you and Dafydd as well, prisoners—rather than kill us. Even my charges against him at the Accounting Office will look weaker, if they come from someone being held prisoner by the very one he charged."

"They'd not find against you, surely?" said Dafydd, who had been standing by throughout this. "Since they will make their decision upon the facts of the matter, not upon how things look."

"I wouldn't think so," said Jim. "But now that the subject's come up it's something I'd like to ask Carolinus about—if he were here. However, you were saying something about these knights, or whatever they are, of Malvinne's being thrown into confusion by something unexpected. They're dressed and armed to fight from horseback; and undoubtedly will have their horses with them. Granted, they're more heavily armed and protected than our men. But what if they had to fight on foot, and our men-at-arms still had their horses, and light lances? Could something be done by our men against theirs then, do you think?"

Jim looked at Brian.

An evil gleam kindled itself in Brian's eyes.

"Most assuredly, James," he said. "The very armor of Malvinne's men would hamper them, on foot; whereas our light-armored men-at-arms on their horses would be able to run them down with their lances with little trouble. But how do you mean to deprive Malvinne's men of their horses?"

"I just had a thought," said Jim. "We don't want to finish riding to the castle this afternoon, in any case, do we?" He did not wait, for agreement was obvious. "If we hide ourselves along the edge of the woods, but well within it, we can watch, this evening, which is only a few hours off, when they return to the castle. We can count their numbers accurately, as well as getting an idea of what kind of opponents we face. Meanwhile, Wat can go on scouring the neighborhood for bowmen, or anybody else who can fight with us. I've no idea whether he'll find anyone or not—"

"Think not you that," said Brian. "You are already known as a good master, in your household and on all your lands. The word has come back to me. I would venture to say we'll get at least half a hundred men of all ages and description— though how many of these may be useful, I don't know. But do you have further thoughts, James?"

"Yes," said Jim, "see what you think of this. We stay hidden this afternoon and tonight. At night, particularly with the help of local people who know how to move in the woods, we shift around to the woods behind the castle, where we spread our men out in a semicircle; so that they can come at all of Malvinne's people behind the castle at once, from many angles. Meanwhile we'll investigate the manner in which the horses are tied, while they are waiting during the day. It may be that there is something we can do to weaken the means that holds them to their tethers—in such a way that Malvinne's men on the morrow will not realize that the holding of their horses has been weakened."

"Good idea, that," commented Brian.

"Then," went on Jim, "sometime tomorrow we do something to alarm their tied-up horses, so that they break loose. Then we do the best we can to herd them into the woods, or at least away from Malvinne's men. Then the rest of us charge on horseback from the woods, and see what we can do against the men on foot."

"It's a good plan, James!" said Brian. "Fine, indeed. But, how do you plan to frighten their horses into pulling themselves free and running off? Were you perhaps thinking of changing yourself into a dragon and flying suddenly down upon them? That would cause any group of horses to flee."

"I'm afraid we can't use that way," said Jim. "I may not have made it clear; but Malvinne isn't the only magician without magic. I'm another. I was only a D-class magician to begin with, with a small balance in the Accounting Office. I used it up in France fairly early."

"But," Brian stared at him. "The magic in the castle—the invisibility—"

"Thank Carolinus," said Jim. "He allowed me to charge things against his own account temporarily."

"You mean," demanded Brian, "you can work no magic at all now, James?"

"I can work magic," said Jim, "but nothing will happen, because I've got nothing in my account with the Accounting Office to make it work. So my turning myself into a dragon, for the moment at least, is impossible. I can do no more than any one of us can do in our own proper bodies."

"That's a singular damn uncomfortable state of affairs!" said Brian thoughtfully, rubbing the stiff, light brown stubble that had sprouted on the lower half of his face. "I can think of no other way at the moment to frighten those horses enough to make them pull loose and run."

"All horses are afraid of fire," said Jim, "particularly those that are fastened and can't run from it. What if we began matters by having several of our men gallop from the woods near one end of the castle, towing bundles of twigs set on fire behind them? If they came suddenly and went fast, the armored men wouldn't have time to stop them. The burning bundles would frighten the horses by themselves, and the grass out there is long and dry at this time of year. Almost certainly, we could start it to burning, that way—or at least to smoldering. That'd not only scare the horses but give Malvinne's men something to think about."

"By Saint Dunstan!" said Brian. "I think you've something there that could set them all about just as we charge, James!"

He glanced up at the sun for a second.

"There're at least three hours until sunset," he went on. "For my part, I can't wait to get behind that castle of yours and discover how their horses are fastened. But it's best we wait where we are until we've seen them return inside, counted their numbers, and learned what we can from that view of them. I vow it will not be easy to wait!"

"For myself," said Dafydd, "there will be much to do, with our own bowmen and with those Wat may find."

As it happened, recruits from the countryside began arriving almost as Dafydd was saying this. Wat had evidently followed the sensible course of setting up headquarters at the first stopping place he had come to, and sending out messengers from there in every direction.

Jim was amazed at the number of these as they continued to come in. He was forced once more to realize something that he had failed to appreciate fully, about this world that was his home nowadays.

He was quite familiar with the fact that the knights loved to fight; and that the men-at-arms and bowmen were not far behind them in that respect. Once fired up, they were not stopped easily. But it had never really struck him that the friendly and subservient plowmen, woodchoppers, and general workers of this land he owned as the Lord of Malencontri, would share this same cheerful joy at the prospect of what might well be a deadly battle.

Young and old, they came in, from boys no more than eight or nine to white-bearded, stooped, old men stiff with arthritis, with knives at their belts and carrying scythes, mattocks, axes and—if nothing else—plain wooden clubs.

Most of them were not going to be of much use against fully armored and experienced warriors, even if these latter were fighting on foot rather than on horseback. Nonetheless, Jim's heart was curiously touched and his spirits warmed by the eager response of his local people. It was, he gathered, partially attributable to the fact that he was considered to be such a good Lord—although he had never thought of himself as being anything unusual that way.

Apparently, simply not misusing them was enough to get them to consider him to be good. But of even more importance was the fact that they literally could hardly wait to get into a fight. It was mind-boggling to someone from the twentieth century. Apparently, a battle of any kind was excitement—like a latter-day circus or parade—and excitements of any kind were rare bright spots in the lives of most.

These, plus the men-at-arms and archers, spread themselves out among the trees facing the castle, far enough back in the shadow of the trees, so that they could not be seen watching. The sun descended; and just at sunset the two bodies of Malvinne's armored horsemen rode into sight around the two opposite ends of the castle, approached the drawbridge, which was down, and clattered up it and through the gate into the castle courtyard.

"Eighty men, all right," said Brian as the last one disappeared into the shadow of the gate.

"Did I not say so?" snarled Aargh.

"Indeed you did, Sir Wolf," said Brian, "and it was not that I did not trust your counting, but that I had to see for myself—not so much their numbers, but what armor and weapons they wore, and how they rode. These are no ragtag troops, James. They are all veterans and used to the saddle. They will be as used to their weapons when the time comes."

"I didn't have much hope they wouldn't be," said Jim gloomily.

"Nor did I," said Brian. "But, on the bright side, did you also notice that while they rode together, they rode in no particularly comradely fashion? Either they have little love for each other; or the day's waiting, as I suggested, has worn them down to where they will need food and drink to thaw out their good humor."

The drawbridge was pulled up.

"Now," said Brian, "the quicker we move to the back of the castle while there is still light to examine the ground, the better. We'll be in shadow from the castle itself there, which will help to cloak us, but may hide some aspect of the ground as well."

They moved, accordingly, to the trees fringing the cleared ground behind the castle. Here, not only was most of the ground in shadow from the castle itself, but by and large the back of Malencontri was one massive wall of stone, affording few lookout points, except from the battlements at the top.

Jim, Brian, and Dafydd, stripped of armor and weapons, and looking as much as possible like locals, moved out to inspect the open space where Malvinne's forces would be hiding in the daytime. They wandered in no particular pattern, but covered the ground thoroughly. There was nothing surprising in their presence, if they were seen from the castle; since it was only to be expected that some of the poorer common sort would comb the ground where their betters had spent the day, hoping to pick up something of value or use that might have been lost or thrown aside.

A low whistle from Brian caught Jim's attention. He looked over to see Brian surreptitiously beckoning him, and went to join the other knight.
Brian was bent over a patch of trampled grass, that was very obviously where the horses had been.

"See," he said to Jim under his breath, "their horses are but tied to pegs driven into the ground. It should be possible to scrape away a little earth where peg meets ground, cut part-through the peg and then push the dirt back. That way the peg should hold against any ordinary tug from the horse, but will be easy to break if the animal is really frightened. Let's wait until the darkness is a little deeper, and spend the time marking the position of the pegs. Then we can work on them when we have full night to hide us from any watchman's eyes."

They did so; and about half an hour later a full fifteen hidden figures—Jim, Brian, Dafydd and a number of the new recruits—were busy with knives, more by feel than otherwise, cutting partway through the stakes and then hiding the cut with a thin covering of earth.

They were done, and retreated into the woods before moonlight should show them still down there. It was not customary for the ordinary sort to leave their houses after dark—as much for the need to wake with the sunrise and begin work, as to hide from superstitious fears of what the night might threaten.

Into their small homes the locals took the bowmen and the men-at-arms. Brian, Jim, and Dafydd chose to camp out around a fire in the woods, far enough away and masked enough by trees that the flames would not be seen from the castle. None of the little dwelling places that had accepted those of lesser rank had quarters that Brian considered respectable for a knight to use; and besides, with the three of them isolated this way, they could discuss plans in privacy.

Jim had his own private reasons for not stepping into one of the huts of his own people. Those same huts would be alive with fleas, lice, and other vermin. He had not stayed completely clear of such on his trip to France and back; but he wanted to keep himself as clean as possible until he was able to get into the castle, have his clothes thoroughly boiled and cleaned, and take a bath in the privacy of his quarters with Angie.

The evening was still busy with people coming and going. The bundles of twigs that were to be set on fire had to be made. Dafydd also had specific instructions to give his bowmen. He had managed to pick at least a dozen passable archers out of the thirty or forty who had presented themselves. The job of these would be mainly to keep any bowmen or crossbowmen on the battlements from shooting down into the crowd below once the attack started. At least they could encourage the marksmen above to keep their heads down. The chief men-at-arms also had to be given specific orders.

Still and all, by what Jim judged to be something like ten o'clock, everyone was gone. The fire had burned down, well on its way toward becoming a bed of embers. The three rolled themselves in saddle blankets, and both Dafydd and Brian dropped off, as if tomorrow were to be no different than any other day. It was a knack that Jim had remarked and envied in them before this.

In his own case, he lay awake for some little time, thinking not so much about the fight, as about the conditions under which Angie was being kept in the castle as a prisoner. Comforting himself finally with the belief that it would not pay Malvinne to abuse the three women of the castle until he knew that Jim and his two Companions were firmly in his grasp, he finally fell asleep.

He woke, like the rest, at daybreak. They had barely got their campfire going to warm themselves, when several of Jim's locals brought them food and homemade beer for breakfast. Jim, to his own surprise, was as ravenously hungry as Dafydd and Brian seemed always to be. He told himself that perhaps he was beginning to fall into the pattern of things here, after all.

They filled their saddle flasks with beer, and tied packages of some of the food, that would not spoil too quickly, to their saddles; and set about getting their forces in position. This, Brian had emphasized, needed to be done before the armed horsemen came out from the castle, so that no noise or movement should attract attention from either them or the castle beyond.

In due time, the unsuspecting foes came, dismounted, tied their horses to the pegs in the ground, and settled down to a number of games, running from dice to a sort of crude form of chess.

And the hard part began.

Now, as Brian had emphasized the night before, they must wait until the knights, men-at-arms, or whoever Malvinne's fighting men were, should have settled down to what they thought was another weary day of waiting. The wait, this time, was almost as hard on those hidden in the woods around them as on the heavily armored men themselves.

Almost, but not quite. For one thing, those waiting in the woods were in shade, and had relative freedom of movement. The men stationed behind the castle cursed the sunlight loudly and hunted small patches of shade as the sun rose and the shadow cast by the castle dwindled.

Then, finally, came the moment Brian had been waiting for. At midday, servants came out from the castle, bearing a meal for the armed men. To the satisfaction of everyone watching, those being fed ate heartily. Not only was there no need to stint themselves, but clearly they did not expect Jim, Brian, Dafydd, and the rest to show up until somewhere between midafternoon and the end of the day.

Sated at last, they lolled around on the grass, too full even to continue the games with which they had been killing time. Brian—who was the natural field commander, accepted as such by everyone from Jim on down—sent word to those hidden in the semicircle of the enclosing woods to be ready.

Chapter 43

As the armed and armored men,
sated, dozed in the sun that now afforded them no patches of shade at all behind
the castle, the raucous challenge of a cock pheasant sounded from the woods
beyond the right end of the castle. It was answered almost immediately by a
counter-challenge from the woods at the west end.

Suddenly, three galloping horses, their pace hardly lessened by the bundle of
blazing twigs each was dragging behind it, raced from each end of the enclosing
woods; and came at full speed across the open space, toward each other and the
pegged-down horses.

Malvinne's warriors, drowsing on the ground, started up on their elbows, then
began clumsily to scramble to their feet. By the time most of them had made it,
the six horsemen had passed each other, and the dead brown grass over which
they had dragged the burning twigs was alight. The tied-down horses were
screaming in fright, breaking loose from the pegs and running off in all
directions.

By now the galloping riders were lost in the trees again, each having
thoughtfully cut loose and left behind his burning bundle of twigs. The tethered
horses were also gone.

The dry grass burned merrily, setting up a fair amount of smoke; not enough to obscure the field, but enough to get into the noses and eyes of the warriors and make both run with water. While they were still trying to get themselves into some sort of order, a new thunder of hooves attracted their attention, and more horsemen burst on them from the woods all around.

But these were not unarmed locals—as the riders of the first six horses had been. These were men-at-arms in light armor, with lances, who drove straight for their targets. The targets were those who had just lost their own horses; and scramble as they might to get out of the way and draw their swords, two-thirds of Malvinne's fighters were flat on the ground in minutes, seeing knife-points at their visors and hearing demands to yield.

Fifteen or twenty were still on their feet, and had drawn together into a tight clump, with shields up and weapons ready, in a formidable, hedgehog sort of defense that should not have been as easy to flatten as the individual men had been.

Nonetheless, even the impact of a lance held by a horseman in light armor, riding a relatively light horse, was effective. Those in the outer ring of the hedgehog went down, or were only upheld by their comrades.

Eventually, the hedgehog was split into pieces. At this point Jim and Brian ceased being field generals and entered the fight at first hand. The disheartened men they encountered as they charged on horseback, were in no condition to resist them. It was not long before no warrior of Malvinne's was standing. Meanwhile, overhead, crossbows had begun to shoot from the walls, and archers outside had begun to shoot back.

Thanks more to the wizardlike archery of Dafydd and his three superb original recruits, than to the skill of the bowmen they had picked up in the field before coming back and the homegrown ones, who—most of them—had never shot at anything much larger than a rabbit before, an end was put to this. Those shooting from the castle were either hurt, killed, or cowed into ceasing.

Brian looked about the field of recumbent bodies.

"Who is leader here?" he shouted.

One heavily armed figure struggled wearily to its feet.

"I, Charles Bracy du Mont," he croaked.

"Do you and your men all yield, or do we start cutting throats?" shouted Brian.

It was no idle threat. The locals who had gathered to Jim's aid, had now emerged from the trees in a number of a hundred or more, all with their knives out, and eager expressions on their faces.

"I . . . yield," said Bracy du Mont.

"And your men?" This time it was Jim, speaking sharply.

"And all those with me," said the other exhaustedly, slumping as he stood.

"Disarm them and bind their hands behind them!" ordered Brian. Bracy du Mont's head came up sharply.

"How?" he shouted. "Tie us up? I, and most here are belted knights! We give our parole!"

"Knights who fight in the service of the Dark Powers have no parole," said Brian. "Tie them all up!"

"And now?" asked Jim of Brian, as the last of the captured men able to walk were trussed up and gathered together.

"Now, we march them, tied, around to the front of the castle," answered Brian grimly. "It's my guess these were the greatest part of Malvinne's force—and Dafydd's bowmen have silenced those upon the battlements. Let's see if, now, Malvinne has sense enough to surrender the castle to us—"

Brian's words were broken into suddenly by an interruption that certainly would have caused a great deal of consternation, if most of those on the field behind the castle had not been too busy to see it approaching. Secoh landed with a thump about fifteen feet in front of Jim.

"Jim!" he cried joyfully, as a couple of arrows aimed by the less expert local bowmen flew past him, happily at a distance that could be unremarked by Secoh. "It's good to see you! On behalf of the mere-dragons I officially bring you their welcome home!"

"Well . . . thank them," said Jim, just beginning to get himself back together again after the shock of Secoh's sudden arrival. "They must have really moved to get together and agree on that resolution in the short time I've been back."

"Well," said Secoh, "actually, they haven't had time for that, yet. So I took it on myself to deliver the message, anyway. And the Cliffside Dragons want to know why you've been back in the neighborhood for more than twenty hours and still haven't returned their passport to them."

"Are they insane, dragon?" exploded Brian. "We've been far too busy to think of passports!"

"Exactly what I said to them myself," answered Secoh. "But you know how it is, each dragon's favorite jewel, and all . . . If you'd give me the passport right now, Jim, I could fly it off to them without any more delay."

"He'll do no such thing—" Brian was beginning, in what appeared to be a fine fury, when Jim put a hand on his arm to check his words.

"I think I'd better, Brian," said Jim. "It'll just take a few minutes.

"If you don't mind," he said to Brian, Dafydd, and everybody else within hearing, "I'm going to need privacy—I mean I'll need to be privy—for this. Because it has to do with magic, you see."

"But Jim," said Brian, "I thought you told us that your magic—"

He checked himself this time; and just in time too, in Jim's estimation.

"This is a special case, Brian," said Jim. "I'll be back in a moment."

He went off into the trees. He had actually wondered himself, the evening after talking to Carolinus on the battlefield in France, why, if Carolinus had been correct in saying that Jim had only been drawing on his account to do his magic, he would still have the ability to shrink down the passport into a size small enough for him to swallow. But the spell had still worked. The only solution he had been able to think of was that in this one particular case he was still being allowed the use of Carolinus's magic account.

Now, among the shadows of the trees, after some moments trying to recall the exact procedure, he was able to cough up the passport in pill form. It grew quickly of its own accord to the size of the full sack of jewels he had been given originally; and he carried this, in both arms, back to give to Secoh.

"I think it was wise of you to give me the passport back now, James," Secoh said, taking it gratefully. "I'll take it right to Cliffside—er, just a moment. My own jewel contribution, you know."

He placed the sack on the ground, untied the top, and reached down inside. He groped around for several moments, with a definitely worried look on his face, which suddenly gave way to bright cheerfulness. His arm emerged with his claw clutching the pearl he had originally donated.

"Excellent!" he said, looking at it. He tucked it into one cheek of his long lower jaw, hastily retied the top of the sack and spread his wings. "I'll see you very soon, James!"

He took off, mounted quickly until he caught a high thermal, and glided away in the direction of Cliffside.

"Well now," said Brian, in none too pleased a voice, "if that's over, perhaps we can get these prisoners moved around to the front of the castle?"

"By all means," answered Jim hastily.

They began their march around the castle. By natural right, Jim, Brian, and Dafydd led. Behind them, the bulk of the experienced men-at-arms and archers went before the prisoners, who moved in a sort of ragged, four-abreast column, followed by the straggling host of local volunteers, their knives out and ready—just in case.

They came around the northeastern end of the castle. The drawbridge was down, and Malvinne was standing on the ground in front of it, with a figure all in plate armor, its visor down, shield on one arm, and a mace in the other. Behind these two, stretching up the gangplank and through the gateway behind to the interior courtyard, were several more ranks of such weaponed and armored fighters as they had just vanquished behind the castle. They all appeared to be simply waiting for the arrival of Jim, Brian, Dafydd, and the rest.

The whole affair took on an almost organized, if not formal, appearance. On their horses, the first three led the rest at a walk, out, around, and back in again, so that they ended with Jim, Brian, and Dafydd seated on their horses with their column behind them. The three were about ten feet in front of Malvinne and the silent, ominously armored and armed, figure beside him.

While the sky was not overcast this day, it was plentifully supplied with clouds, and no sunlight was striking directly on the scene. The dulled light gave the motionless metal figure beside Malvinne a heavy glint.

"James," said Brian under his breath, and keeping his gaze fixed straight ahead on Malvinne, "I fear me that from here on you must command and do the speaking."

"I'd planned to," said Jim harshly, without making any attempt to lower his voice. He was thinking of Angie and the others, prisoners somewhere in the castle.

He dismounted from his horse. Following his lead, Brian and Dafydd dismounted with him and came forward.

"You planned what, James?" said Malvinne as he halted a couple of steps in front of the other magician.

"I plan to have you out of this castle of mine very quickly," said Jim. Now that he was face-to-face with Malvinne, he found himself coldly angry. What right had this defrocked AAA magician to go around acting as if he could make his own rules?

"*Your* castle, James?" said Malvinne, cocking a head at him like an interested bird. "I believe you inhabited it only a short while."

"Nonetheless," said Jim, "it's mine—on a grant from King Edward."

"Hmmm," said Malvinne thoughtfully. "Would it interest you to know that there's another paper taking it away from you, in London right now, just waiting for the King's signature? You know that under certain conditions he'll sign just about anything, just to be left alone?"

"Why should I believe that?" said Jim. "And if I did, what's it got to do with the situation here? You're occupying my castle and I want you out. Out—and any damage you've done to it or harm to the people in it, I'll hold you to account for!"

"You're thinking perhaps of our meeting shortly at the request of the Accounting Office?" said Malvinne. "You might stop to consider that those charges you made may look a little flimsy, when it's understood that they're made by a man who's my prisoner."

"I'm not your prisoner," said Jim.

"Ah, but you will be," responded Malvinne. "As I was saying—they might sound like an attempt by a very weak, young magician to defend himself in a bad situation by accusing a senior practitioner of the Art in order to divert attention from his own situation."

"I don't believe the Accounting Office works that way," said Jim becoming a little weary of this chitchat. "In any case, as I said, I'm not your prisoner."

"But, as *I* said, I think you will be," said Malvinne. His voice took on formal tones. "Now, before the people here assembled, I charge you with having lied about me, both as regards the charges and on many other occasions."

Jim felt a sudden sense of something wrong, which pushed the earlier cold anger from him. What Malvinne had just done, in the terms of this world, was issue the kind of personal challenge one knight would issue to another. Jim himself was of course a knight; and most undoubtedly the other had been knighted somewhere along the way, or at least ennobled, so that he was of the gentlemanly class in a temporal sense.

"You're challenging me?" he echoed, hoping to prod the other into providing a little more information.

"Yes, I am," said Malvinne. "Well—not I exactly, since I'm elderly. So I'll make use of the fact I'm a magician, and therefore of the class entitled to choose a Champion to fight for me. In fact I've already done so. My Champion is here beside me."

He turned to the silent, metallic, visored figure beside him.

"Are you not at my side now, my Champion?" he inquired.

The figure slowly raised its visor; and Jim stared.

The face was one he had seen only once before, but would never forget. It was the face of the man he thought still running and hiding on the continent. The face of Sir Hugh de Bois de Malencontri, whom he had last faced on a spit of land reaching out to the Loathly Tower, more than a year ago, after Secoh had been tricked by Sir Hugh into calling Jim down to where Sir Hugh's crossbowmen could cover him with their weapons.

"I am here, and I am your Champion," said the square, heavy-boned face revealed by the visor. He smiled, not pleasantly. "Nor am I something made of snow, Sir James, as you may be thinking. It is I, myself, standing in front of the castle that was my own, and shortly will be my own again with the signature of the King on that paper in London, once it has been proved that you are Malvinne's prisoner. For we are now to have a trial by battle, and it shall be God's"—the word took a bitter twist in Sir Hugh's mouth—"will, that you show yourself a false and recreant knight, with no claim either to your spurs or to this land and castle!"

He had been stripping off one of his gauntlets as he spoke; and as he finished he flung it in Jim's face.

Jim made a sudden discovery. It was why people who have gauntlets flung in their face by way of challenge tend thereafter to be eager immediately to take up the challenge. The metal-reinforced glove struck Jim in the face like a weapon. Suddenly, his nose was bleeding, a bad cut on his lip was bleeding, and it felt as if one of his teeth had been knocked loose. The only thing in his mind, abruptly, was getting down to business with Sir Hugh as quickly as possible.

But the glove had fallen from his face to the ground before him; and before he could pick it up, Brian had caught him by one arm and dragged him back enough steps so that he could speak to him in a voice so low that Malvinne and Sir Hugh could not overhear.

"James!" Brian sounded almost as if he would shake Jim out of his present explosion of emotion. "James! Listen to me! You cannot fight Sir Hugh! Hear me, you cannot fight him. You are a magician yourself, even if less in rank than Malvinne, but equally entitled to choose a Champion. I will be your Champion. I must pick up that glove for you. Do not touch it yourself!"

"The hell you will!" said Jim a little thickly through an already swelling upper lip. "I'm going to cut that bastard into so many pieces—"

"If you could, I'd be all for it!" said Brian, still in the same low, urgent tone of voice. "But listen to me Jim! This is Brian, who has been teaching you to fight all this last winter. I tell you, you stand no more chance against Sir Hugh, than a child against the Lancelot of legend, himself. He is a knight of great experience. I agree with you—he's a bastard. But, he is nonetheless a bastard who is one of the best fighters I know. I trust in God above all things, but I will not tempt God this time by letting you go out to fight him. As a trial by combat, this is a farce! Do you hear me, Jim?"

"I hear you," growled Jim, licking the blood from his cut lip, "but listen to me, Brian. I, and nobody else, am going to fight him!"

"James, if you love me—" Brian was beginning, as Jim pushed him aside, strode forward, and reached down to scoop up Sir Hugh's glove. He held it firmly in his hands and grinned bloodily at Sir Hugh.

"I accept this challenge in my own right, in God's name!" he said, using the formula that he had learned from Sir Brian months ago.

Chapter 44

The common folk were delighted. There was going to be a circus after all. Or, if not a circus, the next thing to it, which was an official combat between two knights, one of which was their own Lord, Sir James, who stood high in their affection.

People like themselves ordinarily never had a chance to see any such legal combat. This would be something to tell their grandchildren about; even though, under the circumstances, most of the usual procedure involved in such a combat would be missing.

The important element remained, that two knights were about to hack in deadly fashion at each other in front of all spectators; and the winner would be adjudged to have been chosen by God to have the right on his side.

Two temporary tents had been put up; not so much for preparation of the two knights to be so engaged, or provisioned for quick surgery, or whatever other crude medical help could be given either one if they were specially wounded, but to follow the pattern of such things.

As a result, Brian had Jim by himself for a little bit, and during that time in the tent was busily giving him instructions on how to fight the battle.

"You were a fool James, to pick up that gauntlet," he said. "But there, let it be.

Clearly it was God's will that you and you alone should fight Sir Hugh at this time instead of myself."

Brian crossed himself.

"No one has greater faith in the Divine Will than myself," he said, "but you will need something like a miracle, James, to win this with Sir Hugh. Now, attend me closely."

Jim's initial fury had calmed down. He still was coldly determined to go out and do the best he could to chop Sir Hugh into little pieces, but he was now calm enough to recognize the common sense in what Brian was saying and be ready to listen.

He was only too aware of his own inadequacies as far as being able to handle the weapons of the fourteenth century; and he most thoroughly believed Brian, when the other told him that Sir Hugh would be a very accomplished opponent to meet.

"Go ahead, Brian," he said, having cleaned his face with a wet cloth. The tooth was not quite as loose as he thought it might be. Hopefully, it would grow solidly back into its socket. "I'm ready to hear anything you've got to tell me. So go ahead. What's the best way for me to fight him?"

"Good, James," said Brian. "Going into such a battle all hot and unthinking is the worst way to do it. Sir Hugh will certainly not be hotheaded when he steps out there, and neither should you be. Now, let's look at the situation as it stands. You are a novice, in spite of a few small bickers like the one at the relieving of my castle. To all intents and purposes, you should be a plaything in Hugh's hands. However, he is not without his own faults, which you may find advantage in."

"For example?" asked Jim.

"I was just about to list them," said Brian. "Let's look first at what we have. You've little skill with weapons, but you're both young and strong. Sir Hugh has great skill with weapons, and is also strong, but somewhat older. Also he is twenty-five to thirty pounds heavier. Much of that will be in muscle—which is a reason for you to avoid his blows as much as possible—but some will be fat. Finally, we have your one main advantage, which is that you are unusually quick of movement. James, by sheer movement, you may evade most of his blows, or even draw Sir Hugh into a trap where his sword will be out of position and you will be in position to strike."

"Go on," said Jim.

"He will prefer to use the mace he was carrying just now," said Brian. "That, with his weight of arm, will make him very dangerous indeed if he can get a blow home, even upon plate armor. A shield will not long stand up to a mace. Also, be your helm never so well padded, a solid blow from a mace can kill you. They have not yet picked a marshal of the field to carry the baton, and cast it down when the combat is to cease. However, they will assuredly do so, since it is Malvinne's announced intent to take you prisoner, rather than get you killed. This gives you one other, small advantage. You are free to kill Sir Hugh if you have the chance. But he will try to avoid killing you—that is, unless in the heat of combat his own feelings run away with him."

"And those are all the advantages I have?" demanded Jim.

"Patience, James," said Brian, "I was just about to say more of your advantages. In a nutshell, Sir Hugh's are weight and experience. In a nutshell, yours are youth, speed, and agility. You have never mastered making a running mount on your horse. But I've already seen you leap higher than I will ever hope to do. So, the way you should fight this combat, is to avoid Sir Hugh's blows, make him follow you around, tire him out, and only then move in on him."

"It's that mace—" Jim was beginning, when Brian interrupted him.

"We will try and make him discard the mace for another weapon," Brian said. "Let me announce that you are carrying my long, two-handed sword."

"That?" said Jim.

He had never liked his practice with the two-handed sword. To his way of thinking it was large and clumsy. Also Sir Brian favored a basic position that seemed to Jim very awkward indeed.

You took hold of the sword hilt with both hands as if you were going to chop with it like an ax. But, instead of advancing against your enemy with it held out before you directly, you held it firmly, but with your hands level with your forehead and the blade in a point-down position vertically parallel to your body.

Brian swore that particular position, in spite of its awkward appearance, allowed you to ward off blows quickly from any direction; and also to strike out at either leg or head of your opponent without warning. Jim had practiced it and had to admit there was some truth in what Brian said. But he still thought there must be a better way of using the weapon.

"Why the two-handed?" he asked Brian.

"Because it greatly increases your reach—and your arms have several inches advantage on Hugh de Bois already," said Brian. "The result being that if you were to use the two-handed and he stayed with his mace, he would be at a disadvantage reaching you. In effect, you could strike him, while still out of reach yourself. Also, it saves you the weight of a shield; which, since the object is to tire him down, will be a considerable advantage."

"I understand that, all right," said Jim, still dubious.

"But he will not hold to his mace, when he sees you," Brian went on as if Jim had not spoken. "He also will change to a two-handed sword."

"Ah," said Jim, beginning to see the glimmer of an advantage in this.

"The end result," said Brian, "is that he will move from the area of his strength into the area of yours."

"Ah," said Jim again.

"Whether he is as well schooled in the two-handed sword, we cannot tell," Brian went on. "In any case, your plan must be to stay away from him and work with your sword both on his sword arm and on his legs. The two-handed is not like a broadsword which you can shift to another hand, if the arm holding it becomes hurt. You will be without shield. So remember, rely on your speed and your agility, James, and you've at least a chance!"

Jim's spirits were beginning to rise. To begin with he had been merely obsessed with fury. Then, as Brian had started to talk, doubt had begun to creep in. Now that doubt had moved away from him. He did have faith in what his own legs could do—more so, even, than Brian knew.

"Now we will get you armored, armed, and ready, James," said Brian.

Twenty minutes later the two of them emerged from the tent to find that Theoluf and one of Malvinne's plate-armored men had been named as wardens of the lists. They were each holding a small rod of freshly cut wood as batons. They were also scowling at each other from opposite sides of what was to be the field of battle, which had been roped off from the spectators.

Under ordinary conditions, a stand would have been arranged to seat the officials and the principals watching the fight. But since no such thing was available at Malencontri, at the center of the field, on the side before the castle, there was a cluster of individuals around Carolinus; who had appeared, complete with a staff as tall as himself, and holding a third baton in his other hand.

Jim and Brian went toward him. Sir Hugh was already there. Carolinus had evidently simply shown up and taken up the position of judge without anyone asking him to hold it. Malvinne was still protesting this as they went over.

"You do not trust a fellow magician, Malvinne?" Carolinus was saying.

Malvinne sputtered.

"You know what I mean!" he was saying. "You are as biased in this matter as I am!"

"I don't see why I should be, Stinky," said Carolinus, quite calmly. "It's true that one of the contestants is a pupil of mine; but the honor of a mage of my rank can surely disregard that. Besides, where are you going to find anyone else to fill this role? Anyone under the influence of the Dark Powers would not be acceptable in a trial before God; and no godly person would perform the service for you, particularly since you're under charges by the Accounting Office. I think you're stuck with me."

"Very well!" said Malvinne malevolently. "But I'm going to report any partisanship of yours when I face my charges."

"Report away, Stinky," said Carolinus, "and meanwhile, you might get out of my way so that I can see the field and the contestant with his associate approaching."

His last words had the result of directing everybody's attention to Brian and Jim as they came up.

It was a time for ritual questions and answers. Jim gave the proper response.

"I will bear a two-handed sword only," he announced.

"Very good," said Carolinus. "That is accepted. Your opponent has requested that there be no fighting on horseback. Will you agree to this?"

Jim was only too ready to agree to this, and he knew that Brian beside him felt exactly the same way. Jim's weakest point was jousting. He also knew why Malvinne had suggested it. On foot, it might be possible for Sir Hugh to knock him unconscious or make him yield. But with lance on horseback, there was no way that Sir Hugh would be able to judge between a use of his weapon that would kill, or only just disable. As Brian had reminded Jim, Malvinne wanted him in the shape of a prisoner.

"I am agreeable," said Jim.

Carolinus turned to Sir Hugh.

"And I understand you will be carrying mace and shield?" he asked the former Lord of Malencontri.

"No," said Sir Hugh, with a grim smile at Jim. "So as not to seem to take any advantage, I will give up my shield and carry, as he does, a two-handed sword only."

"Excellent," said Carolinus in that same cold, official voice. "You may now retire to opposite ends of the lists. The marshals will be instructed to hold up their batons. When they allow their arms holding the batons to fall, you may start walking toward each other. After that, may God defend the right!"

Jim turned away, Brian still beside him, and began heading toward the eastern end of the list. He had turned without thinking, perfectly automatically, but it was well he did. Sir Hugh's slight pause, while he got rid of his mace and had it replaced by a two-handed sword, had given Jim the chance to take the end of the list that would put the sun at his back.

Shortly now, the sun would be straight overhead, in any case; and there would probably be little difference in who started where. Besides, as they moved around, Jim might well find himself facing east whether he wanted to or not. Nonetheless, for the moment it was another small advantage.

In spite of the clouds, the day *was* warming.

For some strange reason they had had good weather not only in England but during the crossing to France and while they were in France itself. Now, once more back in England, the weather was still good. Jim wondered idly, as he plodded toward the far end of the list, if the Dark Powers had something to do with this. Or was something as large as weather beyond their control?

He reached the end of the list and turned. Sir Hugh was still walking toward his end. A moment later, he reached it, and turned to face Jim. They were now about fifty yards apart. The marshals lifted their arms simultaneously, so that they held the batons up over their heads. Then, at a word from Carolinus, they dropped them.

Jim began the long walk toward his opponent.

Sir Hugh was also approaching him. The other was carrying, Jim saw, his own two-handed sword in the same position of readiness that Jim was carrying his.

The great sword did not look awkward, held in that position by Sir Hugh. Rather it looked merely comfortable, as if long practice had trained the other to carry it that way. For a moment Jim felt a fear that the very way he was holding his sword would give his inexperience away to Hugh. Then he shoved this thought from his mind and concentrated on more immediate things.

He put his mind to thinking about the various moves he could remember from his twentieth-century days, playing volleyball and basketball. He had been a natural at both. Right now he was trying to think which moves, if any, would prove useful to him in this coming bout.

One thing that would come in handy, he thought, would be the fact that he had learned to fake an opponent out with a move of his body, without moving his feet. Also, Sir Hugh might not be familiar with the sidestep and sudden spin that could bring him partway around on the flank of an opponent before the other could realize what was happening. He looked ahead.

Sir Hugh had grown considerably in the scene before him. They were getting very close together. Now they were only a few steps apart. As they stepped within reach of each other's weapons, without warning Sir Hugh let go of his hilt, dropped his weapon, then crouched, and caught it again a good eight inches lower. With the point now barely above the ground, he lunged upward, driving that point toward Jim's helmet.

The only thing that saved Jim in this moment was the fact that he had already made up his mind to feint right with his body, but with his feet in place, then execute the quick sidestep and spin, after the basketball motion he had been thinking of. Consequently, he was already in motion when Sir Hugh began his lunge, and the sharp point of the long sword licked empty air. Thinking that the other was wide open for a return blow, Jim commenced a swing with his blade at Sir Hugh's near shoulder.

But Sir Hugh, still in the crouching position, managed to pivot and, raising his sword into blade-up guard position, was able to block most of the force of the blow; so that only the tip of Jim's blade licked against the metal of his shoulder. A shout went up from the locals, who counted this, clearly, as an effective hit. Jim, himself, knew it had not been. He stepped swiftly backward as Sir Hugh's blade glanced off his own in the guard position, and drove once more at Jim's helm.

Again, Hugh reached empty air, for Jim was out of range. Sir Hugh straightened his knees in what was almost a spring, to bring himself back once more within striking range. He had the large sword again in blade-down position;

and this time it swept forward to cut at Jim's leg, but changed in midswing to direct itself once more at Jim's shoulders or head.

Jim spun right, and the blade missed. But he was beginning to see some purpose in what Sir Hugh was doing. The other knight was hoping to disable Jim without actually killing him, with some kind of head blow—preferably one that would twist his helmet around on his shoulders, so that he could no longer see through the visor. Jim blocked Hugh's blade, and was unpleasantly startled by the power behind it. Brian had not exaggerated when he said that Sir Hugh had a strong upper body.

They continued, Hugh advancing, Jim dodging and retreating. Gradually, the tactics of the two men became obvious to the watchers and Malvinne's armed men, now seated on the grass in front in rows, with their hands still tied behind them.

These began to jeer and catcall. Jim had no time to pay attention to this, but out of the corner of his eye he saw his own and Brian's men-at-arms moving between the ranks of seated men. The jeering stopped—cut off, in one instance, rather abruptly.

The combat continued. Jim was watching for signs that Sir Hugh might be tiring, but saw none. Unhappily, at the same time, he became conscious that he, himself, was tiring. This continual quick movement, as the sun heated up their armor, was taking the strength out of him.

It occurred to him that with his spins and evades, he might be being a little too fancy—using up energy, where Sir Hugh was conserving it.

He tried to think of what he would do if he abandoned his plan. But no alternative came to mind. He had ample evidence from a number of glancing, but very noticeable, blows from Sir Hugh that the other was far and away his superior at close quarters.

Jim's legs were holding up all right. He had never doubted that they would. But his arms and shoulders were getting tired from manipulating the heavy sword.

The common people from Jim's lands who were watching did not jeer, but there was a glumness about them. Clearly, they, like Malvinne's warriors, had come to the conclusion that Jim was afraid of his opponent and doing his best to evade him.

Well, thought Jim sourly, they were right—at least in part.

But evasion could not go on forever. Sooner or later they would have to reach the point of trading blows, and Jim did not like to think of what would happen to him when they came to that point.

He had this thought so firmly fixed in mind that it was not until after receiving another of Sir Hugh's glancing blows—this time in his side as he spun away once more from the other man—that he realized the blow had not been as heavy as some the other man had struck earlier.

It had never occurred to him that Sir Hugh's arms might also tire. He had expected it from his own arms, but he had unconsciously assumed that the other was as capable in the upper part of his body as Jim was in his lower. Cautiously he invited a blow that he could at least partially block. Sure enough, it seemed to him that Sir Hugh was not striking with the strength he had struck with before.

It was a common thing among boxers, Jim knew, to become arm-weary in the course of a bout. This was often increased by an opponent's pummeling of the muscles of those same arms. Jim had been scoring his few blows against Sir Hugh's arms. It was just possible this was having an effect.

Now that he had concentrated on this business of arm weariness, Jim was becoming more and more conscious of the growing weakness in his own arms. Eventually, this must bring him to the point where he could not strike an effective blow, that would tell against the other through his armor. In short, his time was limited. Which meant that somewhere along the line he would have to take the initiative and close with Sir Hugh. Then it would be the other man's weakened arms against his own.

Meanwhile, he was still doing his best to tire out Sir Hugh's legs. He was spinning clear around behind the other knight now and striking at him almost from straight behind. In Jim's helmet, sweat ran down off his forehead and dripped in his eyes. His whole suit of armor felt as if its inner padding had been soaked in water. He wondered if Hugh was suffering such difficulties; and the next time he spun close to Hugh, he deliberately listened.

Yes, Sir Hugh was panting hoarsely within his own helm.

But now Jim's arms were getting very tired. It was time to gamble. He started one of his usual fakes and spins, but this time did not complete it. He stood still and took the full swing of Sir Hugh's sword against his own.

The impact jarred his arms to his elbows. But it did not seem to have the deadly power of Sir Hugh's earlier blows. Sudden hope flared up in Jim. His arms had just about reached their limit of being able to strike an effective blow, anyway. He stood where he was, parried another blow from Hugh and struck back, without dodging.

Neither one was using the point-down guard position any more. Both were simply holding their swords point-forward and taking alternate swings at each other. A sudden sense of intoxication began to fill Jim from this new, stationary way of fighting. He was through with shadowboxing; and it was a relief to simply catch blows and strike back. The enthusiasm mounted in him as he heard Hugh's hoarse panting, even over his own gasping for air within his helmet. For a moment he played with the idea that Sir Hugh was tired to the point where now they were a match. All he had to do was keep chopping away like this, and shortly victory would be his.

He was still thinking this when Sir Hugh's blade, coming from nowhere it seemed, slashed full against the front of his helmet and turned it partly around on his head. What he had feared had happened—but not completely. He could still see the bars on the left-hand side of his visor with his right eye.

One-eyed, his sense of perspective was gone and as a result, his judgment of distance. Fury opened up in him like the door of a lit blast furnace. He had done exactly what he told himself he would not do, what Brian had warned him against. He had tried to match his strength against Sir Hugh's where the other was strong. Both he and Hugh were out on their feet, but one decisive blow by either would decide the combat. There were not many blows left in either one of them. He was rocked on his feet suddenly by the full impact from Sir Hugh's sword against the metal capping the point of his right shoulder, on his blind side.

"Got you. . . . you bastard!" the other gasped.

He realized then that they had both gone beyond the point of taking prisoners. Hugh, in particular, was out to kill him; and now he seemed in good position to do so. Another glancing blow turned Jim's helmet even further around. Now he could hardly see his opponent at all. Any moment now Sir Hugh would be able to choose the place where the edge of his blade would land, and that would be the beginning of the end for Jim.

The next blow would be the finish. Jim suddenly thought of his duel with the pirate chieftain, when he and Brian, with a handful of men-at-arms, had led the relief of Castle Smythe. His legs were still good.

He leaped. His leap carried his waist almost level with Sir Hugh's upper chest. It was the last thing the other knight was expecting; and for just a moment he hesitated in delivering the blow he was about to strike.

In that moment Jim's powerful legs drove his heels out in a double kick against the armored shoulders he had been pounding with his blade all through the combat.

Sir Hugh went down, flat on his back. A second later, Jim was standing on the one arm of the other's that still held the hilt of the two-handed sword. He put the tip of his own sword between the bars of Sir Hugh's helmet.

"You yield?" he gasped.

"I yield," came back from Sir Hugh croakingly—just as cries of "*Hold!*" came from both sides of the field. Jim looked up to see both marshals running toward him, their batons thrown down. Beyond them Carolinus's baton was on the ground before him. Clearly, they thought him as filled with the lust to kill as Sir Hugh had been—and probably he had been, at that. At any rate, it was over now.

He stepped back, taking his foot off the wrist of the hand that had held Sir Hugh's sword, but which had now let go.

He kicked the sword out of the reach of the fallen knight. And stood a moment, rocking on his feet with weariness, before the heat of his armor, the exhaustion of the battle, the reaction of having won, all combined against him. The landscape spun around him as he fell.

Chapter 45

J im could not have been unconscious
for more than a few seconds. He was roused by the voice of Carolinus calling him.

When with great effort he staggered to his feet, hardly anything about him
seemed to have changed from the moment before. But there were changes
happening. The clouds were now rushing together to form a solid, heavy, dark
blanket over them. A wind had come up from nowhere and was blowing in all
directions at once. Now from his right, now from his left, now—it seemed—
directly down from overhead. The staff in Carolinus's hands had grown half again
its length, and he gripped it higher up.

Brian and Dafydd had appeared beside the magician, and were now also
holding to the staff with both hands. Stranger even, Aargh had appeared from
nowhere and taken a grip on the staff near its bottom, with his teeth. Even from
where he stood, James could see that the wolf's great jaws were locked, completely
closed. The vicious, yellow teeth must be completely through the wood.

All of these seemed to be trying to hold the staff upright against the buffeting of
the wind, which increased steadily. The other spectators were huddling away from
it like sheep in a storm, pressed back across the drawbridge, up against the bulk of
the castle wall, as if that would support them.

"James!" it was Carolinus's voice again. "Come! Hurry!"

Jim turned toward him.

"Take hold of the staff!" shouted Carolinus. "Strip off your gauntlets, and help hold the staff with your bare hands. Quickly!"

Jim obeyed. The minute his fingers closed around the wood of the staff, it seemed that a further change came over everything about him. It was as if he had taken off dark glasses and could now suddenly see clearly.

What he saw was that the staff was radiating small lightnings out at right angles from the upright wood. These lightnings ran away from the staff on either side, to encompass the people behind them; and forward, to encompass those on the field. The lightnings went farther and ran around the castle, up its gray stone corners and along its battlemented top, enclosing it in an outline of barbed and brilliant light, flashing and flickering with constant life.

"Help hold, James!"

Carolinus's words were whipped from his mouth by the wind. They reached Jim's ears only faintly, in spite of the fact that the other man was no more than a foot from him. His white beard tugged and tore, this way and that, as if it would fly from his face under the force of the winds.

"Put all your strength into it!" called Carolinus's voice. "We must hold! For the protection of your people and your castle and everything you keep dear. Hold!"

The clouds were thick and heavy and low, now. It was so dark that Jim could hardly see across the cleared space in front of the castle to the trees. Sir Hugh still lay without moving, as he had lain when he had yielded to Jim a few moments before. Higher up in the sky and a little ways off from that, directly over the cleared area and the castle, Jim saw a lightening of the clouds; as if a cave had been hollowed out in them, and that cave had light of its own. In its space he saw, like ghost figures against the clouds, the King and Queen of the Dead seated on their thrones; and below them a horde of those they called their bodyguard. Together, they were watching from the clouds.

The wind increased. Far off in the woods to Jim's right, he heard a crashing sound, as if several great trees at once had been felled by a downward hammer blow of the wind. A moment later there was a second crash a little closer; and then a third crash, even closer yet. An icy chill crept over Jim. It was exactly as if some great, invisible giant was walking toward the castle, crushing the trees like grass under its feet as it came.

"Accounting Office!" cried the wind-thinned voice of Carolinus. "Give us strength! They are attacking the fabric that holds the Kingdoms! Give us strength!"

The wind lashed and struck and tugged at the staff, trying hard to pull it from the grasp of their hands and Aargh's teeth. It was very close to succeeding. Then, from somewhere that was both outside and within him at once, Jim felt new energy pouring into him. It had no body, no mass, no feel of anything solid or gaseous. It was simply an incoming.

As it came, he seemed to feel himself grow—not physically, or even mentally, but in some strange way he could not define. His vision sharpened even more. But this time, it was with an inner vision. With the extra energy it came to him that he understood and saw much more than he had ever understood or viewed before.

It seemed that he looked upon fields of knowledge he had never realized existed. Almost, he could see, as through a number of panes of different, lightly tinted glass, his own twentieth-century world, that he and Angie had left a year before. His grip on the staff tightened. He looked at Carolinus, and he saw Carolinus smiling at him through his wind-whipped beard.

Now, they held the staff firmly upright, for all the wind could do; and the lightnings that sprang from it were thicker and stronger, drawing lines of protection about the people and the castle.

Still, what sounded like the footsteps of an invisible giant were getting closer and closer.

Suddenly, Malvinne, who had been standing within the bright line of protection, broke away and ran out into the field—half of the distance at least to where the shape of Sir Hugh still lay motionless in his armor. He fell on his knees, raising his arms to the dark clouds above.

"Stinky, you fool! Come back!" shouted Carolinus.

His voice was strong now and carried even over the wind. Malvinne could not have helped hearing it; but he paid no attention. He lifted his arms even higher to the clouds, his hands appealing.

"Help me!" he cried to them. "Help me, now! I have been faithful!"

"Stinky!" cried Carolinus, a note of pain in his voice. "Listen to me—"

Still, Malvinne ignored him, holding his arms to the clouds, stretching up to them. His attention was all on them, alone.

The giant's steps were very close now. Jim saw, or felt, or heard—it was all these things together—something like a string being stretched to the breaking point, a string ringing with the single note of its tension. Then, suddenly it snapped; and ceased to sound.

"I have been faithful. . . ." Malvinne's voice came faintly once again through the roar of the wind.

There was a sudden turbulence in the clouds above where Malvinne knelt. The King and Queen of the Dead were already fading in their enclave farther off. Jim felt the new energy that had flowed into him, beginning to go; and the clouds did not break, but a brightness began to come through them, as if they were thinning from above.

He saw Malvinne then, for the last time; a limp figure, hanging like a dead man from the end of a string, being pulled up and up and up in the direction of where the fading ghosts of the King and Queen of the Dead had been. As he got higher, he grew harder to see, almost as transparent as they, until finally they were one with the clouds, indistinguishable, and he was one with the clouds, indistinguishable from them and the clouds.

Then, at last, the clouds broke. Sunlight poured down through them upon the castle and its surrounding grounds. The wind died; and the last of the energy that had suddenly come to fill Jim, left him. As it went, his own strength failed; and darkness moved in to enclose him.

He was not even conscious of falling. But again, he woke within seconds. Dafydd and Brian were holding him up and stripping the armor off him. Carolinus stood by, now with a staff that was no taller than the one he had brought originally. His face was white, and he looked a thousand years old. But the staff seemed to uphold him; and when the last of the armor was off Jim, he reached out an arm that was surprisingly strong and caught one of Jim's arms, holding him upright by himself.

"Go you," said Carolinus to Brian and Dafydd, "to those who wait for you."

Dafydd and Brian hesitated a moment, then turned together and ran toward the castle. Held up by Carolinus, Jim found himself walking after them. Now, from the suddenly empty open gateway above the drawbridge, three figures came running down. They were Geronde Isabel de Chaney, Danielle—now heavy with child—and Angie.

"Angie!" Jim cried; and with an excess of strength he had not realized he had, he broke from Carolinus and enclosed Angie within his arms as she came running to him.

Only a few steps ahead, Brian also was holding his Lady close; and to Jim's left, Dafydd's long arms were wrapped around Danielle, who was both crying and laughing at once.

"My golden bird, my golden bird," said Dafydd, his cheek against her hair and rocking her gently in his arms.

"What kind of a golden bird am I?" answered Danielle, between tears and laughter. "Look at me. Look at me!"

"I am looking," said Dafydd, releasing her enough so that he could reach down and stroke the great swell of her lower body. "At this greatest thing that my golden bird could give to me. What else could I ask, now, except more of the same?"

They fell together, again embracing, Dafydd now laughing himself, but with his own eyes shiny.

Jim and Angela held each other for a long moment without words. Then Angie's voice sounded softly in Jim's left ear.

"You're home," she murmured, "home, at last."

"Yes," said Jim.

"To stay," said Angie.

"Yes," said Jim.

And knew he lied. And knew that Angie knew he lied.

But for now the words were true enough.